John Gillies

Memoirs of the Life of the Reverend George Whitefield

John Gillies

Memoirs of the Life of the Reverend George Whitefield

ISBN/EAN: 9783337339227

Printed in Europe, USA, Canada, Australia, Japan

Cover: Foto ©Raphael Reischuk / pixelio.de

More available books at **www.hansebooks.com**

MEMOIRS

OF THE

LIFE

OF THE REVEREND

GEORGE WHITEFIELD, M. A.

Late Chaplain to the Right Honorable

THE COUNTESS OF HUNTINGDON:

IN WHICH

Every Circumstance worthy of Notice, both in his private
and public Character, is recorded.

Faithfully selected from his Original PAPERS,
JOURNALS and LETTERS.

ILLUSTRATED BY

A Variety of interesting and entertaining ANECDOTES,
from the best Authorities.

WITH

A particular ACCOUNT of his DEATH and FUNERAL;
and Extracts from the SERMONS, which
were preached on that Occasion.

COMPILED

By the REV. JOHN GILLIES, D. D.

To which is now added,

AN EXTRACT FROM MR. WHITEFIELD's TRACTS.

Yea, doubtless, I count all things but loss, for the excellency of
the knowledge of CHRIST JESUS, MY LORD: For whom I have
suffered the loss of all things, and do count them but dung
that I may win CHRIST. PHIL. iii. 8.

And I will very gladly spend, and be spent for you. 2. Cor. xii. 15.

For he that winneth souls is wise. PROV. xi. 30.

And they that be wise, shall shine as the brightness of the
firmament: and they that turn many to righteousness, as the
stars, for ever and ever. DAN. xii. 3.

NEW-LONDON, (CONN.) PRINTED BY S. GREEN,
FOR CORNELIUS DAVIS, N. YORK.

THE
CONTENTS.
CHAP. I.

CHAP. II.

CHAP. III.

CHAP. IV.

CHAP. V.

A 2

CHAP. XVI.

CHAP. XIX.

CHAP. XX.

CHAP. XXI.

MEMOIRS

OF THE

LIFE

OF

THE REVEREND

Mr. GEORGE WHITEFIELD.

CHAP. I.

From his Birth, to his going to the Univerfity of Oxford, Anno 1732.

THIS eminent and pious fervant of Chrift, Mr. GEORGE WHITEFIELD, was born at Gloucefter, on the fixteenth day of December, *O. S.* 1714. His father, Thomas Whitefield, nephew of the Rev. Mr. Samuel Whitefield, of Rockhampton, in Gloucefter-shire*, was firft bred to the employment of a wine-merchant

* The Rev. Mr. Samuel Whitefield, great-grand-father of George, was born at Wantage in Berkfhire, and was Rector of North Ledyard in Wiltfhire. He removed afterwards to Rockhampton. He had five daughters, two of whom were married to clergymen, Mr. Perkins and Mr. Lovingham: And two fons, Samuel, who fucceeded his father in the Cure of Rockhampton, and died without iffue; and Andrew, who was a private gentleman, and lived retired upon his eftate. Andrew had fourteen children, of whom Thomas was the eldeft, the father of Mr. George Whitefield.

B

merchant in Briſtol ; but afterwards kept an Inn in the city of Glouceſter. In Briſtol he married Miſtreſs Elizabeth Edwards, who was related to the Blackwells and Dimours, of that city ; by whom he had ſix ſons and one daughter*. Of theſe, George was the youngeſt, who being bereaved of his father, when only two years old, was regarded by his mother with a peculiar tenderneſs, and educated with more than ordinary care.

HE was early under religious impreſſions ; but the bent of his nature, and the general courſe of his younger years, as himſelf acknowledges † with expreſſions of ſhame and ſelf-condemnation, was of a very different kind.

BETWEEN the years of twelve and fifteen, he made a good progreſs in the Latin claſſics, at the public ſchool ; and his eloquence began to appear, even at that early period, in the ſpeeches which he delivered at the annual viſitations. It is probable the applauſe he received on theſe occaſions, contributed to his fondneſs for theatrical amuſements : From whence it has been inſinuated, that' he learned his oratory upon the ſtage. This, however, ſeems to have no other foundation, than his acting a part,

ſome-

---

* Elizabeth, the daughter, was twice reputably married at Briſtol. John, his ſon, lies interred with the family, in St. Mary Decrypt Church in Glouceſter. Joſeph died an infant. Andrew ſettled in trade at Briſtol, and died in the twenty-eighth year of his age. James was Captain of a ſhip, and died ſuddenly at Bath. Thomas and Richard are ſtill living. The father died December, 1716. The mother continued a widow ſeven years, and was then married to Mr. Loagden, an Ironmonger in Glouceſter, by whom ſhe had no iſſue. She died December, 1751, in the ſeventy-firſt year of her age.

† See the two firſt parts of his Life at the beginning.— Confeſſions of a like nature, are to be found in the writings of St. Auguſtin.

fometimes, with his fellow-fcholars; particularly, in certain dramatic performances prepared for them by their mafter: For that he was more indebted as an orator to nature, than to art of any kind, mut be evident to all perfons of difcernment who were acquainted with him. Such could not fail to obferve, that his eloquence was in a great meafure the effect of his genius, and proceeded chiefly from that peculiar affemblage of extraordinary talents with which God had endowed him.

NOTWITHSTANDING this, it appears from his conduct, that he either had not yet difcovered where his talents lay, or could not find means to qualify himfelf for entering into any profeffion where they might be properly exercifed: for when he was about fifteen years of age, he declined the purfuit of learning, and talked of getting an education that would better fit him for bufinefs. During this period, he ftill continued to refide with his mother; and as her circumftances were not then fo eafy as before, he did not fcruple to affift her in the bufinefs of the tavern. But the prevailing bent of his genius began now ftrongly to difcover itfelf; for even in this unfavorable fituation he compofed feveral fermons, one of which he dedicated to his eldeft brother: And after having vifited him at Briftol, he came home with a refolution to abandon his prefent employment, and to turn his thoughts a different way.

AFTER this, being for fome time difengaged from every purfuit, and but poorly fupported out of his mother's fcanty fubfiftence, he was in no fmall danger of being utterly ruined by the influence of his former companions: but it pleafed God to break the fnare by filling him with an abhorrence of their evil deeds.

ABOUT this time, the impreffions of religion began again to recover their influence in his breaft: And
when

when he was feventeen years of age, he received the facrament of the Lord's fupper. He now became more and more watchful, both over his heart and converfation. He was frequently employed in fafting and prayer; fpent much of his time in reading books of devotion; attended public worfhip twice every day; and fo deeply was he engaged in thefe exercifes, that his thoughts were conftantly fet on the great things of religion.

CHAP. II.

From the time of his going to the Univerfity of Oxford, to his embarking for Georgia, Anno 1737.

WHEN Mr. WHITEFIELD arrived at eighteen, he was fent to the Univerfity of Oxford, where he was again expofed to the fociety of the wicked: But remembering his former danger and deliverance, by the grace of GOD, he refifted all their folicitations, and cultivated an acquaintance with the Methodifts, as the only perfons that feemed to preferve a fenfe of religion, through the whole of their deportment.

IT would be going beyond our purpofe to give an account of the rife of Methodifm: For this, the reader is referred to the Rev. Mr. John Wefley's firft Journal. But it may not be improper to notice the fpirit of the age, when it firft appeared.—At that time, ferious and practical Chriftianity in England was in a very low condition; fcriptural, experimental religion, (which in the laft century ufed to be the fubject of the fermons and writings of the clergy) was become quite unfafhionable; and the only thing

infifted

infifted on was a defence of the out-works of Chriftianity againft the objections of infidels. What was the confequence? The writings of infidels multiplied every day, and infidelity made a rapid progrefs among perfons of every rank, not becaufe they were reafoned into it by the force of argument, but becaufe they were kept ftrangers to Chrift and the power of the gofpel. We have a moft affecting defcription of this, by Bifhop Butler, whom none will fufpect of exaggerating the fact :* "It is come, "I know not how, to be taken for granted, by many "perfons, that Chriftianity is not fo much as a fubject "of inquiry; but that it is, now at length, difco- "vered to be fictitious; and accordingly they treat "it, as if in the prefent age, this were an agreed "point among all people of difcernment; and no- "thing remained but to fet it up as a principal fub- "ject of mirth and ridicule; as it were by way of "reprifals, for its having fo long interrupted the "pleafures of the world." Such was the ftate of religion in England, and Scotland was greedily fwallowing down the poifon, when it pleafed GOD to raife up the Methodifts, as inftruments to revive his work in the midft of abounding impiety, and to bring multitudes who had fcarcely a form of godlinefs, to experience its quickening and renewing power.

HAPPY was it for Mr. WHITEFIELD, that there was a fociety of Methodifts, at that time, in Oxford; but efpecially that he became acquainted with the Rev. Mr. Charles Wefley, by whom he was treated with particular kindnefs. Such benefit did he receive under his miniftry, that he always accounted him his fpiritual father. And Mr. Wefley's reciprocal affection for him, ftands recorded in the verfes at the beginning of Mr. WHITEFIELD's fecond and third Journals.

LIKE

* Preface to his Analogy, May, 1736.

LIKE the other Methodiſts, Mr. WHITEFIELD now began to live by rule, and to improve every moment of his time to the beſt advantage. He received the communion every Sabbath, viſited the ſick, and the jail priſoners, and read to the poor. For daring to be thus ſingularly religious, he ſoon incurred the diſpleaſure of his fellow-ſtudents, and felt the effects of it in their unkind behavior. In the mean time, he was greatly diſtreſſed with melancholy thoughts, which were augmented by exceſſive bodily auſterities. And at laſt, by reading, and perhaps, miſunderſtanding ſome myſtic writers, he was driven to imagine, that the beſt method he could take, was to ſhut himſelf up in his ſtudy, till he had perfectly mortified his own will, and was enabled to do good without any mixture of corrupt motives. He likewiſe imagined that he muſt relinquiſh external duties, and public worſhip, and laſtly, (which was no ſmall trial and affliction to him) that he muſt deny himſelf the pleaſure of converſing with his religious friends. In this pitiable ſtate of mind, Mr. Charles Weſley found him one day, when he went to ſee him ; apprized him of his danger, if he perſiſted in that way of life, and recommended to him his brother as a perſon of greater experience ; who readily gave him, from time to time, his friendly advice. Soon after this, however, he carried his abſtinence and faſting to ſuch an extreme, that his body was ſo emaciated and feeble, that he could hardly walk up ſtairs. His tutor therefore thought proper to call a phyſician, and it appeared by the event, he had rightly judged in doing ſo : for it pleaſed GOD to make the phyſician's care and medicines ſucceſsful to his recovery.

His bodily health being reſtored, his ſoul was likewiſe filled with peace and joy in believing on the Son of GOD. This joy was ſo great for ſome time, that go where he would, he could not help praiſing

GOD

God continually in his heart, and with fome difficulty reftrained himfelf from doing it aloud. As he was urged to go into the country for confirming his health, he returned to his native air at Gloucefter, where (his mind being now happily enlightened) he preferred the facred writings to all other books, and read them with conftant prayer ; in which exercife he found unfpeakable delight and benefit. But inclination confpired with duty, to hinder him from confining his religion to himfelf : Having a heart formed for fociety and friendfhip, he could not think of fhutting himfelf up in his clofet ; but made it his bufinefs to converfe with young perfons, about his own time of life, in oider to awaken them to a fenfe of religion. God was pleafed foon to give fuccefs to his endeavors this way; for feveral of them joined with him, and notwithftanding the contempt they knew it would bring upon them, met together from time to time for religious exercifes. He alfo there read to fome poor people in the town, twice or thrice a week, and read and prayed with the prifoners in the county goal every day.

Being now about twenty-one years of age, he was fent for by Doctor Benfon, Bifhop of Gloucefter ; who told him, That though he had purpofed to ordain none under three-and-twenty, yet he fhould reckon it his duty to ordain him whenever he applied. Upon which, at the earneft perfuafion of his friends, he prepared for taking orders.

His behavior on this occafion was very exemplary. He firft ftudied the Thirty-nine Articles, that he might be fatisfied of their being agreeable to Scripture. Then, he examined himfelf by the qualifications of a minifter mentioned in the New Teftament, and by the queftions that he knew were to be put to him at his ordination. On the Saturday, he was much in prayer for himfelf and thofe who were to be ordained ed with him. On the morning of his ordination, (which was at Gloucester, Sunday, June 20, 1736) he rose early, and again read, with prayer, St. Paul's Epistles to Timothy ; and after his ordination, went to the Lord's table.

THE Sunday following, he preached his Sermon on *The Necessity and Benefit of Religious Society*, to a very crowded auditory ; and that same week, he set out for Oxford, whither he inclined to go, rather than to the parish which the Bishop would have given him ; because it was the place where he might best prosecute his studies, and where he hoped his labors might be most useful.* Soon after this, he was invited to officiate at the Chapel of the Tower of London. The first time he preached in London, was August, 1736, at Bishopsgate Church. Having a very young look, the people were surprised at his appearance, and seemed to sneer as he went up to the pulpit ; but they had not heard him long, when their contempt was turned into esteem, and their smiles into grave attention. He continued at the Tower

two

* " Last Sunday in the afternoon, I preached my first ser-
" mon in the church where I was baptized, and also first re-
" ceived the Sacrament of the Lord's supper.—Curiosity
" drew a large congregation together. The sight, at first, a
" little awed me. But I was comforted with a heart-felt
" sense of the Divine Presence : And soon found the advan-
" tage of having been accustomed to public speaking, when
" a boy at school ; and of exhorting and teaching the pri-
" soners, and poor people at their private houses, whilst at
" the University. By these means, I was kept from being
" daunted over-much. As I proceeded, I perceived the fire
" kindled, till at last, though so young, and amidst a crowd
" of those who knew me in my childish days, I trust, I was
" enabled to speak with some degree of Gospel-authority.—
" Some few mocked ; but most, for the present, seemed
" struck : and I have since heard, that a complaint had been
" made to the Bishop, that I drove fifteen mad, the first ser-
" mon. The worthy prelate, as I am informed, wished that
" the madness might not be forgotten before next Sunday."

two months, preaching, catechifing, and vifiting the foldiers; and feveral ferious young men came to hear his morning difcourfes on the Lord's day. In the mean time, the letters which the Rev. Meffieurs Wefleys and Ingham wrote home from Georgia, made him long to go and preach the Gofpel in thofe parts; yet he waited till Providence fhould make his way more clear, and returning to Oxford, he found himfelf very happy in his former employments, and had much pleafure in reading *Henry's Commentary on the Bible*, and in the company of fome religious young men, who met together in his chamber every day.

In November, 1736, he was again called from Oxford, to minifter at Dummer in Hampfhire.—This was a new fphere of action among poor illiterate people; but he was foon reconciled to it, and thought he reaped no fmall profit by converfing with them. Neverthelefs, he continued his ftudies with unwearied application: Dividing the day into three parts; eight hours for fleep and meals, eight for public prayers, catechifing and vifiting; and eight for ftudy and retirement. During his ftay here, he was invited to a very profitable curacy in London; but did not accept of it, as he was ftill intent upon going abroad. Providence, at length, feemed to open a door to him; for he received letters, containing what he thought to be an invitation to go to Georgia, from Mr. John Wefley, whofe brother came over about this time to procure more laborers. It is eafy to judge how readily this propofal would be embraced: and now that he thought himfelf clearly called, (many things concurring to make his ftay at home lefs noceffary) he fet his affairs in order, and in January, 1737, went to take leave of his friends in Gloucefter and Briftol. At Gloucefter, the congregations, when he preached, were very large and very ferious. At Briftol, many perfons were forced to return from the churches
where

where he was invited to preach, for want of room.
He went also to Bath, where he was kindly received,
and preached twice.   But he did not stay long at any
of thefe places, being obliged to go to Oxford about
the latter end of February ; from whence he came
up to London, to wait upon General Oglethorp, and
the Truftees for Georgia.   He was foon introduced
to the Archbifhop of Canterbury, and the Bifhop of
London, who both approved of his going abroad.
While he continued at London, waiting for General
Oglethorp, he preached more frequently than he had
done before, and greater numbers of people flocked
to hear him.   But finding that the General was not
likely to fail for fome time ; and being under particular obligations to the Rev. Mr. Sampfon Harris,
minifter at Stonehoufe in Gloucefterfhire, he went at
his requeft, to fupply his charge, till he fhould dif-
patch fome affairs in London.   There he was very
happy in his public miniftrations, but efpecially in
his retirements, which he ufed afterwards to reflect
upon with great fatisfaction.   On Mr. Harris' return,
he left Stonehoufe, and upon repeated invitations
went a fecond time to Briftol, where he preached as
ufual, about five times a-week.   Here the multitudes
of his hearers ftill encreafed.†   He was attended by
perfons of all ranks and denominations ; private religious focieties were erected ; a collection for the
poor prifoners in Newgate, was made twice or thrice
a-week ; and large encouragement was offered to
him, if he would not go abroad.   During his ftay at
Briftol, which was from the end of May to the
twenty-firft of June, he paid a fecond fhort vifit to
Bath, where the people crouded, and were ferioufly
affected,

---

† " Some hung upon the rails, others climbed up the leads
" of the church, and all together made the church itfelf fo
" hot, with their breath, that the fteam would fall from the
" pillars like drops of rain."

affected, as at Brittol, and no lefs than 160*l*. was collected for the poor of Georgia.

June 21, he preached his farewel-fermon at Briftol; and towards the end of the difcourfe, when he came to tell them, "it might be they would fee "him no more," the whole congregation was exceedingly affected; high and low, young and old, burft into a flood of tears. Multitudes, after fermon, followed him home weeping; and the next day he was employed from feven in the morning till midnight, in talking and giving advices to thofe who came to him, about the concerns of their fouls and falvation.

From Briftol he went to Gloucefter, and preached to a very crowded auditory; and after ftaying a few days went on to Oxford, where he had an agreeable interview with the other Methodifts, and came to London about the end of Auguft.

Here he was invited to preach and affift in adminiftering the facrament in a great many churches. The congregations continually increafed; and generally on the Lord's-day, he ufed to preach four times to very large and very much affected auditories, and to walk ten or twelve miles in going to the different churches. His friends began to be afraid he would hurt himfelf: but he ufed to fay, "He found, by "experience, the more he did, the more he might "do for God."

His name was now put into the news-papers, (though without his confent or knowledge,) as a young gentleman going volunteer to Georgia, who was to preach before the focieties at their general quarterly meeting. This ftirred up the people's curiofity more and more. He preached on that occafion, his fermon on *Early Piety*, which was printed at the requeft of the focieties. After this, for near three months fuccefively, there was no end of

people's

people's flocking to hear him, and the managers of charity-fchools were continually applying to him to preach for the benefit of the children ; for that pur-pofe they procured the liberty of the churches on other days of the week befides the Lord's day ; and yet thoufands went away from the largeft churches, not being able to get in. The congregations were all attention, and feemed to hear as for eternity. He preached generally nine times a-week, and often adminiftered the facrament early on the Lord's-day morning, when you might fee the ftreets filled with people going to the church with lanthorns in their hands, and hear them converfing about the things of God.

As his popularity increafed, oppofition increafed proportionably. Some of the clergy became angry ; two of them fent for him, and told him, they would not let him preach in their pulpits any more, unlefs he renounced that part of the preface of his fermon on *Regeneration,* (lately publifhed) wherein he wifh-ed " that his brethren would entertain their audito-" ries oftener with difcourfes upon the new birth.'' Probably fome of them were irritated the more, by his free converfation with fome of the ferious Dif-fenters, who invited him to their houfes, and repeat-edly told him, " That' if the doctrines of the new-" birth, and juftification by faith, were preached " powerfully in the churches, there would be few " Diffenters in England." Nor was he without oppofition even from fome of his friends. But under thefe difcouragements, he had great comfort in meet-ing every evening with a band of religious intimates, to fpend an hour in prayer, for the advancement of the gofpel, and for all their acquaintance, fo far as they knew their circumftances. In this he had un-common fatisfaction : once he fpent a whole night with them in prayer and praife ; and fometimes at
                              midnight,

midnight, after he had been quite wearied with the labors of the day, he found his ſtrength renewed in this exerciſe, which made him compoſe his ſermon upon *Interceſſion*.

THE nearer the time of his embarkation approached, the more affectionate and eager the people grew. Thouſands and thouſands of prayers were put up for him. They would run and ſtop him in the alleys of the churches, and follow him with wiſhful looks. But above all, it was hardeſt for him to part with his weeping friends at St. Dunſtan's, where he helped to adminiſter the ſacrament to them, after ſpending the night before in prayer : This parting was to him almoſt inſupportable.

C H A P. III.

From the time of his embarking for Georgia, *to his re-embarking for* England, 1738.

IN the latter end of December, 1737, he embarked for Georgia. *This was to him a new, and at firſt appearance, a very unpromiſing ſcene. The ſhip was full of ſoldiers, and there were near twenty women among them. The captains, both of the ſoldiers and ſailors, with the ſurgeon, and a young cadet, gave him ſoon to underſtand, that they looked upon him as an impoſtor, and for a while treated him as ſuch. The firſt Lord's-day, one of them played on the hautboy, and nothing was to be ſeen but cards, and little heard, but curſing and blaſphemy.
This

* Here begins a manuſcript of Mr. WHITEFIELD's, from which ſeveral paſſages are taken in the following account. It is referred to by M. S.

C

This was a very difagreeable fituation; but it is worth while to obferve, with what prudence he was helped to behave among them, and how God was pleafed to blefs his patient and perfevering endeavors to do them good.

He began with the officers in the cabin, in the way of mild and gentle reproof; but this had little effect.* He therefore tried what might be done between decks, among the foldiers. And though the place was not very commodious, he read prayers and expounded twice a-day. At firft he could not fee any fruit of his labor, yet it was encouraging to find it fo kindly received by his new red-coat parifh-ioners (as he calls them) many of whom fubmitted chearfully to be chatechifed about the leffons they had heard expounded.

In this fituation things continued for fome time. But all this while, he had no place for retirement, and there was no divine fervice in the great cabin, both which he greatly defired. At laft he obtained his wifh : one day finding the fhip captain a little inclined to favor him, he afked him to fuffer him now and then to retire into the round-houfe, where the captain flept, and offered him money for the loan of it. The captain would not take the money, but readily granted his requeft. Soon afterwards, the military captain having invited him to a difh of coffee, he took the liberty to tell him, "That though " he was a volunteer on board, yet as he was on " board, he looked upon himfelf as his chaplain, and " as fuch, he thought it a little odd, to pray and

" preach

* "I could do no more for a feafon, than whilft I was " writing, now and then turn my head by way of reproof, to " a Lieutenant of the foldiers, who fwore as though he was " born of a fwearing conftitution. Now and then, he would " take the hint, return my nod with a, ' Doctor, I afk your " pardon,' and then to his cards and fwearing again." M. S.

" preach to the fervants, and not to the mafter :"
and added 'withal, " That if he thought proper, he
" would make ufe of a fhort collect now and then,
" to him, and the other gentlemen in the great
" cabin." After paufing a while, and fhaking his
head, he anfwered, " I think we may, when we have
" nothing elfe to do." This aukward hint was
all he got for the prefent ; yet he was encouraged
thereby to hope, that the defired point would be foon
gained.

THEY were detained in the Downs, by contrary
winds, for near a month ; the foldiers on board became by this time more and more civilized, and the
people at Deal heard him gladly. There he preached
thrice, at the invitation of the minifters, and often
expounded in the houfe where he lodged. This
work was very delightful to him ; but he was fuddenly called away by a fair wind, about the end of
January, 1738, juft after he had preached in upper
Deal church.

BEING returned to the fhip, he began to comfort
himfelf with fome promifing appearances of doing
good in the great cabin. As he had no better place,
he generally every night retired with his friend,
Mr. Haberfham, and his brother, and two fervants,
behind the round-houfe, for prayer and other religious exercifes. Sometimes, he perceived Captain
Whiting was hearkening within. One day, finding
on the Captain's pillow, the *Independent Whig*, he
exchanged it for a book entitled, *The Self-Deceiver*.
Next morning the Captain came fmiling, and enquired who made that exchange ; Mr. WHITEFIELD
confeffed the charge, and begged his acceptance of
the book, which he faid he had read, and liked very
well. From thence forward a vifible alteration was
feen in him. The other Captain alfo, about the fame
time, met him as he was coming from between decks,
and

and defired, "that they might have public fervice, "and expounding, twice a-day, in the great cabin."

In about a fortnight, they reached Gibralter, whither they were bound to take in fome more foldiers. There, one Major Sinclair had been fo kind as to provide a lodging for him unafked, who with the other military gentleman, even Governor Sabine, and General Columbine, received him moft courteoufly. Being apprehenfive, that at a public military table, he might be more than hofpitably entertained, by way of prevention, he begged leave to remind his Excellency of an obfervation made in the book of Efther, on the court of the great Ahafuerus, "That none did compel." He took the hint, and genteelly replied, "That no compulfion of any kind fhould be "ufed at his table." And every thing was carried on with great decorum. The officers attended at public worfhip with order and gravity ; the minifters alfo behaved with great civility ; and all concurred to give him invitations to preach, which he did twice or thrice in the week ;* and in the evenings and mornings, when not on board, he expounded, converfed and prayed with a religious fociety of foldiers, who had liberty from the Governor to affemble at any time in the church. His evening expofitions were attended, not only by the foldiers, but by officers, minifters and towns-people ; and from all that could be judged, his labors were not without the divine blefling.

Finding another fociety of religious foldiers there, belonging to the Church of Scotland, he fent
them,

---

* " Strange and unufual was the fcene, both with refpect " to the place and people. The adjacent promontories, and " the largenefs of the rock of Gibralter, helped me to en- " large my ideas of Him, who *in his ftrength fetteth faft the* " *mountains, and is girded about with power.* And the place " being, as it were, a public rendezvous of all nations, I " thought I faw the world in epitome." M. S.

them, as well as the former, fome proper books, talked with feveral of them, and endeavored to unite both focieties together ; urging on them the neceffity of a catholic, difinterefted love, and of joining in prayer for the advancement of the kingdom of Chrift. This exhortation alfo, by the bleffing of God, had a good effect ; and two or three of the latter fociety being draughted out for Georgia, defired leave to go in the fhip with Mr. WHITEFIELD, which was readily allowed them.

BEFORE the embarkation of the foldiers, by the General's confent, he gave them a parting difcourfe in the church. And after embarkation, from time to time, as the weather permitted, he preached to them on board their refpective fhips.* Colonel Cochran, who commanded, was extremely civil : and foon after their fetting fail, there was fuch a change upon Captain Mackay, that he defired Mr. WHITEFIELD would not give himfelf the trouble of expounding and praying in the cabin, and between decks ; for he would order a drum to be beat morning and evening, and himfelf would attend with the foldiers on the deck. This produced a very agreeable alteration ; they were now as regular as in a church. Mr. WHITEFIELD preached with a Captain on each fide of him, and foldiers all around ; and the two other fhips' companies, being now in the trade-winds, drew near, and joined in the worfhip of God. The great cabin was now become a Bethel ; both Captains were daily more and more affected ; and a crucified Savior, and the things pertaining to the kingdom of God,

---

* He not only preached to them; but gave them notice, that he intended fpeaking to them, one by one, to fee what account they could give of their faith. — *Ibid.* At this time he began his " Obfervations on felect Paffages of Scripture turn- " ed into Catechtical Queftions," printed in Vol. IV. of his Works.

God, were the ufual topics of their converſation.
Once, after public fermon, Captain Mackay defired
the foldiers to ſtop, whilſt he informed them, that to
his great ſhame, he had been a notorious ſwearer
himſelf, but by the inſtrumentality of that gentleman,
pointing to Mr. WHITEFIELD, he had now left it
off, and exhorted them for CHRIST's ſake, that they
would go and do likewiſe. The children were cate-
chiſed; there was a reformation throughout the
whole foldiery. The women cried, " What a change
" in our Captain." The bad books and packs of
cards, which Mr. WHITEFIELD exchanged for Bibles, and other religious books, (abundance of which
were given to him to diſperſe by the *Society for promoting Chriſtian Knowledge*) were now thrown over-
board; and a fever, that prevailed in general through
the whole ſhip, helped to make the impreſſions ſink
deeper. For many days and nights, he viſited betwixt twenty and thirty ſick perſons, crawling between decks upon his knees, adminiſtring medicines
or cordials to them, and ſuch advice as ſeemed ſuit-
able to their circumſtances. The ſailors did not
eſcape the fever; Captain Whiting gladly went with
him to viſit them. One of them in particular, who
had been a moſt notorious ſcoffer, ſent for him in a
bitter agony, crying out upon and lamenting his
wicked life. The Cadet, who was a cabin paſſenger,
being alſo ſeized, was wounded deeply, told Mr.
WHITEFIELD the hiſtory of his life, and informed
Captain Mackay of his deſire to leave the army, and
to return to his original intention (having had an
Univerſity education) of devoting himſelf to the
ſervice of the Church of GOD. Mr. WHITEFIELD
himſelf was alſo ſeized, but by the bleſſing of GOD,
he ſoon recovered, and was ſtrong enough, in about a
week, to come out to the burial of the Cook of the
ſhip, who had boaſted, " That he would be wicked

" till

" till two years before he died, and then he would " be good." But he was fuddenly taken ill, and died in about fix hours.*

IT was the beginning of May, when they drew near to land. After preaching his farewel-fermon, he arrived at the parfonage-houfe at Savannah, May 7, 1738, about four months after his firft embarkation at Deptford.

UPON this voyage (many years after) he made the following reflection : " A long, and, I truft, " not altogether unprofitable voyage. What fhall " I render to the Lord for all his mercies ? Befides " being ftrengthened to go through my public work, " I was enabled to write letters, and compofe fer- " mons, as though I had been on land. Even at " this diftance of time, the remembrance of the " happy hours I enjoyed in religious exercifes on the " deck, is refrefhing to my foul. And though nature " fometimes relented at being taken from my friends, " and the little unufual inconveniences of a fea-life ; " yet, a confcioufnefs that I had in view the glory of " GOD, and the good of fouls, from time to time " afforded me unfpeakable fatisfaction."†

ONE Mr. Delamot, who had gone volunteer with Mr. John Wefley, and was left behind him as fchool-mafter at Savannah, received Mr. WHITEFIELD at the parfonage-houfe, which he found much better than expectation. Here fome ferious perfons, the fruits of Mr. Wefley's miniftry, foon came to fee him. On the morrow he read prayers and expounded in the court houfe, and waited upon the magiftrates ; but being taken ill, he was confined for above a week with a fever and ague.

WHEN

* " This was the only adult, except a foldier (who had " killed himfelf at Gibralter by perpetual drinking) that died " out of all that were on board." M. S.

† M. S.

WHEN he was recovered, and able to look about him, he found every thing bore the afpect of an infant colony ; and, what was more difcouraging ftill, he faw it was likely to continue fo, by the very nature of its conftitution. " The people (fays he) were " denied the ufe both of rum and flaves. The lands " were allotted them, according to a particular plan, " whether good or bad ; and the female heirs pro- " hibited from inheriting. So that, in reality, to " place people there, on fuch a footing, was little " better than to tie their legs, and bid them walk. " The fcheme was well meant at home ; but, as too " many years experience evidently proved, was ab- " folutely impracticable in fo hot a country abroad. " However, that rendered what I had brought over " from my friends, more acceptable to the poor " inhabitants, and gave me an ocular demonftration, " which was what I wanted, when the hint was " given* of the great neceffity and promifing utility " of a future orphan houfe, which I now determined, " by the divine affiftance, to fet about in earneft. " The Saltzburghers at Ebenezer, I found had one ; " and having heard and read of what profeffor " Franck had done in that way in Germany, I con- " fidently hoped that fomething of the like nature " might be owned and fucceeded in Georgia. Many " poor orphans were there already, and the number " was likely foon to increafe.

" As opportunity offered, I vifited Frederica and " the adjacent villages, and often admired, confid- " ering the circumftances and difpofition of the firft " fettlers, that fo much was really done. The fettlers " were chiefly broken and decayed tradefmen from " London,

* " It was firft propofed to me by my dear friend Mr. " Charles Wefley, who, with General Oglethorpe, had con- " certed a fcheme, for carrying on fuch a defign, before I " had any thoughts of going abroad myfelf." Vol. III. page 453.

" London, and other parts of England ; and feveral
" Scotch adventurers ; fome Highlanders, who had
" a worthy minifter, named Macleod ; a few Mora-
" vians ; and the Saltzburghers, who were by far
" the moft induftrious of the whole. With the wor-
" thy minifters of Ebenezer, Meffrs. Grenaw and
" Boltzins, I contracted an intimacy. Many praying
" people were in the congregation, which with the
" confideration that fo many charitable people in
" England had been ftirred up to contribute to
" Georgia, and fuch faithful laborers as Meffrs.
" Wefleys and Ingham had been fent, gave me great
" hopes, that unpromifing as the afpect at prefent
" might be, the colony might emerge in time out of its
" infant ftate. Some fmall advances Mr. Ingham had
" made towards converting the Indians, who were
" at a fmall fettlement about four miles from Savan-
" nah. He went and lived among them for a few
" months, and began to compofe an Indian Gram-
" mar ; but he was foon called away to England ;
" and the Indians (who were only fome run-away
" Creeks) were, in a few years, fcattered or dead.
" Mr. Charles Wefley had chiefly acted as Secretary,
" to General Oglethorpe, but he foon alfo went to
" England to engage more laborers ; and not long
" after, his brother, Mr. John Wefley, having met
" with unworthy treatment, both at Frederica and
" Georgia, foon followed. All this I was apprized
" of, but think it moft prudent not to repeat
" grievances. Through divine mercy I met with
" refpectful treatment from magiftrates, officers, and
" people. The firft I vifited now and then, the
" others, befides preaching twice a-day, and four
" times of a Lord's-day, I vifited from houfe to
" houfe : I was, in general, moft cordially received ;
" but from time to time found, that ' *Cœlum non ani-*
" *mum mutant, qui trans mare currunt.*' Though
" lowered

" lowered in their circumstances, a sense of what
" they formerly were in their native country, re-
" mained. It was plain to be seen, that coming over
" was not so much out of choice, as constraint :
" choosing rather to be poor in an unknown country
" abroad, than beholden to relations, or live among
" 'those who knew them in more affluent circum-
" stances at home. Among some of these the event
" however proved, that the word took effectual root.
" I was really happy in my little foreign cure, and
" could have cheerfully remained among them, had
" I not been obliged to return to England, to receive
" priest's orders, and make a beginning towards
" laying a foundation to the Orphan-house. And
" thus the place I intended to hide myself in, became,
" through my being obliged to return for these
" purposes, a means of increasing that popularity
" which was already begun, but which by me was
" absolutely unforeseen, and as absolutely unde-
" signed."*

ABOUT the middle of August, having settled one
that came with him as schoolmaster in a neighboring
village, and left his friend Mr. Habersham, at Savannah, after an affectionate parting with his flock, he
set out for Charleston, in South-Carolina.

HERE he paid his first visit to Commissary Garden, and at his entreaty preached the next Sunday
morning and evening, in a grand church resembling
one of the new churches in London. The inhabitants seemed at his first coming up, to despise his
youth ; but their countenances were altered before
                                    worship

* " During my stay there, the weather was most intensely
" hot, sometimes burning me almost through my shoes. See-
" ing others do it, who were as unable, I determined to enure
" myself to hardiness, by lying constantly on the ground ;
" which, by use, I found to be so far from being a hardship,
" that afterwards it became so, to lie on a bed." M. S.

worſhip was over. Mr. Garden thanked him moſt cordially, and apprized him of the ill treatment Mr. Weſley had met with in Georgia, and aſſured him, that were the ſame arbitrary proceedings to commence againſt him, he would defend him with his life and fortune. He alſo ſaid ſomething about the colony of Georgia, that much encouraged him, as if he thought its flouriſhing was not very far off ; and that Charleſton was fifteen times bigger now, than when he (Mr. Garden) firſt came there.

C H A P. IV.

From his embarking at Charleſton *for* London, *to his preaching firſt in* Moorfields, 1739.

SEPTEMBER 6, 1738, Mr. WHITEFIELD embarked in a ſhip bound from Charleſton to London. They had a very uncomfortable paſſage. For near a fortnight, they were beat about not far from the bar ; they were ſoon reduced to an allowance of water ; and the ſhip itſelf was quite out of repair. They were alſo very poorly off for proviſions. When they were about a third part of their paſſage, they met with a Jamaica-man, who had plenty of every thing. He ſent for Mr. WHITEFIELD on board, and offered him a moſt commodious birth ; but he did not think it right to leave his ſhip-mates in diſtreſs, and therefore returned to his own ſhip, with ſuch things as they were pleaſed to give him. The remaining part of the voyage was ſtill more perilous. The only thing comfortable, was, that in the midſt of theſe trials, deep impreſſions were

made

made on fome that were on board. All conftantly
attended public worfhip twice, and fome thrice-a-day.
Once the Captain cried out, " Lord, break this hard
" heart of mine."   Others were impreffed ; particularly one Captain Gladman, a paffenger, on whom
a great change was wrought, and afterwards, at his
own earneft requeft, became Mr. WHITEFIELD's
fellow-traveller.   At length, after nine weeks toffing
and beating to and fro, they found themfelves in
Limerick harbor.*

AT Limerick, Bifhop Burfcough received him
very kindly, and engaged him to preach in the ca-
thedral, the good effects of which he heard of many
years after.   From thence he went to Dublin, where
he preached, and was courteoufly received by Dr.
Delany, Bifhop Rundell, and Archbifhop Bolton, who
had heard of him from a gentleman of Gibraltar.
And after a paffage of twenty-four hours from Dublin, he arrived at Park-gate, Thurfday, November
30, preached twice on the Lord's-day at Manchefter,
and came to London the Friday following, December 8.

HERE he had a conference with the Moravian
brethren, who were lately come to London ; and
though he could not directly fall in with their way
of expreffing themfelves, yet he heartily agreed with
them in the old Proteftant Doctrine of juftification
in the fight of GOD, by Faith alone in the imputed
righteoufnefs of Chrift ; and was not a little delighted to find a great increafe of the work of GOD,
both as to light and love, doctrine and practice,
                                through

* " I wifh I could never forget what I felt, when water,
" and other provifions, were brought us from afhore. One
" Mr. MacMahon, a country gentleman, came from his feat
" at midnight, on purpofe to relieve us, and moft kindly in-
" vited me, though unknown, to his houfe, to ftay as long as
" I pleafed." M.S. and Journals.

through the inſtrumentality of Mr. Charles and eſpecially of Mr. John Weſley.

SOME of the clergy now began to ſhew their diſpleaſure more and more; ſo that in two days time five churches were denied him. And though the Archbiſhop of Canterbury, and the Biſhop of London, both received him civilly, it was but coldly : And the latter enquired " Whether his Journals were not " a little tinctured with enthuſiaſm ?" He replied, that they were written only for himſelf, and private friends, and were publiſhed entirely without his conſent or knowledge, or ſo much as his conſent being aſked at all.* The Truſtees for the Colony of
Georgia,

---

* It was certainly wrong to publiſh them, without his con-ſent and reviſal; otherwiſe, the publication of them was a very proper way to prevent the miſrepreſentation of facts, either by calumny and detraction on the one hand, or by ex-aggeration on the other. And it is a great pity he did not con-tinue them. They would have been the beſt poſſible memoirs of his life. But we ſee how the offence given by, or taken at, ſome paſſages, might help determine him " to proceed (as he afterwards ſays) in a more compendious way." The Journals were, indeed, moſtly written amidſt his inceſſant la-bors in preaching, travelling, and writing a multitude of letters. And the whole was told with that unguarded ſim-plicity, which though it charms the candid, and diſpoſes them to forgive or overlook many things, yet gives frequent han-dle to the critical and ſevere. It muſt alſo be owned, that his unſuſpecting honeſty made him ſometimes receive, with too little caution, the characters of perſons and ſocieties, from thoſe whom he took to be the friends of religion, and who perhaps, were really ſo, but were miſinformed. Being there-fore convinced, upon ſecond thoughts, that both his Journals, and the two firſt parts of his Life, needed correction, he pro-miſed a new edition of them, which he accordingly publiſhed in 1756. And in the preface he ingenuouſly acknowledges, that upon a review, he had found " many miſtakes, (which " are now rectified) and many paſſages that were juſtly ex-" ceptionable," (which are now eraſed.) And in a note, up-

ON

D

Georgia, received him more cordially, were pleafed to exprefs their fatisfaction at the accounts fent them of his conduct, during his ftay in the Colony : and being requefted, by letters fent unknown to him, from the Magiftrates and inhabitants, they moft willingly prefented him to the Living of Savannah, (though he infifted upon having no falary) and as readily granted him five hundred acres of land, whereon to erect an Orphan-houfe ; to collect money for which, together with taking Prieft's Orders, were the chief motives of his returning to England fo foon.

NEAR a month elapfed, before a board fat, to make him thefe returns. But during that interval, he was not idle. He and his brethren went on in their ufual courfe, taking hold of every opportunity of doing good, and preaching occafionally as churches were allowed them.* And though the church wardens and clergy were averfe, yet the common people were rather more eager than ever. But what furprized him moft, was to fee many of the heads and members of the London Societies, (who, by the accounts given by Dr. Woodward and Horneck,† he

thought

___

on September 24, 1740, he fays, " In my former Journal, " taking things by hearfay too much, I fpoke and wrote too " rafhly, both of the Colleges and Minifters of New-England; " for which, as I have already done when at Bofton laft, from " the pulpit, I take this opportunity of afking public pardon " from the prefs. It was rafh and uncharitable, and though " well meant, I fear, did hurt." But thefe corrections, while they fhew the author's candour and humility, do not affect the hiftory of his extraordinary labors and fuccefs in the work of the Gofpel.

* " GOD gave us a moft pleafant Gofpel Chriftmas feafon, " and fuch a happy beginning of a New Year, as I had never " feen before." M. S.

† See Dr. Woodward's Account of the Rife and Progrefs of the Religious Societies in the City of London, &c.

thought were founded on a good bottom) make such virulent opposition. · However, numbers of them were of another mind, and other Societies were soon formed in various parts of the town. A large room in Fetter-lane, was the general place of rendezvous, where they had frequent meetings, and great satisfaction in social prayer.* At the same time, in the churches that were open, the people crowded, and were affected more than ever. And he and his brethren were so much engaged, that for some days he could walk, and preach, and visit Societies with very little sleep, and religious exercises seemed to be their meat and drink.

JANUARY 11, 1739, he set out for Oxford, to receive Priest's Orders from his good friend Bishop Benson, which he did the next Lord's day : and having preached and administered the Sacrament at the Castle, and preached again in the afternoon, to a crowded congregation, he returned to London, January 15.

As he had collected so much for the Charity-schools last year, he reasonably supposed that the pulpits would not be denied him for the use of the Georgia Orphan-house this year. But the religious concern advancing, and spreading more and more, opposition also increased. A pamphlet was published against his sermon *On Regeneration.* Several Clergymen made strong objections against him and his brethren, for expounding in societies ; and some people were threatened with prosecution by their parish ministers, for suffering them to expound in their

* " It was a Pentecost season indeed. Sometimes whole " nights were spent in prayer. Often have we been filled as " with new wine. And often have I seen them overwhelmed " with the Divine Presence, and crying out, ". Will God, " indeed, dwell with men upon earth !—How dreadful is this " place .—This is no other than the house of GOD, and the " gate of Heaven !" M. S.

their houfes.   Yet this did not difcourage either
preachers or hearers.   The more they were oppofed,
the more they were ftrengthened.   New awakenings were heard of in various parts ; and " What
fhall I do to be faved?" was the repeated queftion
of every day.

ALL the pulpits were not as yet fhut up: Two
or three churches were allowed him to preach in,
and to collect for the Georgia Orphans, and for
erecting a Church for the poor Saltzburghers at
Ebenezer.   One Mr. Broughton behaved nobly on
this occafion.   Application being made to him, to
deny Mr. WHITEFIELD his pulpit, he anfwered,
" Having got the Lecturefhip of St. Helen's by
" Mr. WHITEFIELD's influence, if he infifts upon it,
" he fhall have my pulpit."   Mr. WHITEFIELD did
infift upon it, but (Mr. Broughton lofing the Lecturefhip) he afterwards blamed himfelf much for his
conduct.

IN Briftol he had the ufe of the churches for two
or three Sundays, but foon found they would not be
open very long.   The Dean was not at home : The
Chancellor threatened to filence and fufpend him.
In about a fortnight, every door was fhut, except
Newgate, where he preached, and collected for the
poor prifoners, and where people thronged, and
were much impreffed : but this place, alfo, was foon
fhut againlt him, by orders from the Mayor.

BEFORE his firft embarkation for Georgia, when
he talked of going abroad, numbers in Briftol ufed
to reply, " What need of going abroad ? Have we
" not Indians enough at home ? If you have a mind
" to convert Indians, there are colliers enough in
" Kingfwood."   And before he left London, whilft
preaching at Bermondfey church, and feeing fo many
thoufands that could not come in, he had a ftrong
inclination to go out and preach to them (though
he

he then ufed notes) upon one of the tomb ftones in the church-yard. And this he mentioned to fome friends, who looked upon the motion, at firft, very unfavorably ; yet were willing to take it into farther confideration. At Briftol he thought he had a clear call to try this method. The colliers, he had heard, were very rude, and very numerous ; fo uncultivated, that nobody cared to go among them ; neither had they any place of worfhip ; and often, when provoked, they were a terror to the whole city of Briftol. He therefore looked upon the civilizing of thefe people ; and much more, the bringing of them to the profeffion and practice of Chriftianity, as a matter of great importance.* After much prayer, and many ftruggles with himfelf, he one day went to Hannam Mount, and ftanding upon a hill, began to preach to about a hundred colliers, upon Matt. v. 1, 2, 3. This foon took air. At the fecond and third time the numbers greatly increafed, till the congregation, at a moderate computation, amounted to near twenty thoufand. But with what gladnefs and eagernefs, many of thefe defpifed outcafts, who had never been in a church in their lives, received the word, is above defcription. "Having (as he " writes) no righteoufnefs of their own to renounce, " they were glad to hear of a Jefus, who was a " friend to publicans, and came not to call the right- " eous, but finners to repentance. The firft difcovery " of their being affected, was to fee the white gut- " ters made by their tears, which plentifully fell " down their black cheeks, as they came out of their " coal-pits. Hundreds and hundreds of them were " foon

* "I thought it might be doing the fervice of my Creator, " who had a mountain for his pulpit, and the heavens for his " founding board ; and who, when his Gofpel was refufed " by the Jews, fent his-fervants into the highways and " hedges." M. S.

" foon brought under deep convictions, which (as
" the event proved) happily ended in a found and
" thorough converfion. The change was vifible to
" all, though numbers chofe to impute it to any
" thing, rather than to the finger of GOD. As the
" fcene was quite new, and I had but juft begun to
" be an extempore preacher, it often occafioned
" many inward conflicts. Sometimes, when twenty –
" thoufand people were before me, I had not, in my
" own apprehenfion, a word to fay, either to GOD or
" to them. But I was never totally deferted, and
" frequently (for to deny it would be lying againft
" GOD) fo affifted, that I knew by happy experience,
" what our Lord meant by faying, ‘ Out of his belly
" fhall flow rivers of living water.’ The open fir-
" mament above me, the profpect of the adjacent
" fields, with the fight of thoufands and thoufands,
" fome in coaches, fome on horfeback, and fome in
" the trees, and at times all affected and drenched in
" tears together, to which fometimes was added the
" folemnity of the approaching evening, was almoft
" too much for, and quite overcame me."*

BESIDES the colliers, and thoufands from neighboring villages, perfons of all ranks flocked daily
out of Briftol. And he was foon invited to preach,
by fome of the better fort, in a large bowling-green
in the city itfelf. Many indeed fneered to fee a
ftripling, with a gown, mount a table, upon what
they called unconfecrated ground. And for once, or
twice, it excited the contempt and laughter of the
higher rank, who formerly were his admirers, when
he preached in the churches. But GOD enabled him
to ftand the laugh, and to preach the Gofpel of
CHRIST with earneftnefs and conftancy ; and was
pleafed to attend it with his bleffing. From all
quarters, people flocked under great concern about
their fouls. Sometimes he was employed almoft

* M. S.   from

from morning to night, giving anſwer to thoſe who came in great diſtreſs, crying out, " What ſhall we do to be ſaved ?" More aſſiſtance was wanted ; he therefore wrote to Mr. John Weſley, who had never yet been at Briſtol, and having received a favorable anſwer, recommended him and his brother, in the ſtrongeſt manner to the people, and humbly prayed that the laſt might be firſt ; for he was determined to purſue his ſcheme of the Orphan-houſe, and return again to his retreat at Georgia.

Mr. Weſley being come, he took an affectionate leave of his friends at Briſtol, and made a ſecond excurſion to Wales, where an awakening had begun ſome years before, by the inſtrumentality of the Rev. Mr. Griffith Jones, and was now carried on by the miniſtry of one Mr. Howel Harris, a layman. They met at Cardiff, and in company with many others, went to Huſk, Ponty-pool, Abergavenny, Comihoy, Carleon, Trelex, and Newport, and preached in all theſe places, Mr. WHITEFIELD firſt in Engliſh, and Mr. Harris afterwards in Welch, to many thouſands. The ſerious perſons among them, of the Free Grace Diſſenters, rejoiced ; but many of high-flying principles, and of another ſtamp, were equally enraged, and expreſſed their diſlike by mockings and threats. All theſe, however, he was enabled to bear with patience, and without the leaſt diſcouragement.

About the 8th of April, from Wales he went to Glouceſter, the place of his birth, where a church was allowed him for once or twice, but no more. However, he preached frequently in Boothall (the place where the judges ſit,) and in his brother's field, to many thouſands.* His concern for his countrymen,

---

* At the time of Mr. WHITEFIELD's preaching in Glouceſter, old Mr. Cole, a diſſenting miniſter, uſed to ſay, " Theſe " are the days of the Son of Man indeed." This Mr. Cole, Mr. WHITEFIELD when a boy, was taught to ridicule. And being

men, his fellow-citizens, and his own relations, made
him forget all bodily weaknefs (to which about this
time, he was frequently fubject,) and readily to
comply with invitations given to preach at Painfwick,
Cheltenham, Evefham, Badfey, Stroud, Chafford,
places abounding with inhabitants, and where there
is ground to hope, many received much fpiritual
benefit. To wander thus about from place to place;
to ftand at bowling-greens, at market-croffes, and
in high-ways, efpecially in his own country, where,
had he conferred with flefh and blood, he might have
lived at eafe ; to be blamed by friends, and have
every evil thing fpoken againft him by his enemies,
was (efpecially when his body was weak, and his
fpirits low) very trying ; but ftill he was inwardly
fupported.

    APRIL 21, he again went to Oxford ; and, after
ftaying a few days with the Methodifts there, came

to

being afked once by one of his congregation, What bufinefs he
would be of? He faid, " A minifter ; but he would take care
" never to tell ftories in the pulpit, like old Cole." About
twelve years afterwards, the old man hearing him preach,
and tell fome ftory to illuftrate the fubject he was upon, and
having been informed what he had before faid, made this remark to one of his elders, " I find that young WHITEFIELD
" can now tell ftories, as well as old Cole." He was much
affected with Mr. Whitefield's preaching, and fo humble, that
he ufed to fubfcribe himfelf his curate ; and went about
preaching after him in the country from place to place. But
one evening, whilft preaching, he was ftruck with death,
and then afked for a chair to lean on, till he concluded his
fermon, when he was carried up ftairs, and died. Mr. WHITE-
FIELD's reflection upon this, is, " O bleffed GOD ! if it be
" thy holy will, may my exit be like his !"

    As to Mr. WHITEFIELD's telling ftories in the pulpit, fome
perhaps may find fault ; but, befide, that he had an uncommon fund of paffages, proper enough to be thus told, and a
peculiar talent of telling them ; it was certainly, a mean of
drawing multitudes to hear him, who would not have attended to the truths of the Gofpel, delivered in the ordinary
manner.

to London, where he attempted to preach at Iflington Church, the incumbent, Mr. Stonehoufe, being a friend to the Methodifts; but in the midft of the prayers, the church-warden came, and demanded his licence, or otherwife he forbad his preaching in that pulpit. He might, perhaps, have infifted on his right to preach, yet for peace fake he declined; and, after the communion fervice was over, he preached in the church-yard.

OPPORTUNITIES of preaching in a more regular way being now denied him, and his preaching in the fields being attended with a remarkable blefling, he judged it his duty to go on in this practice, and ventured the following Sunday into Moorfields.— Public notice having been given, and the thing being new and fingular, upon coming out of the coach, he found an incredible number of people affembled — Many had told him that he fhould never come again out of that place alive. He went in, however, between two of his friends; who, by the preffure of the crowd were foon parted entirely from him, and were obliged to leave him to the mercy of the rabble. But thefe, inftead of hurting him, formed a lane for him, and carried him along to the middle of the Fields (where a table had been placed, which was broken in pieces by the crowd,) and afterwards back again to the wall that then parted the upper and lower Moorfields; from whence he preached without moleftation, to an exceeding great multitude in the lower Fields. Finding fuch encouragement, he went that fame evening to Kennington-Common, a large open place, near three miles diftant from London, where he preached to a vaft multitude, who were all attention, and behaved with as much regularity and quietnefs, as if they had been in a church.*

* " Words cannot well exprefs the glorious difplays of " Divine Grace, which we faw, and heard of, and felt." M.S.

C H A P. V.

From his preaching in Moorfields, *&c. to his laying the Foundation of the Orphan-houfe in* Georgia, 1740.

FOR feveral months, after this, Moorfields, Kennington-Common, and Blackheath, were the chief fcenes of action. At a moderate computation, the auditories often confifted of above twenty thoufand. It is faid their finging could be heard two miles off, and his voice near a mile. Sometimes there were upwards of a hundred coaches, befides waggons, fcaffolds, and other contrivances, which particular perfons let out for the convenience of the audience. Having no other method to take, he was obliged to collect for the Orphan-houfe in the fields, or not at all, which was humbling to him, and his friends, who affifted him in that work. But the readinefs with which the people gave, and the prayers which they put up when throwing in their mites, were very encouraging.* In the mean while, Mr. John Wefley was laboring with great zeal at Briftol, his brother, Mr. Charles, in London and elfewhere, Mr. Ingham had been preaching in many churches of Yorkfhire, Mr. Kinchin in Oxford, and Mr. Rogers in Bedfordfhire. Thus the feed fown was gradually increafed, and the embargo which was now laid on the fhipping, gave him leifure for more journies through various parts of England ; and GOD was pleafed to crown his labors with amazing fuccefs.

SOME demur happening in Briftol, he went there

a

---

* "Once upwards of twenty pounds were collected in "halfpence." M. S.

a few days; put Mr. John Wesley (who had now made a progress in building the Kingswood school, and also had begun a room at Bristol) in full power; and took him along with him, and introduced him as a field preacher, at Gloucester and other places. Every where the word seemed to sink deeper and deeper into the hearts of the hearers. Singing and praying were heard in Kingswood, instead of cursing and swearing; and in many other places the fruits of righteousness evidently appeared.

MANY false reports were now spread abroad, concerning him. Not a journey he could make, but he was either killed or wounded, or died suddenly. One groundless fiction was continually invented after another. And the Bishop of London laid hold of this occasion for publishing a charge to his clergy to avoid the extremes of enthusiasm and lukewarmness. But amidst these discouragements, he was not left without the countenance and friendship of several persons of influence.

THE embargo being taken off, and upwards of a thousand pounds collected for the Orphan-house, he sailed the second time for America, August 14, 1739, with a family consisting of eight men, one boy, and two children, besides his friend Mr. Seward.

AFTER a passage of nine weeks,* he arrived at Philadelphia in the beginning of November, and was immediately invited to preach in the churches, to which people of all denominations thronged, as in England. From thence he was invited to New-York, by Mr. Noel, the only person with whom he had any acquaintance in that part of America. Upon his arrival,

* For the manner in which he employed his time on board, see his Journals and Letters of this period.—A little before he sailed, he finished his Answer to the Bishop of London's Pastoral Letter. And during the voyage, he wrote his Letter to the Religious Societies of England. See Vol. IV. of his Works.

arrival, they waited on the Commiſſary ; but he refuſed him the uſe of his church. Mr. WHITEFIELD there preached in the fields, and on the evening of the ſame day, to a very thronged and attentive audience in the Rev. Mr. Pemberton's meeting-houſe ; and continued to do ſo twice or thrice a-day for above a week ; and by all that could be judged, with very great ſucceſs.

ON his way to and from Philadelphia, he alſo preached at Elizabethtown, Maidenhead, Abingdon, Neſhamini, Burlington, and New-Brunſwick, in the New-Jerſeys, to ſome thouſands gathered from various parts, among whom there had been a conſiderable awakening, by the inſtrumentality of one Mr. Freelinghauſen, a Dutch miniſter, and the Meſſrs. Tennents, Blair, and Rowland. He had alſo the pleaſure of meeting with old Mr. Tennent, as well as his ſons, and with Mr. Dickinſon.* It was no leſs pleaſing than ſtrange to him, to ſee ſuch gatherings in a foreign land ; miniſters and people ſhedding tears ;

ſinners

* "Mr. Tennent, and his brethren in preſbytery, intend "breeding up gracious youths for our Lord's vineyard. The "place wherein the young men ſtudy now, is a log-houſe, "about twenty feet long, and near as many broad. From "this deſpiſed place, ſeven or eight worthy miniſters of Jeſus "have lately been ſent forth, and a foundation is now laying "for the inſtruction of many others. The work, I am per- "ſuaded, is of God, and therefore will not come to nought." Journals, November 22, 1739.

The event has verified his judgment about this inſtitution. It is now a large college at Princetown in New-Jerſey : and has already had many worthy preſidents (ſome of whoſe names are well known in the learned world) ſuch as Mr. Dickinſon, Mr. Burr, Mr. Jonathan Edwards, Mr. Samuel Davies, Dr. Finley, and at preſent Dr. Witherſpoon, by whoſe abilities, care, and activity it is, under Providence, in a very flouriſhing condition.

And there has been lately (ſummer 1770) a remarkable revival of religion among the ſtudents, both in the college and grammar-ſchool.

finners ſtruck with awe; and ſerious perſons, who had been much run down and deſpiſed, filled with joy. Mean-time the Orphan-houſe affairs went on well. The things brought from England, were ſold for their benefit. A ſloop was purchaſed, of which Captain Gladman was maſter; and a young man, who had lately received ſerious impreſſions under Mr. WHITEFIELD's preaching, willingly offered himſelf as mate. Many little preſents were made to his family for ſea-ſtores, and the intended houſe. And about the end of November, he took his leave of his family, and ordered them to proceed in their voyage to Savannah, while himſelf, with Mr. Seward and two more, determined to go thither by land.

NUMBERS followed, ſome twenty, ſome ſixty miles out from Philadelphia. He preached at Cheſter, Wilmington, Newcaſtle, (where he was met on the way by Mr. Roſs, miniſter of the place) Chriſtian-bridge, and Whitely Creek, where Mr. William Tennent (whoſe meeting-houſe is in the neighbor-hood) had erected a tent for him. Here he obſerved new ſcenes of field preaching, or rather preaching in the woods, opened to him. At Whitely-Creek, perhaps the congregation did not conſiſt of leſs than ten thouſand. Earneſt invitations were given him to come and preach elſewhere; which he had great encouragement to do from the viſible ſucceſs of his labors; but he haſted to be with his family at Savannah.

In his way thither, he alſo preached in Maryland, at North-Eaſt and Joppa, and at Annapolis, the ca-pital, where he was received with much civility by the Governor; and at Upper-Marlborough.

In Virginia alſo, he preached at Williamſburgh, where he was courteouſly received by the Governor, and by Mr. Blair, the Commiſſary, whom he ſpeaks of with great regard.

E   WHEN

WHEN he came to North-Carolina, he thought it
seemed to be the greateſt waſte, and the moſt uncultivated of ſpots, both in a temporal and ſpiritual
ſenſe. Yet here, in a place called Newbern-Town,
his preaching was attended with an uncommon influence. And it was not without effect at Newton, on
Cape Fear river, where were many from Scotland
amongſt the congregation, who had lately come over
to ſettle in North-Carolina.

IMMEDIATELY on coming into South-Carolina
province, (he ſays) a viſible change was obſervable
in the manners of the people. And when he came
to Charleſton, (which was on Saturday, January 3,
1740) he could ſcarce believe but he was amongſt
Londoners, both in reſpect of gaicty of dreſs, and
politeneſs of manners.

HERE he ſoon perceived, that by field-preaching
he had loſt his old friend the Commiſſary, who once
promiſed to defend him with life and fortune. However, at the requeſt of the Independent miniſter,
(who continued his friend to his dying day,) he
preached in his meeting-houſe. At the firſt ſermon,
all was gay and trifling, no impreſſion ſeemingly
made at all. But next morning in the French church,
the ſcene was quite altered. A viſible and almoſt
univerſal concern appeared. Many of the inhabitants earneſtly deſired him to give them one ſermon
more ; for which purpoſe he was prevailed upon to
put off his journey till the next day ; and there was
reaſon to think his ſtay was not in vain.

NEXT morning, he and his companions ſet out in
an open canoe for Savannah ; and in their way, for
the firſt time, lay in the woods, upon the ground,
near a large fire, which keeps off the wild beaſts ;
upon which he makes this reflection,* " An emblem,
" I thought of the divine love and preſence keeping
" off evils and corruptions from the ſoul."

* M. S.   ON

On his arrival at Savannah, January 11, he was very happy to meet his family who had got there three weeks before him ; and to find by letters from England, New-York, &c. that the work of God prospered. But it was a melancholy thing to see the colony of Georgia reduced even to a much lower ebb than when he left it, and almost deserted by all but such as could not well go away. Employing these, therefore, he thought would be of singular service, and the money expended, might be also a means of keeping them in the colony.

Before his arrival, Mr. Habersham had pitched upon a plot of ground for the Orphan-house, of five hundred acres, about ten miles from Savannah, and had already begun to clear and stock it. The orphans, in the mean time, were accommodated in a hired house. On this, many years after, he makes the following reflections : " Had I proceeded according to the rules of prudence, I should have first " cleared the land, built the house, and then taken " in the orphans ; but I found their condition so " pitiable, and the inhabitants so poor, that I imme- " diately opened an infirmary, hired a large house at " a great rent, and took in, at different times, " twenty-four orphans. To all this I was encou- " raged, by the example of Professor Franck. But " I forgot to recollect, that Professor Franck built in " Glaucha, in a populous country, and that I was " building in the very tail of the world, where I " could not expect the least supply, and which the " badness of its constitution, which every day I ex- " pected would be altered, rendered by far the most " expensive part of all his Majesty's dominions.— " But had I received more and ventured less, I should " have suffered less, and others more."*

The first collection he made in America, was at the Rev. Mr. Smith's meeting-house in Charleston,

* M. S.   whither

whither he went about the middle of March, to fee his brother, the Captain of a fhip from England. He was defired, by fome of the inhabitants, to fpeak in behalf of the poor orphans ; and the collection amounted to feventy pounds fterling. This was no fmall encouragement to him at that time, efpecially as he had reafon to think it came from thofe who had received fpiritual benefit by his miniftrations.

HAVING returned to Savannah, he went to the fpot of ground where he intended the Orphan houfe fhould be built ; and, upon the 25th day of March, 1740, laid the firft brick of the great houfe, which he called BETHESDA, i. e. *a houfe of mercy.** By this time, near forty children were taken in, to be provided with food and raiment ; and counting the workmen and all, he had near a hundred to be daily fed. He had very little money in bank ; and yet he was not difcouraged ; being perfuaded, that the beft thing he could do at prefent for the infant colony, was to carry on the work.

* Long after this he writes, " Bleffed be God, I have not " been difappointed in the hope, that it would be a houfe, and " place of mercy to many, both in refpect to body and foul." M. S.

CHAP.

CHAP. VI.

From his laying the Foundation of the Or-
phan-houfe in Georgia, *to his Arrival in*
England, 1741.

Mr. WHITEFIELD again, therefore, fet off in a
floop for Newcaftle in Pennfylvania, where he arrived
about the middle of April. In this fhort paffage of
ten days, he was much difcouraged both by weaknefs
of body, and low fpirits. But, as he obferved afterwards, Providence was infinitely better to him than
his fears, and exceeded his moft fanguine expectations. For, during the fpace of two months, he
was ftrengthened to preach, generally twice, and
frequently, befides travelling, thrice a-day. At Philadelphia, the churches were no longer allowed him;
but he preached in the fields to congregations that
confifted fometimes of near ten thoufand, and with
great apparent fuccefs. Large collections were made
for the Orphan-houfe; once, not lefs than an hundred
and ten pounds fterling. Societies for praying and
finging were fet on foot; and in every part of the
town, many were concerned about their falvation.
Some were wrought upon in a more inftantaneous,
others in a more progreffive, fome in a more filent,
others in a more violent manner.*

At New-York, New-Brunfwick, Staten-Ifland,
Bafkingridge, Whitely-Creek, Frogs-Manor, Reedy-
Ifland, there was great concern, upon the mind both
of the preacher and hearers.

SOME-

---

* "Many negroes came; fome of them enquiring, "Have
I a foul?" M. S.

SOMETIMES he was almoſt dead with heat and
fatigue. Thrice a-day he was lifted up upon his
horſe, unable to mount otherwiſe ; then rode and
preached, and came in and laid himſelf along upon
two or three chairs. He did not doubt but ſuch a
courſe would ſoon take him to his deſired reſt. Yet
he had many delightful hours with Meſſrs. Tennents,
Blair, &c. " Night ſays he, was as it were turned
"into day, when we rode ſinging through the woods.
" I could not help recommending theſe men, wherever
" I went, in the ſtrongeſt manner, becauſe I ſaw they
" gloried in the croſs of Chriſt*."

WITH

*M. S. In a journal written by Mr. William Seward, (Mr.
WHITEFIELD's companion in travel) we have the following
particulars belonging to this period.

" April 9, 1740. Mr. WHITEFIELD propoſed my going to
England upon ſeveral important affairs, particularly to bring
over Mr. Hutchins to take care of the Orphan-houſe in his ab-
ſence—To acquaint the Truſtees of Georgia with the ſtate of
the colony, and the means under God, for the better eſtabliſhment thereof, it being now upheld almoſt wholly by the ſol-
diery and Orphan-houſe, moſt of the people who are uncon-
cerned in either, being gone or going—The proper means are
principally three. 1. An allowance of negroes. 2. A free
title to the lands. 3. An independent magiſtracy, viz. ſuch as
are able and willing to ſerve without fee or reward. My bu-
ſineſs with the Truſtees will be farther, to bring over the
money lodged in their hands for building the church at Savannah. I am moreover, to collect ſubſcriptions for a negro
ſchool in Pennſylvania, where our brother WHITEFIELD pro-
poſes to take up land in order to ſettle a town for the reception of ſuch Engliſh friends whoſe hearts God ſhall incline to
come and ſettle there.

" April 13. Mr. Tennent informed us of the great ſucceſs
which had attended our brother WHITEFIELD's preaching,
when here laſt. For ſome time, a general ſilence was fixed
by the LORD on people's minds, and many began ſeriouſly to
think on what foundation they ſtood—A general outward reformation has been viſible. Many miniſters have been quickened in their zeal to preach the word in ſeaſon and out of
ſeaſon. Congregations are increaſed, and ſome few, it is

hoped,

WITH great joy he reached Savannah on the 5th of June, bringing his orphans, in money and provisions, upwards of five hundred pounds sterling. Next day, when they came to public worship, young and old were

hoped, will be brought, through their convictions, into a found and saving conversion.

" April 14. Mr. Jones, the Baptist minister, told us of two other ministers, Mr. Treat and Mr. Morgan, who were so affected with our brother WHITEFIELD's spirit, that the latter had gone forth, preaching the glad tidings of salvation, towards the sea coast in the Jerseys, and many other places which lay in darkness and the shadow of death. The former told his congregation, that he had been hitherto deceiving himself and them ; and that he could not preach to them at present, but desired they would join in prayer with him.

" April 15. We were informed that an Indian trader was so affected with brother WHITEFIELD's doctrine, that he is gone to teach the Indians, with whom he used to trade.

" April 18. This day was published our brother WHITE-FIELD's Letter to the Inhabitants of Maryland, Virginia, North and South Carolina, about their abuse of the poor negroes. (See his Works, Vol. IV.)

" Heard of a drinking club that had a negro boy attending them, who used to mimic people for their diversion. The gentlemen bid him mimic our brother WHITEFIELD which he was very unwilling to do ; but they insisting upon it, he stood up and, said, " I speak the truth in Christ, I lie not ; unless you repent you will all be damned." This unexpected speech broke up the club, which has not met since.

" —Notice was given of a new lecture at German-Town every Thursday, by four ministers.

" April 22. Agreed with Mr. Allen for five thousand acres of land on the forks of Delaware, at 2200l. sterling, the conveyance to be made to Mr. WHITEFIELD, and after that assigned to me, as security for my advancing the money.— Mr. WHITEFIELD proposes to give orders for building the negro school on the purchased land, before he leaves the province.

" April 24. Came to Christopher Wigner's plantation in Shippack, where many Dutch people are settled, and where the famous Mr. Spalemburg resided lately. It was surprizing to see such a multitude of people gathered together in such a

wilderness

were all diffolved in tears. Some, who came to vifit them, were alfo deeply impreffed ; particularly Mr. Hugh Bryan and his family,* and fome of his relations.

wildernefs country, thirty miles diftant from Philadelphia.—Our brother was exceedingly carried out in his fermon, to prefs poor finners to come to Chrift by faith, and claim all their privileges ; viz. Not only righteoufnefs and peace, but joy in the Holy Ghoft : and after he had done, our dear friend Peter Bochler preached in Dutch, to thofe who could not underftand our brother in Englifh.

"Before our brother left Philadelphia, he was defired to vifit one who was under a deep fenfe of fin from hearing him preach. And in praying with this perfon, he was fo carried beyond himfelf, that the whole company (which were about twenty) feemed to be filled with the Holy Ghoft, and magnified the God of heaven.

"April 25. Rofe at three o'clock : and though our brother WHITEFIELD was very weak in body, yet the Lord enabled him to ride near fifty miles, and to preach to about five thoufand people at Amwell, with the fame power as ufual. Mr. Gilbert Tennent, Mr. Rowland, Mr. Wales, and Mr. Campbel, four godly minifters, met us here.

"April 26. Came to New-Brunfwick.—Met Mr. Noel from New-York a zealous promoter of our Lord's kingdom. He faid their foci_ty at New-York was increafed from feventy to one hundred and feventy, and was daily increafing ; and that Meffrs. Gilbert and William Tennents, Mr. Rowland, and feveral others, were hard laborers in our Lord's vineyard.

"April 28. Had a moft affectionate parting with our dear brother WHITEFIELD, and our other brethren."

The reft of Mr. Seward's Journal was written moftly during his paffage to England, where he arrived June 19, and with which it concludes. Mr. WHITEFIELD, in the new edition of his Journals, 1756, obferves, " April 28, 1740. This " was the laft time I faw my worthy friend ; for before my " return to England, he was entered into his reft, having left " behind, a glorious teftimony of the transforming efficacy of " converting grace. This hath alfo been the happy cafe of " his brother Benjamin, who lately finifhed his courfe with " joy."

* For a more particular account of Mr. Bryan's family, and of his vifit to Mr. WHITEFIELD, and what followed upon

it,

tions. Several from Beaufort in South-Carolina, then received their first impressions. All these things gave him great encouragement. And though his family was now great (near a hundred and fifty, including workmen) and the plan laid down would have required some thousands to support it ; and although very often he had not twenty pounds in cash, he was still kept from being disheartened ; and his friends believing the work to be of God, continued cheerfully to assist him.

THOUGH he was very weak in body, yet the cry from various quarters for more preaching, and the necessity of supplying so large a family, made him go again to Charles-Town, where, as well as at Dorchester, Ashley-Ferry, Ponpon, and John's-Island, he preached to very attentive and affected auditories. Charles-Town was the place of the greatest success, and of the greatest opposition. The Commissary poured out his anathemas, refused to give him the sacrament, and published some letters against him. But all in vain. He preached twice almost every day, to great crouds, in the Independent and Baptist meeting-houses ; besides expounding in the evening in merchants' houses. Thus he went on successfully (though often ready to die with the excessive heat) till the end of August : when, having received most pressing invitations from the Rev. Dr. Colman and Mr. Cooper, ministers in Boston ; and being desirous of seeing the descendants of the good old Puritans, and their seats of learning ; and having encouragement that something might be done for the Orphan-house, he embarked in the Orphan-house sloop for New-England, in company with several Charles-Town friends ; and arrived at Rhode-Island, September 14. HERE

it, See No. I. of "Living Christianity delineated in the Diaries "and Letters of Mr. Hugh Bryan and Mrs. Mary Hutson." Recommended by the Rev. Dr. Conder and Dr. Gibbons.

·HERE several gentlemen foon came to vifit him, among whom was the Rev. Mr. Clap, an aged diffenting minifter, in whom he thought he faw what manner of men the old Puritans were, who firft fettled New-England, and was much delighted with his converfation. They went together to the incumbent's houfe, to afk the ufe of the church, which was granted : and in it he preached three days, twice a day, to deeply affected auditories.

THIS he thought was a happy entrance into New-England. But he was ftill more agreeably furprifed, when, before he got to Bofton, he was met feveral miles from the city, by the Governor's fon, and fome of the minifters, and principal inhabitants, who conducted him to Mr. St—nf—rd's (brother-in-law to Dr. Colman) who with his colleague Mr. Cooper, and many others, came and joined in prayer.

JONATHAN Belcher, Efq. was then Governor of the Maffachufetts colony, and Joliah Willard, Secretary. Both thefe gentlemen were his fincere friends ; fo were the minifters, Meffrs. Webb, Foxcraft, Prince, Dr. Sewall, Gee, &c. To avoid, however, giving any juft offence, he went to the Englifh church to morning prayers ; but finding, by converfation with the Commiffary, and fome other clergy, that there was no accefs there, he began preaching in the afternoon, at Dr. Colman's meeting-houfe, and fo went round (except when he preached on the common) to the other meeting-houfes, efpecially the largeft of them, for fome time together.

GOVERNOR Belcher generally attended, Secretary Willard, and feveral of the Council, fet the fame example, and all feemed to vie who fhould fhow the greateft refpect. Congregations were exceeding large, both within and without ; and were much affected. Old Mr. Walter, who fucceeded Mr. Elliot, commonly called the Apoftle of the Indians, at Rox-bury,

bury, faid it was Puritanifm revived : and Dr. Colman faid, when preaching at his meeting-houfe the
Sunday following, that " it was the happieft day he
" ever faw in his life."

HE preached alfo at Cambridge, Marblehead,
Ipfwich, Newbury, Hampton, York, Portfmouth, Salem, and Moulden, to large congregations. The
gentlemen of the greateft repute had their houfes
open, in every place ; collections were readily made
for the orphans ; and, in about a week, having preached fixteen times, and rode a hundred and feventy
miles. he returned to Bofton, October 6.

HERE the congregations were ftill encreafed. At
his farewel fermon, it was fuppofed there were near
twenty thoufand people. He received a great number of letters, and could have fpent whole days in
converfing with thofe that came to him under foul
concern. Minifters and ftudents attended. Little
children were imprefíed. The contributions for the
orphans were very confiderable, amounting in town
and country, to near five hundred pounds fterling.

HE fet out next for Northampton : having read
in England an account of a remarkable work of converfion there, publifhed by their paftor the Rev. Mr.
Jonathan Edwards ; and having a great defire to fee
him, and to hear the account from his own mouth.

AT Concord, Sudbury, Marlborough, Worcefter,
Leicefter, Hadley, places all lying in the way, pulpits
and houfes were every where opened, and a continued
influence attended his preaching. At Northampton,
when he came to remind them of what GOD had
formerly done for them, it was like putting fire to
tinder. Both minifter and people were much moved ;
as were the children of the family, at an exhortation which their father defired Mr. WHITEFIELD to
give them.

AFTER leaving Northampton, he preached in
Weftfield,

Weftfield, Springfield, Suffield, Windfor, Hartford, Weathersfield, Middletown and Wallingford, to large and affected congregations. And October 23, reached New-Haven, where he was affectionately received by Mr. Pierpont, brother in law to Mr. Edwards, and had the pleafure of feeing his friend Mr. Noel, of New-York, who brought him letters from Georgia. Here alfo he was much refrefhed with the converfation of feveral gofpel minifters. It being affembly time, and the Governor and Burgeffes then fitting, he ftayed till Lord's day, and had the pleafure to fee numbers daily impreffed. The good old Governor particularly, was much affected and at a private vifit which Mr. WHITEFIELD paid him, faid, " Thanks be to GOD for fuch refrefhings in our way " to heaven."

ON Monday mcrning he fet forward, and preached with ufual fuccefs at Milford, Stratford, Fairfield, Norwalk, and Stamford, where he was vifited by fome minifters under deep concern.

THIS was on the borders of New-York province, into which he now again entered, and preached at Rye and Kingfbridge, on his way to the city of New-York, where he arrived October 30. Here for three days fucceffively, and afterwards at Staten-Ifland, Newark, Bafkingridge, his preaching appeared to be attended with more fuccefs than ever. At Trenton he had a long conference with fome minifters about Mr. Gilbert Tennent's complying with an invitation to go and preach in New England. After prayer, and confidering the arguments both for and againft this propofal, they thought it beft he fhould go ; which, however diffident of himf-lf, he was perfuaded to do. And his miniftrations were attended with an extraordinary bleffing to multitudes, as is particularly narrated elfewhere*.   SATURDAY -

* See Prince's Chriftian Hiftory, or Hiftorical Collections of the fuccefs of the gofpel, Vol. II. where the facts are fet down in the order of time.   About

SATURDAY, November 8, Mr. WHITEFIELD came back to Philadelphia, and next day preached to several thousands in a house built for that purpose, since his last departure. Here he both heard of, and

About this time Mr. WHITEFIELD wrote his Letter to some Church-Members of the Presbyterian Persuasion, in Answer to certain Scruples and Queries which they had proposed. See Works, Vol. IV.

What sort of reception he had in New-England, will farther appear from the following letters of some eminent ministers of Boston, and adjacent towns, published by the Rev. Mr. Josiah Smith, of Charleston, in the South-Carolina Gazette.

October 1, 1740.

Rev. and dear Sir,

" Your kind letter by Mr. WHITEFIELD, and your other, are both now before me. You raised our expectations of him very much, as did his Journals more, and Mr. P. of New-York concurred with them ; but we own, now that we have seen and heard him, that our expectations are all answered and exceeded, not only in his zealous, and fervent abounding labours, but in the command of the hearts and affections of his hearers.—He has been received here as an angel of God, and servant of Jesus Christ. I hope this visit to us, will be of very great use and benefit to ministers and people. He has found his heart and mouth much opened to speak freely and boldly to us, and he finds it received with joy." The same Gentleman, November 29, 1740, writes thus:—" Mr. WHITEFIELD left us seven weeks ago; the last week we heard of him at Philadelphia. I hear that much of the presence of God is with him. He has left a blessing behind him, we hope, with us. Our people high and low, old and young, are very swift to hear. The excellent meekness of Mr. WHITEFIELD's Answer to the Querists, will honour him to you."

Another, in a Letter, October 22, 1740, expresses himself thus : " Though it is always a singular pleasure to me to hear from you, yet your two letters by Mr. WHITEFIELD, had a new circumstance of pleasure from the dear hand that presented them. I perceive you was impatient to know what

and faw many, who were the fruits of his former miniftrations; and continued among them till No- vember 17, preaching twice a-day. Afterwards he preached in Gloucefter, Greenwich, Piles-Grove, Cohanfie,

what fort of entering in he had among us. We (minifters, rulers, and people) generally received him as an angel of God. When he preached his farewel fermon in our com- mon, there were twenty-three thoufand, at a moderate computation. We are abundantly convinced, that you fpoke the words of truth and fobernefs in your fermon relating to him. Such a power and prefence of God with a preach- er, and in religious affemblies, I never faw before; but I would not limit the Holy One of Ifrael. The prejudices of many are quite conquered, and expectations of others vaftly outdone, as they freely own.—A confiderable num- ber are awakened, and many Chriftians feem to be greatly quickened. He has preached twice at Cambridge; he has one warm friend there, Mr. ——, the tutor, who has fol- lowed him to Northampton, and will, for ought I know, to Georgia. But Mr. WHITEFIELD, has not a warmer friend any-where, than the firft man among us. Our Governor has fhewed him the higheft refpect, carried him in his coach from place to place, and could not help following him fif- ty miles out of town.—I hope the religion of the country will fare the better for the impreffions left on him."——The fame Gentleman writes, December 2, 1740. " The man greatly beloved, I fuppofe, may be with you before now. That his vifit here will be efteemed a diftinguifhing mer- cy of heaven by many, I am well fatisfied. Every day gives me frefh proofs of Chrift's fpeaking in him. A fmall fet of gentlemen amongft us, when they faw the af- fections of the people fo moved under his preaching, would attribute it only to the force of found and geftures. But the impreffions on many are fo lafting, and have been fo tranf- forming, as to carry plain fignatures of a divine hand going along with him.—Another Gentleman writes, October 11, 1740, and thanks me for recommending to him, fo worthy a perfon as the Rev. Mr. WHITEFIELD, who has preached Chrift, and the great truths of the gofpel among them, with remarkable fervour of fpirit, and to a general acceptance; and hopes that there are many awakened by his

Cohansie, Salem, Newcastle, Whiteley-Creek, Frog's-
Manor, Nottingham; in many, or most of which
places,

his ministry.—Another of the same date writes, That he
had conceived very highly of him by some clauses in my
private letter, and the sermon I preached by way of
apology, &c. But, confesses he had not gone high enough in his opinion of him, and that his expectations are
more than answered in him.—Another, November 21, 1740,
" Blesses God that he was sent thither; that he had so many opportunities of seeing him, and sitting under his ministry. That he appeared to him a wonderful man indeed; that his preaching was accompanied with a divine
power and energy, beyond any man's he had ever heard
before: and the effects of his ministry were very marvellous among them."—I shall conclude with the following
passage of another Gentleman, in a letter of November
7, 1740. " I received yours by the Rev. Mr. WHITEFIELD,
with whom I coveted a great deal more private conversation than I had opportunity for, by reason of the throngs
of people almost perpetually with him.—But he appears to be
full of the love of GOD, and fired with an extraordinary
zeal for the cause of CHRIST, and applies himself with
the most indefatigable diligence that ever was seen among
us, for the promoting the good of souls. His head, his heart,
his hands seem to be full of his Master's business. His discourses, especially when he goes into the expository way, are
very entertaining. Every eye is fixed upon him, and every
ear chained to his lips. Most are very much affected;
many awakened and convinced; and a general seriousness
excited. His address more especially to the passions, is
wonderful, and beyond what I have ever seen. I think I
can truly say, that his preaching has quickened me, and
I believe it has many others besides, as well as the people.
Several of my flock, especially the younger sort, have been
brought under convictions by his preaching; and there is
this remarkable amongst them of the good effects of his
preaching, that the word preached now by us, seems more
precious to them, and comes with more power upon them.
My prayer for him is, that his precious life may be length-
ened out, and that he may be an instrument of reviving
dying religion in all places whithersoever he comes, who
seems to be wonderfully fitted for, as well as spirited to
it.'

places, the congregations were numerous, and deeply affected.

NOVEMBER 22, he got to Bohemia in Maryland, and from thence he went to Reedy-Ifland. At both places his preaching was attended with great influence. And at the laft (their floop being detained by contrary winds near a week,) he preached frequently. All the captains and crews of the fhips that were wind-bound conftantly attended, and great numbers crowded out of the country, fome as far as from Philadelphia; and as great concern as ever came upon their minds.

DECEMBER 1, he fet fail from Reedy-Ifland for Charlefton in South-Carolina, and here he makes the following remark: " It is now the feventy-fifth " day fince I arrived at Rhode-Ifland. My body was " then weak, but the Lord has much renewed its " ftrength. I have been enabled to preach, I think, " an hundred and feventy-five times in public, befides " exhorting frequently in private. I have travelled " upwards of eight hundred miles, and gotten up- " wards of feven hundred pounds fterling, in goods, " provifions, and money, for the Georgia orphans. " Never did I perform my journies with fo little fa- " tigue, or fee fuch a continuance of the divine pre- " fence in the congregations to whom I have preach- " ed. Praife the Lord, O my foul."*

AFTER a pleafant paffage of eight or nine days, and preaching again at Charlefton and Savannah, he ar- rived on the 14th of December at the Orphan-houfe, where he found his family comfortably fettled. At Rhode-Ifland he had providentially met with Mr. Jon- athan Barber, whofe heart was very much knit to him, and who was willing to help him at the Orphan houfe. Him, therefore, he left fuperintendant for the fpiritual, and Mr. Haberfham for the temporal affairs; and
having

* Journals, December 1, 1740.

having fpent a very comfortable Chriftmas with his Orphan family, he fet off again for * Charlefton, where he arrived January 3, 1741, and preached twice every day as ufual, to moft affectionate auditories, till the 16th of January, when he went on board for England. He arrived the 11th of March at Falmouth, rôde poft to London, and preached at Kennington-Common the Sunday following.

C H A P. VII.

From his Arrival in England, *in the Year* 1741, *to his leaving* Scotland, *the fame Year.*

THE new and unexpected fituation in which he now found himfelf, will be beft defcribed in his own words: " But what a trying fcene appeared here! In my zeal, during my journey through America, I had written two well-meant, though injudicious letters, againft England's two great favourites. The Whole Duty of Man, and Archbifhop Tillotfon, who, I faid, knew no more of religion than Mahomet. The Moravians had made inroads upon the focieties. Mr. John Wefley, fome way or other, had been prevailed on to preach and print in favour of perfection, and univerfal redemption; and very ftongly againft election, a doctrine, which I thought and do now believe,

was

* At Charlefton, the Commiffary was going to proceed againft him for correcting and preparing for the prefs, a letter written by Mr. Hugh B——n, in which it was hinted, that the clergy break their canons. He alfo laid him under fufpenfion for omitting to ufe the form of prayer, prefcribed in the communion book, when officiating in a diffenting congregation.—But Mr. WHITEFIELD gave fecurity for his appearance, and appealed home.

F 3

was taught me of God, therefore could not possibly recede from. Thinking it my duty so to do, I had written an answer at the Orphan-house, which though revised, and much approved of by some good and judicious divines, I think had some too strong expressions about absolute reprobation, which the apostle leaves rather to be inferred, than expressed. The world was angry at me for the former, and numbers of my own spiritual childred for the latter. One that got some hundreds of pounds by my Sermons, being led away by the Moravians, refused to print for me any more. And others wrote to me that God would destroy me in a fortnight; and that my fall was as great as Peter's. Instead of having thousands to attend me, scarce one of my spiritual children came to see me from morning to night. Once at Kennington-Common, I had not above a hundred to hear me. At the same time, I was much embarrassed in my outward circumstances. A thousand pounds I owed for the Orphan-house. Two hundred and fifty pounds bills, drawn upon Mr. Seward, now dead, were returned upon me. I was also threatened to be arrested for two hundred pounds more. My travelling expences also to be defrayed. A family of a hundred to be daily maintained, four thousand miles off, in the dearest place of the King's dominions. Ten thousand times would I rather have died, than part with my old friends. It would have melted any heart to have heard Mr. Charles Wesley and me weeping after prayer, that, if possible, the breach might be prevented. Once I preached in the Foundary (a place which Mr. John Wesley had procured in my absence) on Gal. iii. but no more. All my works was to begin again. One day, I was exceedingly refreshed in reading Beza's life of Calvin, wherein were these words, "Calvin turned out of Geneva, but behold a Church.

a Church arifes." A gentlewoman who lent me three
hundred pounds to pay the prefent Orphan houfe
demand : and a ferious perfon (whom I never faw
or heard of) giving me a guinea, I had fuch con-
fidence, that I ran down with it to a friend, and expreffed my hope, that God who fent this perfon with
the guinea, would make it up fifteen hundred ; which
was the fum I thought would be wanted.

"NEVER had I preached in Moorfields on a week
day. But, in the ftrength of God, I began on
Good-Friday; and continued twice a-day, walking
backward and forward from Leadenhall, for fome
time preaching under one of the trees, and had
the mortification of feeing numbers of my fpiritual children, who but a twelvemonth ago could
have plucked out their eyes for me, running by me
whilft preaching, difdaining fo much as to look at
me, and fome of them putting their fingers in their
ears, that they might not hear one word I faid.

"A like fcene opened at Briftol, where I was
denied preaching in the houfe I had founded : Bufy bodies, on both fides, blew up the coals. A
breach enfued. But as both fides differed in judgment, and not in affection, and aimed at the glory of our common Lord ; though we hearkened too
much to tale-bearers on both fides, we were kept
from anathematizing each other, and went on in
our ufual way ; being agreed in one point, endea-
vouring to convert fouls to the ever bleffed Mediator *."

In---

---

* About this time he was ordered to attend in the Parliament Houfe, to give information concerning the ftate of
the Colony in Georgia. " April 13, 1741. I have been at
the Parliament Houfe. The Georgia affair was adjourned.
It was fomewhat of a trial to be in the houfe. I then remembered

In confequence of this, one Mr. Cennick, a preacher, who could not fall in with Mr. Wefley's fentiments, and one or two more in like circumftances, having joined Mr. WHITEFIELD, they began a new houfe in Kingfwood, and foon eftablifh ed a fchool among them, that favoured Calviniftical Principles. And here, and in feveral other places, they preached to very large and ferious congregations, in the fame manner as he had done in America.

THITHER he intended to return as foon as poffible. Mean time, it being inconvenient, on account of the weather, to preach morning and evening in Moorfields; fome Free grace Diffenters (who ftood by him clofely in that time of trial) got the loan of a piece of ground, and engaged with a carpenter to build a large temporary fhed, to fcreen the auditory from cold and rain, which he called a Tabernacle, as it was only intended to be made ufe of for a few months, during his ftay in his native country. The place fixed upon, was very near the Foundery, which he difliked, becaufe he thought it looked like erecting altar againft altar; but, upon this occafion he remarks, " All was wonderfully over ruled for good and for the furtherance of the Gofpel. A frefh awakening immediately began. Congregations grew exceeding large, and at the people's defire, I fent (neceffity reconciling me more and more to laypreaching) for Meffrs. Cannick, Harris, Seagrave, Humphries, &c. &c. &c. to affift *."

　　　　　* M. S.　　　　　FRESH

membered what the Apoftle faid, " We are become a fpectacle to men." My Appeal will come to nothing, I believe. I have waited upon the Speaker. He received me very kindly."

Again. " He treated me kindly, and affured me, that " there would be no perfecution in the King's reign."

FRESH doors were now opened to him, and invitations fent to him from many places, where he had never been. At a Common, near Braidtree in Effex, upwards of ten thoufand perfons attended. At Halftead, Dedham, Cofslefhall, Weathersfield, Colchefter, Bury, and Ipfwich, the congregations were very large and much affected †.

At this time alfo, he was ftrongly folicited by religious perfons, of different perfuafions, to vifit Scotland. Several letters had paft between him and the Meffrs. Erfkines, fome time before ‡, and he had a great defire to fee them. He therefore took his paffage from London to Leith, where (after five days, which he employed in writing many excellent letters to the Orphans, &c. he arrived July 30, 1741. Several perfons of diftinction moft gladly received him, and would have had him preach at

Edinburgh

---

† "Sweet was the converfation I had with feveral minifters of CHRIST. But our own clergy grew more and more fhy, now they knew I was a Calvinift; though no doubt (as Mr. Bedford told me when going to the Bifhop of London) our Articles are Calviniftical." M. S.

‡ See his Journals, and his Letters to the Rev. Mr. R. E. and the Rev. Mr. E. E.

In his laft to Mr. E. E. before coming to Scotland he writes, "May 16, 1741. This morning I received a kind letter from your brother Ralph, who thinks it beft for me wholly to join the Affociate Prefbytery, if it fhould pleafe GOD, to fend me into Scotland. This I cannot altogether come into. I come only as an occafional preacher, to preach the fimple Gofpel to all that are willing to hear me, of whatever denomination. I write this, that there may not be the leaft mifunderftanding between us. I love and honour the Affociate Prefbytery in the bowels of Jefus Chrift: but, let them not be offended, if in all things, I cannot immediately fall in with them."

To the fame purpofe he writes to Mr. R. E. May 23, 1741.

Edinburgh directly; but he was determined that the Rev. Meffrs. Erfkines fhould have the firft offer; and therefore went immediately to Dunfermline, and preached in Mr. Erfkine's Meeting houfe.

GREAT perfuafions were ufed to detain him at Dunfermline, and as great to keep him from preaching for, and vifiting the Rev. Mr. Wardlaw, who had been colleague to Mr. Ralph Erfkine above twenty-years; and who, as well as the Rev. Mr. Davidfon, a diffenting minifter in England, that went along with Mr. WHITEFIELD, were looked upon as perjured, for not adhering to the Solemn League and Covenant. This was new language to him, and therefore unintelligible.—But that he might be better informed, it was propofed that the Rev. Mr. Moncrief, Mr. Ebenezer Erfkine, and others, members of the affociate Prefbytery, fhould convene in a few days, in order to give him farther light.

IN the mean time, Mr. Ralph Erfkine accompanied him to Edinburgh, where he preached in the Orphan-houfe Park (field-preaching being no novelty in Scotland) to a very large and affected auditory, upon thefe words, " The Kingdom of God is not Meat and Drink, but Righteoufnefs, and Joy in the Holy Ghoft." The next day he preached in the Weft Kirk, and expreffed great pleafure in hearing two Gofpel Sermons from the Rev. Mr. Gufthart, and the Rev. Mr. Macvicar.—And the following day, he preached in the Cannongate Church, where Mr. Ralph Erfkine went up with him into the pulpit.

ACCORDING to promife, he returned with him to Dunfermline, where Mr. E. Erfkine, and feveral of the Affociate Prefbytery were met together, When Mr. WHITEFIELD came, they foon propofed

to

THE REV. GEORGE WHITEFIELD.

to proceed to bufinefs. He afked them for what
purpofe ? They anfwered, to difcourfe, and fet him
right about Church Government, and the Solemn
League and Covenant. He replied, they might fave
themfelves that trouble, for he had no fcruple about
it, and that fettling Church Government, and preaching about the Solemn League and Covenant, was
not his plan. He then told them fomething of his
experience, and how he was led into his prefent
way of acting. One of them, in particular, faid
he was deeply affected. And Mr. E. Erfkine defired they would have patience with him, for that
having been born and bred in England, and never
ftudied the point, he could not be fuppofed to be
perfectly acquainted with it. But Mr. M. infifted,
that he was therefore more inexcufable, for England had revolted moft with refpect to Church Government ; and that he being born and educated
there, could not but be acquainted with the matter in debate. Mr. WHITEFIELD told him, he had
never made the Solemn League and Covenant the
fubject of his ftudy, being too bufy about matters
which he judged of greater importance. Several
replied, that every pin of the Tabernacle was precious. He anfwered, that in every building there
were outfide and infide workmen ; that the latter,
at prefent, was his province : that if they thought
themfelves called to the former, they might proceed in their own way, and he would proceed in
his. He then afked them ferioufly, what they would
have him to do? The anfwer was, that he was
not defired to fubfcribe immediately to the Solemn
League and Covenant, but to preach only for them,
till he had further light. He afked. Why only for
them ? Mr. R. E. faid, " They were the Lord's
people." He then afked, Were no other the Lord's
people but themfelves ? If not, and if others were
the

the Devil's people, they had more need to be preached to; that for his part, all places were a-like to him; and that if the Pope himself would lend him his pulpit, he would gladly proclaim in it the righteousness of the Lord Jesus Christ. Something passed about taking two of their breth-ren with him to England, to settle Presbytery there; and then with two more, to go and settle Presbytery in America. But he asked, Suppose a number of Independents should come, and declare, that after the greatest search, they were convinced that Independency was the right Church Govern-ment, and would disturb nobody, if tolerated, should they be tolerated? They answered, No.—Soon af-ter this the company broke up. And Mr. M. preached upon Isa. xxi. 11, 12. " Watchman, what of the night? &c." And took occasion to declaim strongly against the Ceremonies of the Church of England, and to argue*, " That one who held Communion with that Church, or with the backslidden Church of Scotland, could not be an Instrument of Reformation." The consequence of all this, was, an open breach. Mr. White-field retired thoughtful and uneasy to his closet: and, after preaching in the fields, sat down and dined with them, and then took a final leave†.

MANY.

---

* " I attended; but the good man so spent himself in the former part of his sermon, in talking against prelacy, the Common Prayer-Book, the surplice, the rose in the hat, and such like externals; that when he came to the latter part of his text, to invite poor sinners to Jesus Christ, his breath was so gone, that he could scarce be heard. What a pity that the last was not first, and the first last!"

† " Having dropt something about persons building a Ba-bel, Mrs.—— said, It was a hard saying. Upon which, I replied,

MANY waited at Edinburgh to know the iſſue of
the conference, who were not diſappointed in the
event.   Thither he returned, after preaching at Innerkeithing. and the Queen's-ferry ; and continued
preaching always twice, often thrice (and once ſeven
times a-day) for ſome weeks together.   The churches
were open, but not being able to hold half the congregations, he generally preached twice a-day in the
Orphan-Hoſpital Park to many thouſands.   Perſons
of the beſt faſhion, as well as of the meaner rank, attended* ; at ſome of their houſes he generally expounded every evening. And every day, almoſt, there
were new evidences of the ſucceſs of his labors. Numbers of miniſters† and ſtudents came to hear him, and
aged, experienced Chriſtians told him, they could ſet
their ſeal to what he preached.

IN this firſt viſit to Scotland, he preached at
Edinburgh, Glaſgow, Aberdeen, Dundee, Paiſley,
Perth, Stirling, Crief, Falkirk, Airth, Kinglaſſie,
Culroſs, Kinroſs, Couper of Fife ; and alſo, at Stone-
hive, Benholm, Montroſe, Brechin, Forfar, Couper
of Angus ; and at Innerkeithing, Newbottle; Gala-
ſhields, Maxton, and Haddington ; and in the weſt
country, at Killern, Fintry, and Balfrone.   To other
places to which he was invited, he did not go § at
                                                this

---

replied, I feared it was a true one, and that they would find
the Babel fall down about their ears. I was never received
into their houſe any more.   Thus was I called to make another ſacrifice of my affections.   But what I had met with in
England, made this the more eaſy."   M. S.

* Among his particular friends were the Marquis of Lo-
thian, the Earl of Leven, Lord Rae, Lady Mary Hamilton,
Lady Frances Gardiner, Lady Jean Nimmo, Lady Dirleton.
See his Letters from Auguſt to December 1741.

† Particularly, one Mr. Wilſon, of Maxton.

§ Among theſe was Cambuſlang, and ſome places in the
north of Scotland.

                        G

this time. But (having collected above five hundred pounds, in money and goods, for his Orphans) he left Edinburgh in the latter end of October, to go through Wales, in his way to London.

CHAP. VIII.

Letters from Ministers and private Christians in Scotland, *representing Mr.* WHITE-FIELD's *reception and success there, in the Year* 1741.

HIS reception, ministrations, and success at the principal places in Scotland, will farther appear from the following Letters.

At Edinburgh, one of the ministers of that city, thus writes to him. " April 20, 1742.* Rev. and Dear Sir, Knowing that many are careful to inform you, from time to time, what passes here, I have hitherto delayed answering your most acceptable Letter, until I should tell you with the greatest certainty, what were the blessed effects of your ministrations amongst us ; and can now assure you, that they were not more surprising than lasting. I don't know or hear of any wrought upon by your ministry, but are holding on in the paths of truth and righteousness. They seem possessed of a truly Christian spirit. Jesus is precious to their souls ; and like the morning light, they are advancing with increasing brightness to the perfect day. Since you left Scotland, numbers in different corners have been awakened. Many in a hopeful way. Religion in this sinful city revives and flourishes. Ordinances are
more

* Glasgow Weekly History, No. XXVII.

more punctually attended on. People hear the word with gladnefs, and receive it in faith and love. New meetings for prayer and fpiritual conference are erecting every where. Religious converfation has banifhed flander and calumny from feveral tea-tables, and Chriftians are not afhamed to own their dear Lord and Mafter. Praife is perfected out of the mouths of babes and fucklings ; and fome ftout-hearted finners captivated to the obedience of Chrift.

"I CANNOT eafily exprefs, with what pleafure I write thefe things ; and doubtlefs, they will give you no lefs joy in reading them. Should not thefe droppings of the dew of heaven encourage our faith and hope of a plentiful effufion of the Spirit, which will at once change our barren wildernefs into a fruitful field? Should not this haften your return, that we may take fweet council together, and enter into the houfe of God in company? You are often on our hearts. We long to fee you face to face. May much of your great Mafter's prefence ever attend, and come along with you."

Mr. George Muir, (afterwards the Rev. Doctor Muir,) late Minifter of Paifley, thus wrote to James Aitken, fchool-mafter in Glafgow.* "Edinburgh, Auguft 8, 1743. As you defire, I have with the affiftance of Mr. Archibald Bowie, Mr. Dun, and the Sergeant, informed myfelf a little, with refpect to the number and fituations of the praying Societies in this place, which you will take as follows: They are, as near as we can guefs, between twenty-four and thirty in number, fome of which will neceffarily be obliged to divide, by reafon of too many meeting together ; and that will increafe the number. A-mongft them are feveral meetings of boys and girls, who, in general, feem not only to be growing in

grace

* Prince's Chriftian Hiftory, No. XXXIV.

grace, but really increasing in knowledge. The little lambs appear to be unwilling to rest upon duties, or any thing short of Christ; as a young gentleman of my acquaintance told me, when under a temptation to think, that he was surely seeking some imaginary refuge, instead of the Savior, he was made to cry out in prayer, ' Lord, I want nothing else, and will have nothing short of the very Christ of God.' There are several meetings of young women, who (although I never, as yet visited any of them) I am informed, hold on very well. The Sergeant tells me, that at one of these meetings, on the morning of the Lord's-day, he has known them all wet with floods of tears, melted down with love to Christ, and affection to one-another for Christ's sake. I have myself been much ravished (when in a meeting in the room below, where some of these resort) to hear them sing the Lord's praises with such melodious voices. There are numbers of young men who meet for the excellent purpose of glorifying God, and promoting Christian knowledge; amongst some of whom I have the honor to be a member; many of them are Divines, who are useful in instructing the weaker sort of us; and that they endeavor to do with the greatest anxiety and desire. A good number of old men, substantial, standing Christians, meet for their edification and instruction, (the glory of their God being always their chief end) and are thereby often revived, and very much refreshed. The generality of these sorts above-mentioned, do walk very circumspectly, and really make it appear to the world, that they have been with Jesus: which is very much evidenced in their chearfully bearing reproaches for Christ's sake. And upon the whole, we hope there is such a flame kindled, as shall never be extinguished. And with respect to two particular societies, whereof Mr.

Bowie

Bowie is a member, he gave me the enclofed* in writing; which you will perufe and return. This is not all; for feveral country people are beginning to affemble together in little meetings, to worfhip their GOD : particularly, the Sergeant informs me of one about two miles from this place, where feveral ploughmen, and other illiterate perfons, meet for the moft noble ends and purpofes ; and are going moft fweetly on, much increafed in grace and knowledge, and fome are daily added to their number. I am informed from the eaft country, (where there have been no focieties fince the feceffion) that about Old Cambus, fix miles from Dunbar, many are now meeting together for focial prayer, and mutual con-verfation about matters of religion, wherein the
Lord

* To Mr. Muir. " Edinburgh, Auguft 6, 1743. As you defire a fhort account of the two focieties I am concerned in, I fhall give it in a very few words. They confift of twenty-five, or twenty-fix members each ; and, except a very few, are all perfons whofe concern about religion began in the late awakening. I never faw the ends of fuch focieties anfwered near fo well, as among thefe. I think, I may fafely declare, that I was never witnefs to fo much of real Chriftian exercife among any perfons I have known, as I have obferved, to my great fatisfaction, among moft of them. It is moft amazing to obferve, how much fome of them, who at their firft con-cern, were brutifhly ignorant of every thing good, have now made fuch advances in knowledge, that they excel thofe who were formerly before them. The concern about their own falvation is not only remarkable, but the abiding earneftnefs they fhow in their prayers, for the increafe of the Redeemer's kingdom, is moft defirable ; and the care they fhow in watch-ing over one-another, is one convincing evidence of their bro-therly love, and true Chriftian tendernefs. I might fay a great deal more, but muft conclude. I am, &c.
A. BOWIE."
There is alfo notice taken of fome remarkable converfions, and of the reformation obferved in the Edinburgh Hofpitals, in Numbers X. XI. XV. of Glafgow Weekly Hiftory.

Lord is with them of a truth. And in that place, there is more eager thirfting for the word, than ufual, and the minifters are learning to fpeak with new tongues. And one of my acquaintance, who was in this place laft winter, has happily been the LORD's inftrument in beginning thefe focieties. How beautiful and refrefhing is it, my·dear friend, to hear of fo many following after the defpifed JESUS? Should we not take it as a token for good, that young ones inftead of fpending their fpare hours in idle, vain, and unprofitable play, do now affemble, and join in calling upon the Lord. Is it not a good fign to hear many poor foolifh virgins, (inftead of being employed in the vanities of the generality of their fex) meeting together for prayer; and many prodigal youths, inftead of revelling, and drunkennefs, chambering, and wantonnefs, now breathing after the knowledge of JESUS CHRIST, and him crucified? O that the LORD would more and more exert his almighty power amongft us. There are feveral other focieties for prayer, near about this city, profpering very well."

THE Rev. Mr. Mac Culloch of Cambuflang, thus writes to Mr. WHITEFIELD, a few months after his firft vifit to Glafgow;* "As it is matter of great joy and thankfulnefs to God, who fent you here, and gave you fo much countenance, and fo remarkably crowned your labors when here at Glafgow with fuccefs; fo I doubt not but the following account, of the many feals to your miniftry in and about that city, will be very rejoicing to your heart, as our glorious Redeemer's Kingdom is fo much advanced, and the everlafting happinefs of immortal fouls promoted.

"I AM well informed by fome minifters, and other judicious and experienced Chriftians, that there are to the number of fifty perfons already got notice

of

---

* Glafgow Weekly Hiftory, No. XIII.

of, in and about Glasgow, that by all that can be judged by persons of the best discerning in spiritual things, are savingly converted by the blessing and power of God, accompanying your ten sermons in that place; besides several others under convictions, not reckoned in this number, whose state remains, as yet, a little doubtful. And besides, several Christians of considerable standing, who were much strengthened, revived, and comforted, by means of hearing your sermons; being made to rejoice in hope of the glory of God, having obtained the full assurance of faith.

" Among those lately converted, here are several young people who were formerly openly wicked and flagitious, or at best but very negligent as to spiritual concerns, but are now in the way of salvation.— Some young converts are yet under doubts and fears; but a considerable number of them have attained to joy and peace in believing.

" Several lately wrought upon in a gracious way, seem to outstrip Christians of considerable standing, in spiritual mindedness, and many other good qualifications: and particularly, in their zeal for the conversion of others, and love to the ordinances, without a spirit of bigotry, or party zeal.

" These converts by your ministry are discovered from time to time; a good many are but lately got notice of, that were not known before; which was partly occasioned by their convictions not being so strong and pungent at the first, as they proved afterwards, partly by the discouragement they met with in the families where they resided, a d partly by the reserved tempers of the persons themselves, and their bashfulness, because of their former negligences and open enormities. These things give ground to hope, there may be more discovered afterwards, that are not yet known.

BESIDES

" BESIDES thefe awakened, by the power of GOD accompanying your fermons, there are others awakened fince, by means of the great vifible change difcovered in their former intimate acquaintance, that were then converted, when they faw the change fo remarkable, and the effects fo abiding.

" YOUNG converts are exceeding active to promote the converfion of others, efpecially their relations and near concerns, by their exhortations, and letters to diftant friends in the country ; and there are fome inftances of the good effects of thefe endeavors.

" THEY have all a great love to one another, and all good Chriftians, and a great fympathy with fuch of their number, as are under doubts and fears. Such of them as have not received comfort, by their earneft and deep concern, and clofe attendance on the means of grace, are hereby inftrumental to excite Chriftians of older ftanding to more diligence in religion.

" THESE, dear Brother, are a few hints of fome of the moft remarkable things, as to the fuccefs of your labors at Glafgow, by the divine bleffing. May a rich and powerful bleffing, give a plentiful increafe to them every-where, where you come with the glad tidings of the great falvation."

AT Aberdeen, one of the minifters of that city, thus writes of him, to a perfon of diftinction —October 3, 1741.* Honored Sir, At your defire, I fhall not refufe, (however much reafon I may have for declining to offer my judgment, or opinion, in things of this nature) to acquaint you freely of what I think of the Rev. Mr. WHITEFIELD, or rather what is the opinion of perfons of more acquaintance with the good ways of GOD.

" HE is, I believe, juftly efteemed by all who are perfonally acquainted with him, an eminent inftrument of reviving, in thefe declining times, a juft fenfe

and

* Glafgow Weekly Hiftory, No. XXVIII.

and concern for the great things of religon. We
have, of late, been much employed, and a great noife
has been made about the leffer matters of the law :
and are now much broken in judgment about things,
many of which, I muft own, I do not underftand†.
The cry has been, and ftill continues loud, ‘ Lo here
is Chrift, and lo there.’ And now the Lord has raifed
up this eminent inftrument, from a quarter, whence
we could not have expected it, to call us to return to
him; from whom, it is plain, we have deeply revolted.
His being by education and profeffion of a different
way, from what, I cannot but think, is moft juftly
profeffed among us, feems to me, to add no fmall
weight to his teftimony ; as does alfo his age. The
Lord by this is, as it were, attracting our eyes and
attention to one, who, had he been formerly of us,
would doubtlefs like others, be defpifed. And yet, I
cannot but look upon it as a fad inftance of a departing GOD, that, inftead of regard, he meets not only
with contempt, but with oppofition alfo, from thofe
who ought to act a very different part. Did he
                                    preach

† Of thofe who differed from their brethren, as to their
judgment about many things, was Mr. B——, one of the minifters of Aberdeen. After he had prayed and preached againft
Mr. WHITEFIELD, in his hearing, and quoted fome paffages
of his firft printed fermons, as heterodox : Sermon being ended, Mr. Ogilvie gave notice, That Mr. WHITEFIELD would
preach in about half an hour. The interval being fo fhort,
the magiftrates retired into the Seffion-houfe, and the congregation patiently waited, big with expectation, (fays Mr.
WHITEFIELD,) of hearing my refentment. At the time appointed, I went up, and took no other notice of the good
man's ill-timed zeal, than to obferve in fome part of my difcourfe, That if the good old gentleman had feen fome of
my later writings, wherein I had corrected fome of my
former miftakes, he would not have expreft himfelf in fuch
ftrong terms. The people being thus diverted from contro-
verfy with man, were deeply impreffed with what they heard
from the word of GOD.”

preach another JESUS, or another doctrine, he ought
justly to be rejected : but this is not the case. And
yet this very thing is advanced as an argument against
him : It is said, he advances nothing new. And I
allow it.   This gives his friends joy.   But these reverend gentlemen should mind, that there are two
things in Gospel ordinances, purity and power. The
first, in mercy, we still have in some good measure
(though complaints of the want of this are very open ;)
but the last, we sadly confess the want of, and this is
what attends the Gospel dispensed by him.   And sure
I am, that even the credible report of it should much
endear him to all, who wish well to the interests of
our dear, though too unknown, and altogether lovely
LORD JESUS.

" His calmness and serenity under all he meets
with, yea his joy in tribulation, is to me so surprising,
that I often think, the Lord sent him to this place, in
particular, to teach me how to preach, and especially
how to suffer.

" HIS attachment to no party, but to CHRIST and
true Grace alone, has long appeared to me a peculiar
excellency in him.   Christianity has been so long
broken into so many different sects and parties, that
an honest Pagan might justly be at loss, was he among
us, where to find the religion of JESUS.

" ONE now appears, who loudly calls us (and
whose voice the LORD seems to back with power) to
look into the original plan of that religion we profess : sure nothing more just, nothing more reasonable.
He tells us, wherein the Kingdom of GOD does consist.
And yet how sad is it, he should be despised. Who
knows but this may be the Lord's last voice to us, before he takes his kingdom from us ?

" As to what you ask of his reception in this city ;
I invited him, nay, urged him, to undertake this journey, in consequence of a correspondence with him, for
more

more than two or three years. I did it with the
concurrence of a very few. His journey was delayed,
till bad reports had imbittered the minds of almost all
against him : so that when he came, I could scarce
obtain liberty for him to preach even in the fields.
Ali that I could do, was what I had refolved long before ; I gave him with great pleasure, and full freedom, my pulpit, which, for that day, was in the
church which our magiftrates and principal people of
note frequent. And at once, the LORD, by his preaching, melted down the hearts of his enemies, (except
—— and ——— ;) fo that, contrary to our cuftom, he
was allowed the fame place and pulpit in the evening
of that day, and the other church as often as he
pleafed.

"WHILE he ftayed among us in this city, he anfwered our expectations fo much, that he has fcarce
more friends any where of its bulk than here, where,
at firft, almoft all were againft him. And the word
came alfo with fo much power, that I hope feveral
of different denominations, will blefs the LORD for
evermore, that they ever heard him. And in his
way from us, I faw in part, and have heard more
fully fince, what fatisfies, that this was of the LORD,
and for the good of many.——P. S. I fuppofe you
have heard, that our magiftrates waited on him while
here, and made him free of this place ; though that
is a compliment rarely paid to ftrangers, of late."

Mr. Willifon, minifter at Dundee, wrote as follows, to his friend at Edinburgh. "October 8,
1741.* Honored Sir, I am favored with yours,
wherein you defire my thoughts of Mr. WHITEFIELD,
and an account of his labors and fuccefs with us.
Although my fentiments may be little regarded by
many, yet when you put me to it, I think I am
bound to do juftice to the character of this ftranger,
                                        which

* Glafgow Weekly Hiftory, No. XIII.

which I fee few willing to do. I am not much furprized, though the devil, and all he can influence, be
up in arms againft the youth, feeing he makes fuch
bold and vigorous attacks upon his kingdom and
ftrong holds. As you, Sir, do obferve it to be with
you, fo it is with us. He is hated, and fpoken evil
againft by all the epifcopal party, and even the moft
of our clergy do labor, to diminifh and expofe him :
this is not to be much wondered at, feeing his incef-
ant labors for CHRIST and fouls, is fuch a ftrong
reproof to them ; befides what he fays publicly,
againft the fending out of unconverted minifters, and
their preaching an unknown CHRIST ; this muft be
galling to carnal men. I look upon this youth, as
raifed up of GOD for fpecial fervice, and fpirited for
making new and fingular attempts, for promoting
true Chriftianity in the world, and for reviving it
where it is decayed : and I fee him wonderfully fitted
and ftrengthened, both in body and mind, for going
through with his projects, amidft the greateft difcouragements and difficulties. I fee the man to be all of
a piece ; his life and converfation to be a tranfcript
of his fermons. It is truly a rare thing, to fee fo
much of GOD about any one man. To fee one fo eminent for humility, in the midft of applaufe ; for meeknefs and patience, under reproaches and injuries ;
for love to enemies ; for defire to glorify CHRIST,
and fave fouls ; contentment in a mean lot, acquiefcing
in the will of GOD in all cafes, never fretting under
any difpenfation, but ftill praifing and giving thanks
for every thing. It is rare to fee in a man, fuch a
flaming fire for GOD and againft fin, whe in the
pulpit ; and yet moft eafy and calm in converfing
with men out of it ; careful not to give offence to
them, and yet never courting the favor of any. GOD
has beftowed a large meafure of gifts and graces upon
him, for the work he is engaged in, and has made
him

him a chofen veffel, to carry his name among the
Gentiles, and to revive his work in feveral other
churches.   O that God may order his coming to poor
Scotland, in fuch a cloudy time, for the fame end !
And who knows, but God might be intreated, if we
could wreftle with him, notwithftanding all our pro-
vocations ! Things appeared moft unlikely, in other
places, fome-while ago, where now Christ is riding
in triumph, going forth conquering and to conquer.
This worthy youth, is fingularly fitted to do the
work of an Evangelift ; and I have been long of
opinion, that it would be for the advantage of the
world, were this ftill to be a ftanding office in the
church.   And feeing the Lord has ftirred him up to
venture his life, reputation, and his ALL for Christ;
refufe the beft benefices in his own country, and run
all hazards by fea and land, and travel fo many
thoufand miles to proclaim the glory of Christ, and
riches of his free-grace, of which he himfelf is a
monument ; and efpecially, feeing God has honored
him to do all this with fuch furprifing fuccefs among
finners of all ranks and perfuafions, and even many
of the moft notorious, in awakening and turning them
to the Lord ; I truly think we are alfo bound to
honor him, and to efteem him highly in love for his
Mafter's, and for his work's fake, according to 1.
Theff. v. 13. And for thofe who vilify and oppofe
him, I wifh they would even notice a Gamaliel's
words, Acts v. " Let him alone, left haply ye be
" found to fight againft God :" Or rather, that they
would regard the Apoftle Peter's words, apologizing
for his going in with the uncircumcifed, Acts xi.
when the Holy Ghoft fell upon them ; ' What was I
' that I could withftand God ?' I have myfelf been
witnefs to the Holy Ghoft falling upon him and his
hearers, oftener than once, I do not fay in a miracu-
lous, though in an obfervable manner.   Yea, I have
                                                    already

H

already feen the defirable fruits thereof in not a few ; and hope, through the divine blefling on the feed fown, to fee more. Many here are blefling GOD, for fending him to this country, though Satan has raged much againſt it.

"THE LORD is a fovereign agent, and may raife up the inſtruments of his glory, from what churches or places he pleafes ; and glorifies his grace the more, when he does it from thofe focieties, whence and when it could be leaſt expected. Though Mr. WHITEFIELD be ordained, according to his educa- tion, a miniſter of the Church of England ; yet we are to regard him as one, whom GOD has raifed up, to witnefs againſt the corrupticns of that Church ; whom GOD is ſtill enlightening, and caufing to make advances towards us. He has already conformed to us, both in doctrine and worfhip, and lies open to light to conform to us in other points. He is tho- roughly a Calviniſt, and found to the doctrines of Free Grace, in the doctrine of Original Sin, the New Birth, Juſtification by CHRIST, the neceffity of imputed Righteoufnefs, the operations of the Holy Ghoſt, &c. Thefe he makes his great theme, drives the point home to the confcience, and GOD attends it with great power. And as GOD has enlightened him gradually in thefe things, fo he is ſtill ready to receive more light, and fo foon as he gets it, he is moſt frank in declaring it.

"GOD, by owning him fo wonderfully, is pleafed to give a rebuke to our intemperate bigotry, and party-zeal, and to tell us, that neither circumcifion nor uncircumcifion availeth any thing, but the new creature."—" P. S. Many with us are for preferring miniſters, according to the party they are of, but commend me to a pious, CHRIST-exalting, and foul- winning miniſter, whatever be his denomination. Such are miniſters of Chriſt's fending, and of fuch,

he

he faith, ' He that receiveth you, receiveth me, and and he that defpifeth you, depifeth me ;' which is a rule of duty to us*.''

THE

* The compiler lately received a tranfcript from the diary of a very worthy Chriftian in Edinburgh, who died about two years ago, in which are the following paffages. '' Sabbati, Auguft 9, 1741. What is furprifing, is, that numbers of all ranks, all denominations, and all characters, come conftantly to hear him, though his fermons abound with tenfe truths which would be unwelcome from the mouth of others. He is indefatigable in his work. Three hours before noon he appoints, for people under diftrefs to converfe with him, when he is much confined. Then he writes numbers of letters. And this week he is to add a morning lecture to his work. I have reafon, among many others, for blefling GOD for fending him to this place.

'' Sabbati, Auguft 30, 1741. Mr. W—d preached Mondaymorning and afternoon, Tuefday-forenoon in the Can, gate Church, evening in the park, and gathered 25l. 7s. 6d. for the poor Highlanders. Next day he went to Newbettle, and preached twice. On Thurfday to Whitburn ; Friday-morning at Torphichen; Friday-evening at Linlithgow ; Saturdaymorning and afternoon, both at Falkirk. And this day he is at Airth. To-morrow he will preach twice at Stirling. Culrofs, Tuefday forenoon ; Dunfermline, afternoon. Wednefday, twice at Kinrofs. Thurfday, Perth. From Friday to Monday, at Dundee. Monday, Kinglaffie, and came to Edinburgh on Tuefday. Bleffed be GOD, he feldom preaches without fome one or other laid under concern. Surely GOD has fent him to this place for good. The Devil never raged more by his emiffaries. It is remarkable, there never was a minifter, no nor any other man, againft whom the mouths of the licentious have been more opened. Since he came, I have found myfelf more defirous to be watchful, leff my foot flip at any time, and to guard againft many things, which before I thought indifferent.

'' Thurfday, October 27, 1741. Yefterday Mr. WHITEFIELD left this place, to return to England. His departure was a great grief to many, whom the LORD has mercifully awakened, under his miniftry, the number of which, I believe, is very great. Mr. W—d alone, among about thirty young communicants that came to converfe with him, found about a dozen, who told him, They were fift effectually touched under

der

THE four preceding letters fhew the acceptable-
nefs and fuccefs of Mr. WHITEFIELD's miniftrations
in moft of the great towns in Scotland.   As to fmaller places, the following extract of a letter from the
Rev. Mr. Thomas Davidfon (his fellow-traveller) to
the Rev. Mr. Henry Davidfon of Gallafhiels, dated
Culrofs, December, 3, 1741, will be an agreeable
fpecimen.

" OUR

der his miniftry ; and gave very good accounts of a work of
GOD upon their fouls. Some of the moft abandoned wretches
are brought to cry, ' What fhall I do to be faved?' I have often had the opportunity of converfation with him, and, I think,
I never heard him, or converfed with him, but I learned fome
good leffon. I do not remember to have heard one idle
word drop from him, in all the times I have been in company with him ; and others, that have been much more with
him, give him the fame teftimony. On Tuefday laft, he
preached and exhorted feven times. I heard him to my
great fatisfaction, the fourth time, in the park. From that
he went to the Old People's Hofpital, to give them an exhortation ; but indeed, I never was witnefs to any thing of the
kind before. All the congregation (for many followed him)
were fo moved, that very few, if any, could refrain from crying out. I am fure, the Kingdom of GOD was then come
nigh unto them, and that a woe will be unto them that flight-
ed the offers of a Savior then made to them. From that, he
went to Heriot's Hofpital, where a great change is wrought
upon many of the boys ; for there, as well as in the Maiden-
Hofpitals, Fellowfhip-meetings are fet up, which is quite new
there ; for the boys at that Hofpital were noted for the wick-
edeft boys about town. I was with him in a private houfe in
the evening. When he came there he was quite worn out.
However, he expounded there, which was the feventh difcourfe that day ; and, what was very furprifing, he was much
frefher after he had done, than at the beginning.

" November 29, 1741. I had agreeable accounts of fome
of the children who were wrought upon by the miniftry of
Mr. W—d. I heard this day of a good many, that I heard
not of formerly, who were not only laid under concern, but
feemed to have a work of grace wrought upon their heart,
appearing by a moft remarkable change in their converfation,

"OUR journey to the North was as comfortable as any we had. In several places, as he came along, the Lord I thought countenanced him in a very convincing manner, particularly at a place called Lundie, five miles north from Dundee, where there is a considerable number of serious Christians, who, hearing that he was to come that way, spent most part of the night before in prayer together. Although his preaching there was only in a passing way, having to ride to Dundee after it, and it was betwixt three and four before he reached the place; yet he had but scarce well begun, before the power of God was indeed very discernible. Never did I see such a pleasing melting in a worshipping assembly. There was nothing violent in it, or like what we may call screwing up the passions; for it evidently appeared to be deep and hearty, and to proceed from a higher spring."

As a conclusion of this article, concerning Mr. WHITEFIELD's first reception and ministrations in Scotland, the reader will not be displeased to see the following extract from the papers of a gentleman deceased, who was eminent for learning and knowledge of the world, and who had a general acquaintance with those who professed the greatest regard to religion.

MESSRS.

tion, and eager desires after farther degrees of knowledge of the LORD's ways, which leads them to attend every opportunity they can have for instruction.

"Sabbath, December 6. 1741. Since Mr. WHITEFIELD's coming here, I find Christians freer in conversation than formerly; which is a great mercy both to themselves and all about them; the experience of which I have had by this past week, in several places where I have been. I had occasion to see a soldier who was lately wrought upon by Mr. WHITEFIELD's means. He seems to have come a great length in a little time, and gives a very judicious account of the Lord's dealings with his soul."

H 2

" Messrs. Ebenezer and Ralph Erskine corresponded with him for two, or three years, and invited him to Scotland. But afterwards reflecting, that if they held communion with an episcopal minister, because a good man and successful preacher, they could not vindicate their renouncing communion with such ministers in the Church of Scotland: They wrote to him not to come. However, on the invitation of some ministers and people of the established Church, he came, and preached his first sermon in Mr. Ralph Erskine's pulpit at Dunfermline, (a town ten or twelve miles from Edinburgh, on the other side of Forth.) At a second visit to Dunfermline, he had a conference with all the seceding brethren, where he honestly avowed that he was a member of the Church of England, and as he thought the Government and Worship of it lawful, was resolved, unless violently thrust out of it, to continue so, rebuking sin and preaching CHRIST: And told them he reckoned the Solemn League and Covenant a sinful oath, as too much narrowing the communion of saints, and that he could not see the divine right of Presbytery. On this they came to a Presbyterial resolution to have no more to do with him; and one of them preached a sermon to shew that one who held communion with the Church of England, or backslidden Church of Scotland, could not be an instrument of reformation. This, however, did not hinder multitudes, both of the Seceders and established Church of Scotland, from hearing his sermons. His soundness in the faith, his fervent zeal, and unwearied diligence for promoting the cause of CHRIST; the plainness and simplicity, the affection and warmth of his sermons; and the amazing power that had accompanied them in many parts of England, and in almost all the North American Colonies, joined to his meekness, humility, and truly candid and catholic spirit, convinced them there

was

was reason to think well of him, and to countenance his ministry. Conversions were become rare, little liveliness was to be found even in real Christians, and bigotry and blind zeal were producing animosities and divisions, and turning away the attention of good men from matters of infinitely greater importance. In this situation, an animated preacher appears, singularly qualified to awaken the secure, to recover Christians to their first love, and first works, and to reconcile their affections one to another.

"THE episcopal clergy gave him no countenance, though some few of their people did. And in the established Church of Scotland, some of the more rigid presbyterians would not hold communion with him, on account of his connection with the Church of England, and his seeming to assume the office of an Evangelist, peculiar, in their apprehension, to the first ages of the church : while some, who affected to be thought more sensible, or more modish and polite, were mightily dissatisfied, with him for preaching the Calvinistic Doctrines of Election, Original Sin, Efficacious Grace, Justification through Faith, and the Perseverance of the Saints ; and for inveighing against the play-house, dancing assemblies, games of chance, haunting taverns, vanity and extravagance in dress, and levity in behavior and conversation.

"SOME gentlemen and ladies who went to hear, would not go a second time, because he disturbed them by insisting on man's miserable and dangerous state by nature, and the strictness and holiness essential to the Christian character. But, upon many of his hearers in Edinburgh, of all ranks and ages, especially young people, deep impressions were made, and many of them waited on him privately, lamenting their former immoral lives, or stupid thoughtlessness about religion, and expressing their anxious concern about obtaining an interest in CHRIST, and the sancti-

fying

fying influences of the SPIRIT. In the greatest part
of these, the impressions have appeared to be saving,
from their circumspect exemplary conduct since that
time, or from their comfortable or triumphant deaths.
Many Presbyterians begin to think more mildly and
candidly than before, of the ministers and members
of the Church of England."*

* This year, 1741, he received the compliment of honorary Burgefs Tickets from the Towns of Stirling, Glafgow,
Paifly, and Aberdeen. And in 1742, from Irvine. And 1762,
from Edinburgh.

C H A P. IX.

From his leaving Edinburgh 1741, *to his
Return to that City in the Year* 1742.

MR. WHITEFIELD, having left Edinburgh in the
latter end of October, 1741, fet out for Abergavenny,
in Wales, where, having fome time ago formed a
refolution, to enter into the married ftate, he married
one Mrs. James,* a widow between thirty and forty
years of age ; of whom he fays, " She has been a
houfe-keeper many years, once gay, but for three
years laft paft, a defpifed follower of the Lamb of
God." From Abergavenny he went to Briftol, where
he preached twice a-day with his ufual fuccefs. Upon
returning to London in the beginning of December,
he received letters from Georgia, concerning his orphan family, which, with refpect to their external
circumftances, were a little difcouraging. On the
other hand, he had moft comfortable accounts of the
fruits of his miniftry in Scotland. This made him
think

* Her maiden name was Elizabeth Burnell.

think of paying another visit there in the Spring. Meantime, he had the pleasure of seeing his labors attended with the divine blessing at London and Bristol. And from Gloucester he thus writes, " December 22, 1741.—Last Thursday evening the Lord brought me hither. I preached immediately to our friends in a large barn, and had my Master's presence. On Friday and Saturday, I preached again twice. Both the power and the congregation increased. On Sunday Providence opened a door for my preaching in St. John's, one of the parish churches. Great numbers came. On Sunday afternoon, after I had preached twice at Gloucester, I preached at Mr. F——'s at the hill, six miles off, and again at night, at Stroud. The people seemed to be more hungry than ever, and the Lord to be more amongst them. Yesterday morning I preached at Painswick, in the parish church, here in the afternoon, and again at night in the barn. God gives me unspeakable comfort, and uninterrupted joy. Here seems to be a new awakening, and a revival of the work of God. I find several country people were awakened, when I preached at Tewksbury, and have heard of three or four that have died in the Lord. We shall never know what good field-preaching has done, till we come to judgment. Many, who were prejudiced against me, begin to be of another mind : and God shows me more and more, that when a man's ways please the Lord, he will make even his enemies to be at peace with him. To-morrow morning I purpose to set out for Abergavenny, and to preach at Bristol, in Wilts, Gloucester and Gloucestershire, before I see London."

In the latter end of December he came to Bristol, where he continued near a month, preaching twice every day, and writing to his friends in London and Scotland. He also set up a general monthly meeting

to

to read corresponding letters. From Briftol he returned to Gloucester, and January 28, 1742, writes
—"On Friday laft I left Briftol, having firft fettled
affairs, almoft as I could with. At Kingfwood I
adminiftered the facrament on Wednefday night.
It was the Lord's paffover. On Thurfday we had a
fweet love-feaft ; on Friday the Lord was with me
twice at Tockington ; on Saturday morning I broke
up fome fallow ground at Newport ; and in the
evening preached to many thoufands at Stroud ; on
Monday morning at Painfwick, and ever fince twice
a-day here. Our congregations. I think, are larger
than at Briftol. Every fermon is bleffed."

On his way to London, Feb. 23, he was ftill farther encouraged by receiving letters from America,
informing him of the remarkable fuccefs of the gofpel
there, and that God had ftirred up fome wealthy
friends to affift his orphans in their late ftraits*. Upon
his return to London, he went on with greater zeal
and fuccefs, if poffible, than ever. " Our Savior (fays
he, writing to a brother, April 6, 1742) is doing great
things in London daily. I rejoice to hear that you
are helped in your work. Let this encourage you :
go on, go on, the more we do, the more we may do
for Jefus. I fleep and eat but little, and am conftantly
employed from morning till midnight, and yet my
ftrength is daily renewed. O free grace ! It fires
my foul, and makes me long to do fomething for
Jefus. It is true, indeed, I want to go home ; but
here are fo many fouls ready to perifh for lack of
knowledge, that I am willing to tarry below as long
as my Mafter has work for me."

FROM

---

* " The everlafting God reward all their benefactors. I
find there has been a frefh awakening among them. I am
informed, that twelve negroes, belonging to a planter lately
converted at the Orphan houfe, are favingly brought home to
Jesus Christ."

FROM this principle of compaſſion to periſhing ſouls, he now ventured to take a very extraordinary ſtep. It had been the cuſtom for many years paſt, in the holiday ſeaſons, to erect booths in Moorfields, for mountebanks, players, puppet-ſhows, &c. which were attended from morning till night, by innumerable multitudes of the lower ſort of people. He formed a reſolution to preach the goſpel among them ; and executed it. On Whitmonday, at ſix o'clock in the morning, attended by a large congregation of praying people he began. Thouſands, who were waiting there, gaping for their uſual diverſions, all flocked round him. His text was John iii. 44. They gazed, they liſtened, they wept ; and many ſeemed to be ſtung with deep conviction for their paſt ſins. All was huſhed and ſolemn. " Being thus encouraged (ſays he,) I ventured out again at noon, when the fields were quite full ; and could ſcarce help ſmiling, to ſee thouſands, when a merry-andrew was trumpeting to them, upon obſerving me mount a ſtand upon the other ſide of the field, deſerting him, till not ſo much as one was left behind, but all flocked to hear the goſpel. But this, together with a complaint that they had taken near twenty or thirty pounds leſs that day than uſual, ſo enraged the owners of the booths, that when I came to preach a third time in the evening, in the midſt of the ſermon, a merry-andrew got up upon a man's ſhoulders, and advancing near the pulpit, attempted to ſlaſh me with a long heavy whip ſeveral times. Soon afterwards they got a recruiting ſergeant, with his drum, &c. to paſs thro' the congregation. But I deſired the people to make way for the King's officer, which was quietly done. Finding theſe efforts to fail, a large body, quite on the oppoſite ſide, aſſembled together, and, having got a great pole for their ſtandard, advanced with ſound of drum, in a very threatening manner, till they came near the

the skirts of the congregation. Uncommon courage was given to both preacher and hearers. I prayed for support and deliverance, and was heard. 'For just as they approached us with looks full of resentment, I know not by what accident they quarrelled among themselves, threw down their staff, and went their way, leaving, however, many of their company behind, who, before we had done, I trust, were brought over to join the besieged party. I think I continued in praying, preaching, and singing (for the noise was too great at times to preach) about three hours. We then retired to the Tabernacle, where thousands flocked. We were determined to pray down the booths; but blessed be God, more substantial work was done. At a moderate computation, I received (I believe) a thousand notes from persons under conviction ; and soon after, upwards of three hundred were received into the society in one day. Some I married, that had lived together without marriage. One man had exchanged his wife for another, and given fourteen shillings in exchange. Numbers, that seemed as it were to have been bred up for Tyburn, were at that time plucked as firebrands out of the burning."

" I cannot help adding, that several little boys and girls, who were fond of sitting round me on the pulpit, while I preached, and handing to me people's notes, though they were often pelted with eggs, dirt, &c. thrown at me, never once gave way ; but on the contrary, every time I was struck, turned up their little weeping eyes, and seemed to wish they could receive the blows for me. God make them, in their growing years, great and living martyrs for him, who out of the mouth of babes and sucklings perfects praise."

CHAP.

CHAP. X.

From his Arrival in Scotland, 1742, *to his Return to* London *the fame Year.*

SOON after this, he embarked a fecond time for Scotland, and arrived at Leith, June 3, 1742.*

But here it is proper to take a view of the ftate of things in that country upon his arrival. It had pleafed GOD to blefs his firft vifit to Scotland, not only for the converfion of particular perfons, and the comfort and quickening of private Chriftians, but to roufe them to more than ordinary concern about the falvation of their neighbours, and to excite pious and
                                              confcientious

* "Edinburgh, Sabbath, June 6, 1742. On Thurfday laft our dear friend Mr. WHITEFIELD returned to this place, to the great comfort of many honeft Chriftians, efpecially of thofe to whom he was made a mean of conviction and converfion when laft here.—He feems to have improved much in Chriftian knowledge. He is much refrefhed with the accounts of the work of GOD in the weft country.—I have heard him preach five excellent difcourfes, all calculated for the building up of Chriftians (though he never fails to put in a word for the conviction of finners;) and, I think, can fay, that I have never heard him without fome influence attending his preaching, efpecially in private houfes. O may the impreffions made on my heart never wear off, left at any time I fhould be in danger of dropping my watch, and becoming untender."

"Sabb. October 17, 1742. It is a great recommendation of Mr. WHITEFIELD to me, that though the Seceders give him every bad character that can be devifed, viz. a forcerer, &c. yet he takes all patiently, and where-ever he goes, fpeaks well of them, fo far as he can: for none can approve of thofe grofs parts of their conduct: therefore thefe he choofes to caft a mantle of love over." Diary formerly quoted.

I

confcientious minifters to greater diligence in their work. Prayers were put up, with fome degree of faith and hope, that GOD would now give fuccefs to their labors ; and not fuffer them always to complain that they fpent their ftrength in vain. Nor were thefe prayers long unanfwered : for in the month of February, 1742, an extraordinary religious concern began to appear publicly at Cambuflang ; and foon after at Kilfyth and other places : the news of which fpread quickly through the land, and engaged general attention. Of this a juft, though fhort defcription is given in the following letter, written by the Rev. Mr. Hamilton (then minifter in the Barony parifh, now in the High-Church of Glafgow) to Mr. Prince, minifter in Bofton.* " Glafgow, Sept. 13, 1742. We in the fouth and weft of Scotland, have great reafon to join in thankfulnefs to God, with you, for the days of the REDEEMER's power that we are favored with. Mr. WHITEFIELD came to Scotland in fummer 1741, for the firft time : and in many places where he preached, his miniftrations were evidently bleffed, particularly in the cities of Edinburgh and Glafgow, where a con-fiderable number of perfons were brought under fuch impreffions of religion, as have never yet left them ; but they are ftill following on to know the LORD. However, this was only the beginning of far greater things : for about the middle of February laft, a very great concern appeared among the people of Cambuf-lang, a fmall parifh, lying four miles fouth-eaft of Glafgow, under the paftoral infpection of the Rev. Mr. William MacCulloch, a man of confiderable parts and great piety. This concern appeared with fome circumftances very unufual among us : to wit, fevere bodily agonies, out-cryings, and faintings in the con-gregation. This made the report of it fpread like fire, and drew vaft multitudes of people from all quarters to

that

* Prince's Chriftian Hiftory, No. X.

that place. And, I believe, in lefs than two months after the commencement of it, there were few parifhes within twelve miles of Cambuflang, but had fome, more or fewer awakened there, to a very deep, piercing fenfe of fin : and many at a much greater diftance. I am verily perfuaded with your worthy brother Mr. Cooper, in his preface to Mr. Edward's fermon, that God has made ufe of thefe uncommon circumftances, to make his work fpread the fafter. But, bleffed be God, Cambuflang is not the only place where thefe impreffions are got. The fame work is fpreading in other parifhes, and under their own minifters, particularly at Caulder, Kilfyth, and Cumbernaud, all to the north, and north-eaft of Glafgow. And I doubt not, that fince the middle of February, when this work began at Cambuflang, there are upwards of two thoufand perfons awakened, and almoft all of them, by the beft accounts I have, in a promifing condition ; there being very few inftances of impoftors, or fuch as have loft their impreffions ; and many whom we are bound to think are true Scripture-converts, and evidencing it by a fuitable walk and converfation. There is evidently a greater ferioufnefs and concern about religion appearing in moft of our congregations than formerly : a greater defire after the word ; people applying themfelves more clofely to their duty ; and erecting new focieties for prayer and fpiritual conference : which gives us the joyful profpect of a confiderable enlargement in the Meffiah's kingdom.

My parifh has likewife had fome fhare in this good work. There has been above an hundred new communicants among them, this fummer, who never did partake of the bleffed facrament before : which is five times as many as ever I admitted in any former year : moft of them were awakened at Cambuflang ; fome of them in their own church ; and in others the impreffions have been more gradual, and not attended

with

with thefe uncommon circumftances before-mentioned.
And it is to be obferved, that before we admit any
perfon to the LORD's table, we particularly examine
them, and are fatisfied with their knowledge of the
principles of religion, of the nature and ends of the
facrament, and the impreflions of religion they have
on their minds.''*

To the fame purpofe is the Rev. Mr. Willifon's
letter to Dr. Colman, minifter in Bofton : dated
Dundee, Feb. 28, 1743.† "I muft inform you a
little of the work of GOD began here. I told you
in my laft, that after Mr. WHITEFIELD's firft coming,
and preaching three months in Scotland, there were
fome beginnings of a revival of religion in fome of
our principal cities, at Edinburgh and Glafgow,
which ftill continue and increafe, efpecially fince Mr.
WHITEFIELD's fecond coming in June laft. But
befides thefe cities, the Lord hath been pleafed to
begin a work much like that in New-England, in
feveral places in the weft of Scotland. The firft
parifh awakened, was Cambuflang; the next was the
parifh of Kilfyth, about nine miles north-eaft of
Glafgow, and afterwards the parifhes of Calder,
Kirkintilloch, Cumbernaud, Campfie, Kilmarnock,
Gargunnock, and a great many others in the country.

                               The

---

* Extract of a Letter from a perfon of diftinction to the
Compiler.

"Edinburgh, February, 1772. I would not afcribe all the
revival of religion in Scotland, to (the inftrumentality of) Mr.
WHITEFIELD. At Cambuflang, it began, before he had been
there ; but in Edinburgh, and all the other places in Scotland,
that I heard of, after diligent enquiry, it began with his firft
vifit. This honor he had from his divine Mafter, and it ought
not to be taken from him. And every time he came to Scotland, it is an undoubted fact, that an uncommon power attended his miniftry ; and many were always brought under
ferious and lafting impreflions."

† Prince's Chriftian Hiftory, No. XI.

The awakenings of people, have been, in a good many, attended with out-cryings, faintings, and bodily diftreffes : but in many more, the work has proceeded with great calmnefs. But the effects in both forts, are alike good and defirable, and hitherto we hear nothing of their falling back from what they have profeffed at the beginning ; and ftill we hear of fome new parifhes falling under great concern here and there, though the great cryings and outward diftreffes are much ceafed.

" THE Lord in this backfliding time, is willing to pity us, and fee our ways and heal them, however crooked and perverfe they have been. O fhall not this wonderful ftep of divine condefcenfion, lead us all to repentance, and to go out to meet a returning GOD, in the way of humiliation and reformation. The magiftrates and minifters in Edinburgh, are beginning to fet up focieties for reformation of manners, and new lectures on week-days. May all our cities follow their example. There is a great increafe of praying focieties alfo in Edinburgh and other towns and villages ; and in them they are keeping days of thankfgiving for the partial waterings the Lord is giving us : thofe in Edinburgh, fend printed memorials to others through the nation, to excite them to it."*

THE greateft ftrangers to religion could not avoid hearing of thefe things, but they were very differently

---

* The Rev. Mr. Macknight of Irvine, thus writes to Mr. WHITEFIELD, June 21, 1742. " Bleffed be our glorious GOD, there are fome awakenings amongft us at Irvine ; not only of thofe who have been at Cambuflang, but feveral others are lately brought into concern about their eternal ftate, and among them feveral children ; the news of which I know will rejoice you, and I hope will encourage you to vifit us to help forward this great and glorious work of converting finners."
—*Remarkable Particulars, &c.*

ently affected with them. Whilst some became more thoughtful and serious, many mocked, and some were even filled with rage. On the other hand, the temper and behavior of those who were the subjects of this remarkable work, was the strongest of all arguments that it came from above. Their earnest desire to be rightly directed in the way to heaven; their tender and conscientious walk; their faithfulness in the duties of their stations; their readiness to make ample restitution for any act of injustice they had formerly committed; their disposition to judge mildly of others, but severely of themselves; their laying aside quarrels and law-suits, and desiring to be reconciled, and to live peaceably with all men; such amiable and heavenly qualities, especially when appearing in some who had formerly been of a very opposite character, could not fail to strike every serious observer. In short, it was such a time for the revival of religion as had never before been seen in Scotland.*

THE enmity which wicked and profane men discovered against this work, and the derision with which they treated it, is no more than what might naturally be expected. But it is not so easy to account for the conduct of the Seceders. These, not satisfied with forbearing to approve of it, went the length even to appoint a general fast among them, one of the grounds of which was, the receiving Mr. WHITEFIELD into Scotland; and another, the delusion, as they called it, at Cambuslang and other places. And Mr. Gibb, one of their ministers, wrote

---

* Particulars may be found in the attested Narrative of the Work at Cambuslang; Dr. Webster's Divine Influence the true Spring, &c. and in Mr. Robe's Narratives and Monthly History.—A view of the most memorable passages, is given in Vol. II. Book IV. Chap. VI. of Hist. Coll. relating to the Success of the Gospel, printed in 1754; where is also some account of the abiding fruits of these religious impressions.

wrote a pamphlet inveighing againſt both, in the moſt virulent language. Such was the bigotry, and miſguided zeal of the bulk of the party at that time. It is hoped their ſucceſſors have juſter views of this matter. But it is not proper here to enlarge upon this ſubject.† With reſpect to Mr. WHITEFIELD, the ſpring of their firſt oppoſition to him, ſufficiently appears from his converſation with them at Dunfermline, formerly mentioned. And the following letter, which he wrote at Cambuſlang, Auguſt, 1742, and which was afterwards printed at Glaſgow, gives an account of their objections, and his anſwers, which are perfectly agreeable to the ſpirit of both*.

" I heartily thank you for your concern about unworthy me. Though I am not very ſolicitous what the world ſay of me, yet I would not refuſe to give any one, much leſs a miniſter of JESUS CHRIST (and ſuch an one I take you to be) all reaſonable ſatisfaction about any part of my doctrine or conduct. I am ſorry that the Aſſociate Preſbytery, beſides the other things exceptionable in the grounds of their late faſt, have done me much wrong. As to what they ſay about the ſupremacy, my ſentiments, as to the power and authority of the civil magiſtrate as to ſacred things, agree with what is ſaid in the Weſtminſter Confeſſion of Faith, chapter xxiii. paragraph 3 and 4. And I do own the LORD JESUS to be the bleſſed Head and King of his church.

" THE

---

† The reader who wants to ſee the objections againſt the work at Cambuſlang, &c. fully refuted, may conſult (beſides the books mentioned in the laſt note) Mr. Robe's Letters to Mr. Fiſher ; and Mr. Jonathan Edwards' Diſtinguiſhing Marks of a Work of the SPIRIT of GOD."—And as to the argument from the goodneſs of the fruits, which is a level to the capacities of all, the Compiler thinks it his duty to add, that among his acquaintance, who were the ſubjects of that work, the fruits were generally both *good* and *laſting*.

* Glaſgow Weekly Hiſtory, No. XXIII.

"THE Solemn League and Covenant I never abjured, neither was it ever propofed to me to be
abjured : and as for my miffives, if the Affociate
Prefbytery will be pleafed to print them, the world
will fee that they had no reafon to expect I would
act in any other manner than I have done. What
that part of my experience is, that favors of the
groffeft enthufiafm, I know not, becaufe not fpecified ;
but this one thing I know, when I converfed with
them, they were fatisfied with the account I then
gave of my experiences, and alfo of the validity of
my miffion ; only, when they found I would preach
the gofpel promifcuoufly to all, and for every minifter that would invite me, and not adhere only to
them, one of them particularly faid, ' They were
fatisfied with all the other accounts which I gave of
myfelf, except of my call to Scotland at that time.'
They would have been glad of my help, and have
received me as a minifter of JESUS CHRIST, had I
confented to have preached only at the invitation of
them and their people. But I judged that to be contrary to the dictates of my confcience ; and therefore
I could not comply. I thought their foundation was
too narrow for any high houfe to be built upon. I
declared freely, when laft in Scotland, (and am more
and more convinced of it fince) that they were
building a Babel.* At the fame time, they knew

very

* The event verified this conjecture. In his M. S. notes,
feveral years after, he makes the following remark : " Such
a work (the religious concern at Cambuflang) fo very extenfive, muft meet with great oppofition. My collections for
the orphans gave a great handle ; but the chief oppofition
was made by the Seceders, who, though they had prayed for
me at a moft extravagant rate, now gave out that I was agita-
ted by the devil. Taking it for granted, that all converted
perfons muft take the covenant, and that GOD had left the
Scotch eftablifhed churches long ago, and that he would never

work

very well, I was very far from being against all
church-government, (for how can any church fubfift
without it ?) I only urged, as I do now, that fince
holy men differ fo much about the outward form, we
fhould bear with, and forbear one another, though in
this refpeſt we are not of one mind.   I have often
declared in the moft public manner, that I believe the
Church of Scotland to be the beft conftituted national
church in the world.   At the fame time I would bear
with, and converfe freely with all others, who do not
err in fundamentals, and who give evidence that they
are true lovers of the LORD JESUS.   This is what I
mean by a catholic fpirit.   Not that I believe a Jew
or Pagan, continuing fuch, can be a true Chriftian, or
have true Chriftianity in them ; and if there be any
thing tending that way in the late extraſt which I
fent you, I utterly difavow it.   And I·am fure, I
obferved no fuch thing in it, when I publifhed it,
though upon a clofer review, fome expreffions feem
juftly exceptionable.   You know how ftrongly I affert
all the doſtrines of grace as held forth in the Weft-
minfter Confeffion of Faith, and doſtrinal articles of
the Church of England. Thefe I truft I fhall adhere to
as long as I live, becaufe I verily believe they are the
truths of GOD, and have felt the power of them in
my own heart.   I am only concerned that good men
fhould be guilty of fuch mifreprefentations.   But this
teaches me more and more to exercife compaffion to-
　　　　　　　　　　　　　　　　　　ward

work by the hand of a curate of the Church of England, they
condemned the whole work, as the work of the devil; and
kept a faft through all Scotland, to humble themfelves, becaufe the devil was come down in wrath, and to pray that the
Lord would rebuke the deftroyer (for that was my title).   But
the LORD rebuked thefe good men; for they fplit among
themfelves, and excommunicated one-another.   Having afterwards a fhort interview with Mr. Ralph Erfkine, we embraced each other, and he faid, " We had feen ftrange
things."

ward all the children of GOD, and to be more jealous over my own heart, knowing what fallible creatures we all are.   I acknowledge that I am a poor blind finner, liable to err, and would be obliged to an enemy, much more to fo dear a friend as you are, to point out to me my miftakes, as to my practice, or unguarded expreffions in my preaching or writing. At the fame time I would humble myfelf before my Mafter, for any thing I may fay or do amifs, and beg the influence and affiftance of his blefled fpirit, that I may fay and do fo no more."

So much for Mr. WHITEFIELD's difference with the Seceders. But notwithftanding all this, upon his fecond arrival in Scotland, June, 1742, he was received by great numbers, among whom were fome perfons of diftinction, with much joy : and had the fatisfaction of feeing and hearing more and more of the happy fruits of his miniftry.*   At Edinburgh, he preached twice a-day, as ufual, in the Hofpital park, where a number of feats and fhades, in the form of an amphitheatre, were erected for the accommodation of his hearers.   And in confequence of earneft invitations, he went to the weft country, particularly to Cambuflang ; where he preached no lefs than three times upon the very day of his arrival, to a vaft body of people, although he had preached that fame morning at Glafgow.

The

---

* "Edinburgh, June 4, 1742.   This morning I received glorious accounts of the carrying on of the Mediator's kingdom.   Three of the little boys that were converted when I was laft here, came to me and wept, and begged me to pray for and with them.   A minifter tells me, that fcarce one is fallen back, who was awakened, either among old or young. The Sergeant, whofe letter brother C—— has, goes on well with his company."

And in the M. S. "Societies (or fellowfhip meetings) I found fet up for prayer, efpecially at Glafgow and Edinburgh. Several young gentlemen dedicated themfelves to the miniftry, and became burning and fhining lights."

The laft of thefe exercifes he began at nine at night, continuing till eleven, when he faid he obferved fuch a commotion among the people, as he had never feen in America. Mr. Mac Culloch preached after him, till paft one in the morning, and even then could hardly perfuade the people to depart. All night in the fields might be heard the voice of prayer and praife. As Mr. WHITEFIELD was frequently at Cambuflang during this feafon, a defcription of what he obferved there at different times, will be beft given in his own words* ; " Perfons from all parts flocked to fee, and many, from many parts, went home convinced and converted unto GOD. A brae, or hill, near the manfe at Cambuflang, feemed to be formed by Providence, for containing a large congregation. People fat unwearied till two in the morning, to hear fermons, difregarding the weather. You could fcarce walk a yard, but you muft tread upon fome, either rejoicing in GOD for mercies received, or crying out for more. Thoufands and thoufands have I feen, before it was poffible to catch it by fympathy, melted down under the word and power of GOD. At the celebration of the holy communion, their joy was fo great, that at the defire of many, both minifters and people, in imitation of Hezekiah's paflover, they had, a month or two afterwards, a fecond which was a general rendezvous of the people of GOD. The communion-table was in the field ; three tents at proper diftances, all furrounded with a multitude of hearers : above twenty minifters (among whom was good old Mr. Bonner) attending to preach and affift, all enlivening and enlivened by one-another."

BESIDES his labors at Glafgow and Cambuflang, it is fomewhat furprifing to think, how many other places in the weft of Scotland he vifited within the compafs of a few weeks, preaching once or twice at every one of them, and at feveral three or four times. It

* M. S.   is

is worth while to fet down the Journal of a week or two. In the beginning of July, he preached twice on Monday at Paifley; on the Tuefday and Wednefday, three times each day at Irvine; on Thurfday, twice at Mearns; on Friday, three times at Cumbernaud; and on Saturday, twice, at Falkirk. And again in the latter end of Auguft; on Thurfday, he preached twice at Greenock; on Friday, three times at Kil. bride; on Saturday, once at Kilbride, and twice at Stevenfon; on Sabbath, four times at Irvine, on Monday once at Irvine, and three times at * Kilmarnock;

Tuefday,

* A gentleman now living, of an irreproachable character, thus writes to the Compiler, April 8, 1771. "When Mr. WHITEFIELD was preaching at Kilmarnock, on the 23d of Auguft, 1742, from thefe words, ' And out of his fulnefs have all ' we received, and grace for grace,' I thought I never heard fuch a fermon on the fulnefs of grace that is treafured up in CHRIST JESUS: and can truly fay that I felt the efficacy of the holy SPIRIT upon my foul, during that difcourfe. I afterwards fhut up myfelf in my chamber, during the remaining part of that day; and before I laid myfelf down to reft, I made a folemn and ferious dedication of myfelf to GOD, by way of covenant, extended and fubfcribed the fame with my hands; and, I think, had communion with GOD, in fo doing: to which I have often had recourfe fince, in adhering thereto, and in renewing thereof; though my life fince has been attended with many backflidings from GOD, and have been perfidious in his covenant; yet ftill I rejoice in his falvation through precious CHRIST. And it is refrefhing to behold the place at this very day, as I have often done fince. I from the æra abovementioned, always looked upon Mr. WHITEFIELD as my fpiritual father, and frequently heard him afterwards in Edinburgh and Glafgow with much fatisfaction. It always gave me joy, the mentioning of his name, and grieved me when he was reproached. And I can very well remember, that when Cape Breton was taken, I happened to be then at Edinburgh; and being invited to breakfaft with Mr. WHITEFIELD, I never in all my life enjoyed fuch another breakfaft. He gave the company a fine and lively defcant upon that part of the world, made us all join in a hymn of praife and thankfgiving, and concluded with a moft

devout

Tuefday, once at Kilmarnock,* and four times at Stewarton ; on Wednefday, once at Stewarton, and twice at the Mearns.   He was alfo at Inchannen, New Kilpatrick, Calder, and Kilfyth, (where the religious concern ſtill increaſed) and at Torphichen. He was indeed ſometimes taken very ill, and his fiiends thought he was going oti; " But in the pulpit (fays he) the Lord out of weaknefs, makes me to wax ſtrong, and caufes me to triumph more and more." And even when he retired for a day or two, it was on purpofe to write letters, and to prepare pieces for the prefs, fo that he was as bufy as ever.†

WHEN he was at Edinburgh, he received accounts that the Spaniards had landed in Georgia.   Upon this occafion he wrote to Mr. Haberſham, " I am glad my dear family is removed to Mr. Bryan's, and rejoice that our glorious GOD had raifed him and his brother up, to be ſuch friends in time of need.   My thoughts have been varioufly exercifed, but my heart kept ſtedfaſt and joyful in the LORD of all lords, whofe mercy endureth for ever.   I long to be. with you, and methinks could willingly be found at the

head

---

devout and fervent prayer.   In the evening of that day, he preached a moſt excellent thankſgiving fermon, from the firſt two verfes of the cxxvith pfalm.

* " I never preached with fo much apparent fuccefs before. At Greenock, Irvine, Kilbride, Kilmarnock, and Stewarton, the concern was great: at the three laſt very extraordinary."

† Particularly, a Vindication of the Work of GOD in New-England.   See Works, Vol. IV. and feveral letters about the affairs of the Orphan-houfe, fome of his friends there having met with harſh treatment from the magiſtrates of Savannah.

At this time alfo he publifhed at Edinburgh, a continuation of the account of the Orphan-houfe, from January 1741, to June 1742.—See his Works, Vol. III. where you have the whole account continued from time to time, till April 1770.

K

head of you kneeling and praying, though a Spaniard's fword fhould be put to my throat.   But alas, I know not how I fhould behave, if put to the trial : only we have a promife, that as our day is, fo our ftrength fhall be.   The thoughts of divine love carry me above every thing.   My dear friend, the Spaniards cannot rob us of this ; nor can men or devils.— I humbly hope that I fhall fhortly hear of the fpiritual and temporal welfare of you all."   And he was not difappointed ; for a few weeks after he was informed of his family's fafe return to Bethefda.*

ABOUT the end of October he left Scotland, and rode poft to London, where he arrived in about five days.   —

* The manner in which the Spaniards were repulfed, with remarks upon the kindnefs of Providence to the colony, may be feen in an extract of General Oglethorp's proclamation for a thankfgiving.

C H A R.

CHAP. XI.

From his Arrival in London, *in the Year* 1742, *to his embarking for* America, *in* 1744.

ON Mr. WHITEFIELD's arrival in London, he found a new awakening at the Tabernacle, which they had been obliged to enlarge ; where, as he ob- serves, " from morning till midnight, I am employed ; and, glory be to rich grace, I am carried through the duties of each day with chearfulnefs, and almoft uninterrupted tranquillity.   Our fociety is large, but in good order.   My Mafter gives us much of his gracious prefence, both in our public and private adminiftrations."

In the month of March, 1742, he went into Gloucefterfhire, where the people feemed more defirous to hear than ever.   " Preaching, (fays he) in Gloucefterfhire, is now like preaching at the Tabernacle in London."   And again, (in a Letter, dated, April 7,) " I preached and took leave of the Gloucefter people, with mutual and great concern, on Sunday evening laft.   It was paft one in the morning before I could lay my weary body down.   At five I rofe again, fick for want of reft ; but I was enabled to get on horfeback, and ride to Mr. F——'s, where I preached to a large congregation, who came there at feven in the merning.   At ten. I read prayers and preached. and afterwards adminiftered the facrament in Stonehoufe church.   Then I rode to Stroud, and preached to about 12,000 in Miftrefs G——'s field ; and about fix in the evening to a like number in Hampton-Common.   After this, went to Hampton, and
held

held a general love-feaſt with the United Societies, and went to bed about midnight very chearful, and very happy." Next morning he preached near Durſley, to ſome thouſands ; about ſeven reached Briſtol, and preached to a full congregation at Smith's Hall : and on Tueſday morning, after preaching again, ſet out for Waterford, in South-Wales, where he opened the aſſociation which he and his brethren had agreed upon, and was ſeveral days with them, ſettling the affairs of the ſocieties. He continued in Wales ſome weeks, and preached with great apparent ſucceſs at Cardiff, Lantriſſant, Neath, Swanzey, Harbrook, Llanelthy, Carmarthen, *Larn, Narbatt, Newton, Jefferſon, Llaſſivrʒn, Kidwilly, Llangathan, Landovery, Brecon, Treveeka, Guenfethen, Builth, and the Gore,† and in the latter end of April returned to Glouceſter, after having, in about three weeks, travelled about four hundred Engliſh miles, ſpent three days, in attending aſſociations,‡ and preached about forty times.

                                        In

---

* It was the Great Seſſions. The Juſtices deſired I would ſtay till they roſe, and they would come. Accordingly they did, and many thouſands more ; and ſeveral people of quality."

  † The work begun by Mr. Jones, ſpread far and near, in South and North-Wales, where the Lord had made Mr. Howel Harris an inſtrument of converting ſeveral clergy as well as laymen. Laſt year I viſited ſeveral places, but now I went to more, and in every place found, that not one half had been told me. The power of God at the ſacrament, under the miniſtry of Mr. Rowland, was enough to make a perſon's heart burn within him. At ſeven of the morning have I ſeen perhaps ten thouſand from different parts, in the midſt of ſermon, crying, Gogunniant—bendyitti—ready to leap for joy. Aſſociations were now formed, and monthly or quarterly meetings appointed, and a cloſer connection eſtabliſhed between the Engliſh and Welch, ſo that ſeveral came over to aſſiſt." M. S.

  ‡ At one of theſe aſſociations, a motion was made to ſeparate from the eſtabliſhed Church : but (ſays Mr. WHITEFIELD)
                                        " by

In May he went back to London, " Once more, as he expreſſes it, to attack the prince of darkneſs in Moorfields," in the time of the holidays. The congregations were amazingly great and much affected. And by the contributions which were now and formerly made for his orphans, he had the ſatisfaction of paying all that was due in England, and of making a ſmall remittance to Mr. Haberſham.

About the middle of June, he made another excurſion, and preached at Fairford, Glanfield, Burford, Bengeworth, and Glouceſter ; alſo at Briſtol and Kingſwood, and at Brinkworth, Tetherton, and Hampton. At Briſtol he continued ſome time,— preaching ſtatedly every day twice, and four times on the Sunday. Afterwards he preached at Exeter, to very large congregations, where many of the clergy attended.

In Auguſt he returned to London, but made no long ſtay there. " I thank you, (ſays he to a correſpondent,) for your kind caution to ſpare myſelf; but evangelizing is certainly my province. Every-where effectual doors are opened. So far from thinking of neſtling at London, I am more and more convinced that I ſhould go from place to place."

Accordingly we find him in the months of October, November, and December, preaching and travelling through the country, as if it had been the
middle

" by far the greater part ſtrenuouſly oppoſed it, and for good reaſon : for, as we enjoy ſuch great liberty under the mild and gentle government of his preſent Majeſty King George, I think we can do him, our country, and the cauſe of God, more ſervice, in ranging up and down, preaching repentance towards God, and faith in our Lord Jesus Christ, to thoſe multitudes who would neither come into church or meeting, but who are led by curioſity to follow us into the fields. This is a way, to which God has affixed his ſeal for many years paſt."

middle of Summer.   At Avon, in Wilts, Tetherton, Clack, Brinkworth, Chippenham, Wellington, Cullompton, Exeter, Axminster, Ottery, Biddeford,† St. Gennis in Cornwall,‡ Birmingham,§ Kidderminster,* and Bromsgrove.   Nor did he feel his health-much impaired, though it was so late in the season.   He observes, indeed that he had got a cold ; but adds, " The Lord warms my heart."

FEBRUARY 1744, an event happened to him, which, amidst all his success, tended to keep him humble, and served to cure him of a weakness to which he had been liable, the trusting to groundless impressions.   It was the death of his only child, concerning whom he was so impressed, that he made no scruple of declaring before the birth, that the child would be a son, and that he hoped he would live to preach the gospel.   Several narrow escapes which

Mrs.

† Here is a clergyman about eighty years of age, but not above one year old in the school of CHRIST. He lately preached three times, and rode forty miles the same day. A young Oxonian who came with him, and many others, were deeply affected. I cannot well describe with what power the word was attended. Dear Mr. Hervey, one of our first Methodists at Oxford, and who was lately a curate here, had laid the foundation."

‡ " Many prayers were put up by the worthy Rector and others, for an out-pouring of GOD's blessed Spirit. They were answered. Arrows of conviction flew so thick, and so fast, and such an universal weeping prevailed from one end of the congregation to the other, that good Mr. J——, their minister, could not help going from seat to seat, to speak, encourage, and comfort the wounded souls."

§ " It is near eleven at night, and nature calls for rest. I have preached five times this day, and weak as I am, through CHRIST strengthening me, could preach five times more."

* " I was kindly received by Mr. Williams. Many friends were at his house. I was greatly refreshed to find what a sweet savour of good Mr. Baxter's doctrine, works, and discipline remained to this day."

Mrs. Whitefield had during her pregnancy, confirmed him in his expectations ; which were fo high, that after he had publicly baptized the child at the Tabernacle, all went away big with hopes of his being fpared to be employed in the work of God. But thefe fond expectations were foon blafted by the child's death, when he was about four months old. This was, no doubt, very humbling to the father ; but he was helped to make the wifeft and beft improvement of it. "Though I am difappointed, fays he, (writing to his friend) of a living preacher by the death of my fon ; yet I hope what happened before his birth, and fince at his death, has taught me fuch leffons, as if duly improved, may render his miftaken parent more cautious, more fober-minded, more experienced in Satan's devices, and confequently more ufeful in his future labors to the church of God."

March 3, he attended the affizes at Gloucefter. The occafion was, in the Summer 1743, the Methodifts had been perfecuted and abufed by the mob, particularly at Hampton, where feveral were hurt, and the life of their preachers threatened. Mr. Whitefield having tried other methods in vain, refolved, with the advice and affiftance of his brethren, to feek the protection of law : and accordingly got an information lodged againft the Hampton rioters in the court of King's Bench. Facts being proved by a variety of evidence, and the defendants making no reply, the rule was made abfolute ; and an information filed againft them. To this they pleaded *Not Guilty*, and therefore the caufe was referred in courfe to the affizes in Gloucefter. There he attended, and got the better of his adverfaries. After a full hearing on both fides, a verdict was given for the profecutors, and all the defendants were brought in guilty of the whole information lodged againft them. This profecution had a very good effect. The rioters were

greatly

greatly alarmed at the thoughts of having an execution issued out against them. But the intention of the Methodists was, to let them see what they could do, and then to forgive them.*

SOME time before this, several anonymous papers, entitled, " Observations upon the Conduct and Behavior of a certain Sect, usually distinguished by the name of Methodists," had been printed, and handed about in the religious societies of London and Westminster, and given to many private persons, with strict injunctions to part with them to no one. Mr. WHITEFIELD having accidentally had the hasty perusal of them ; and finding many queries concerning him and his conduct, contained in them ; and having applied for a copy, which was refused him, he thought it his duty to publish an advertisement, desiring (as he knew not how soon he might embark for Georgia) a speedy, open publication of the said papers, that he might make a candid and impartial answer. He had reason to believe the Bishop of London was concerned in composing or revising them : but that he might not be mistaken, after the publication of the advertisement, he wrote the Bishop a letter, wherein he desired to know, whether his Lordship was the author or not ; and also desired a copy. The Bishop sent word, " he should hear from him." Some time after, one Mr. Owen, printer to the Bishop, left a letter for Mr. WHITEFIELD, informing him that he had orders from several of the Bishops, to print the Observations, &c. with some few additions, for their use ; and when the impression was finished, Mr. WHITEFIELD should have a copy. For these reasons, Mr. WHITEFIELD thought it proper to direct his Answer to the Observations, to the Bishop of London, and the other Bishops concerned in the publication of them. This answer occasioned the Rev. Mr. Church's Expostulatory

* See an account of this trial in his Works, Vol. IV.

tory Letter to Mr. WHITEFIELD; to which he soon replied, with thanks to the author for prefixing his name.[*]

HAVING resolved to make another visit to America, whither Mr. Smith, a merchant, then in England, in the name of thousands, invited him. With him he took passage in a ship going from Portsmouth; but being informed, just before he was about to take his farewel, that the captain refused to take him, for fear, as he alledged, of spoiling the sailors, he was obliged to go as far as Plymouth. "In my way, says he, I preached at Wellington, where one Mr. Darracott had been a blessed instrument of doing much good. At Exeter also, I revisited, where many souls were awakened to the divine life. At Biddeford, where good Mr. Hervey had been curate, we had much of the power of GOD; and also at Kingsbridge. But the chief scene was at Plymouth and the dock, where I expected least success."[‡] It is remarkable, that just before his success at Plymouth, he was in danger of being killed. Four gentlemen, it seems, came to the house of one of his particular friends, kindly enquiring after him, and desiring to know where he lodged. Soon afterwards, Mr. WHITE-FIELD received a letter, informing him that the writer was a nephew of Mr. S—, an attorney at New-York; that

---

[*] See his Works, Vol. IV. where is also his Answer to the Second Part of the Observations, &c. in a second letter to the Bishop's, written during his voyage to America that year.

[‡] M. S. Upon mentioning Biddeford, he adds here a character of Mr. Hervey; it is pity he did not write it down.—— However, we have a sketch of it ——
' Your sentiments concerning Mr. H—'s book, are very just. The author of it, is my old friend; a most heavenly-minded creature, one of the first of the Methodists, who is contented with a small cure, and gives all that he has to the poor. He is very weak, and daily waits for his dissolution.'

that he had the pleafure of fupping with Mr. WHITE-
FIELD at his uncle's houfe ; and defired his company
to fup with him, and a few more friends, at a tavern.
Mr. WHITEFIELD fent him word, that it was not
cuftomary for him to fup abroad at taverns, but fhould
be glad of the gentleman's company to eat a morfel
with him at his lodging ; he accordingly came and
fupped ; but was obferved frequently to look around
him, and to be very abfent. At laft he took his leave,
and returned to his companions in the tavern ; and
being by them interrogated, what he had done, he
anfwered, " That he had been ufed fo civilly, he had
not the heart to touch him." Upon which, it feems,
another of the company, a lieutenant of a man of war,
laid a wager of ten guineas, that he would do his bufinefs for him. His companions, however, had the
precaution to take away his fword. It was now about
midnight, and Mr. WHITEFIELD having that day
preached to a large congregation, and vifited the
French prifoners, was gone to bed : when the landlady came and told him that a well-dreffed gentleman
defired to fpeak with him, Mr. WHITEFIELD, ima-
gining it was fomebody under conviction, defired him
to be brought up. He came, and fat down by the
bed-fide, congratulated him upon the fuccefs of his
miniftry, and expreffed much concern at being detained from hearing him. Soon after he broke out in the
moft abufive language, and in a cruel and cowardly
manner, beat him in his bed. The landlady and her
daughter hearing the noife, rufhed into the room,
and feized upon him ; but he foon difengaged himfelf
from them, and repeated his blows on Mr. WHITE-
FIELD, who being apprehenfive that he intended to
fhoot or ftab him, underwent all the furprize of a fudden and violent death. Afterwards a fecond came
into the houfe, and cried out from the bottom of the
ftairs, " Take courage, I am ready to help you." But

by

by the repeated cry of *murder*, the alarm was now so great that they both made off. " The next morning, (says Mr. WHITEFIELD) I was to expound at a private house, and then set out for Biddeford. Some urged me to stay and prosecute ; but being better employed, I went on my intended journey, was greatly blessed in preaching the everlasting gospel, and upon my return was well paid for what I had suffered : curiosity having led perhaps two thousand more than ordinary, to see and hear a man that had like to have been murdered in his bed. And I trust, in the five weeks time† while I waited for the convoy, hundreds were awakened and turned unto the LORD. At the dock, also, near Plymouth, a glorious work had begun. Could the fields between Plymouth and the Dock, speak, they could tell what blessed seasons were enjoyed there."

† M. s.

C H A P. XII.

From his embarking for America, *in* 1744, *to his going to the* Bermudas, *in the Year* 1748.

AS soon as the convoy came*, Mr. WHITEFIELD embarked in the beginning of August 1744, though in a poor state of health. The tediousness of the voyage, he imagined, occasioned no small addition to a violent pain in his side. However, he says, " Blessed be GOD, in a week or two after we sailed, we began to have

a

---

* " August 4. Our convoy is now come. I desire you all to bless GOD for what he is doing in these parts; for preaching in the Dock is now like preaching at the Tabernacle.
Our

a church in our ship. We had regular public prayer morning and evening, frequent communion, and days of humiliation and fasting." After a passage of eleven weeks*, he arrived at York in New-England. Colonel Pepperell went with some friends in his own boat, to invite him to his house. But he was not in a proper condition to accept the invitation, being so ill of a nervous cholic, that he was obliged, immediately after his arrival, to go to bed. His friends were very apprehensive ; but he himself had much inward peace. Great care was taken of him by a physician who had been a notorious Deist, but was awakened, the last time he was in New-England. For some time he was, indeed, very weak : " Yet (he writes) in three weeks, I was enabled to preach: but, imprudently going over the ferry to Portsmouth, I caught cold, immediately relapsed, and was taken, as every one thought, with death, in my dear friend Mr. Sherburne's house. What gave me most concern was, that notice had been given of my being to preach. Whilst the Doctor was preparing a medicine, feeling my pains abated, I on a sudden cried, ' Doctor, my pains are suspended : by the help of God, I will go and preach, and then come home and die.' In my own apprehension, and in all appearance to others, I was a dying man. I preached. The people heard me as such. The invisible realities of another world lay open to my view. Expecting to stretch into eternity, and to be with my Master before the morning, I spoke with peculiar energy.

Such

Our morning-lectures are very delightful. O ! the thousands that flock to the preaching of CHRIST's Gospel."

P. S. " I must tell you one thing more. There is a ferry over to Plymouth. The ferry-men are now so much my friends, that they will take nothing of the multitudes that come to hear me preach ; saying, ' GOD forbid that we should sell the word of GOD."

* His Letter to the Clergy of the Diocess of Litchfield and Coventry is dated during this voyage.

THE REV. GEORGE WHITEFIELD.   109

Such effects followed the word, I thought it was worth dying for a thousand times.   Though wonderfully comforted within, at my return home, I thought I was dying indeed.   I was laid on a bed upon the ground, near the fire, and I heard my friends say, ' He is gone.' But GOD was pleased to order it otherwise.   I gradually recovered ; and soon after, a poor negro-woman would see me.   She came, sat down upon the ground, and looked earnestly in my face, and then said, in broken language, ' Master, you just go to heaven's gate. But JESUS CHRIST said, Get you down, get you down, you must not come here yet ; but go first, and call some more poor negroes.' I prayed to the LORD, that if I was: o live, this might be the event.

" IN about three weeks I was enabled, though in great weakness, to reach Boston ; and every day was more and more confirmed, in what I had heard about a glorious work, that had been begun and carried on there, and in almost all parts of New-England, for two years together. Before my last embarkation from Georgia, Mr. Colman, and Mr. Cooper, wrote me word, that upon Mr. Tennent's going out as an itinerant, the awakening greatly increased in various places,* till, at length, the work so advanced everywhere, that many thought the latter-day glory was indeed come, and that a nation was to be born in a day. But, as the same sun that lightens and warms the earth, gives vent to noxious insects ; so the same work, that for a while carried all before it, was sadly blemished through the subtilty of Satan,§ and the want of more experience in ministers and people, who

had

---

* See Prince's Christian History, (or Historical Collections, &c. Vol. II. page 304) where are attestations of above a hundred-and-twenty ministers to the goodness of the work.

§ Thus it was at the reformation in Germany.

L

had never feen fuch a fcene before. Oppofers, who
waited for fuch an occafion, did all they could to
aggravate every thing. One rode feveral hundred
miles, to pick up all the accounts he could get of
what was wrong in what he called only ' a religious
ftir.' And God having been pleafed to fend me firft,
all was laid upon me. Teftimonies figned by various
minifters came out againft me,† almoft every day.—
And the diforders were alfo at the higheft ; fo that
for a while, my fituation was rendered uncomfortable.‡   But amidft all this fmoke, a bleffed fire broke
out.

† He wrote an Anfwer to a Teftimony by Harvard College.
See Works, Vol. IV.

‡ While fome publifhed teftimonials againft Mr. WHITE-
FIELD, others publifhed teftimonials in his favor ; as Mr. Hob-
by, Mr. Loring : Fifteen Minifters convened at Taunton,
March 5, 1745. And the following paragraph is in Prince's
Chriftian Hiftory, No. XCIV.

" Saturday, November 24, 1744. The Rev. Mr. WHITE-
FIELD was fo far revived, as to be able to fet out from Portfmouth to Bofton, whither he came in a very feeble ftate the
Monday evening after : fince which, he has been able to preach
in feveral of our largeft houfes of public worfhip, particularly the Rev. Dr. Colman's, Dr. Sewall's, Mr. Webb's, and
Mr. Gee's, to crowded affemblies of people, and with great
and growing acceptance. At Dr. Colman's defire, and the
confent of the church, on the Lord's day after his arrival, he
adminiftered to them the Holy Communion. And laft LORD's
day he preached for Mr. Cheever of Chelfea, and adminiftered
the Holy Supper there. The next day preached for the Rev.
Mr. Emerfon, of Malden. Yefterday he fet out to preach at
fome towns to the northward, propofes to return hither the
next Wednefday-evening, and after a few days, to comply
with the earneft invitations of feveral minifters, to go and
preach to their congregations in the fouthern parts of the
province. He comes with the fame extraordinary fpirit of
meeknefs, fweetnefs, and univerfal benevolence, as before.
In oppofition to the fpirit of feparation and bigotry, is ftill for
holding communion with all Proteftant churches. In oppofition to enthufiafm, he preaches a clofe adherence to the Scriptures,

out. The awakened fouls were as eager as ever to hear the word.* Having heard that I had expounded early in Scotland, they begged I would do the fame in Boston. I complied, and opened a lecture at fix in the morning. I feldom preached to lefs than two thoufand. It was delightful to fee fo many of both fexes, neatly dreffed, flocking to hear the word, and returning home to family prayer and breakfaft, before the oppofers were out of their beds. So that it was commonly faid, that between early rifing, and tar-water, the phyficians would have no bufinefs.'

It was now Spring, 1745, and at that time the firft expedition was fet on foot againft Cape Breton. 'Colonel Pepperell, who was then at Boston, and conftantly attended Mr. WHITEFIELD's lecture, was pleafed, the day before he accepted a commiffion, to be General in that expedition, to afk Mr. WHITEFIELD's opinion of the matter. He told him, with his ufual franknefs, " That he did not, indeed, think
the

tures, the neceffity of trying all imprefflions by them, and of rejecting whatever is not agreeable to them, as delufions. In oppofition to Antinomianifm, he preaches up all kinds of relative and religious duties though to be performed in the ftrength of Chrift : and in fhort, the doctrines of the Church of England, and of the firft fathers of this country. As before, he firft applies himfelf to the underftandings of his hearers, and then to the affections. And the more he preaches, the more he convinces people of their miftakes about him, and increafes their fatisfaction."

* " A man of good parts, ready wit, and lively imagination, who had made it his bufinefs, in order to furnifh matter for preaching over a bottle, to come and hear, and then carry away fcraps of my fermons; having one night got fufficient matter to work upon, as he thought, attempted to go out ; but being pent in on every fide, he found his endeavors fruitlefs. Obliged thus to ftay, and looking up to me, waiting for fome frefh matter for ridicule, GOD was pleafed to prick him to the heart. He came to Mr. P. full of horror, confeffed his crimes, and longed to afk my pardon."

the scheme proposed for taking Louisburgh, very promising : that the eyes of all would be upon him. If
he did not succeed, the widows and orphans, of the
slain soldiers, would be like lions robbed of their
whelps ; but if it pleased GOD to give him success,
envy would endeavor to eclipse his glory ; he had
need, therefore, if he went, to go with a single eye ;
and then, there was no doubt, but if Providence
really called him, he would find his strength proportioned to the day." About the same time, Mr.
Sherburne, another of Mr. WHITEFIELD's friends,
being appointed one of the Commissaries, told him,
' He must favor the expedition, otherwise the serious
people would be discouraged from enlisting ; not only
so, but insisted he should give him a motto for his flag,
for the encouragement of the soldiers.' This he refused to do, as it would be acting out of character. But
Mr. Sherburne would take no denial. He therefore,
at last, gave them one, *Nil desperandum Christo Duce.*
" If CHRIST be Captain, no fear of a defeat." Upon
which great numbers enlisted. And before their
embarkation, the officers desired him to give them a
sermon. This he readily complied with, and preached from these words : " As many as were distressed,
as many as were discontented, as many as were in
debt, came to David, and he became a Captain over
them." He spiritualized the subject, and told them,
how distressed sinners came to JESUS CHRIST, the Son
of David ; and in his application, exhorted the soldiers to behave like the soldiers of David, and the
officers to act like David's worthies ; then he made
no manner of doubt, there would be good news from
Cape Breton. After this, he preached to the General
himself ; who asked him, If he would not be one of
his chaplains ? But he excused himself, and said, " He
should think it an honor, but believed, as he generally
preached three times a day, in various places, to large

congre-

congregations, he could do more fervice by ftirring up the people to pray, and thereby ftrengthening his, and his foldiers' hands." And in this practice he perfifted during the fiege of Louifburgh. "I believe (adds he,) if ever people went with a difinterefted view, the New Englanders did then. Though many of them were raw and undifciplined, yet numbers were fubftantial perfons who left their farms, and willingly ventured all for their country's good. An amazing fcene of providences appeared,* and though fome difcouraging accounts were fent during the latter end of the fiege ; yet in about fix weeks, news was brought of the furrender of Louifburgh. Numbers flocked from all quarters, to hear a thankfgiving fermon upon the occafion. And I truft the blefling beftowed on the country, through the thankfgivings of many, redounded to the glory of God."

THE New England people had fome time ago, offered to build him a large houfe to preach in ; but as this fcheme might have abridged his liberty of itinerating, he thanked them for their kind offer, and at the fame time begged leave to refufe the accepting of it. As his bodily ftrength increafed, and his health grew better, he began to move farther fouth-ward ; and after preaching eaftward, as far as Cafco-bay, and North Yarmouth, he went through Connecticut, Plymouth, Rhode-Ifland, preaching to thoufands, generally twice a-day. "And though, (fays he†) there was much fmoke, yet every day I had more and more convincing proof, that a blefled gofpel fire had been kindled in the hearts both of minifters and people. At New-York, where I preached as ufual, I found that the feed fown, had fprung up abundantly : and at the eaft end of Long-Ifland faw many inftances. In my way to Philadelphia, I had

the

* See Mr. Prince's Sermon upon that occafion.

† M. S.　　　L 2

the pleafure of preaching, by an interpreter, to fome converted Indians, and of feeing near fifty young ones in one fchool, near Free hold, learning the Affembly's Catechifm. A bleffed awakening had been begun, and carried on among the Delaware Indians, by the inftrumentality of Mr. David Brainard,* fuch a one as hath not been heard of fince the awakening of New-England by the venerable Mr. Elliott, who ufed to be ftiled the Apoftle of the Indians; his brother followed him. Mr. William Tennent, whofe party I found much upon the advance, feemed to encourage their endeavors with all his heart.

"His brother, Mr. Gilbert Tennent, being earneftly folicited thereto, I found fettled in the place formerly erected at the beginning of the awakening. The gentlemen offered me eight hundred pounds a year, only to preach among them fix months, and to travel the other fix months where I would. Nothing remarkable happened, during my way fouthward. But when I came to Virginia, I found that the word of the LORD had run and was glorified. During my preaching at Glafgow, fome perfons wrote fome of my extempore fermons, and printed them almoft as faft as I preached them. Some of thefe were carried to Virginia, and one of them fell into the hands of Samuel Morris. He read and found benefit.‡ He then read them to others; they were awakened and convinced. A fire was kindled; oppofition was made; other laborers were fent for; and many, both white people and negroes, were converted to the LORD.

"IN North Carolina, where I ftayed too fhort a time, little was done. At Georgia, through the badnefs of the inftitution, and the Truftees' obftinacy

in

* See his Life and Journals.

‡ See this more fully narrated, Hift. Coll. Book IV, Chap. V. Sect. 22.

in not altering it, my load of debt and care was greatly increafed, and at times almoft overwhelmed me.   But I had the pleafure of feeing one, who came as a player from New-York, now converted unto GOD, and a preacher of JESUS CHRIST.   One Mr. Ratteray brought me ten pounds ; and at my return northward, frefh fupplies were raifed up.   The generous Charlefton people raifed a fubfcription of three hundred pounds, with which I bought land, being cheap during the war ; and a plantation, and a few negroes were purchafed at Indian-land.   Thus, for a while, the gap was ftopped.   I preached a fermon upon the Rebellion.   Was very fick at Philadelphia ; kindly received at Bohemia, and at New-York.

"As itinerating was my delight, and America, as being a new world, particularly pleafing, I now began to think of returning no more to my native country.   But travelling, care, and a load of debt, contracted not for myfelf, but the Orphan-houfe, weighed me down.   And being much troubled with ftitches in my fide, I was advifed to go to Bermudas, for the recovery of my health."*   He accordingly embarked, and landed there the 15th of March, 1748.

CHAP.

* In his Letters during this period, are the following paffages :

"Auguft 26, 1746. The door, for my ufefulnefs, opens wider and wider.   I love to range in the American woods, and fometimes think, I fhall never return to England any more.

"October 8. I have had fome fweet times with feveral of the Lutheran minifters at Philadelphia.

"November 8. I have lately been in feven counties in Maryland, and preached to great congregations.

"May 21, 1747. I have now been upon the ftretch, preaching conftantly for almoft three weeks.   My body is often extremely weak, but the joy of the LORD is my ftrength, and by the help of GOD, I intend going on till I drop, or this
poor

C H A P. XIII.

From his Arrival at the Bermudas, *on his Return to* London *in* July, 1748.

MR. WHITEFIELD met with the kindeft reception at Bermudas, and for above a month, he preached generally twice a-day, traverfing the ifland from one end to the other : but his activity, ufefulnefs, and treatment, will beft appear by an extract from his manufcript journal of that period.

"THE poor carcafe can hold out no more. Thefe fouthern colonies lie in darknefs, and yet, as far as I find, are as willing to receive the Gofpel, as others. If fome good book: could be purchafed, to difpofe of among poor people, much good might be done.

"June 1. The congregations yefterday were exceeding large. I am fick and well, as I ufed to be in England; but the Redeemer fills me with comfort. I am determined, in his ftrength, to die fighting.

"June 4. I have omitted preaching one night, to oblige my friends, that they may not charge me with murdering my-felf; but I hope yet to die in the pulpit, or foon after I come out of it.

"June 23. Since my laft, I have been feveral times on the verge of eternity. At prefent, I am fo weak, that I can-not preach. It is hard work to be filent, but I muft be tried every way.

"June 29. GOD has been pleafed to bring my body to the very brink of the grave, by convulfions, gravel, a nervous cholic, and a violent fever. For this week paft, I have not preached; but fince my leaving Philadelphia, about three days ago, I feemed to have gathered ftrength, and hope once more, to-morrow, to proclaim amongft poor finners, the unfearchable riches of JESUS CHRIST. I purpofe to go to Bofton, and return by land, fo as to reach Charlefton by November.

" THE simplicity and plainness of the people, together with the pleasant situation of the island, much delighted me. The Rev. Mr. Holiday, minister of Spanish-Point, received me in a most affectionate Christian manner, and begged I would make his house my home. In the evening, I expounded at the house of Mr. Savage, of Port-Royal, which was very commodious, and which also he would have me make my home. I went with Mr. Savage, in a boat lent us by Captain ——, to the town of St. George, in order to pay our respects to the Governor. All along we had a most pleasant prospect of the other part of the island; but a more pleasant one I never saw. One Mrs. Smith, of St. George's, for whom I had a letter of recommendation from my dear old friend Mr. Smith of Charleston, received me into her house. About noon, with one of the council and Mr. Savage, I waited upon the Governor. He received us courteously, and invited us to dine with him and the council at a tavern. We accepted the invitation, and all behaved with great civility and respect. After the Governor rose from the table, he desired, if I stayed in town on the Sunday, that I would dine with him at his own house.

" SUNDAY, March 20, read prayers, and preached twice this day, to what were esteemed here large auditories, in the morning at Spanish-Point church, and in the evening at Brackish-Pond church, about two miles distant from each other. In the afternoon I spoke with greater freedom than in the morning, and I trust not altogether in vain. All were attentive—
some

" July 4. At present, I am very weakly, and scarce able to preach above once or twice a-week.

" September 11. We saw great things in New-England. The flocking and power that attended the word, was like unto that seven years ago. Weak as I was, and have been, I was enabled to travel eleven hundred miles, and preach daily. I am now going to Georgia to winter.

fome wept.   I dined with Colonel Butterfield, one of the council, and received feveral invitations to other gentlemen's houfes.   May GOD blefs and reward them, and incline them to open their heart to receive the LORD JESUS ! Amen, and Amen !

"WEDNESDAY, March 23, dined with Captain Gibbs, and went from thence and expounded at the houfe of Capt. F—le, at Hunbay, about two miles diftant.   The company was here alfo large, attentive, and affected.   Our LORD gave me utterance : I expounded on the firft part of the viiith chapter of Jeremiah.   After lecture, Mr. Riddle, a counfellor, invited me to his houfe, as did Mr. Paul, an aged prefbyterian minifter, to his pulpit ; which I complied with upon condition the report was true, that the Governor had ferved the minifters with an injunction that I fhould not preach in the churches.

"FRIDAY, March 25.   Was prevented preaching yefterday by the rain, which continued from morning till night ; but this afternoon GOD gave me another opportunity of declaring his eternal truths to a large company at the houfe of one Mr. B—s, who laft night fent me a letter of invitation.

"SUNDAY, March 27.   Glory to GOD ! I hope this has been a profitable Sabbath to many fouls : It has been a pleafant one to mine.   Both morning and afternoon I preached to a large auditory, in Bermudas, in Mr. Paul's meeting-houfe, which I fuppofe contains above four hundred.   Abundance of negroes, and many others, were in the veftry, porch, and about the houfe.   The word feemed to be clothed with a convincing power, and to make its way into the hearts of the hearers.   Between fermons, I was entertained very civilly in a neighboring houfe : Judge Bafcome and three more of the council came thither ; each gave me an invitation to his houfe.   O how does the LORD make way for a poor ftranger in a ftrange land !

land ! After the fecond fermon, I dined with Mr.
Paul, and in the evening expounded to a very large
company at Counfellor Riddle's. My body was fomewhat weak, but the Lord carried me through, and
caufed me to go to reft rejoicing. May I thus go to
my grave, when my ceafelefs uninterrupted reft fhall
begin !

"MONDAY, March 28. Dined this day at Mrs.
D—l's, mother-in-law to my dear friend the Rev.
Mr. Smith ; and afterwards preached to more than a
large houfe full of people, on Matt. ix. 12. Towards
the conclufion of the fermon, the hearers began to be
more affected than I have yet feen them. Surely the
LORD JESUS will give me fome feals in this ifland !
Grant this, O REDEEMER, for thy infinite mercy's
fake !

"THURSDAY, March 31. Dined on Tuefday at
Colonel Corbufiers ; and on Wednefday, at Colonel
Gilbert's, both of the council, and found, by what I
could hear, that fome good had been done, and many
prejudices removed. Who fhall hinder, if GOD will
work ? Went to an ifland this afternoon, called Ireland, upon which live a few families ; and to my furprize, found a great many gentlemen, and other people, with my friend Mr. Holiday, who came from
different quarters to hear me. Before I began preaching, I went round to fee a moft remarkable cave,
which very much difplayed the exquifite workman-
fhip of Him, who in his ftrength fetteth faft the mountains, and is girded about with power. Whilft I was
in the cave, quite unexpectedly I turned and faw
Counfellor Riddle, who with his fon came to hear
me, and whilft we were in the boat, told me that he
had been with the Governor, who declared he had
no perfonal prejudice againft me, and wondered I did
not come to town and preach there, for it was the
defire of the people ; and that any houfe in the town,
the

the court-houfe not excepted, fhould be at my fervice.
Thanks be to God, for fo much favor!—If his caufe
requires it, I fhall have more.—He knows my heart :
I value the favor of man no farther than as it makes
room for the gofpel, and gives me a larger fcope to
promote the glory of God.   There being no capacious houfe upon the ifland, I preached for the firft
time here in the open air.   All heard very attentively, and it was very pleafant after fermon to fee
fo many boats full of people returning from the
worfhip of God.   I talked ferioufly to fome in our
own boat, and began to fing a pfalm, in which they
readily joined.

   " Sunday, April 3.   Preached twice this day at
Mr. Paul's meeting-houfe, as on the laft Sabbath, but
with greater freedom and power, efpecially in the
morning, and I think to as great, if not greater auditories.   Dined with Colonel H—vy, another of the
council ; vifited a fick woman, where many came to
hear, and expounded afterwards to a great company
at Capt. John Dorrel's, Mrs. D—l's fon, who with
his wife courteoufly entertained me, and defired me
to make his houfe my home.—So true is that promife
of our Lord's, ' That whofoever leaves father or
mother, houfes or lands, fhall have in this life a hun-
dred-fold with perfecution, and in the world to come,
life everlafting.'   Lord, I have experienced the one ;
in thy good time grant that I may experience the
other alfo !

   " Wednesday, April 6.   Preached yefterday at
the houfe of Mr. Anthony Smith, of Baylis Bay, with
a confiderable degree of warmth, and rode afterwards to St. George's, the only town in the ifland.
The gentlemen of the town had fent me an invitation by Judge Bafcome, and he with feveral others,
came to vifit me at my lodgings, and informed me,
that the Governor defired to fee me.   About ten I
                                             waited

waited upon his Excellency, who received me with great civility, and told me he had no objection against my person or my principles, having never yet heard me, and he knew nothing in respect to my conduct in moral life, that might prejudice him against me; but his instructions were, to let none preach in the island, unless he had a written licence to preach somewhere in America or the West-Indies: at the same time he acknowledged that it was but a matter of mere form. I informed his Excellency that I had been regularly inducted to the parish of Savannah; that I was ordained priest by letters dismissory from my Lord of London, and under no church censure, from his Lordship; and would always read the church prayers, if the clergy would give me the use of their churches. I added further, that a minister's pulpit was looked upon as his free-hold, and that I knew one clergyman who had denied his own Diocesan the use of his pulpit. But I told his Excellency I was satisfied with the liberty he allowed me, and would not 'act contrary to his injunction. I then begged leave to be dismissed. because I was to preach at eleven o'clock: His Excellency said, he intended to do himself the pleasure to hear me. At eleven the church-bell rung, the church-bible, prayer book, and cushion, were sent to the town house — The Governor, several of the council, the minister of the parish, and assembly men, with a great number of town's-people, assembled in great order. I was very sick, through a cold I catched last night; but I read the church-prayers, (the first lesson was the xvth of the first book of Samuel) and preached on those words, 'Righteousness exalteth a nation.' Being weak and faint, and having much of the head-ach, I did not do that justice to my subject as I sometimes am enabled to do; but the Lord so helped me, that, as I found afterwards,

the

M

the Governor and the other gentlemen expreſſed their approbation, and acknowledged they did not expect to be ſo well entertained. Not unto me, O LORD, not unto me, but unto thy free grace be all the glory!

"AFTER ſermon, Dr. F——b's, and Mr. P——t, the collector, came to me, and deſired me to favor them and the gentlemen of the town with my company to dine with them. I accepted the invitation. The Governor and the Preſident and judge Baſcome were there. All wondered at my ſpeaking ſo freely and fluently without notes. The Governor aſked me whether I uſed minutes.—I anſwered, No. He ſaid it was a great gift. At table his Excellency introduced ſomething of religion, by aſking me the meaning of the word Hades. Several other things were ſtarted about free-will, Adam's fall, predeſtination, &c. to all which GOD enabled me to anſwer ſo pertinently, and taught me to mix the *utile* and *dulce* ſo together, that all at table ſeemed highly pleaſed, ſhook me by the hand, and invited me to their reſpective houſes. The Governor, in particular, aſked me to dine with him on the morrow, and Dr. F——b, one of his particular intimates, invited me to drink tea in the afternoon. I thanked all, returned proper reſpects, and went to my lodgings with ſome degree of thankfulneſs for the aſſiſtance vouchſafed me, and abaſed before GOD at the conſideration of my unſpeakable unworthineſs. In the afternoon, about five o'clock, I expounded the parable of the prodigal ſon to many people at a private houſe, and in the evening had liberty to ſpeak freely and cloſely to thoſe that ſupped with me. O that this may be the beginning of good goſpel-times to the inhabitants of this town! LORD, teach me to deal prudently with them, and cauſe them to melt under thy word!

"FRIDAY, April 8. Preached yeſterday with great clearneſs and freedom, to about four-ſcore
people,

people, at a houfe on David's ifland, over againft St. George's town; went and lay at Mr. Holiday's, who came in a boat to fetch me; and this day I heard him preach, and read prayers; after which, I took the facrament from him. I'oneft man, he would have had me adminifter and officiate; but I chofe not to do it, left I fhould bring him into trouble after my departure. However, in the afternoon, I preached at one Mr. Tod's, in the fame parifh, to a very large company indeed.—The LORD was with me. My heart was warm, and what went from the heart, I truft went to the heart, for many were affected. O that they may be converted alfo! Then it will be a *Good Friday* indeed to their fouls.

"SUNDAY, April 10. Dined and converfed yefterday, very agreeably, with Judge Bafcome: who feems to have the greateft infight into the difference between the Arminian and Calviniftical fcheme of any one I have yet met with upon the ifland.—In the afternoon, I vifited a fick paralytic; and this day I preached twice again at Mr. Paul's meeting-houfe. The congregations were rather larger than ever, and the power of GOD feemed to be more amongft them. I think I fee a vifible alteration for the better, every LORD's day.—Bleffed be GOD! In the evening I expounded at Mr. Jofeph Dorrell's, (where I dined) to a very large company; then went to his kinfman's, my ufual lodging, on Saturday and Sunday evenings, who with his wife and other friends, feemed kinder and kinder daily.— Good meafure, preffed down, and running over, may the LORD, both as to fpirituals and temporals, return into all their bofoms!

"SATURDAY, April 16. Preached fince LORD's-day at five different houfes, to concerned and affected congregations, at different parts of the ifland, but was more indifpofed, one night, after going to bed,

than

than I had been for some time.   On two of the days
of this week, I dined with the Prefident and Captain
Spafford, both which entèrtained me with the utmoft
civility.

"SUNDAY, 17. Still GOD magnifies his power
and goodnefs more and more.   This morning we
had a pleafing fight at Mr. Paul's meeting houfe.   I
began to preach, and the people to hear and be
affected as in days of old at home.   Indeed the profpect is encouraging Praife the LORD, O my foul!
After preaching twice to large congregations in the
meeting houfe, I at the defire of the parents, preached
in the evening a fermon at the funeral of a little boy
about five years of age.   A great number of people
attended, and the LORD enabled me fo to fpeak, as to
affect many of the hearers.—Bleffed be the LORD for
this day's work! Not unto me, O LORD, not unto
me, but unto thy free grace be all the glory!

" SUNDAY, April 24.   The laft week being rainy,
I preached only five times in private houfes, and this
day but once in the meeting houfe ; but I hope neither time without effect.   This evening expounded
at Counfellor Riddle's, who with the other gentlemen, treats me with greater refpect every day.—
Colonel Gilbert, one of the council, has lent me his
horfe during my ftay, and Mr. D——ll this morning
informed me of a defign the gentlemen had, to ráife
a contribution to help me difcharge my arrears, and
fupport my orphan family.   Thanks be given to thy
name, O GOD! Thou knoweft all things ; thou knoweft that I want to owe no man any thing, but love
and provide for Bethefda after my deceafe.   Thou
haft promifed thou wilt fulfil the defires of them that
fear thee.   I believe, LORD, help my unbelief, that
thou wilt fulfil this defire of my foul.   Even fo,
Amen!

" SATURDAY, April 30.   Preached fince LORD's-
day,

day, two funeral sermons, and at five different houses in different parts of the island to still larger and larger auditories, and perceived the people to be affected more and more. Twice or thrice I preached without doors. Riding in the sun, and preaching very earnestly, a little fatigued me; so that this evening I was obliged to lie down for some time. *Faint, yet pursuing:* must be my motto still.

"SUNDAY, May 1. This morning was a little sick; but I trust GOD gave us a happy beginning of the new month. I preached twice with power, especially in the morning, to a very great congregation in the meeting-house; and, in the evening, having given previous notice, I preached about four miles distant, in the fields, to a large company of negroes, and a number of white people, who came to hear what I had to say to them. I believe, in all, there were near fifteen hundred people. As the sermon was intended for the negroes, I gave the auditory warning, that my discourse would be chiefly directed to them, and that I should endeavor to imitate the example of Elijah, who when he was about to raise the child, contracted himself to its length. The negroes seemed very sensible and attentive. When I asked them, whether all of them did not desire to go to heaven, one of them, with a very audible voice said, 'Yes Sir.' This caused a little smiling; but in general, every thing was carried on with great decency; and, I believe, the LORD enabled me to so to discourse, as to touch the negroes, and yet not give them the least umbrage to slight or behave insolently to their masters. If ever a minister in preaching need the wisdom of the serpent to be joined with the harmlessness of the dove, it must be when discoursing to negroes. Vouchsafe me this favor, O GOD, for thy dear Son's sake!

M 2 "MONDAY,

" Monday, May 2. Upon enquiry, I found that some of the negroes did not like my preaching, because I told them of their curfing, fwearing, thieving and lying. One or two of the worft of them,-as I was informed, went away. Some faid, they would not go any more : They liked Mr. M——r better, for he never told them of thefe things ; and I faid, their hearts were as black as their faces. They expected they faid, to hear me fpeak againft their mafters. Bleffed be God that I was directed not to fay any thing, this firft time, to the mafters at all, though my text led me to it. It might have been of bad confequence, to tell them their duty, or charge them too roundly with the neglect of it, before their flaves. They would mind all I faid to their mafters, and, perhaps, nothing that I faid to them. Every thing is beautiful in its feafon. Lord, teach me always that due feafon, wherever I am called, to give either black or white, a portion of thy word ! However, others of the poor creatures, I hear, were very thankful, and came home to their mafters' houfes, faying they would ftrive to fin no more. Poor hearts ! Thefe different accounts affected me ; and upon the whole, I could not help rejoicing, to find that their confciences were fo far awake.

" Saturday, May 7. In my converfation thefe two days, with fome of my friends, I was diverted much, in hearing feveral things that paffed among the poor negroes, fince my preaching to them laft Sunday. One of the women, it feems, faid, ' That if the book I preached out of was the beft book that was ever bought at, and come out of London, fhe was fure it had never all that in it, which I fpoke to the negroes.' The old man, who fpoke out loud laft Sunday, and faid ' Yes,' when I afked them, Whether all the negroes would not go to heaven ? Being queftioned by fomebody, Why he fpoke out fo ? Anfwered,

fwered, ' That the gentleman put the queftion, once
or twice, to them, and the other fools had not the
manners to make him any anfwer, till at laft, he
feemed to point at me, and I was afhamed that nobody fhould anfwer him, and therefore I did.' Another, wondering why I faid, ' Negroes had black
hearts ;' was anfwered by his black brother thus :
' Ah, thou fool, doft thou not underftand it ? He
means black with fin.' Two more girls were over-
heard by their miftrefs, talking about religion, and
they faid, ' They knew, if they did not repent, they
muft be damned.' From all which I infer, that thefe
Bermudas negroes are more knowing than I fuppofed ;
that their confciences are awake, and confequently
prepared, in a good meafure, for hearing the gofpel
preached unto them.

" SUNDAY, May 8. This alfo, I truft has been
a good Sabbath. In the morning I was helped to
preach powerfully to a melting, and rather a larger
congregation than ever, in Mr. Paul's meeting-houfe,
and in the evening, to almoft as large a congregation
of black and white, as laft Sunday, in the fields, near
my hearty friend Mr. Holiday's houfe. To fee fo
many black faces, was affecting. They heard very
attentively, and fome of them now began to weep.
May GOD grant them a godly forrow, that worketh
repentance not to be repented of !

" FRIDAY, May 13. This afternoon preached
over the corpfe of Mr. Paul's eldeft fon, about twenty-
four years of age ; and by all I could hear and judge
of, by converfing with him, he did indeed die in the
LORD. I vifited him twice laft LORD's-day, and
was quite fatisfied with what he faid, though he had
not much of the fenfible prefence of GOD. I find he
was a preacher upon his death-bed. For he exhorted
all his companions to love CHRIST in fincerity, and
bleffed his brother and fifter, and, I think, his father
and

and mother, just before his departure. A great many people attended the funeral. I preached on Luke vii. 13. "And when the LORD saw her, he had compaffion on her, and faid unto her, Weep not."— Many were affected in the application of my difcourfe, and, I truft, fome will be induced, by this young man's good example, to remember their Redeemer in the days of their youth. Grant it, O LORD, for thy dear SON's fake!

"SUNDAY, May 15. Praife the LORD, O my foul, and all that is within thee, praife his holy name! This morning I preached my farewel-fermon, at Mr. Paul's meeting houfe; it was quite full, and, as the Prefident faid, above a hundred and fifty whites, befides blacks, were around the houfe. Attention fat on every face; and when I came to take my leave, oh! what a fweet unaffected weeping was there to be feen every-where. I believe there were few dry eyes. The negroes likewife without doors, I heard wept plentifully.—My own heart was affected, and though I have parted from friends fo often, yet I find every frefh parting almoft unmans me, and very much affects my heart. Surely a great work is begun in fome fouls at Bermudas. Carry it on, O LORD; and if it be thy will, fend me to this dear people again. Even fo, LORD JESUS. Amen.

"AFTER fermon, I dined with three of the Council, and other Gentlemen and Ladies, at Captain Bafcome's; and from thence we went to a funeral, at which Mr. M——r preached; and after that I expounded on the LORD's Transfiguration, at the houfe of one Mrs. Harvey, fifter to dear Mr. Smith of Charlefton. The houfe was exceeding full, and 't was fuppofed above three hundred ftood in the yard. The LORD enabled me to lift up my voice like a trumpet. Many wept. Mr. M——r returned from the funeral with me, and attended the lecture, as did the

the three Counfellors, with whom I converfed very freely. May God reward them, and all the dear people of the ifland, for thofe many and great favors they have conferred on me who am the chief of finners, and lefs than the leaft of all faints!

Sunday, May 22. Bleffed be God! the little leaven thrown into the three meafures of meal, begins to ferment, and work almoft every day, for the week paft. I have converfed with fouls loaded with a fenfe of their fins, and as far as I can judge, really pricked to the heart. I preached only three times, but to almoft three times larger auditories than ufual. Indeed the fields are white, ready unto harveft. God has been pleafed to blefs private vifits. Go where I will, upon the leaft notice, houfes are crowded, and the poor fouls that follow are foon drenched in tears. This day I took, as it were, another farewel. As the fhip did not fail, I preached at Somerfet in the morning, to a large congregation in the fields, and expounded in the evening to as large a one at Mr. Harvey's houfe, round which ftood many hundreds of people. But in the morning and evening how did the poor fouls weep. The Lord feemed to be with me in a peculiar manner, and though I was ready to die with heat and ftraining, yet I was enabled to fpeak louder, and with greater power, I think, than I have been before. Gifts and grace, efpecially in the evening, were both in exercife. After the fervice, when I lay down on the bed to reft, many came weeping bitterly around me, and took their laft farewel. Though my body was very weak, yet my foul was full of comfort. It magnified the Lord, and my fpirit rejoiced in God my Savior. Abundance of prayers and bleffings were put up for my fafe paffage to England, and fpeedy return to Bermudas again. May they enter into the ears of the Lord of Sabaoth! For, God willing, I intend vifiting thefe dear

people

people once more. In the mean while, with all humility and thankfulness of heart will I here, O Lord, set up my Ebenezer: For hitherto, surely, thou hast helped me! I cannot help thinking that I was led to this island by a peculiar providence. My dear friend, Mr. Smith of Charleston, has been especially instrumental thereto. Thanks be to the Lord for sending me hither. I have been received in a manner I dared not expect, and have met with little, very little opposition indeed. The inhabitants seem to be plain and open-hearted. They have also been open-handed. For they have loaded me with provisions for my sea-store; and in the several parishes, by a private voluntary contribution, have raised me upwards of a hundred pounds sterling. This will pay a little of Bethesda's debt, and enable me to make such a remittance to my dear yoke-fellow, as may keep her from being embarrassed, or too much beholden in my absence. Blessed be God, for bringing me out of my embarrassments by degrees; May the Lord reward all my benefactors a thousand-fold! I hear that what was given, was given exceeding heartily, and people only lamented that they could do no more."

AFTER having transmitted to Georgia, what was given to him for the Orphan-house, and dreading to go back to America in that season of heat, for fear of relapsing, and having pressing calls to England, he took the opportunity of a brig, and in twenty-eight days arrived at Deal*. The next evening. July 6, 1748,

* During this voyage, among other Letters, he wrote the following:

"June 24, 1748. (on board.) Yesterday I made an end of revising all my Journals. Alas! alas! in how many things I have judged and acted wrong. I have been too rash and hasty in giving characters both of places and persons. Being fond of Scripture-language, I have often used a stile too apostolical,

1748, he reached London, after an abfence of near four years.

C H A P.

poftolical, and at the fame time, I have been too bitter in my zeal. Wild-fire has been mixed with it, and I find that I frequently wrote and fpoke in my own fpirit, when I thought I was writing and fpeaking by the affiftance of the SPIRIT of GOD. I have likewife too much made inward impreflions my rule of acting, and too foon and too explicitly publifhed what had been better kept in longer, or told after my death. By thefe things, I have hurt the bleffed caufe I would defend, and alfo ftirred up needlefs oppofition. This has humbled me much, and made me think of a faying of Mr. Henry's, ' Jofeph had more honefty than he had policy, or he never would have told his dreams.' At the fame time, I cannot but praife GOD, who filled me with fo much of his holy fire, and carried me, a poor weak youth, through fuch a torrent both of popularity and contempt, and fet fo many feals to my unworthy miniftrations. I blefs him for ripening my judgment a little more, for giving me to fee and confefs, and I hope, in fome degree, to correct and amend fome of my former miftakes."

At this time, alfo, he finifhed his "Abridgment of Mr. Law's Serious Call;" which he endeavored to make more ufeful, by excluding whatever is not truly evangelical, and illuftrating the fubject more fully from the Holy Scriptures.— See his Works, Vol. IV.

C H A P. XIV.

From his Arrival in London, 1748, *to his going to* Ireland, *in the Year* 1751.

ON Mr. WHITEFIELD's vifiting a few of his friends, immediately after his return, he found him-felf in no very agreeable fituation. His congrega-tion at the Tabernacle was fadly fcattered. And as to his outward circumftances, he had fold all his houf-hold furniture, to help to pay the Orphan-houfe debt, which yet was far from being cancelled. But under all thefe difcouragements, he was ftill fupported. His congregation was foon re-united, and received him with the greateft joy. And at this time a very unexpected thing happened to him. Lady Hunting-don, before his arrival, had ordered Mr. Howel Har-ris to bring him to her houfe at Chelfea, as foon as he came afhore. He went, and having preached twice, the Countefs wrote to him, that feveral of the Nobility defired to hear him. In a few days the Earl of Chefterfield, and a whole circle of them attended: and having heard once, defired they might hear him again. " I therefore preached again, fays he, in the evening, and went home, never more furprized at any incident in my life.* All behaved quite well, and were in fome degree affected. The Earl of Chefter-field thanked me, and faid, ' Sir, I will not tell you what I fhall tell others, how I approve of you :' or words to this purpofe. At laft Lord Bolingbroke came to hear, fat like an archbifhop, and was pleafed to fay, ' I had done great juftice to the divine attri-butes in my difcourfe.'‡ Soon afterwards her Lady-

* M. S.   –   fhip

‡ It is alfo faid, that David Hume, Efq. of Edinburgh, was

a

ship removed to town, where I preached generally twice a-week to very brilliant auditories. Blessed be God, not without effectual success on some."

In September 1748, he made a third visit to Scotland, where he met with a hearty welcome. Great multitudes flocked to hear him, both at Edinburgh and Glasgow. " I have reason, says he, to believe some have been awakened, and many quickened and comforted. My old friends are more solidly so than ever, and a foundation I trust, has been laid for doing much good, if the Lord should call me thither again. Two Synods†, and one Presbytery, brought me upon the

a hearer of Mr. WHITEFIELD's, and was much taken with his eloquence. Such testimonies are set down, not for their weight, but their singularity.

† He means the Synods of Glasgow and Perth, and the Presbytery of Edinburgh. What happened in the Synod of Glasgow, may be seen in a pamphlet, entitled, " A fair and impartial Account of the Debate in the Synod of Glasgow and Air, 6 October, 1748, against employing Mr. WHITEFIELD;" published at Edinburgh the same year, and supposed to be written by the Rev. Dr. Erskine, who was then minister at Kirkintilloch. The short history of the matter is this. A motion was made, tending to prohibit or discourage ministers from employing Mr. WHITEFIELD. The speeches made in support of the motion, were upon the following topics. His being a priest of the Church of England. That he had not subscribed the Formula. His imprudencies. Chimerical scheme of the Orphan-house. Want of evidence, that the money he collects is rightly applied. Asserting that assurance is essential to faith. Encouraging a dependence on impulses and immediate revelations. Declaring on slender evidence, some people converted, and others carnal and unregenerated. Often, indeed, pretending to repent of his blunders, and retract; but as often relapsing into them. And lastly, his being under a sentence of suspension by Commissary Garden, from which he had appealed to the High Court of Chancery, and made oath to prosecute that appeal in a twelve-month; and yet it was never prosecuted.

On

N

the carpet ; but all has worked for good." While
he was in Scotland, he endeavored to do all the
fervice he could to the New-Jerfey College, and in
conjunction

On the other hand, the minifters who were againft the motion, fpoke in this manner. I blufh to think, faid one, that any
of our brethren fhould befriend a propofal fo contrary to that
moderation and catholic fpirit, which now is, and I hope ever
fhall be the glory of our Church.   I am fenfible, many things
in the Church of England need refermation ; but I honor her,
notwithftanding, as our fifter church.   If Bifhop Butler, Bifhop Sherlock, or Bifhop Secker, were in Scotland, I fhould
welcome them to my pulpit.   In this I fhould imitate Mr.
Samuel Rutherford, as firm a prefbyterian as any of us, who
yet employed Bifhop Ufher.   There is no Law of CHRIST, no
Act of Affembly prohibiting me to give my pulpit to an Epifcopal Independent, or Anabaptift Minifter, if of found principles in the fundamentals of Religion, and of a fober life.
Our Church exprefsly enjoins, Act XII. April 1711, that great
tendernefs is to be ufed to foreign Proteftants. The requiring
ftrangers to fubfcribe our Formula, before they preach with
us, would lay as effectual a bar againft employing thofe of
Congregational Principles, or Prefbyterian Non-fubfcribers,
as thofe of the Church of England.
    As to Mr. WHITEFIELD, faid another, there are few min-
ifters whofe character has been fo well attefted, by the moft
competent judges, both at home and abroad.   One thing I
cannot but obferve : thofe who have fpoken moft warmly a-
gainft Mr. WHITEFIELD, in this debate, acknowledge they
have made little or no enquiry into his character: whereas
thofe on the other fide, have made a very careful enquiry ;
and that enquiry has turned out entirely to their fatisfaction.
With regard to his imprudencies, there is a great difference
betwixt blunders owing to a bad heart, and thofe that are owing only to a mifinformed judgment ; efpecially, when the
miftakes that occafioned them, have mifled feveral great and
good men.   Whether Mr. WHITEFIELD's fcheme of the Orphan-houfe be prudent or not, it is demonftrable it was honeftly meant. The magiftrates of Savannah publifhed three
years ago, in the Philadelphia Gazette, an affidavit that they
had carefully examined Mr. WHITEFIELD's receipts and dif-
burfements, and found that what he had collected in behalf
of the Orphans, had been honeftly applied ; and that befides,
                                                              he

conjunction with some ministers who wished well to
that institution, advised the sending over a minister
from America, to make application in person. Which
was afterwards done in the year 1754, when Mr.

Tennent

he had given considerably to them of his own property. As
to his maintaining, that assurance is essential to faith; encouraging an unwarrantable regard to impressions; and being
too hasty in pronouncing men carnal or converted; his sentiments in these particulars, have been altered for upwards of
two years. And now he scarce preaches a sermon, without
guarding his hearers against relying on impressions, and telling
them that faith, and a persuasion we are justified, are very
different things, and that a holy life is the best evidence of a
gracious state. These retractions are owing to a real change
of sentiment. Letters from correspondents in New-England
shew, that this change is at least, of two years date, and that
ever since it happened, he has preached and acted with remarkable caution. Lastly, with respect to the prosecution of
his appeal, Mr. WHITEFIELD exerted himself to the utmost to
get his appeal heard, but could not prevail on the Lord's
Commissioners so much as once to meet on the affair; they,
no doubt, thinking of Mr. Garden's arbitrary proceedings
with the contempt they deserved. But say some, "Mr.
WHITEFIELD being under a suspension not yet reversed, is now
no minister." But for what was he suspended? Why, for no
other crime, than omitting to use the form of prayer prescri-
bed in the communion book, when officiating in a Presbyterian congregation. And shall a meeting of Presbyterian ministers, pay any regard to a sentence which had such a foundation?

The issue of the debate was a rejecting of the motion by a
vote, 27 to 13; and a resolution which was so express as to
be a decent burial of it; laying no new restriction on ministers from inviting strangers, but leaving things precisely as
they were before. And they who chose to give Mr. WHITE-
FIELD their pulpits, never after met with any molestation.
Upon the whole, the attacks made on Mr. WHITEFIELD's character, proved the occasion of informing the Synod of the
falshood of many aspersions thrown out against him, of the
great increase of his prudence and caution, and the remarkable change of his sentiments and behaviour, so far as either
were offensive. And thus what was intended for his reproach,
turned out to his honor.

Tennent and Mr. Davies applied to the General
Affembly, and obtained an appointment of a general
collection. He alfo began to think of making his
Orphan houfe not only a receptacle for fatherlefs
children, but alfo a place of literature and academ-
ical ftudies. Such a place, he thought, was much
wanted in the fouthern parts of America ; and if
conducted in a proper manner, would be of great
fervice to the colony. He therefore, after his return
to England, wrote to the Truftees, fignifying that
this was his intention, if they would be pleafed to
put the colony upon another footing, and allow a
limited ufe of negroes, without which, he had long
been of opinion, that Georgia never could be a flourifhing province. Mean-time, he went on in his
ufual way, and with his ufual fuccefs at London,
Eriftol, and Gloucefter, during the winter. And in
February, 1749, made an excurfion to Exeter and
Plymouth, where he found a ftrange alteration in the
people, fince he had been firft there, about five years
before ; they now received him with the greateft joy,
and were importunate to hear him ; and many of
them gave proofs of a folid converfion to GOD.——
" Now, (fays he) Plymouth feems to be quite a new
place to me." As his health was impaired in London, he loved to range (as he calls it) after precious
fouls. Though he never wanted to make a fect, or
to fet himfelf at the head of a party.

" I HAVE feen enough of popularity, (fays he) to
be fick of it ; and did not the intereft of my bleffed
Mafter require my appearing in public, the world
fhould hear but little of me hence-forward." Yet he
could not think of remitting his diligence in the
work of the gofpel. " I dread the thoughts of
flagging in the latter ftages of my road," is an expreffion that he often ufes in writing to his friends.
He was frequently very ill ; but he imagined preaching

ing and travelling did him service. "Fear not your weak body, (says he, in a letter to Mr. Hervey,) we are immortal till our work is done. CHRIST's laborers must live by miracles; if not, I must not live at all; for GOD only knows what I daily endure.—My continual vomitings almost kill me, and yet the pulpit is my cure, so that my friends begin to pity me less, and to leave off that ungrateful caution, 'Spare thyself.' I speak this to encourage you.*

IN March, 1749, he returned to London from an excursion of about six hundred miles in the west, where he had the pleasure of seeing that his former visits had been blessed with abundant success. In May he went to Portsmouth, and preached every day for more than a week, to very large and attentive auditories. Many were brought under convictions, prejudices seemed to be universally removed, and people, that a few days before were speaking all manner of evil against him, were very desirous of his longer stay to preach the gospel among them.

JUNE 24, he writes from Bristol: "Yesterday GOD brought me here, after having carried me a circuit of about eight hundred miles, and enabled me to preach, I suppose, to upwards of a hundred thousand souls. I have been in eight Welch counties, and, I think, we have not had one dry meeting. The work in Wales is much upon the advance, and likely to increase daily. Had my dear Mr. Hervey been there, to have seen the simplicity of so many dear souls, I am persuaded he would have said, *sit a ini mea cum Methodistis.*" IN

---

* About this time, he wrote "Remarks on a Pamphlet, entitled, The Enthusiasm of Methodists and Papists compared." Wherein (with a candor very uncommon in controversial writings) he says, "several mistakes in some parts of my past writings and conduct are acknowledged, and my present sentiments concerning the Methodists explained." See his Works, Vol. IV.

In the month of July and August he was at London, Bristol, Plymouth, Biddeford and Exeter. When he returned to London, he had the pleasure of a visit from two German ministers, who had been laboring among the Jews, and, it is said, had been made instrumental in converting many of them.

In the month of September he went into Northamptonshire and Yorkshire; and preached at Oundle, Abberford, Leeds, and Haworth, where good Mr. Grimshaw (who was so indefatigable in his endeavors to bring souls to CHRIST) was minister. In his church they had above a thousand communicants, and in the church-yard about six thousand hearers. At Leeds, the auditory consisted of above ten thousand. Thither Mr. WHITEFIELD was invited by one of the Rev. Mr. Wesley's preachers, and by the societies. And Mr. Charles Wesley coming there, gave notice of him to the people, and also introduced him to the pulpit in Newcastle, where he preached four times, and twice without doors.

It being now late in the year, he did not go forward to Scotland, but returned to London, after having preached about thirty times in Yorkshire, and above ten times in Cheshire, and Lancashire. He was also at Sheffield and Nottingham. And the congregations were every where large and serious. Only in one or two places, he had a little rough treatment; but this he did not mind, while he had reason to think many received real benefit. He arrived in London about the middle of November, and continued there till the beginning of February, employed in his usual manner. Having offered to assist, occasionally, at West-street chapel, it was accepted. Accordingly he preached four or five times there, and administered the sacrament twice or thrice. Congregations were very large.

FEBRUARY 6, 1750, he writes from Gloucester.
"Though

" Though I left London in a very weak condition, and the weather was but bad, I came here on Friday-evening, and was ſtrengthened to preach on Saturday, and likewiſe on Sunday evening, and twice the ſame day in the country, at the New-houſe and at Hampton." And again from Briſtol, February 12. " Since I wrote laſt, we have been favored both in Glouceſter city, and in the country, with pleaſant and delightful ſeaſons. I have preached about twenty times, within theſe eight or nine days ; and though frequently expoſed to rain and hail, am much better than when I left London." From Briſtol he went to Exeter, and to Plymouth, and in his way met with the Rev. Mr. Pearſall, a diſſenting miniſter at Taunton and Mr. Darracott at Wellington ; both of whom he ſpeaks of in his Letters with the higheſt regard. At Plymouth he preached twelve times in ſix days, and the longer he preached, he had the greater number of hearers. His friends grew more zealous, and the fury of his enemies began to ſubſide. From thence he travelled near to the Land's end, preaching in a great many places, ſuch as Taviſtock, St. Ginny's,† Port Iſaac, Camelford, St. Andrews, Redruth, Gwinnop, St. Mewens. All this he accompliſhed before the 21ſt of March, when we find him again at Exeter. " Invitations, (ſays he) are ſent to me from ſeveral places. I want more tongues, more bodies, more ſouls for the LORD JESUS. Had I ten thouſand, he ſhould have them all."

In April he was at London and Portſmouth. And in May went to Aſhby, to wait on Lady Huntingdon, who had been ill. In his way thither, he had a moſt
comfortable

---

† " Four of Mr. Weſley's preachers were preſent, and three clergymen, Mr. Bennet, aged fourſcore, Mr. Thompſon, and Mr. Grigg." " I found, as I went along, a moſt bleſſed work ad been carried on by the inſtrumentality of the Mr. Weſleys, and their fellow-laborers." M. S.

comfortable interview with the Rev. Dr. Doddridge, Mr. Hervey*, and Dr. ———. But at Aſhby, where it might have been leaſt expected, there was a riot made before Lady Huntingdon's houſe, while the goſpel was preaching : and in the evening ſome people, in their return home, narrowly eſcaped being murdered. The Juſtice being informed, ſent a meſſage, in order to bring the offender before him. " So that I hope, (ſays Mr. WHITEFIELD) it will be, over-ruled for great good, and that the Goſpel, for the future, will have free courſe."

AFTER he left Aſhby, he preached at Radcliff Church, Nottingham and Sutton with great ſucceſs.

" At

---

* Mr. Hervey thus wrote of his interview to a friend : " I have ſeen lately, that moſt excellent miniſter of the ever-bleſſed JESUS, Mr. WHITEFIELD. I dined, ſupped, and ſpent the evening with him at Northampton, in company with Dr. Doddridge, and two pious, ingenious clergymen of the Church of England, both of them known to the learned world by their valuable writings. And ſurely, I never ſpent a more delightful evening, or ſaw one that ſeemed to make nearer approaches to the felicity of heaven. A gentleman of great worth and rank in the town, invited us to his houſe, and gave us an elegant treat ; but how mean was his proviſion, how coarſe his delicacies, compared with the fruit of my friend's lips ; they dropped as the honey comb, and were a well of life. Surely, people do not know that amiable and exemplary man, or elſe, I cannot but think, inſtead of depreciating, they would applaud and love him. For my part, I never beheld ſo fair a copy of our LORD, ſuch a living image of the SAVIOR, ſuch exalted delight in GOD, ſuch enlarged benevolence to man, ſuch a ready faith in the divine promiſes, and ſuch a fervent zeal for the divine glory ; and all this, without the leaſt noroſeneſs of humor, or extravagancies of behavior ; ſweetened with the moſt engaging chearfulneſs of temper, and regulated by all the ſobriety of reaſon, and wiſdom of Scriptures ; inſomuch, that I cannot forbear applying the wiſe man's encomium of an illuſtrious woman, to this eminent miniſter of the everlaſting Goſpe : " Many ſons have done virtuouſly, but thou excelleſt them all."

' At Nottingham, (fays he) feveral came to me, enquiring, What they fhould do to be faved ? I preached
there four times. One evening Lord S. and feveral
gentlemen, were prefent, and behaved with great
decency. Many thoufands attended. Yefterday-morn-
ing I breakfafted with three diffenting minifters ; and
Mr. P——s, who told me, that Lady P—— defired
he would prefs me to preach at the church. Yefterday, in the afternoon, I preached at Sutton : and this
morning at Mansfield." After leaving that place, he
went to Rotherham and Sheffield. He was at Leeds
in the end of May, and obferves, " Methinks, I am
now got into another climate, where there are many of
God's people." From thence he went to Manchefter,
Rofindale, and feveral other parts of Lancafhire, Kendal, Whitehaven, Cockermouth, preaching generally
twice a-day, and arrived at Edinburgh, July 6. Having preached near a hundred times fince he left London, and by a moderate computation, to above a
hundred thoufand fouls. " It is amazing (he writes)
to fee how people are prepared, in places where I
never was before. What fhall I render to the Lord ?"-

At Edinburgh and Glafgow, (in which places he
fpent the month of July, 1750) he was received, as
ufual, in the moft loving and tender manner, preaching generally twice a day to great multitudes, whofe
ferioufnefs, and earneft defire to hear him, made him
exert himfelf rather beyond his ftrength. " By
preaching always twice, (fays he) and once thrice,
and once four times in a day, I am quite weakened ;
but I hope to recruit again. I am burning with a
fever, and have a violent cold; but Christ's prefence
makes me fmile at pain, and the fire of his love burns
up all fevers whatfoever." He left Edinburgh, Auguft
4, and foon found himfelf much better for riding. At
Berwick, one of the minifters fent him an offer of his
pulpit, and he was informed that many more round
that

that town were willing to do the fame. At his return to London, he preached feveral times at West-ftreet Chapel. He had alfo the pleafure of Mr. Hervey's company, who, at his defire, came up to town, and lodged in his houfe. In the months of September and October he made excurfions to Fortfmouth, Chatham, Gloucefter, Birmingham, Everfham, Wednefbury, and Nottingham ; " ranging about (as he expreffes it) to fee who would believe the Gofpel-report." And was particularly fuccefsful at Chatham and Canterbury.

He fpent the winter in London, in his ufual bufy and laborious way, and with equal fuccefs. He was confined, near a fortnight, to his room by a violent fever, and inflammation of the lungs ; but before the 17th of December, he was able to preach again. And in the latter end of January, 1751, he rode poft to Afhby, being alarmed with the accounts of Lady Huntingdon's dangerous illnefs, and the afflictions with which it has pleafed God to vifit her family. He writes from Afhby, January 29. " Bleffed be God, Lady Huntingdon is fomewhat better. Entreat all our friends to pray for her. Her fifter-in-law, Lady Frances H——, lies dead in the houfe. She was a retired Chriftian, lived filently, and died fuddenly without a groan. May my exit be like hers. Almoft all the family have been fick in their turns."

Having left London, March 5, he went again into Gloucefterfhire, and to Briftol, and preached at Taunton and Wellington, in his way to Plymouth. April 11, he was at Exeter, and writes thus to Mr. Hervey : Some good, I truft, is to be done, this fpring to many fouls. This weftern circuit, I believe has been bleffed already. I have preached about forty times fince I left London, and have been enabled feveral times to ride forty miles a-day. I find this fenfibly refrefhes me. I wifh you could fay fo too.

At

At Plymouth we had fweet feafons ; and on Tuefday laft I met with a young clergyman, who was
awakened under my preaching feven years ago.   He
has been at Cambridge, and was ordained by the
Bifhop of Exeter.   He is followed much, and I fuppofe, will foon be reproached for his Mafter's fake.
I hope you will find ftrength to proceed in your book."

From Exeter he fet out on a tour through Wales,
where, in about three weeks, he rode near five hundred miles, and preached generally twice a-day ; and
from hence, he made his vifit to Ireland, which had
been in his thoughts fome time.

CHAP. XV.

From his firft Vifit to Ireland, *to his opening
the New Tabernacle at* London, *in the Year*
1753.

AFTER a paffage of five days from Wales, he arrived May 24, 1751, at Dublin, where he was gladly
received, and lodged at the houfe of Mr. L——, and
preached every morning and evening, as ufual in other
places : " Surely (fays he) here are many converted
fouls, among whom are two or three ftudents, and
feveral foldiers.   At firft the greatnefs and hurry of
the place furprized me ; but thanks be to the Lord
of the harveft, here, as well as elfewhere, the fields
are white, ready unto harveft.   Congregations are
large, and hear as for eternity."   And again : Athlone, June 10.   For this week paft, I have been
preaching twice almoft every day in fome country
towns.   I find, through the many offences that have
lately been given, matters were brought to a low
ebb.

ebb. But the cry now is, " Methodifm is revived again."* At Limerick he preached feven times to large and affected auditories, and twice at Cork, (where the Methodifts had lately been mobbed) to a great body of people, with all quietnefs. From thence he went to Bandon and Kinfale, where a like blefling attended his preaching. At his return to Cork, the numbers and affections of his hearers increafed. At Belfaft alfo he was detained fome days beyond his intention, by the people's importunity, and preached at Lifburn, Lurgun, the Maize, and Lambag, towns and places adjacent. So many attended, and the profpect of doing good was fo promifing, that he was forry he had not come to the north of Ireland fooner. But he hafted to pay another vifit to Scotland, before he embarked for America, which he was intent upon doing before winter.

He therefore came over in the beginning of July, 1751, from Belfaft to Irvine, where, at the defire of the magiftrates, he preached to a great congregation; and fo proceeded to Glafgow. From this place he writes, July 12. " Though I preached near eighty times in Ireland, and God was pleafed to blefs his word, yet Scotland feems to be a new world to me. To fee the people bring fo many Bibles, turn to every paffage when I am expounding, and hanging, as it were, upon me to hear every word, is very encouraging. I feel an uncommon freedom here ; and talking with the winter as well as with the fummer faints, feeds and delights my heart."§ At this time he

* In the MSS. he fays, " I took a journey from near Haverford-weft to Ireland, where a yet greater work had been begun and carried on to a high degree, amidft prodigious oppofition ; numbers converted, not only from Popery, but to Jesus Christ, at Athlone, Dublin, Limerick, Cork, and various other places."

§ Here it may be proper, once for all, to take notice of some

he was glad to underſtand that Mr. Dinwiddie, brother-in-law to the Rev. Mr. MacCulloch, of Cambuſlang, was made Governor of Virginia. In that
province there had been a conſiderable awakening
for

ſome particulars relating to Mr. WHITEFIELD's viſits to
Scotland, which he continued till within a few years of his
death.

Though after the years 1741, and 1742, there was no ſuch
extenſive new awakenings, Mr. WHITEFIELD's coming was
always refreſhing to ſerious perſons, and ſeemed to put new
life into them : and alſo to be the means of increaſing their
number. His preaching was ſtill eminently uſeful in various
reſpects. In the firſt place it had an excellent tendency to
deſtroy the hurtful ſpirit of bigotry, and exceſſive zeal for
ſmaller matters ; and to turn men's attention to the great
and ſubſtantial things of religion. Another effect was, that
it drew ſeveral perſons to hear the goſpel, who ſeldom went
to hear it from other miniſters. Again, young people in general were much benefitted by his miniſtry, and particularly
young ſtudents, who became afterwards ſerious evangelical
preachers. Laſtly, his morning diſcourſes, which were moſtly
intended for ſincere, but diſconſolate ſouls, were peculiarly
fitted to direct and encourage all ſuch in the Chriſtian life.
And his addreſſes in the evening to the promiſcuous multitudes who then attended him, were of a very alarming kind.
There was ſomething exceedingly ſtriking in the ſolemnity of
his evening congregations in the Orphan-houſe park at Edinburgh, and High-church-yard of Glaſgow, eſpecially towards
the concluſion of his ſermons, (which were commonly very
long, though they ſeemed ſhort to the hearers) when the whole
multitude ſtood fixt, and like one man hung upon his lips
with ſilent attention, and many under deep impreſſions of the
great objects of religion, and the concerns of eternity.——
Theſe things will not ſoon be forgotten ; and it is hoped the
many good effects, which, by the divine bleſſing attended
them, never will.

His converſation was no leſs reviving than his ſermons.
Many in Edinburgh and Glaſgow are witneſſes of this, eſpecially at Glaſgow, when in company with his good friends,
Mr. MacLaurin, Mr. Robert Scott, &c. one night challenge
the ſons of pleaſure with all their wit, good humor, and gaie-
ty,

for some years past, especially in Hanover-county and the places adjacent. As the ministers of the establishment did not favor the work, and the people had put themselves under the care of the New-York synod,

ty to furnish entertainment so agreeable. At the same time every part of it was not more agreeable, than it was useful and edifying.

His friends in Scotland, among whom were many of all ranks, from the highest to the lowest, were very constant and steady in their great regard for him. And his opposers grew more and more mild. Some anonymous pamphlets were written against him at his first coming : But these soon died and were forgotten. Afterwards a number of stories were handed about to his disadvantage ; but upon enquiry, it was found either that matters were misrepresented or exaggerated; or that there was no foundation for such reports at all. In short, when they were traced to their origin, they rather turned out to his honor. He used to smile at good Mr. MacLaurin's honest zeal, who on such occasions spared no pains to come at the truth, and when he had discovered it, was no less eager to communicate the discovery to others, for the vindication of Mr. WHITEFIELD's character, in which he thought the credit of religion was concerned. The following instance is well remembered : One Lieutenant Wright alledged, that Mr. WHITEFIELD had kept back money sent by a gentlewoman to her son in America ; this coming to Mr. MacLaurin's ears, he was restless till he procured a meeting betwixt Mr. WHITEFIELD and his accuser. They met ; Mr. Wright did not retract what he had said. Upon which a letter was instantly wrote to the mother at London ; and her answer being received, a confutation of the calumny was published in the Glasgow Courant in the following terms : " October 31, 1748. A story having been spread in this town of Mr. WHITEFIELD's having received twenty pounds sterling from a gentlewoman in London, to give to her son in Georgia ; whereas he had received only three guineas, which he had returned to the gentlewoman when he came back from Georgia, her son having been gone from thence before his arrival; a letter was wrote to London to clear up this affair, to which the gentlewoman has sent this answer : ' Sir, this is to assure you, that I received of Mr. John Stevens the three guineas, which was the full sum that I gave you for my son. I hope it is only a false aspersion

fynod, they met with difcouragements from thofe in power. However, Mr. Samuel Davies (afterwards prefident of the college of New-Jerfey) being licenfed, was fettled over a congregation ; and the religious concern fo increafed, that one congregation was multiplied to feven. There was now an agreeable profpect that thefe good people would have the fame privileges fecured to them, which diffenting Proteftants enjoy at home. AUGUST

perfion on him ; for I never heard that he fhould fay any fuch thing, being three months in England. I am, &c.' September 13, 1748.' There is likewife a receipt come down, dated September 3, to Mr. Stevens. Both the letter and receipt are to be feen in the hands of the publifher."

But, indeed, Mr. WHITEFIELD's whole behavior was fo open to the eyes of the world ; and his character, after it had ftood many attacks from all quarters, came at laft to be fo throughly eftablifhed, that feveral of his oppofers in Scotland feemed rather to acquire a certain degree of efteem for him ; at leaft, they all thought proper to give over fpeaking againft him.

When he was at Glafgow, he always lodged with Mr. James Niven, merchant above the Crofs ; till towards the end of his life, his afthmatic diforder made the town-air difagree with him. And then he went out in the evenings, and ftayed with his good friend Mr. MacCulloch, at Cambuflang.

A perfon of eminence, whom a fincere efteem of Mr. WHITEFIELD made attentive to his reception and miniftrations in Scotland, from firft to laft, writes thus to the compiler :

" Edinburgh, January, 1772. I think more might be faid with great juftice, concerning the effects of his miniftry in Scotland, after the firft two years ; as there was always a remarkable revival followed each of his vifits ; which many of the minifters teftified from their particular knowledge, efpecially by the number of new communicants —Mention might be made of the great number of minifters in Scotland, that employed him, and of the many affectionate letters he received from them, of which there were a good many printed both in the London and Glafgow Weekly Hiftories, from fome of the moft eminent men in the Church, who had employed him to preach in their pulpits, and continued fo to do, when opportunity offered ; except in the Prefbytery of Edinburgh ; and even there, the Magiftrates always allowed him a church to preach in, every time he came."

AUGUST 6, he fet out from Edinburgh for London, in order to embark a fourth time for America. He had thrown up much blood in Edinburgh; but the journey he was now upon had a good effect in recovering him from that illnefs; and as he went along, he was much refrefhed with the accounts he received of the happy fruits of his miniftry at Kendal the year before. After a forrowful parting with his friends in England, which grew ftill more diftreffing to him, he went aboard the Antelope, Captain MacLellan, bound for Georgia with Germans; and took along with him feveral children.

HE arrived at Savannah, October 27, and found the Orphan houfe in a flourifhing condition. "Thanks be to God (fays he) all is well at Bethefda. A moft excellent tract of land is granted to me very near the houfe, which in a few years, I hope will make a fufficient provifion for it. From November, 1751, to the beginning of April, 1752, he was partly at Bethefda, and partly in South Carolina, ftill upon the ftretch in his Mafter's work. I intend, (fays he) by his affiftance, now to begin; for as yet, alas! I have done nothing." And again, "O that I may begin to be in earneft! It is a new year; God quicken my tardy pace, and help me to do much work in a little time! this is my high ambition."

BEING warned by what had happened to him formerly, he did not venture to ftay the fummer feafon in America; but took his paffage in the end of April, for London. At his arrival, he perceived he had returned in a very good time; for Georgia was foon to be taken into the hands of Government, and put on the fame footing with other colonies, which gave ground to hope that it would foon become a flourifhing province. This was joyful news. He now thought Providence was appearing for Georgia and Bethefda. He determined therefore to fell his

plantation,

plantation, and to carry all his ſtrength to the Orphan-houſe.

ABOUT the middle of June, he planned a new
rout. " Next week, (ſays he) God willing, I ſhall
go to Portſmouth, from thence to Bath, then to the
weſt, then to Wales, and from thence, may be, to
Scotland and Ireland." Accordingly we find his
letters of this period, dated at Portſmouth, ·Briſtol,
Cardiff, Haverford-weſt. In returning to Briſtol, he
attended an aſſociation, where were preſent about
nine clergy, and near forty other laborers, of whom
he writes : " I truſt all are born of God, and deſirous
to promote his glory, and his people's good. All
was harmony and love."

AUGUST 17, he was in London. His letter of
this date, to his acquaintance Dr. F——, the cele-
brated electrical philoſopher, deſerves particular notice. " I find you grow more and more famous in
the learned world. As you have made a pretty
conſiderable progreſs in the myſteries of electricity,
I would now humbly recommend to your diligent un-
prejudiced purſuit and ſtudy, the myſtery of the new
birth. It is a moſt important, intereſting ſtudy, and
when maſtered, will richly anſwer and repay you for
all your pains. One at whoſe bar we are ſhortly to
appear, hath ſolemnly declared, that without it, we
cannot enter the kingdom of heaven. - You will ex-
cuſe this freedom. I muſt have *aliquid Chriſti* in all
my letters."

FROM London he took another tour to Edinburgh,
where he arrived in the beginning of September,
1752. In his way he preached twice at Lutterworth,
(the famous John Wickliff's pariſh) and at Leiceſter ;
and in both places was informed afterwards that
good was done. At Newcaſtle, he was as it were
arreſted to ſtay, and preached four times to great
congregations.   AT

AT Edinburgh and Glafgow (in which places he
continued till the 10th of October) he was employed
as ufual.   He writes from Glafgow, September 29.
" At Edinburgh great multitudes, among whom were
abundance of the better fort, attended twice every
day.   Many young minifters and ftudents have given
clofe attendance, and I hear of feveral perfons that
have been brought under deep convictions.   I intend
to fend you copies of two letters from a Highland
fchoolmafter, who is-honored of God to do much
good among the poor Highland children."   " I have
brave news fent me from Leicefter and Newcaftle,
and have ftrong invitations to Yorkfhire and Lancafhire.   What a pity it is that the year goes round
fo foon."*

IN his way back to London, he preached at Berwick, Alnwick, Morpeth, and Newcaftle.   From
Sheffield he writes, November 1.   " Since I left
Newcaftle, I have fcarce known fometimes, whether I
have been in heaven or on earth.   At Leeds, Burftall, Howarth, Halifax, &c. thoufands and thoufands
have flocked twice or thrice a-day to hear the word
of life.   I am now come from Bolton, Manchefter,
Stockport, and Chinly.   Yefterday I preached in a
Church.   Four ordained minifters, friends to the
work of God, have been with me.   The word hath
run fo fwiftly at Leeds, that friends are come to
fetch

* In 1752, the General Affembly of the Church of Scotland, upon a divifion of the houfe, by a few votes depofed
Mr. Gillefpie ; which afterwards gave occafion to the fociety
called the Prefbytery of Relief.   Mr. WHITEFIELD being informed of the circumftances of that affair, writes thus—" I
wifh Mr. Gillefpie joy.   The Pope I find has turned Prefbyterian.—The Lord reigns, that is enough for us."   And again,
—" Now will Mr. Gillefpie do more good in a week, than before, in a year.   How blind is Satan !   What does he get by
cafting out CHRIST's fervants ?   I expect that fome great
good will come out of thefe confufions."

fetch me back, and am now going to Rotherham, Wakefield, Leeds, York and Epworth. GOD favors us with weather, and I would fain make hay whilst the sun shines.—O that I had as many tongues, as there are hairs upon my head ! the ever-loving, ever-lovely JESUS, should have them all. Fain would I die preaching."

NOVEMBER 10, he arrived at London, and proceeded in his usual way at the Tabernacle. December 15, he says. " My hands are full of work ; and I trust I can say, the LORD causes his work to prosper in my unworthy hands. More blessed seasons we never enjoyed. Our sacramental occasions have been exceedingly awful and refreshing."

HE now began to think of erecting a new Tabernacle, a large building eighty feet square ; which he accomplished in the spring and summer following.

ABOUT this time also, we find Mr. Hervey and him employed in revising each other's manuscripts. Of Mr. Hervey's he says : " For me to play the critic on them, would be like holding up a candle to the sun. However, I will just mark a few places, as you desire. I foretel their fate ; nothing but your scenery can screen you. Self will never bear to die, though slain in so genteel a manner, without shewing some resentment against its artful murderer." Again, ' I thank you a thousand times for the trouble you have been at in revising my poor compositions, which I am afraid you have not treated with a becoming severity. How many pardons shall I ask for mangling, and I fear murdering your *Theron* and *Aspasio*. If you think my two sermons will do for the public, pray return them immediately. I have nothing to comfort me but this, that the LORD chuses the weak things of this world to confound the strong, and things that are not, to bring to nought the things that are. I write for the poor, you for the polite and noble ;
—GOD

—GOD will assuredly own and bless what you write.'

HE was much affected about this time with the death of one Mr. Steward, a Minister that began to be popular in the church, but soon entered into his rest. "When I met the workmen to contract about the building, I could scarce bear to think of building Tabernacles. Strange! that so many should be so soon discouraged, and we continued. Mr. Steward spoke for his LORD, as long as he could speak at all. He had no clouds nor darkness. I was with him till a few minutes before he slept in JESUS."

MARCH 1, 1753, he laid the foundation of the new Tabernacle, and preached from Exod. xx. 24. During the building thereof, he preached in Moorfields, Spittalfields and other places in London, and made excursions to Chatham, Sheerness, and Braintree.

IN the month of April, he went to Norwich for a few days, preaching twice a-day to thousands, who attended with the greatest eagerness. At his evening sermons, some rude people made opposition, but without effect. At this time also he published his Expostulatory Letter to Count Zinzendoff, which is in the 4th vol. of his works.

IN May he made another excursion to Narboth, Pembroke, Haverford-west, &c. where congregations were large, and a gracious melting seemed to be among the people. Within little more than a fortnight he rode three hundred and fifty miles, and preached above twenty times.

SUNDAY, June 10, 1753, he opened his new Tabernacle, preaching in the morning from 1. Kings, viii. 11. and in the evening from 1. Chron. xxix. 9.

CHAP.

CHAP. XVI.

From his opening the New Tabernacle in Moorfields, *so his preaching at the Chapel in* Tottenham-Court Road, 1756.

MR. WHITEFIELD having preached in London at
his Tabernacle for a few days with his usual fervor
and success, and to large congregations, in the end
of the month of June, set out towards Scotland.   In
his way he had desirable meetings at Oulney and
Northampton.   He preached also at Liecester, and
Nottingham, where a great multitude came to hear,
and at Sheffield.   In his way to Leeds, next morning,
he preached at Rotherham and Wakefield.   At the
former place he had been disturbed twice or thrice,
and was almost determined to preach there no more.
But he found this would have been a rash determina-
tion ; for some who had been bitter persecutors, now
received him gladly into their house, and owned that
God had made him instrumental in their conversion.
At Leeds he had great success.   At York also he
preached four times.   Twice they were disturbed,
and twice had very agreeable seasons.   At Newcastle
he preached seven times, and once at Sunderland to
great multitudes who were deeply impressed. At five
in the morning the great room was filled, and on the
Lord's day, the congregation without was exceeding
large. In short, the prospect all around was so promising, that he almost repented of his engagement to
go to Scotland, and resolved to come back as soon as
possible.

HE proceeded however according to his promise,
and having spent some days at Edinburgh and Glasgow

gow in his ufual laborious and earneft manner, and
with ufual acceptance, he returned to England, Auguft 7.*

ALL this time he preached twice or thrice a-day,
and once five times. This he found rather too much
for his ftrength. But he ftill went on, often expreffing his defires and hopes foon to fee his divine Mafter
in glory.

ON his return to England, he went from Newcaftle to Stockton, Ofmotherly, York and Leeds. He
affifted at the facrament at Howarth, where they had
a very extraordinary feafon, and a vaft number of
communicants. He went as far as Bolton, Manchefter and Stockport. The more he preached, the more
eager the people feemed to be. The laft part of his
circuit was to Lincolnfhire, Rotherham, Sheffield,
Nottingham, and Northampton. He returned to
London in the latter end of September, having travelled

* After he had been in Glafgow, the following paragraph
appeared in the Newcaftle Journal, Auguft 11, 1753. " By a
Letter from Edinburgh we are informed, that on the fecond
inftant Mr. WHITEFIELD, the Itinerant, being at Glafgow,
and preaching to a numerous audience near the Play-houfe
lately built, he inflamed the mob fo much againft it, that they
ran directly from before him, and pulled it down to the
ground. Several of the rioters are fince taken up, and committed to goal."
It would not have been worth while to tranfcribe this,
were it not another fpecimen of the unaccountable liberties
taken by fome of the oppofers of Mr. WHITEFIELD in telling
their ftories concerning him. The fact was this. Mr. WHITE-
FIELD being informed that the Players had lately come to
Glafgow, and had met with fome encouragement, took occafion in his fermons to preach againft Play-houfes, and to re-
prefent their pernicious influence on religion and morality,
efpecially in a populous, commercial city, and the feat of a
Univerfity. But there was no riot. It was the proprietor
of the Play-houfe (at that time a flight temporary booth, fupported by the old walls of the Bifhop's caftle) who ordered
his workmen to take it down.

velled about twelve hundred miles, and preached a hundred and eighty times to many thousands.

His stay in London was but short, for in the month of October he took another tour to Stafford-shire. A new scene of usefulness seemed to open to him, while he preached at Culney, at Oxen, near Harborough, Bosworth, Kettering and Bedford ; at all which places he preached in one week. At Birmingham also, and several adjacent places, the people flocked to hear the gospel. At a place near Dudley, called Guarnall, he was informed of a whole company that were awakened by reading his sermons. He met with others awakened years ago, and heard of a notorious persecutor and drunkard, who had been powerfully struck. He loved to break up new ground, as he expresses it ; and had the pleasure to find sometimes that his way was prepared by the blessing which God had given to his writings, particularly at Alperam in Cheshire, and at Liverpool, where a person that had received benefit by reading his sermons, met him at landing, and took him to his house. All was quiet here, and at Chester, where he preached four times, and had several of the clergy in his congregations. But at Wrexham and Nantwich (where a Methodist meeting house had lately been pulled down) he was disturbed by the mob, and forced to remove his congregation to a place a little out of town.

Thus he went on, returning at times for a few days to London. And November 16, writes from Gloucester, " After Lord's-day, I am bound for Bristol and Plymouth, and hope to get into my winter-quarters for some time before Christmas. Glad should I be to travel for Jesus all the year round. It is more to me than my necessary food.

On Sunday, November 25, he opened the new Tabernacle at Bristol, which he observes " was large, but not half large enough ; for if the place could contain

tain

tain them, near as many would attend as in London."
He also preached twice, in his brother's great house,
to the quality. Though it was so late in the year, he
set out for Somersetshire, and preached several times
in the open air, at seven o'clock at night. "My
hands and body, (says he) were pierced with cold;
but what are outward things, when the soul within is
warmed with the love of God? The stars shone exceeding bright: by an eye of faith, I saw Him who
called them all by their names. My soul was filled
with a holy ambition, and I longed to be one of those
who shall shine as the stars for ever and ever." At
this time his friend and fellow-laborer, the Rev. Mr.
John Wesley, had, by his extraordinary labors,
brought his life into great danger, of which Mr.
WHITEFIELD thus writes; "Bristol, December 3,
1753. I am hastening to London, to pay my last respects to my dying friend. The physicians think his
disease is a galloping consumption. I pity the church,
I pity myself, but not him. Poor Mr. Charles will
now have double work. But we can do all things
through CHRIST strengthening us!" His letters to
both the brothers on this occasion are very affectionate and sympathizing. And he soon had the pleasure
of seeing Mr. Wesley recover. December 26, he had
a visit from Messieurs Tennent and Davies from A-
merica, who came over to procure contributions for
the College of New-Jersey. As they were commis-
sioned to apply for a general collection in Scotland,
he gave them recommendatory letters, and heartily
endeavored to promote their design. He stayed in
London all the winter of 1753,* longing for a spring
campaign,

---

* His Letters written about the beginning of the new year,
shew the habitual frame of his mind. "Near forty years old,
and such a dwarf! The winter come already, and so little
done in the summer." Again, "I heartily wish your Lordship,

campaign (as he expresses it,) that he might begin to do something for his divine Master.

MARCH 7, 1754, having got twenty-two poor destitute children under his care, he embarked with them for America, by way of Lisbon, where he stayed from the 20th of March, to the 13th of April.

FROM Lisbon he writes : " The air agrees with my poor constitution extremely, and through divine assistance, I hope what I see will also much improve my better part, and help to qualify me better for preaching the everlasting gospel : again a gentleman hath most gladly received me into his house, and behaves like a friend indeed. To day I dine with the Consul. Every day I have seen or heard something, that hath a native tendency to make me thankful for the glorious reformation." After sight of some popish processions, which were new and very striking to him, he says, " I returned to my lodgings not a little affected, to see so many thousands led away from the simplicity of the gospel, by such a mixture of human artifice and blind superstition, of which, indeed, I could have formed no idea, had I not been an eyewitness." He was still more shocked at the procession of St. Francis ; and most of all at the sight of near two hundred penitents passing along the streets in a moon shine night, dragging along heavy chains fastened to their ancles, which made a dismal rattling, most of whom whipped and lashed themselves with cords, and with flat bits of iron ; and some of them struck so hard, that their backs were quite red, and very much swelled. He wrote a description of this to his friend, with expressions of praise and gratitude to Providence for the great wonder of the Reformation, and for delivering

ship, not the compliments but the blessings of the season ; even all those blessings that have been purchased for a lost world by the death and sufferings of an incarnate GOD." '

delivering Britain from the return of fuch fpiritual flavery, by defeating the unnatural rebellion. "Blef-fed be God, (fays he) the fnare is broken and we are delivered. O for Proteftant practices to be added to Proteftant principles." He further obferves, "The preachers here have alfo taught me fomething; their action is graceful, *Vividi oculi, vividæ manus, omnia vivida.* Surely our Englifh preachers would do well to be a little more fervent in their addrefs. They have truth on their fide; why fhould fuperftition and falfhood run away with all that is pathetic and affec-ting?" His two laft letters from Lifbon contain a long and lively defcription of the fuperftitious farces which he faw acted on Holy Thurfday, as they call it, and Good Friday; which he concludes with very fe-rious reflections, and expreffions of pity towards the poor deluded people, who are not allowed to examine matters by the word of God.

AFTER a paffage of fix weeks from Lifbon, he ar-rived at Beaufort, in South Carolina, May 27, with his Orphan charge, all quite well. Having fettled them in his family in Georgia, which now confifted of above a hundred, and fpent fome time in Carolina, he took a journey to the northward. At Charlefton, (fays he) and other parts of Carolina, my poor labors have met with the ufual acceptance, and I have reafon to hope a Clergyman hath been brought under very ferious impreffions. My health is wonderfully preferved. My wonted vomitings have left me, and though I ride whole nights, and have been frequently expofed to great thunders, violent lightnings, and heavy rains, yet I am rather better than ufual, and as far as I can judge, am not yet to die. O that I may at length learn to begin to live. I am afhamed of my floth and lukewarmnefs, and long to be on the ftretch for God." He arrived at New-York by water, July 27, and preached backwards and forwards from New-York to

Philadelphia,

Philadelphia, and Whitely Creek, till the middle of September. " Every-where, he obferves, a divine power accompanied the word, prejudices were removed, and a more effectual door opened than ever, for preaching the gofpel." The latter end of September, he had once more the pleafure of feeing his good old friend Governor Belchier at Elizabeth-Town (New-Jerfey.) And it being the New-Jerfey commencement, the Prefident and the Truftees prefented Mr. WHITEFIELD with the degree of A. M. The meeting of the fynod fucceeded, before whom he preached feveral times, and had much fatisfaction in their company. " To morrow (fays he) October 1, God willing. I fhall fet out with the worthy Prefident (Mr. Burr) for New-England, and expect to return back to the Orphan-houfe, through Virginia. This will be about a two thoufand miles-circuit ; but the REDEEMER's ftrength will be more than fufficient." He had alfo fome thoughts of going to the Weft-Indies, had it been practicable, before his return to England.

He arrived with Prefident Burr, at Bofton, October 9, and preached there a week with great acceptance. " At Rhode Ifland and Bofton (fays he) fouls fly to the gofpel, like doves to the windows. Oppofition feems to fall daily." When he was at Bofton, he heard to his great joy that a Governor was at length nominated for Georgia, and that his friend Mr. Haberfham was made fecretary ; to whom he writes, " May the King of kings enable you to difcharge your truft, as becomes a good patriot, fubject, and Chriftian !" At this time, he went as far north as Portfmouth (New Hampfhire) preaching always twice and fometimes thrice a day : his reception at Bofton was more favorable than that fourteen years before ; and in general his labors feemed to be attended with as great a bleffing as ever. He took leave of the Bofton

ton people at four in the morning, November 7, and went to Rhode Island ; from thence through Maryland* and Virginia, where the prospect of doing good was so promising, that he was sorry he had not come sooner. Many came forty or fifty miles to hear him ; and a spirit of conviction and consolation seemed to run through all the assemblies. Three churches were opened to him. Prejudices subsided ; some of the rich and great began to think favorably of his ministrations ; and several of the lower class came to him, and acknowledged what God had done for them by his preaching, when there before.

In the month of February, 1755, he got back to Charleston, and from thence went to Savannah ; continuing in these places till the latter end of March, when he embarked for England. And on the 8th of May, arrived at Newhaven in Sussex.

The first thing he took notice of, was the success of the gospel in his native country : " Glory be to the great Head of the Church ! the word hath still free course. The poor despised Methodists are as lively as ever ; and in several churches, the gospel is now preached with power. Many in Oxford are awakened to the knowledge of the truth; and I have heard almost every week of some fresh Minister or another, that seems determined to know nothing but Jesus Christ, and him crucified.† This consideration seems to have reanimated him. He went on preaching earnestly at London, Bristol, Bath, and in Gloucestershire, till the month of August. Then he went to Norwich, and opened the Tabernacle there.

" At

* " At length I have got into Maryland, and into a family, out of which, I trust, five have been born of God."

† In the M.S. he puts down the names of Jones, Romaine, Madan : of whom it appears he intended to have written more particularly.

"At this place, (fays he) notwithftanding offences have come, there has been a glorious work begun, and is now carrying on, (Auguft 30, 1755.) The polite and great feem to hear with much attention, and I fcarce ever preached-a week together with greater freedom."

AFTER this he went his northern circuit, and found reafon to blefs GOD for giving countenance to his labors all the way ; particularly, at Northampton, Liverpool, Bolton, Mancheﬅer, Leeds, Bradford, and York.*   But when he had been fome days at Newcaﬅle, he found it too late to go to Ireland, (as he once propofed) or even to Scotland : He returned therefore to London, October 30, preaching twice and thrice a-day for two months, to many thoufands. At this time, he fays, " Next to JESUS, my King and Country were upon my heart.   I hope I ﬅall always think it my bounden duty, next to inviting finners to the bleﬅed JESUS, to exhort my hearers to exert themfelves againﬅ the firﬅ approaches of Popiﬅ tyranny, and arbitrary power.†   O that we may be enabled to watch and pray, againﬅ all the oppoﬁtion of Antichriﬅ in our hearts ; for after all, there lies the moﬅ dangerous man of fin.   About the end of November. he preached in pain, occaﬁoned by a fore throat, which was like to have terminated in an inﬂammatory quinfey.   This obliged him, much againﬅ his will, to be ﬁlent a few days.   As foon as the
danger

---

* "At York, I hope, a fine gentleman was touched ; and feveral I find were awakened there, and at Newcaﬅle, at my laﬅ viﬁt."

† This refers to the encroachments made by the French upon the Britiﬅ Colonies in America ; and their threatening Great Britain with an invaﬁon ; which occaﬁoned a declaration of war againﬅ France next year.

danger feemed to be over, he fell to work again.*—
He was now applied to by many ferious perfons, to
preach twice a-week at Long-acre Chapel, near the
play-houfes.   Being informed that the place was
licenfed, he complied and preached there for the firft
time, on December 23, 1755; but met with great
difficulties.   The Bifhop of B—— fent him a prohi-
bition.   There was alfo a number of foldiers, drum-
mers, and many of the lower fort of people, hired to
diftnrb him, by making a noife in the neighboring
houfe, or yard, of one Mr. C——; and this not once
or twice, but every time he preached at that Chapel;
being hired by fubfcription, and provided with a
copper furnace, bells, drums, clappers, &c. they made
it their bufinefs to raife the loudeft din they poffibly
could, from the moment he began preaching, to the
end of his fermon.   By which, alfo, mobbers were
encouraged to come and riot at the Chapel-door, during the time of divine fervice, and then infult and
abufe him, and the congregation, after it was over.
The Chapel windows, while he was preaching, were
repeatedly broken by large ftones, which fadly
wounded fome of the hearers.   Upon this occafion,
Mr. WHITEFIELD wrote feveral fpirited letters to
the Bifhop of B——, acknowledging, indeed, his
Lordfhip's candor, and thanking him for his favorable
opinion and good wifhes; (for the Bifhop had wrote
an anfwer to his firft letter) but, at the fame time,
with great ftrength of reafon, and a becoming fenfe
of Britifh liberty, defending his own conduct, and re-
monftrating againft the riotous proceedings of his
adverfaries, "Laft Tuefday night, (fays he) all was
hufhed.   And in order to throw off the popular
odium, I gave it as my opinion, that it was owing
                                                        to

---

* "One Phyfician prefcribed a *perpetual blifter*; but I have
found *perpetual preaching* to be a better remedy.   When this-
grand catholicon fails, it is over with me."

to your Lordſhip's kind interpoſition. ·One Mr. C. and one Mr. M. I am informed, are greatly concerned. I know them not ; and I pray the Lord of all lords never to lay this ill and unmerited treatment to their charge. If no more noiſe is made on their part, I aſſure your Lordſhip, no further reſentment ſhall be made on mine. But, if they perſiſt, · I have the authority of the Apoſtle on a like occaſion, to appeal unto Cæſar. And thanks be to God, we have a Cæſar to appeal to, whoſe laws will not ſuffer any of his loyal ſubjects to be uſed in ſuch an inhuman manner. I have only one favor to beg of your Lordſhip, tHat you would ſend (as they are your Lordſhip's pariſhioners) to the above gentlemen, and deſire them henceforward, to deſiſt from ſuch unchriſtian, (and eſpecially, at this critical juncture,) ſuch riotous and dangerous proceedings. Whether as a Chaplain to a moſt worthy Peereſs, and a Preſbyter of the Church of England, and a ſteady diſintereſted friend to our preſent happy conſtitution, I have not a right to aſk ſuch a favor, I leave to your Lordſhip's mature deliberation." In the mean time, his preaching was owned by God : particularly as to one, who had been a ſubſcriber to hire men to make the noiſe.

In the beginning of February, 1756, he ſent eighty pounds of the collection which he had made at the Tabernacle, on the day of the public faſt, to the ſociety for relieving the poor perſecuted French Proteſtants.*

As the uproar was ſtill continued at Long-acre Chapel, and the facts were ſo flagrant, he was adviſed to proſecute the offenders by law. This being underſtood his life was threatened. A man came up to him, in the pulpit at the Tabernacle, and three

anonymous

---

* This year, 1756, he publiſhed, " A ſhort Addreſs to Perſons of all Denominations, occaſioned by the Alarm of an intended Invaſion." Inſerted in Vol. IV. of his Works.

anonymous letters were sent him, denouncing a certain, sudden and unavoidable stroke, unless he desisted from preaching, and pursuing the offenders.   Judging that others were concerned as well as himself, and that it was an affair that had reference to the welfare of civil government, he sent a copy of one of the letters to the Honorable Hume C———ll, begging the favor of his advice; and was advised by all means, to put all concerned into the court of King's-Bench.   The Earl of Holderness, (one of the secretaries of state) to whom he was introduced on this occasion, received him very courteously, and seemed to have no objection against issuing a reward. for the discovery of the letter-writer.   "I find," says Mr. WHITEFIELD, in his letter to Lady H———n, May 2, 1756, " that all things happen for the furtherance of the Gospel.   I suppose your Ladyship has seen his Majesty's promise of a pardon, to any that will discover the letter-writer; and this brings the further news of my having taken a piece of ground, very commodious to build on, not far from the Foundling Hospital.   I have opened the subscription, and through GoD's blessing. it hath already amounted to near six hundred pounds.   I hope, in a few months, to have what hath been long wanted, a place for the Gospel, at the other end of the town.   This evening, GoD willing, I venture once more to preach at Long acre." The place he here speaks of, is the chapel in Tottenham-Court-Road, which he began to build May 10, 1756.

AFTER this he set out on one of his wonted tours, and having spent three weeks in preaching, with usual success, at Bristol, and in Gloucestershire, at Bradford, Frome, Warminster, and at Portsmouth, he returned to London in the beginning of June.

JULY 27, he writes "The gospel flourishes in London.   I am just returned from preaching it at Sheerness, nefs, Chatham, and in the camp." Next day he fet off for Scotland. How he employed his time in his way thither, appears from the following letter. "Sunderland, Auguft. 14, 1756 : How fwiftly doth my precious time fly away ! It is now a fortnight fince I came to Leeds, in and about which, I preached eight days, thrice almoft every day, to thronged and affected auditories. On Saturday laft at Bradford, in the morning, the auditory confilted of about ten thoufand ; at noon, and in the evening at Burftall, to near double the number. Though hoarfe, I was helped to fpeak fo, that all heard. Next morning, I took a forrowful leave of Leeds, preached at Doncafter at noon, and at York the fame night ; on Wednefday at Wawftall, about fifty miles off ; on Thurfday, twice at Yarm, and laft night, and this morning here." All the way he heard of a great concern, fince he was in thefe parts laft year.

UPON preffing invitation from friends in the North, he proceeded to Edinburgh, where he arrived Auguft 20, and preached there* and at Glafgow, as ufual, till September 22 ; about which time he received a meffage from the new Governor of Georgia in London, defiring to fee and converfe with him before he embarked.

IN

* "Edinburgh, September 9, 1756. For near thefe three weeks, the Rev. Mr. WHITEFIELD hath been preaching in the Orphan-Hofpital-Park, to very crouded auditories, twice every day. As he was frequently very explicit in opening the miferies of Popifh tyranny, and arbitrary power ; and very warm in exhorting his hearers to loyalty and courage at home, and in ftirring them up to pray for the fuccefs of his Majefty's forces, both by fea and land abroad ; we have, reafon to believe, that his vifit at this juncture hath been particularly ufeful." *Glafgow Courant.*

"Edinburgh, September 23. On Tuefday evening, the Rev. Mr. WHITEFIELD, after fermon, made a collection for the poor Highlanders, when upwards of fixty pounds fterling was collected." *Ibid.*

In his way to London, he again vifited Leeds, and went fome days into good Mr. G—— and Mr. J——'s round, preaching upon the mountains to many thoufands. But finding his laft year's diforder was like to return, he was obliged to leave off, and came to London, in the end of October ; and November the 7th, opened his new Chapel in Tottenham-Court. Road, preaching from 1. Cor. iii. 11.

CHAP. XVII.

From his opening his Chapel in Tottenham-Court-Road, *to his Arrival in* Edinburgh, *in the Year* 1759.

H IS conftant work was now preaching about fifteen times a-week, which, with a weak appetite, want of reft,* and much care lying upon his mind, enfeebled his body exceedingly. " But (fays he) the joy of the Lord is my ftrength, and my greateft grief is, that I can do no more for Him, who hath done and fuffered fo much for me."

His new Chapel fucceeded according to his wiflr. On Sunday-mornings hundreds went away, not being able to get in. Some people of diftinction came, and begged they might have a conftant feat ; and he received a very ferious letter, from a perfon who was brought under concern there, though he came at firft out of curiofity, to fee what fort of place it was.†

IN

---

* " I could enlarge, but it is near fix in the morning, and I muft away to preach."

† " A neighboring Doctor calls the place WHITEFIELD'S Soul-trap. I pray the friend of finners, to make it a Soul-trap

In spring 1757, he set out again on his northern circuit, and came to Edinburgh in the month of May, when the General Assembly of the Church of Scotland held their annual meeting. He was much pleased with this circumstance. Many ministers attended his sermons, perhaps a hundred at a time. Thereby prejudices were removed, and many of them seemed to be deeply affected. About thirty of them, as a token of respect, invited him to a public entertainment.

The King's Commissioner also invited him to his table.‡ Thousands, among whom were a great many of the best rank, daily attended his ministrations, and the longer he staid, the more the congregations increased.

From Edinburgh he went to Glasgow, where, having preached twice by the way, he arrived June 8, and continued till the 14th preaching, as usual, in the High Church-yard, to great multitudes, both morning and evening, in one of the churches of the city. The poor in Glasgow being at this time in very mournful circumstances, notwithstanding the various sources of supply, he (with the countenance of the Magistrates) made a collection for them, at his sermon on Monday-evening, which amounted to near sixty pounds. Next day he preached at Paisley; and from thence set out for Ireland.   His

trap indeed, to many wandering creatures. —— S——, the player, makes always one of the auditory, and, as I hear, is much impressed, and brings others with him.''

‡-Some of the Scotch clergy, who were prejudiced against Mr. WHITEFIELD, took upon them to signify to the Commissioner, (Lord C-thc-rt) by some of their friends, that it would be better not to invite Mr. WHITEFIELD to his table; and that it would give offence. This overture his Grace received with indignation.

The Earl of L—— also, who was the King's Commissioner before Lord C-thc-rt, shewed particular atttention to Mr. WHITEFIELD: and from the time of his first coming to Scotland, shewed great and constant regard for him.

His firſt reception was promiſing as formerly. Congregations at Dublin were very large, and much affected. One of the Biſhops told a Nobleman, (who repeated it to Mr. WHITEFIELD) that he was glad he was come to rouſe the people. All ſorts attended, and all ſorts ſeemed to be ſtruck with a religious concern. But on Sunday afternoon, July 3, after preaching in Oxman-town-green, (a place frequented by the Ormond and Liberty boys, as they call them, who often fight there) he narrowly eſcaped with his life. It being war time, he took occaſion to exhort his hearers, (as was his uſual practice) not only to fear God, but to honor the King ; and prayed for ſuccefs to the King of Pruſſia. In the time of ſermon and prayer, a few ſtones were thrown at him, which did no hurt. But when he had done, and thought to return home, the way he came, by the Barracks, to his great ſurprize accefs was denied : and he was obliged to go near half a mile, from one end of the Green to the other, through hundreds of Papiſts, &c. who finding him unattended, (for a ſoldier and four preachers who came with him, had fled) threw vollies of ſtones upon him from all quarters, and made him reel backwards and forwards, till he was almoſt breathlefs, and all over a gore of blood.* At laſt with great difficulty, he ſtaggered to the door of a miniſter's houfe lying next to the Green, which was kindly opened to him. For a while he continued ſpeechlefs and panting for breath ; but his weeping friends having given him ſome cordials, and waſhed his wounds, a coach was procured, in which, amidſt the oaths, imprecations, and threatenings of the Popiſh rabble, he got ſafe home ; and joined in a
                                                        hymn

---

* I received many blows and wounds ; one was particularly large, and near my temples. I thought of Stephen, and was in hopes, like him, to go off in this bloody triumph, to the immediate preſence of my Maſter.

hymn of thankſgiving with his friends, by whom, he ſays, " none but ſpectators could form an idea of the affection with which he was received." Next morning he ſat out for Port Arlington, " Leaving, (ſays he) my perſecutors to his mercy, who of perſecutors has often made preachers. I pray GOD, I may thus be avenged of them."

AFTER preaching at Port Arlington, Athlone, Limerick, and Cork ; in the beginning of Auguſt he returned to England ; and while the weather permitted, continued to range, (as he expreſſes it) preaching with great earneſtneſs every where.— " This ſpiritual hunting, (ſays he) is delightful ſport, when the heart is in the work." At Plymouth he had the pleaſure of ſeeing officers, ſoldiers, ſailors, &c. attending his ſermons with the utmoſt ſolemnity. In Exeter alſo, Briſtol, Glouceſter, and Glouceſterſhire, he had delightful ſeaſons. About the middle of October, 1757, he returned to London.

HIS attendance this winter in both the Chapel and the Tabernacle, together with his thoughtfulneſs, greatly impaired his health. He was troubled with continual vomitings, got little ſleep, and had no appetite. Still, however, he went on as well as he could. " I am brought now, (ſays he) to the ſhort allowance of preaching but once a-day, and twice on a Sunday." But when he was not preaching, he was projecting ſome ſcheme or other for the advancement of religion : for inſtance, the building the alms-houſes for pious widows, on the ground that ſurrounded his Chapel. " I have a plan, (ſays he) for twelve. The whole expence will be four hundred pounds. I have got a proſpect of two. I propoſe allowing each widow half-a-crown a-week. The ſacrament-money will more than do. If this be effected, many godly widows will be provided for, and .

Q

and a ſtanding monument left that the Methodiſts were not againſt good works." It was not long till this plan was put in execution. The foundation of the alms-houſes was laid February 16, 1758, and the widows began to be admitted in June following.

He began his ſummer-circuit this year at Glouceſter : from thence he went to Briſtol, and then to Wales. When he was in Wales, he was brought very low in his health. He was not able to ſit up in company, as he uſed to do ; and could take very little food. Yet continued travelling and preaching twice a day, through various towns in South Wales, where multitudes attended ; on Sundays the numbers were almoſt incredible.

In the month of July he ſet off for Scotland. In his way he preached at Everton, St. Neots, Kayſo, Bedford, Oulney, Weſton, Underwood, Ravenſtone, Northampton, and Newcaſtle. Four clergymen lent him their pulpits. His bodily ſtrength increaſed ſo little by this journey, that he ſometimes had thoughts of turning back. But this he did not think to be his duty. "Through divine ſtrength, (ſays he) I hope to go forward, and ſhall ſtrive, as much as in me lies, to die in this glorious work." Yet it pleaſed God to reſtore his health in a good meaſure, ſoon after his arrival in Scotland. From Edinburgh he writes, Auguſt 19 and 24. " For theſe four months laſt paſt, I have been brought ſo exceeding low in my body, that I was in hopes, every ſermon I preached would waft me to my wiſhed for home. Scotland, I hoped, would finiſh my warfare ; but it has rather driven me back to ſea again. On Tueſday next, I thought to have moved ; but as it is race-week, and my health is improving, friends adviſe me to ſtay, to ſtir them up to run with patience the race that is ſet before us.* HAVING

* " Edinburgh, September 14, 1758. Mr. WHITEFIELD'S preſence, at this time, has been particularly uſeful to the Or-

HAVING left Edinburgh, September 13, he preached in a great many places in the north of England, Alnwick, Newcastle, Durham, Bishop-Aukland, Leeds, &c. and came to London about the end of October.

HE now talked of going over again to America, where his affairs were in a good situation : " Blessed be GOD, (says he) that I can send you word, a never-failing Providence hath put it into my power to pay off all Bethesda's arrears. I am talking every day of coming over ; but how to do it in war-time, or how to get the Chapel and Tabernacle supplied, I cannot as yet be clear in." Not being able, it seems, to get over these difficulties, he continued all winter 1758, in London, and about the middle of May, 1759, opened his spring campaign at Bristol. In the month of June he was in Gloucestershire and York-shire, where people, high and low, rich and poor, flocked, as usual, to hear him, twice a day ;† and from thence re-visited Scotland.

phan-Hospital, for which upwards of two hundred pounds hath been raised from the collection at the doors, and seat-rents. Before he left Glasgow, he made a collection for the Glasgow Charitable Highland Society, for supporting and educating poor Highland children ; a scheme particularly useful at this time, when so many of their parents and friends are abroad in America, in his Majesty's service. During his stay here, he has had occasion to preach three thanksgiving sermons, for the victory at Crevelt, the taking of Cape Breton, and the late defeat of the Russians. By his warm and repeated ex-hortations to loyalty, and a steady adherence to the Protest-ant-interest, on this, and all other occasions, it must be ac-knowledged, even in this view, his visit here has been useful to the community in a civil, as well as religious light."— *Glasgow Courant.*

† " I am growing fat ; but, as I take it to be a disease, hope I shall go home the sooner."

CHAP.

C H A P. XVIII.

From his Arrival at Edinburgh. 1759, *to his opening Lady* Huntingdon's *Chapel at* Bath, *in the Year* 1765.

ABOUT the beginning of July 1759, he came to Edinburgh; his congregations here and at Glasgow were very large, and very attentive, as formerly.* But he complains in his letters, " that with respect to the power of religion, it was a dead time in Scotland in. comparison with London, and several other parts of England."

His visit to Scotland this year, gave occasion to a passage, which was much for his honor, and a full confutation of the mercenary motives ascribed to him by some of his adversaries. One 'Miss Hunter, a young lady of considerable fortune, made a full offer to him of her estate, both money and lands, amounting to about seven hundred pounds, which he gener-
ously

---

* "Edinburgh, August 15, 1759. On Tuesday-morning the Rev. Mr. WHITEFIELD set out on his return for England. It is said, that here and at Glasgow, within these six weeks he has preached near a hundred times, and yet the congregations were always increasing. Whatever this be owing to, every body must judge for themselves : but it is certain he continually exerted all his rhetoric in stirring up a zeal for his God, his King and his country, in the time of danger; and seemed particularly pleased, as were thousands more, that he had an opportunity last LORD's Day-evening, of preaching a thanksgiving sermon to a most thronged auditory, on account of the glorious victory lately vouchsafed to Prince Ferdinand over the French.

"The sum collected for the benefit of the Orphan-Hospital, during his stay here, amounted to two hundred and fifteen pounds."

oufly refufed. And upon his refufing it for himfelf, fhe offered it to him for the benefit of his Orphanhoufe in Georgia. Which he alfo abfolutely refufed. Thefe facts the compiler has from undoubted authority.

He fpent the winter* in London, and got his Chapel enlarged.

March 14, 1760, he made a collection at his Chapel and Tabernacle, of above four hundred pounds, for the diftreffed Pruffians, who had fuffered fo much from the cruelty of the Ruffians, at Newmark, Coftrin, &c.†

In fummer 1760, he went into Gloucefterfhire and Wales, and from thence to Briftol. When he preached at the Tabernacle in Briftol, there were more in the evenings than it could well hold ; and in the fields his congregations confifted of not lefs than ten thoufand.

He now began to undergo a new kind of perfecution (which however has fometimes fallen upon men of the greateft eminence) that of being mimicked and burlefqued upon the ftage.‡ His enemies had in vain ufed violence againft him, and having found that the law would not fuffer them to proceed in that way, they therefore thought they would try what they
could

---

* October 1759, he wrote a preface to Mr. Samuel Clark's Bible. See his Works, Vol. IV.

† For this difinterefted act of benevolence, it is faid, he received the thanks of his Pruffian majefty.

‡ The compiler is uncertain as to the time when this was firft done. Mr. Whitefield firft takes notice of it in his letter dated Auguft 15, 1760. It feems to have taken its rife from the refentment of the play-houfe people, after they failed in their attempt to frighten him from preaching at Longacre chapel, and were farther exafperated by feeing him erect a chapel of his own in Tottenham-court-road.

could do by mockery. For this purpofe, they got for their tool one Samuel Foote, a mimic, who having had fome fuccefs in imitating Mr. WHITEFIELD's perfon, and fpeaking a few ludicrous fentences in his manner, was encouraged to proceed further, and to write a farce (called the Minor) to be acted at the Theatre in Drury-lane.* This performance is otherwife very dull and uninterefting ; but by its impiety, it cannot fail to excite the indignation of the religious and fober-minded. For, in order to expofe Mr. WHITEFIELD to contempt, the author makes no fcruple to treat the very expreffions and fentiments of the Bible with ridicule ; or (to put the moft favorable conftruction upon the matter) he and thofe whom he fent to the Tabernacle and Chapel to procure materials, were fo little acquainted with the facred writings, as not to know, that what they took for Mr. WHITEFIELD's peculiar language, was the language of the word of GOD.‡   Be this as it may,

they

---

* See a Letter to David Garrick, Efq. occafioned by the intended reprefentation of the Minor at Drury-lane Theatre, faid to be written by the Rev. Mr. Madan.

‡ Mr. Foote being manager of the Edinburgh Theatre in winter 1770, the Minor was acted there. The firft night it was pretty thronged, as people fond of any novelty were led to it without knowing any thing of the nature of the performance. But (fuch was the public fenfe of the impurity and indecency of it when known) that on the fecond night, only ten women appeared. When it was acted on Saturday, November 24, a difpute arofe among the fpectators, whether it was proper to bring Mr. WHITEFIELD upon the ftage, as he was now dead? This, however, was done ; and raifed a general indignation in the inhabitants of that city. Next day feveral minifters (the Rev. Dr. Erfkine, Dr. Walker, &c.) took notice of it in their difcourfes from the pulpit. Dr. Walker (whofe church is frequented by the people of higher rank) obferved in his lecture upon 2. Cor. v. 14,—21, that he could not read the 17th verfe, "If any man be in CHRIST, he

is

they loft their labor, for they were fo far from leffen-
ing the number of his congregations, that they increafed them ; and brought thoufands of new perfons
to hear the gofpel ; which was the very thing he always aimed at : and thus Providence gave him the
victory over them.

MARCH 14, 1760, he preached at the Chapel
from Hof. xi. 8, 9. and at the Tabernacle in the evening from the 80th Pfalm and laft verfe. At the former
place he collected two hundred and twenty two
pounds, eight fhillings and nine-pence ; and at the
other, one hundred and eighty two pounds, fifteen
fhillings and nine pence, for the diftreffed Proteltants
in Pruffia. No man was a more ftrict obferver of
public occurrences, or more endeavored to improve
them.

IN the month of September and October 1760, he
made a tour through Yorkfhire ; and was in London,
during the winter, employed as ufual. On the faft-
day, Feb. 13, 1761, he preached early in the morning
at the Tabernacle on Exod. xxxiv. 1, &c. and collected one hundred and twelve pounds ; in the forenoon
he labored at the Chapel, and difcourfed on Joel ii.
15. and afterwards collected two hundred and forty-
two pounds ; and in the evening he preached at the

Taber-

is a new creature," without expreffing the juft indignation
he felt, upon hearing that laft night a profane piece of buf-
foonry was publicly acted, in which this facred doctrine is
ridiculed. Mr. Baine, of the Kirk of Relief, preached a fermon upon the occafion, December 2, from Pfalm xciv. 16.
which was publifhed and fold off in a few days. Towards the
conclufion of the fermon, he fays, " How bafe and ungrateful is fuch treatment of the dead : and that too fo very nigh
to a family of orphans, the records of whofe hofpital will
tranfmit Mr. WHITEFIELD's name to pofterity with honor,
when the memory of others will rot. How illiberal fuch
ufage of one, whofe feafonable good fervices for his King and
Country are well known ; whofe indefatigable labors for his
beloved Mafter were countenanced by Heaven'?

Tabernacle from Gen. vii. 1. and collected two hundred and ten pounds.   These sums were immediately applied to the noble purposes for which they were collected, the relief of the German Protestants, and the sufferers by fire at Boston.*

BUT his health, which had often been very bad† now grew worse and worse, so that in April 1761, he was brought to the gates of death.   After his recovery, being still exceeding weak, and not able to preach as formerly, he left London, and made a visit to Bristol, Exeter and Plymouth, by which he found himself somewhat 'better ; but could not bear long journies and frequent preaching as he used to do‡.

OCTOBER, 1761, he complains, " I have not preached a single sermon for some weeks.   Last Sunday I spoke a little ; but I feel its effects ever since. A sea-voyage seems more necessary to me now than ever.

* Four hundred pounds were assigned to the Germans, and given into the hands of the Rev. Mr. Ziegenhagen.

" Boston, Feb. 27, 1764.   At a meeting of the freeholders, and other inhabitants of the town of Boston, on Friday last, it was voted unanimously, that the thanks of the town be given to the Rev. Mr. GEORGE WHITEFIELD, for his charitable care and pains in collecting a considerable sum of money in Great Britain, for the distressed sufferers by the great fire in Boston, 1760; and a respectable committee was appointed to wait on Mr. WHITEFIELD, to inform him of the vote, and present him with a copy thereof."   Boston Gazette.

† It was happy for him, that he frequently got the assistance of clergymen from the country ; and at this time particularly of the Rev. Mr. Berridge, late Moderator of Cambridge, of whom he writes—" A new instrument is raised up, out of Cambridge University.   He has been here preaching with great flame, and like an angel of the churches indeed." —The compiler is informed that the Rev. Mr. Berridge, at Everton, still continues zealous and successful.

‡ The MS. (which after the year 1748, contains only very short and imperfect hints) ends here.

ever. I know now what nervous diforders are. Bleffed be God that they were contracted in his fervice ;
I do not repent—though I am frequently tempted to
wifh the report of my death had been true, fince my
diforder keeps me from my old delightful work of
preaching." In a journey to Leeds and Newcaftle,
this month, he could bear riding in a poft chaife, but
preaching feldom, his friends being fo prudent as not
to prefs him to it : " I hope however, fays he, I am
travelling in order to preach." Accordingly he prolonged his journey the length of Edinburgh and Glafgow, and did not return to London till the month of
December ; when he found himfelf confiderably better, which (under God) he attributed to his following
the fimple prefcription of four eminent phyficians in
Edinburgh ; being fenfible, as he faid, that their advice had been more blefled, for his recovery, than
all the medicines and directions he had elfewhere.

As foon as his health was in fome meafure reftored, he fell to his beloved work again.   From Briftol,
April 1762, he writes, " Briftol air agrees with me.
I have been enabled to preach five times, this laft
week, without being hurt.   Who knows but I may
yet be reftored fo far as to found the Gofpel-trumpet
for my God ?   The quietnefs I enjoy here, with daily
riding out, feems to be one very proper means."   He
continued thus to preach four or five times a-week,
notwithftanding his weaknefs, till about the middle
of May ; and was fometimes enabled to "take the
field," as he exprefles it, which gave him great joy ;
" Mounts," fays he, " are the beft pulpits, and the
heavens the beft founding boards. O for power equal
to my will ! I would fly from pole to pole, publifh-
ing the everlafting gofpel of the Son of God."   When
he returned to London, the cares and labors that
thronged upon him were ready to bring him low a-
gain.   In the month of July, therefore he made a voyage

age to Holland,† and found himself so much the better
for it, that he writes from Norwich, July 31, " The
expedition to Holland, was, I trust, profitable to myself and others ; and if ever my usefulness is to be
continued at London, I must be prepared for it by
a longer itineration both by land and water. At
present, blessed be GOD, I can preach once a-day ;
and it would do your heart good to see what an influence attends the word. All my old times are revived again."

AUGUST 18, he arrived at Edinburgh, made a
visit to Glasgow. where he preached every day (and
twice at Cambuslang and continued preaching once a-
day at Edinburgh till September 13, when he returned to England : and was glad (now that peace was
expected) of the prospect of embarking soon for A-
merica.

WHILE in England, he found that preaching
once a day did not hurt him, but dared not venture
oftener. At Leeds, Bristol, and Plymouth, he had
very desirable seasons ; but with respect to London,
he says, " As affairs are circumstanced, every thing
there tends to weigh me down." Having therefore
persuaded some of his intimate friends, as trustees, to
take upon them the whole care of the affairs of his
Chapel and Tabernacle, and all his other concerns at
home ; he resolved to sail from Greenock in Scotland.
On his way thither, in the month of March 1763, he
preached at Everton, Leeds, Aberford, Kippax, and
Newcastle, and was also employed in writing his Observations, &c. in answer to Bishop Warburton.

WHEN he came to Scotland, he continued to
preach once a-day, for some weeks ; but being taken
ill of his old disorder at Edinburgh, he was obliged
to be silent (for the most part) for near six weeks afterwards. At last, in the beginning of June, he embarked

† He preached at Rotterdam four times.

barked the fixth time for America, in the fhip Fanny,
Captain Archibald Galbreath, bound from Greenock
to Virginia : where (after a voyage of twelve weeks)
he arrived in the latter end of Auguft.*

His letters in September, October, and November, 1763, are dated from Philadelphia. He found
himfelf ftill an invalid ; yet made fhift to preach
twice a-week. " Here, (fays he) are fome young
bright witneffes rifing up in the church. Perhaps I
have already converfed with forty new-creature minifters of various denominations. Sixteen hopeful
ftudents, I am credibly informed, were converted at
New-Jerfey College laft year. What an open door,
if I had ftrength! Laft Tuefday we had a remarkable feafon among the Lutherans ; children and grown
people were much impreffed."

He wanted much to go forward to Georgia, but
the phyficians were abfolutely againft it, till he got
more ftrength. In the latter end of November he
fet out from Philadelphia for New-York, and on his
way preached feveral times at New-Jerfey College
and Elizabeth-Town, with much acceptance. His
fpirits now grew better, and he could fometimes
preach thrice a week. While he continued at New-
York during the winter, he writes, " Prejudices in
this place have moft ftrangely fubfided. The better
fort flock as eagerly as the common people, and are
fond of coming for private gofpel-converfation.—
Congregations continue very large, and I truft faving
impreffions are made upon many."†   AFTER

* " —— Thanks to a never failing Redeemer, I have not
been laid by an hour through ficknefs, fince I came on board.
A kind captain, and a moft orderly and quiet fhip's company,
who gladly attended when I had breath to preach. Scarce an
oath have I heard upon deck—and fuch a ftillnefs through the
whole fhip, both on week-days and the LORD's-day, as hath
from time to time furprized me."

† " New-York, January 23, 1764. The Rev. Mr. GEORGE
WHITEFIELD

AFTER leaving New-York, he preached at Eaſt-Hampton, Bridge-Hampton, and Southold, upon Long-Iſland ; at Shelter-Iſland alſo ; and at New-London, Norwich, and Providence, on the main land. Then proceeded to Boſton, where he arrived in the latter end of February, 1764, and was received with uſual warmth of affection. But as the ſmall-pox was ſpreading through the town, he choſe to preach for a while in the adjacent places. At Newbury a great influence attended his preaching. He writes from Concord to his friend Mr. S— S—, " How would you have been delighted to have ſeen Mr. Wheelock's Indians ? Such a promiſing nurſery of future miſſion-aries, I believe, was never ſeen in New-England before ; pray encourage it with all your might. I alſo wiſh you could give ſome uſeful puritanical books to Harvard-College Library, lately burnt down.*

IN

WHITEFIELD has ſpent ſeven weeks with us, preaching twice a-week to more general acceptance than ever ; and been treated with great reſpect by many of the gentlemen and merchants of this place. During his ſtay, he preached two charity ſermons ; the one on the occaſion of the annual col-lection for the poor, in which double the ſum was collected that ever was upon the like occaſion ; the other was for the benefit of Mr. Wheelock's Indian School at Lebanon, in New England, for which he collected (notwithſtanding the preſent prejudices of many people againſt the Indians) the ſum of one hundred and twenty pounds. In his laſt ſermon he took a very affectionate leave of the people of this city, who ex-preſſed great concern at his departure. May GOD reſtore this great and good man (in whom the gentleman, the Chriſt-ian, and accompliſhed orator ſhine forth with ſuch luſtre) to a perfect ſtate of health, and continue him long a bleſſing to the world, and the Church of CHRIST." *Boſton Gazette.*

* Some years after the gentlemen of Harvard College ex-preſſed their gratitude to Mr. WHITEFIELD by the following vote. " At a meeting of the Preſident and Fellows of Har-vard-College, Auguſt 22, 1768. The Rev. Mr. GEORGE WHITEFIELD having, in addition to his former kindneſs to

Harvard

In the month of April he had a return of his diforder; but it did not keep him long from preaching: and the Bofton people were exceedingly eager to hear. He was thinking to proceed immediately fouthward, but they fent after him and perfuaded him to come back. June 1, 1764. He writes,— "Friends have even conftrained me to ftay here, for fear of running into the fummer's heat. Hitherto I find the benefit of it. Whatever it is owing to, through mercy I am much better in health than I was this time twelve months, and can now preach thrice a-week to very large auditories, without hurt. And every day I hear of fome brought under concern. This is all of grace."

After a forrowful parting, he left Bofton, and came back to New-York, from whence his letters are dated from the end of June till the latter end of Auguft. "At prefent, (fays he) my health is better than ufual, and as yet I have felt no inconvenience from the fummer's heat.—I have preached twice lately in the fields, and we fat under the bleffed Redeemer's fhadow with great delight. My late excurfions upon Long-Ifland, I truft, have been bleffed. It would furprize you to fee above one hundred carriages at every fermon, in this new world.

In

Harvard-College, lately prefented to the Library, a new Edition of his Journals, and having procured large benefactions from feveral benevolent and refpectable gentlemen;—*Voted,* That the Thanks of the Corporation be given to the Rev. Mr. Whitefield, for thefe inftances of Candor and Generofity.

PRESENT,

The Prefident,
Mr. Appleton,
Mr. Profeffor Winthrop,
Dr. Elliot,
Dr. Cooper,
Treafurer Hubbard.

A true Copy, per
Edward Holyoke,
Prefident.

R

In September and October he was at Philadelphia ; the Provost of the College there read prayers for him. Both the present and late Governor, with the principal gentlemen of the city attended, and thanks were sent to him from the trustees, for speaking for the charity-children, and countenancing the institution.

From Philadelphia he proceeded southward 'thro' Virginia. And November 22, at New Brunswick, in Carolina, he writes, "At Newbern last Sunday, good impressions were made.—From that place to this, I have met with what they call New-Lights,* almost every stage.—I have the names of six or eight of their preachers. This, with every other place, being open and exceedingly desirous to hear the Gospel, makes me almost determine to come back early in the spring."

After preaching at Charleston, he arrived at Savannah in December, where he found affairs prospering to his wish : " The colony, (says he) is rising fast ; nothing but plenty at Bethesda, and all arrears, I trust, will be paid off before I leave it ; so that in a short time I hope to be free from these outward incumbrances." And he was not disappointed in his expectations ; for he writes, " Bethesda, January 14, 1765,—God hath given me great favor in the sight of the Governor, Council and Assembly. A memorial was presented for an additional grant of lands, consisting of two thousand acres. It was immediately complied-with. Both houses addressed the Governor in behalf of the intended College. As warm an answer was given.† Every heart seems to leap for joy
                                                        at

---

* A name given to those who favored the revival of religion under the ministry of Mr. *Whitefield,* Mr. Tennent, &c.

† See the Memorial, Address and Answer, in Vol. III. of his Works, page 469, &c.

at the profpect of its future utility."——Again, " Bethefda, February 15. Yefterday morning the Governor and Lord J. A. G——n, with feveral other
gentlemen, favored me with their company to breakfaft. But how was my Lord furprized and delighted!
After expreffing himfelf in the ftrongeft terms, he
took me afide and informed me, that the Governer
had fhewed him the accounts, by which he found
what a great benefactor I had been ; that the intended College would be of the utmoft utility, to this and
the neighboring provinces ; that the plan was beautiful, rational, and practicable ; and that he was
perfuaded his Majefty would highly approve of, and
alfo favor it with fome peculiar marks of his royal
bounty.*

HAVING left Bethefda in fuch comfortable circumftances, February 18,† he delayed his propofed tour
to the northward, and thought it beft to embark
directly for England, to finifh the affair about the
College. He fpent fome time, however, at Charlefton,
in the month of March, and after a very affectionate
parting, fet out for Philadelphia, preaching, as he
went along, in feveral places :‡ but no fhip offering

at

* He adds, in the fame Letter, " Now farewell, my belev-
ed Bethefda ; furely the moft delightfully fituated place in all
the fouthern parts of America.—What a bleffed winter have
I had ! Peace and love, and harmony, and plenty reign here.
Mr. W—: hath done much in a little time. All are furprized
at it. But he hath worked night and day, and not ftirred a
mile for many weeks."_

† " Thanks be to GOD, all outward things are fettled on
this fide the water. The auditing the accounts, and laying a
foundation for a College, hath filenced enemies, and comforted friends. The finifhing this affair confirms my call to England, at this time."

‡ " All along from Charlefton to this place (Newcaftle) the
cry is, ' For CHRIST's fake ftay and preach to us.' O for a
thoufand lives to fpend for JESUS !"

at Philadelphia, he failed from New-York in the Earl
of Halifax packet, and arrived once more in England, July 5, 1765.*

AFTER his arrival he found himself ftill very weak
in body, and obliged to go on much more flowly than
he ufed to do. Yet this did not difcourage him from
doing what he could, in hopes of foon entering into
his reft. " O to end this life well! (fays he) Methinks I have now but one more river to pafs over.
And we know of one that can carry us over, without
being ankle-deep."

OCTOBER 6, he was called to open Lady Hun-
.tingdon's chapel at Bath,† when he preached from
2. Cor. vi. 16.

* " We have had but a twenty eight days paffage. The
tranfition hath been fo fudden, that I can fcarce believe that
I am in England. I hope, ere long, to have a more fudden
tranfition into a better country." [When he arrived at London, July 21, he was very ill of a nervous fever.]

† " The Chapel is extremely plain, and yet equally grand.
A moft beautiful original. All was conducted with great fo-
lemnity. Though a very wet day, the place was very full.
I preached in the morning, Mr. Townfend in the evening."

C H A P.

C H A P. XIX.

From his opening Lady Huntingdon's *Chapel
at* Bath, *to his embarking for* America, *in
the Year* 1769.

AFTER preaching some little time at Bath, he
returned to London, from whence, January 18, 1766,
he writes to a friend at Sheerness, " I am sorry to
acquaint you, that it is not in my power to comply
with your request. For want of more assistance, I
am confined in town with the care of two important
posts, when I am only fit to be put into some garrison
among the invalids." But he was relieved, for a
little space, early in the spring ; for we find him in
the month of March at Bath and Bristol.

MARCH. 17, he says, " The uncertainty of my
motions hath made me slow in writing ; and a desire
to be a while free from London cares, hath made
me indifferent about frequent hearing from thence.
Last Friday evening, and twice yesterday, I preached
at Bath to very thronged and brilliant auditories."

ABOUT this time. the Stamp Act was repealed ;
on which occasion he greatly exulted. The interest
of the Colonies always lay near his heart, and he
hoped this step would restore peace and happiness
to his country. In his Letter-book is the following
sentence, " March 16, 1766. Stamp-Act repealed,
Gloria Deo."

MR. Occum, an Indian preacher, and Mr.-Whit-
aker, came over from America to solicit contributions for Mr. Wheelock's Indian-school, an institution
which Mr. WHITEFIELD greatly approved. Concerning this he writes, " London, April 25 The
prospect

profpect of a large and effectual door opening among the heathens, blefled be GOD, is very promifing. Mr. Occum is a fettled, humble Chriftian : the good and-great, with a multitude of a lower degree, heard him preach laft week at Tottenham-Court, Chapel, and felt much of the power and prefence of our common LORD. Mr. R——n hath preached, and collected one hundred' pounds ; and I believe feven or eight hundred pounds more are fubfcribed. The truly noble Lord D——h efpoufes the caufe moft heartily, and his Majefty is become a contributor. The King of kings and Lord of lords, will blefs them for it."*

JUNE 19; we find him at Collam, near Briftol, from whence he writes, " As my feverifh heat continues, and the weather is too wet to travel, I have complied with the advice of my friends, and have commenced a hot-well, water drinker twice a-day. However, twice this week, at fix in the morning, I have been enabled to call thirfty fouls to come and drink of the water of life freely. To-morrow evening, GOD willing, the call is to be repeated, and again on Sunday."

HE was alfo at Bath and Briftol in the month of November this year. At Briftol he preached to a very crowded auditory (though the weather was exceeding bad) and adminiftered the facrament ; and at Bath he preached to the moft numerous affembly of nobility he had ever feen attend there.

IN the month of January, 1767, he wrote a recommendatory preface to a new edition of Bunyan's Works ; which is inferted with his Tracts in Vol. IV.

---

* Mr. Occum and Mr. Whitaker came afterwards to Scotland, and preached at Edinburgh and Glafgow, where they got very confiderable contributions ; particularly from Mr. Sprewll's family in Glafgow, and from the Rev. Mr. M'Culloch at Cambuflang.

IV. and March 20, he was called to open Lady Huntingdon's new Chapel at Brighthelmstone in Sussex, when he preached on 2. Peter, iii. 18.

After an excursion to Norwich, in April 1767, he says, "I fear my spring and summer fever is returning. If so, my intended plan of operations will be much contracted. But future things belong to Him who orders all things well."

Yet the very next month we find him preaching at Rodborough, Gloucester, and Haverford-West in Wales ; from whence he writes, May 31, " Thousands and thousands attended by eight in the morning. Life and light seemed to fly all around. On Tuesday, God willing, I am to preach at Woodstock ; on Friday at Pembroke ; here again next Sunday by eight, and then for England." And when he returned to Gloucester, June 10, " Blessed be God, (says he) I am got on this side the Welch mountains. Blessed be God, I have been on the other side. What a scene last Sunday ! What a cry for more of the bread of life ; but I was quite worn down."

September 11. He was at Leeds, having preached at Northampton and Sheffield in the way : and September 20, at Newcastle, from whence he writes, " I have now a blessed Methodist field street-preaching plan before me. This afternoon in the Castle-Garth, to-morrow for Sunderland, then to Yarm, &c. &c.——I have been enabled to preach in the street at several places, and hope to go to Gesborough, Whitby, Scarborough, New-Malton, York, Leeds, Liverpool, Chester, Manchester, &c."—Again (from Thirsk, September 28.) " My body feels much fatigued in travelling ; comforts in the soul over balance."—And (Leeds, October 3.) " Field and street-preaching hath rather bettered than hurt my bodily health."

This winter his negociations about the intended College at Bethesda, came to an issue. A memorial,

addressed

addressed to his Majesty, was put into the hands of the clerk of the privy council, setting forth the great utility of a College in that place to the inhabitants of the southern provinces, and praying that a charter might be granted upon the plan of the College at New-Jersey. This memorial was by him transmitted to the Lord President, and by his lordship referred to the consideration of the Archbishop of Canterbury, to whom also a draft of an intended charter was presented by the Earl of D——h. Upon which an epistolary correspondence ensued betwixt the Archbishop and Mr. WHITEFIELD ; the sum of which was, the Archbishop put the draft of the Charter into the hands of the Lord President, who promised to consider it ; and gave it as his opinion, that, " the head of the College ought to be a member of the church of England. That this was a qualification not to be dispensed with. And also that the public prayers should not be extempore ones, but the liturgy of the church, or some other established form." Mr. WHITEFIELD answered, he could not agree to either of these restrictions, because the greatest part of the Orphan-house collections and contributions came from dissenters ; and because he had frequently declared the intended College was to be founded upon a broad bottom, and no other. " This, (says he,) I judge I was sufficiently warranted to do, from the known, long established, mild, and uncoercive genius of the English government ; also from your Grace's moderation towards Protestant dissenters ; from the unconquerable attachment of the Americans to toleration principles, as well as from the avowed habitual feelings and sentiments of my own heart. This being the case, and as your Grace, by your silence, seems to be likeminded with the Lord P——t ; and as your Grace's and his worship's influence will undoubtedly extend itself to others, I would beg leave, after returning all

due

due acknowledgments, to inform your Grace that I intend troubling your Grace and his Lordfhip no more about this fo long depending concern. As it hath pleafed the great head of the church in fome degree to renew my bodily ftrength, I purpofe now to renew my feeble efforts, and turn charity into a more generous, and confequently into a more extenfively ufeful channel. I have no ambition to be looked upon as the founder of a College ; but I would fain act the part of an honeft man, a difinterefted minifter of Jesus Christ, and a truly catholic, moderate prefbyter of the church of England."*

Accordingly he refolved, in the mean time, to add a public academy to the Orphan-houfe, like what was done at Philadelphia, before its College-Charter was granted and to wait for a more favorable opportunity of making frefh application, for a Charter upon a broader bottom.

October 28, he preached at the Tabernacle, to the Society for promoting- Religious Knowledge among the Poor, when the collection amounted to above a hundred pounds, (about four times as much as ufual) and eighty perfons became new fubfcribers.†

IN

* See his Works, Vol. III. page 472—484, where the fteps he took in this affair are more fully narrated in a Letter to Governor Wright—and Letter MCCCLXXVII. in which he complains to his intimate friend Mr. K—n, "None but God knows what a concern lies upon me now, in refpect of Bethefda. As another voyage, perhaps, may be the iffue and refult of all at laft, I would beg you, and my dear Mr. H—y, to let me have my Papers and Letters, that I may revife and difpofe of them in a proper manner. This can do no hurt, come life, or come death."

† His text was, Luke xi. 2. *Thy kingdom come.* The place was quite full, and many went away for want of room. A great number of diffenting minifters were prefent ; probably more than ever before met to hear a church-clergyman preach.

In the beginning of the year 1768, six pious students were expelled from Edmund Hall in Oxford, for using extempore prayer, reading and singing hymns, and exhorting one another in private religious meetings. Upon this occasion, Mr. WHITEFIELD wrote his letter to Dr. Durell, Vice-Chancellor of the University.*

In the summer, he went once more to Edinburgh, where his Orphan house-Park congregations were as large, attentive, and affectionate as ever.

AUGUST 3, soon after his return to London, Mrs. Whitefield was attacked with an inflammatory fever, and the 9th of August she died. The 14th of the month he preached her funeral sermon, from Rom. viii. 20 : and September 12, he writes, " I have been in hopes of my own departure. Through hard riding and frequent preaching, I have burst a vein. The flux is in a great measure stopped, but rest and quietness are strictly enjoined. We were favored with glorious Gospel gales this day fortnight, and several preceding days, at opening good Lady Huntingdon's Chapel, and place of pious education in Wales."‡

SEPT.

---

preach. He afterwards dined with the ministers and whole company at Draper's-Hall, where he was treated with great respect. All was very harmonious, and gave him great pleasure in reflection.

* See his Works, Vol. IV.

‡ From his Memorandum-Book. " August 24, 1768. Opened good Lady Huntingdon's Chapel and College, in the parish of Talgarth, Brecknockshire, South-Wales. Preached from Exodus xx. 24. 'In all places where I record my Name, I will come unto thee, and I will bless thee,'' "August 25. Gave an exhortation to the students in the College-chapel, from Luke i. 15 'He shall be great in the sight of the LORD.'' " Sunday, August 28. Preached in the Court before the College, (the congregation consisting of some thousands) from 1. Cor. iii. 11. 'Other foundation can no man lay, than that which is laid, which is JESUS CHRIST.'

SEPTEMBER 26, he writes concerning his friend and fellow-laborer, Mr. Middleton : " He is now made perfectly whole. He was buried from the Tabernacle laſt Wedneſday-evening, and a ſubſcription is opened for his four orphans. In the midſt of his torturing pains, being aſked by his daughter, How he was ? He anſwered, ' A heaven upon earth.' Soon afterwards he fell aſleep in JESUS."

FROM his letters dated in November and December, it appears he was in a very poor ſtate of health, yet ſtill continued to preach, as often as he was able.

" BRISTOL, November 12. · Laſt night, I hope, the Redeemer manifeſted forth his glory, Friday-evening, and the following Sunday, I ſhall preach at Bath. In three weeks I expect to reach London, except called before that period, to reſide at the New-Jeruſalem. The pleaſing proſpect lies day and night open before me."

NEXT ſpring, 1769, he ſeems to have recovered a little ; for we find him preaching more frequently. It gave him great pleaſure to ſee ſome more of the nobility joined to Lady H——n's ſociety. " Some more coronets, I hear, are likely to be laid at the Redeemer's feet. They glitter glorioully when ſet in, and ſurrounded with a crown of thorns."

IN the month of May he preached at Kingſwood, Briſtol, Bradford, Frome, Chippenham, Rodborough, Caſtlecomb, Durſley. But deferred his weſtern-circuit on account of the opening the Chapel, at Tunbridge.

JULY 23, 1769, he opened Lady Huntingdon's New Chapel at Tunbridge-Wells. Preached from Geneſis xxviii. 17. " This is none other but the Houſe of GOD, and this is the Gate of Heaven." In the evening, the congregation being too large to be contained in the Chapel, he preached out of doors, from a mount in the Court before the Chapel ; after

which

which he gave a general exhortation : and next day adminiſtered the ſacrament, and preached from 1. Theſ. ii. 11. 12.

Now he ſeriouſly began to prepare for another voyage ; and in the beginning of September he embarked the ſeventh and laſt time for America.*

CHAP. - XX.

From his laſt embarking for AMERICA, *to his Death,* September 30, 1770.

MR. WHITEFIELD was detained near a month in the Downs by contrary winds ;† but he improved his time, as uſual, in writing many excellent letters, preaching on board ; and ſometimes came aſhore and preached, both at Deal and Ramſgate.

THE following extract of Mr. WHITEFIELD's Manuſcript Journal, relative to this period, cannot be unacceptable.

"SATURDAY, September 2. Had a moſt awful parting ſeaſon at Tottenham-Court Chapel Sacrament, laſt Sunday-morning ; the Sermon, from Geneſis xxviii. 12. And the ſame at Tabernacle, (which was more than full) on Wedneſday morning at ſeven o'clock. This day dined at my worthy, faſt, and tried friend, Mr. Keen's ; and having comfortably ſettled, and left all my outward concerns in his hands, I took an affectionate leave, and in campany with ſome dear friends, this evening reached Graveſend ; where

---

* In the Friendſhip, Capt. Ball. "I am comforted on every ſide. A civil Captain and paſſengers. All willing to attend on divine worſhip, and to hear of religious things."

† One ſhip was loſt, but the paſſengers eſcaped in the boat.

where others met us. We supped and conversed together in some degree, I trust, like persons who hoped ere long, to sit down together at the marriage-feast of the supper of the Lamb. Hasten, O Lord, that wished for time !

Sunday, September 3. Preached this morning at the Methodist Tabernacle from John xiith. verse 32d. The congregation was not very large. But God gave me great freedom of speech, and made it indeed a House of God, and Gate of Heaven. In the afternoon, I preached in the market-place, from Genesis iii. verse 15th, to a much larger, but not more devout auditory. In the out-skirts, as might naturally be expected, some were a little noisy, but a great body was very attentive, and I was enabled to lift up my voice like a trumpet. The remainder of the evening was spent as the night before, with my Christian London friends ; who with me, less than the least of all, exceedingly rejoiced at the opportunity of a parting street-market-place preaching, where, I trust, some pennyless bankrupt sinners were made willing to buy Gospel wine and milk, without money, and without price. May the great day show that this hope was not altogether ill-grounded !

"Monday, September 4. Had my dear Christian friends on board to breakfast with me this morning. Conversation was sweet, but parting bitter. 'What mean you (said the Apostle) to weep and break my heart ?' However, through infinite mercy, I was helped to bear up, and after their departure, the Divine Presence made up the loss of all, even with new creature comforts. Lord, if this Divine Presence go not with, and accompany me all the way, for thy infinite mercies' sake, suffer me not to go one step farther.

But I believe thy promise, Lord,
Oh ! help my unbelief.
S   " Tuesday,

" Tuesday, September 5. The Captain not coming down as was expected, we did not weigh anchor till this morning's ebb.

" The winds being contrary, and the weather hazy, we did not arrive in the Downs till the Friday following. *Interim*, I had the opportunity of conversing a little with the pilot, and steerage passengers. All attended divine worship very orderly, and thanked me for my offer of lending them books, and giving them what assistance lay in my power towards making their voyage comfortable. All seemed thankful, and the pilot parted with tears in his eyes. May the great, and never-failing Pilot, the almighty Jesus, renew us, and take us all into his holy protection, and then all must necessarily end in our safe arrival in the haven of eternal rest!

" Tuesday, September 12. Preached last Sunday morning to my little flock on board, and was most agreeably surprized to-day, with a kind unexpected visit from the Rev. Dr. Gibbons. His discourse was very friendly and devout.

Wednesday, September 13. I went ashore and attended on an Ordination solemnity, at the dissenting meeting. Several ministers officiated. Several very important questions were asked, and answered before, and a solemn charge given after, imposition of hands. But the prayer put up in the very act of laying on of hands, by Dr. Gibbons, was so affecting, and the looks and behavior of those that joined, so serious and solemn, that I hardly know when I was more struck, under any one's ministration. The Ordination being over, at the desire of the ministers, and other gentlemen, I went and dined with them. Our conversation was edifying. And being informed that many were desirous to hear me preach. I willingly complied, and I trust some seed was sown the same evening at Deal, which, by God's heavenly

blessing,

bleſſing, will ſpring up to life eternal. The people
of Deal ſeemed very civil, and ſome came to me who
had not forgotten my preaching to them, and their
deceaſed friends and parents, thirty-two years a-go.

"Friday, September 14, 15. I had received
moſt preſſing invitations to viſit Ramſgate, many
weeks ago. Theſe were now repeated by many of
that place, who came to the Ordination at Deal ; ſo
there was no reſiſting their importunity. We reached Ramſgate about two, took ſome refreſhment, and
there I preached about four, not to a very large,
but an attentive and affected auditory. This I did
alſo the morning following ; and was moſt agreeably
entertained with the diſcourſe, and good memory of
one, in particular, who had been my fellow paſſenger, and frequent hearer many years ago, in the
Wilmington, Captain Darling, bound to Piſcataway,
in New-England. The people's behavior here was
ſo undiſſembledly generous, frank, genteel, and Chriſtian, that I know not where I have been more pleaſed
and delighted. Being quite uneaſy, leſt by ſtaying
longer I ſhould be unready, if the wind ſhould turn
favorable, I went early on Sunday morning to Deal,
and from thence immediately on board, and preached
in the afternoon. This morning, came a ſurreptitious
copy of my Tabernacle Farewel Sermon, taken, as
the ſhort-hand writer profeſſes, *verbatim*, as I ſpoke
it. But ſurely he is miſtaken. The whole is ſo
injudiciouſly paragraphed, and ſo wretchedly uncon-
nected, that I owe no thanks to the miſguided, though
it may be well meant zeal of the writer and publiſher,
be who they will. But ſuch conduct is an unavoidable tax upon popularity. And all that appear for
Jesus Christ, and his bleſſed Goſpel, muſt, like
their Maſter, expect to ſuffer from the falſe fire of
profeſſing friends, as well as ſecret malice of avowed
enemies. However, if any one ſentence is bleſſed to
the

the conviction of one finner, or the edification of any individual faint, I care not what becomes of my character, though I would always pray to be preferved from bringing upon myfelf, or others, needlefs, unneceffary contempt.

"MONDAY, September 25. Weighed anchor laft Tuefday-morning, with a fmall favorable gale and fine weather. So many fhips, which had lain in the Downs, moving at the fame time, and gently gliding by us, together with the profpect of the adjacent fhore, made a moft agreeable fcene. But it proved only a very tranfient one. For by that time we got to Fairlee, the wind backened, clouds gathered, very violent gales fucceeded, and for feveral days we were fo toffed, that after coming over againft Brighthelmftone, the Captain rightly judging turned back, (as did many other fhips) and anchored over againft New-Rumley and Dungenefs. LORD, in thine own time, thou wilt give the winds a commiffion to carry us forward toward our defired port."

At laft they got out of the channel, and on the 30th of November, arrived at Charlefton in South Carolina. It had been a dangerous and trying paffage; yet on his arrival, he found himfelf in better health-than at the end of any voyage he had made for feveral years; and the fame day that he came afhore, he preached at Charlefton, where his reception was as hearty, or heartier than ever.*

HERE

* From his Memorandum Book. "For the laft week (November 1769) we were beating about our port, within fight of it, and confined for two days in Five-fathom-hole, juft over the bar. A dangerous fituation, as the wind blew hard, and our fhip, like a young Chriftian, for want of more ballaft, would not obey the helm. But through infinite mercy, on November 30, a pilot-boat came and took us fafe afhore to Charlefton, after being on board almoft thirteen weeks.— Friends received me moft cordially. Praife the LORD, O my foul; and forget not all his mercies. Oh, to begin to be a Chriftian, and Minifter of JESUS."

HERE Mr. Wright came to meet him, and acquainted him that all was in great forwardnefs at Bethefda. And when he arrived there, he writes, " January, 1770. Every thing exceeds my moft fanguine expectations. And the increafe of this Colony is almoft incredible."†

THE great regard which the Colony of Georgia thought themfelves bound to exprefs towards Mr. WHITEFIELD, at this time particularly, appears from the following authentic papers.

" COMMONS Houfe of Affembly, Monday, January 29, 1770. Mr. Speaker reported, that he, with the Houfe, having waited on the Rev. Mr. WHITEFIELD, in confequence of his invitation at the Orphan-houfe Academy ; heard him preach a very fuitable and pious fermon on the occafion ; and with great pleafure obferved the promifing appearance of improvement, towards the good purpofes intended, and the decency and propriety of behavior of the feveral refidents there ; and were fenfibly affected, when they faw the happy fuccefs which has attended Mr. WHITEFIELD's indefatigable zeal for promoting the welfare of the province in general, and the Orphan-houfe in particular. Ordered, That this report be printed in the Gazette.

JOHN SIMPSON, Clerk."

EXTRACT from the Georgia Gazette. " Savannah, January 31, 1770. Laft Sunday, his Excellency the Governor, Council and Affembly, having been invited by the Rev. Mr. GEORGE WHITEFIELD, attended at divine fervice in the Chapel of the Orphanhoufe Academy, where prayers were read by the Rev. Mr. Ellington, and a very fuitable fermon was preached by the Rev. Mr. WHITEFIELD, from Zechariah

iv.

† Two wings were added to the Orphan-houfe, for the accommodation of ftudents ; of which Governor Wright condefcended to lay the foundation, March 25, 1769. See Vol. III.

iv. 10. 'For who hath defpifed the day of fmall things?' to the general fatisfaction of the auditory; in which he took occafion to mention the many difcouragements he met with, well known to many there, in carrying on this inftitution for upwards of thirty years paft, and the prefent promifing profpect of its future and more extenfive ufefulnefs. After divine fervice, the company were very politely entertained with a handfome and plentiful dinner; and were greatly pleafed to fee the ufeful improvements made in the houfe, the two additional wings for apartments for ftudents, one hundred and fifty feet each in length, and other leffer buildings, in fo much forwardnefs; and the whole executed with tafte, and in a mafterly manner; and being fenfible of the truly generous and difintereited benefactions derived to the Province through his means, they expreffed their gratitude in the moft refpectful terms."

Soon after this he writes from Charlefton, February 10. "Through mercy, I enjoy a greater fhare of bodily health than I have known for many years. I am now enabled to preach almoft every day. Bleffed be God, all things are in great forwardnefs at Bethefda, I have converfed with the governor, concerning an act of Affembly, for the eftablifhment of the intended Orphan-houfe College.* He moft readily confents. I have fhown him a draught, which he much approves of; and all will be finifhed at my return

* See a Paper of College-Rules, at the end of Vol. III. of his Works, which was found written with his own hand, and in which he orders the following authors in divinity to be read: Henry, Doddridge, Guyfe, Burkitt, Willifon, Prof, Franck, Bofton, Jenks, Hervey, Hall, Edwards, Trapp, Pool, Warner, Leighton, Pearfon, Owen, Bunyan. And the homilies to be read publicly by rotation. He intended to publifh a new edition of the Homilies, the Preface to which (with Prayers on feveral Occafions) is to be feen in Vol. IV.

turn from the northward. In the mean while the buildings will be carried on."†

His letters of a later date are in the fame ftrain, full of expreffions of gratitude to Providence for the good ftate of his health, and how exceedingly happy he was at Bethefda. And of his purpofe (after he had travelled in the northern parts all fummer) to return to his beloved Bethefda, late in the fall. But this event never happened.

From Philadelphia, May 24, he writes, " I have now been here near three weeks. People of all ranks flock as much as ever. Impreffions are made on many, and, I truft, they will abide. Notwithftanding, I preach twice on the Lord's day, and three or four times a-week befides, yet I am rather better than I have been for many years."

Again, Philadelphia, June 14. " This leaves me juft returned from a one hundred and fifty miles circuit, in which, bleffed be God, I have been enabled to preach every day. So many invitations are fent from various quarters, that I know not which way to turn myfelf."

And, New-York, June 30. " Next week I purpofe to go to Albany. From thence, perhaps, to the Oneida Indians. There is to be a very large Indian Congrefs. Mr. Kirkland accompanies me. He is a truly Chriftian minifter and miffionary. Every thing poffible fhould be done to ftrengthen his hands. Perhaps

† " Since my being in Charlefton, I have fhewn the draught to fome perfons of great eminence and influence. They highly approve of it, and willingly confent to be fome of the Wardens. Near twenty are to be of Georgia, and about fix of this place ; one of Philadelphia ; one of New-York ; one of Bofton ; three of Edinburgh ; two of Glafgow ; and fix of London. Thofe of Georgia and South Carolina, are to be qualified ; the others, to be only honorary correfponding Wardens."

haps I may not fee Georgia till Chriſtmas." In his memorandum book is the following remark.*

AND again, from New-York, July 29, he writes, " During this month I have been above a five hundred miles circuit, and have been enabled to preach and travel through the heat every day. The congregations have been very large, attentive, and affected, particularly at Albany, Schenectady, Great Bamington, Norfolk, Saliſbury, Sharon, Smithfield, Poughkeepſie, Fiſh-Kill, New-Rumbart, New-Windſor, and Peckſhill. Invitations crowd upon me both from miniſters and people, from many quarters. I hope to ſet out for Boſton in two or three days."

WHEN he was at Boſton, September 17, he writes to Mr. W——t at Betheſda, " Fain would I contrive to come by Captain Souder from Philadelphia, but people are ſo importunate for my ſtay in theſe parts, that I fear it will be impracticable. Two or three evenings ago, I was taken in the night with a violent flux, attended with reaching and ſhivering,—but through mercy I am reſtored, and to-morrow morning hope to begin again. I hope it hath been well with you, and all my family ; hoping, ere long, to ſee you, &c."

AND laſtly, to his dear friend Mr. R—— K——n, in London. Portſmouth, New-Hampſhire, September 23. " By this time I thought to be moving ſouthward ; but never was greater importunity uſed to detain me longer in theſe northern parts. Poor New-
England

---

* ' July 2, 1770. Sailed from New-York with Mr. Kirkland, and two kind old friends, and arrived at Albany July 6. Was kindly received by Mr. Bays and Domaine Weſtaloe. Preached the ſame evening, and went the next day to ſee the Cohoes Falls, twelve miles from Albany. O thou wonder-working GOD ! Preached twice on the LORD's Day, at Albany, and the next day at Schenectady, and was ſtruck at the delightful ſituation of the place. Heard afterwards that the word ran, and was glorified both there and at Albany. Grace, Grace !'

England is much to be pitied : Boſton people moſt of all. How groſsly miſrepreſented !—You will ſee by the many invitations, what a door is opened for preaching the everlaſting Goſpel. I was ſo ill on Friday, that I could not preach, though thouſands were waiting to hear. Well! the day of releaſe will ſhortly come ; but it does not ſeem yet : for by riding ſixty miles I am better, and hope to preach here to-morrow. If ſpared ſo long, I hope to ſee Georgia about Chriſtmas.—Still pray and praiſe.—Hoping to ſee all dear friends about the time propoſed, and earneſtly deſiring a continued intereſt in all your prayers, &c."

FROM the 17th to the 20th of September, he preached daily at Boſton ; September 20, at Newton : September 21, he ſet out from Boſton, upon a tour to the eaſtward, pretty much indiſpoſed : preached at Portſmouth in New-Hampſhire, September 23 : and from that to the 29th, continued preaching every day ; thrice at Portſmouth, once at Kittery, and once at Old-York. Saturday-morning, September 29, he ſet out for Boſton ; but before he came to Newbury Port, where he had engaged to preach next morning, he was importuned to preach by the way, at Exeter. At this laſt place he preached in the open air, to accommodate the multitudes that came to hear him, no houſe being able to contain them. He continued his diſcourſe near two hours, was greatly fatigued, and in the afternoon ſet out for Newbury-Port, where he arrived that evening ; went early to bed, it being Saturday night, intending to preach the next day. He awaked ſeveral times in the night, and complained much of a difficulty of breathing. At ſix o'clock, on the LORD's Day-morning, he expired in a fit of the aſthma.

MR. Richard Smith, who accompanied Mr. WHITEFIELD from England to America, the laſt time, and in his journeyings when there, to the time of his death, hath given a particular account of his death and interment, which it may not be improper to insert.

"On Saturday, September 29, 1770, Mr. WHITE-FIELD rode from Portsmouth to Exeter, (fifteen miles) in the morning, and preached there to a very great multitude, in the fields. It is remarkable, that before he went out to preach that day, (which proved to be his last sermon) Mr. Clarkson, senior, observing him more uneasy than usual, said to him, ' Sir, you are more fit to go to bed than to preach.' Mr. WHITEFIELD answered, ' True, Sir,' but turning aside, he clasped his hands together, and looking up, said, ' LORD JESUS, I am weary in thy work, but not of thy work. If I have not yet finished my course, let me go and speak for thee once more in the fields, seal thy truth, and come home and die.' The text he preached from, was 2. Cor. xiii. 5. He dined at Captain Gillman's. After dinner, Mr. WHITEFIELD and Mr. Parsons rode to Newbury. I did not get there till two hours after them. I found them at supper. I asked Mr. WHITEFIELD how he felt himself after his journey. He said, ' he was tired, therefore he supped early and would go to bed.'' He eat a very little supper, talked but little, asked Mr. Parsons to discharge the table, and perform family-duty; and then retired up stairs. He said, ' that he would sit and read till I came to him;' which I did as soon as possible, and found him reading in the Bible with Dr. Watts' Psalms lying open before him. He asked me for some water-gruel, and took about half his usual quantity; and kneeling down by the bed-side, closed the evening with prayer. After a little conversation, he went to rest, and slept till two in the morning, when he awoke me, and asked for a little cider; he drank about a wine-glass full. I asked him how he felt, for he seemed to pant for breath. He told me ' his asthma was coming on him
again;

again ; I muſt have two or three days reſt.   Two or
three days riding, without preaching, would ſet me
up again.'   Soon afterwards he aſked me to put the
window up a little higher (though it was half up all
night) for, ſaid he, ' I cannot breathe, but I hope I
ſhall be better by and by ; a good pulpit-ſweat to-
day may give me relief; I ſhall be better after
preaching.'   I ſaid to him I wiſhed he would not
preach ſo often.   He replied, ' I had rather wear out,
than ruſt out.'   I then told him, I was afraid he took
cold in preaching yeſterday.   He ſaid, ' he believed
he had ;' and then ſat up in the bed and prayed, that
God would be pleaſed to bleſs his preaching where
he had been, and alſo bleſs his preaching that day,
that more ſouls might be brought to Christ, and
prayed for direction whether he ſhould winter at
Boſton, or haſten to the ſouthward ; prayed for a
bleſſing on his Betheſda College, and his dear family
there ; for Tabernacle and Chapel congregations,
and all his connections on the other ſide the water,
and then laid himſelf down to ſleep again.   This was
nigh three o'clock.   At a quarter paſt four, he waked,
and ſaid, ' My aſthma, my aſthma is coming on, I
wiſh I had not given out word to preach at Haverhill
on Monday ; I don't think I ſhall be able ; but I
ſhall ſee what to-day will bring forth.   If I am no
better to-morrow, I will take a two or three days
ride.'   He then deſired me to warm him a little
gruel, and in breaking the fire-wood, I waked Mr.
Parſons ; who thinking I knocked for him, roſe and
came in.   He went to Mr. Whitefield's bed-ſide,
and aſked him how he felt himſelf.   He anſwered, ' I
am almoſt ſuffocated, I can ſcarce breathe : my aſthma
quite choaks me.'   I was then not a little ſurprized,
to hear how quick and with what difficulty he drew
his breath.   He got out of bed, and went to the open
window for air.   This was exactly at five o'clock.

I

I went to him, and for about the space of five minutes, I saw no danger; only that he had a great
difficulty in breathing, as I had often seen before.
Soon afterwards he turned himself to me, and said, *I
am dying*. I said, I hope not, Sir. He ran to the
other window panting for breath, but could get no
relief. It was agreed I should go for Dr. Sawyer,
and on my coming back, I saw death on his face, and
he again said, *I am dying*. His eyes were fixed, his
under-lip drawing inward every time he drew his
breath ; he went towards the window, and we offered him some warm wine with lavender drops, which
he refused. I persuaded him to sit down in the chair,
and have his cloak on ; he consented by a sign, but
could not speak. I then offered him the glass of
warm wine ; he took half of it, but it seemed as if
it would have stopped his breath entirely. In a little
time he brought up a considerable quantity of phlegm
and wind. I then began to have some small hopes.
Mr. Parsons said, he thought Mr. WHITEFIELD
breathed more freely than he did; and would recover.
I said, No Sir, he is certainly dying. I was continually employed in taking the phlegm out of his
mouth with a handkerchief, and bathing his temples
with drops, rubbing his wrists, &c. to give him relief,
if possible ; but all in vain, his hands and feet were
cold as clay. When the Doctor came in, and saw
him in the chair leaning on my breast, he felt his
pulse, and said, ' He is a dead man.' Mr. Parsons
said, ' I do not believe it, you must do something
Doctor.' He said, ' I cannot ; he is now near his
last breath.' And indeed so it was, for he fetched but
one gasp, and stretched out his feet, and breathed no
more. This was exactly at six o'clock. We continued rubbing his legs, and hands, and feet, with
warm cloths, and bathed him with spirits for some
time, but all in vain. I then put him into a warm
bed,

bed, the Doctor ſtanding by, and often raiſed him upright, continued rubbing him and putting ſpirits to his noſe for an hour, till all hopes were gone. The people came in crowds to ſee him ; I begged the Doctor to ſhut the door.

The Rev. Mr. Parſons, at whoſe houſe my dear Maſter died, ſent for Captain Fetcomb, and Mr. Boadman, and others of his Elders and Deacons, and they took the whole care of the burial upon themſelves, prepared the vault, and ſent and invited the bearers. Many miniſters of all perſuaſions came to the houſe of the Rev. Mr. Parſons, where ſeveral of them gave a very particular account of their firſt awakening under his miniſtry, ſeveral years ago, and alſo of many in their congregations, that to their knowledge, under God, owed their converſion wholly to his coming among them, often repeating the bleſſed ſeaſons they had enjoyed under his preaching : and all ſaid, that this laſt viſit was attended with more power than any other, and that all oppoſition fell before him. Then one and other of them would pity and pray for his dear Tabernacle and Chapel congregations, and it was truly affecting to hear them bemoan America and England's loſs. Thus they continued for two hours converſing about his great uſefulneſs, and praying that God would ſcatter his gifts and drop his mantle among them. When the corps was placed at the foot of the pulpit, cloſe to the vault, the Rev. Mr. Daniel Rogers made a very affecting prayer, and openly conſeſſed, that under God, he owed his converſion to the labors of that dear Man of God, whoſe precious re-remains now lay before them. Then he cried out, ' ' O my father, my father !' then ſtopt and wept, as though his heart would break, and the people weeping all through the place. Then he recovered, and finiſhed his prayer, and ſat down and wept. Then one of the Deacons gave out that hymn, *Why do we*

T   *mourn*

mourn departing friends? Some of the people weeping, some singing, and so on alternately. The Rev. Mr. Jewel preached a funeral discourse, and made an affectionate address to his brethren to lay to heart the death of that useful Man of God; begging that he and they might be upon their watch-tower, and endeavor to follow his blessed example. The corps was then put into the vault, and all concluded with a short prayer, and dismission of the people, who went weeping through the streets to their respective places of abode."

THE melancholy news of Mr. WHITEFIELD's death reached London on Monday, November 5, 1770, by the Boston-Gazette, and by three letters from different persons at Boston, to his friend Mr. Keen, who also by the same post received two of his own hand writing, written in health: one seven, the other five days before his death. Mr. Keen had the melancholy event notified the same night at the Tabernacle, and the next night at Tottenham-Court Chapel. His next step was to consider of a proper person to preach the funeral sermon; and recollecting he had often said to Mr. WHITEFIELD, If you die abroad, whom shall we get to preach your funeral sermon? Must it be your old friend the Rev. Mr. John Wesley? And having received constantly for answer, " He is the man," Mr. Keen accordingly waited on the Rev. Mr. Wesley on the Saturday following, and engaged him to preach it on the LORD's Day, November 18, which he did to a very large, crowded, and mournful auditory; many hundreds going away, who could not possibly get in.

IN both the places of worship the pulpits, &c. were hung with black cloth, and the galleries with fine black baize. The pulpits had escutcheons placed in front, and on each of the houses adjoining, hatchments were put up: the motto on each was, *Mea · vita*

rita Salus and Gloria Chriſtus. Six months expired
before the mourning was taken down, and the eſcut-
cheons hung up in each veſtry. The hatchments remained twelve months, and when taken down, one
was placed in the Tabernacle, and the other in the
Chapel, over a neat marble monument Mr. WHITE-
FIELD had erected for his wife, with room left for a
few lines reſpecting himſelf after his deceaſe, as he
purpoſed lying in the ſame vault had he died in England. Accordingly the Rev. Mr. Knight of Halifax,
in Yorkſhire, drew up the following lines.

In Memory of

THE Rev. Mr. GEORGE WHITEFIELD, A. M.
Chaplain to the Right Honorable the Counteſs of
Huntingdon, whoſe Soul, made meet for Glory,
was taken to IMMANUEL's boſom, on the 30th of
September, 1770; and whoſe body now lies in
the ſilent Grave at Newbury-Port, near Beſton,
in New England, there depoſited in the hope of
a joyful Reſurrection to eternal Life and Glory.

HE was a Man eminent in Piety, of a humane, benevolent, and charitable Diſpoſition;
his Zeal in the Cauſe of GOD was ſingular, his
labors indefatigable, and his Succeſs in preaching the Goſpel, remarkable and aſtoniſhing.
He departed his Life in the 56th Year of his
age.

And, like his Maſter, was by ſome deſpis'd;
Like him, by many others, lov'd and priz'd:
But theirs ſhall be the everlaſting Crown,
Not whom the World, but JESUS CHRIST will own.

Mr. WHITEFIELD was not full fifty ſix years of age
at the time of his death: thirty-four years of which
he ſpent in the miniſtry. And if life is to be meaſured
by the greateſt activity and enjoyment; ſuch as being
always

always intent upon some good design, and vigorous
in the pursuit of it ; filling up every day with actions
of importance, worthy of a man and a Christian ;
seeing much of the world, and having a constant flow
of the most lively affections, both of the social and religious kind ; Mr. WHITEFIELD, in these thirty-four
years may be said to have lived more than most men
do, though their lives were prolonged for many ages.

CHAP. XXI.

*A Description of his Person ; a Review of his
Life ; and the most striking Parts of his
Character pointed out.*

HIS person was graceful, and well proportioned :
his stature rather above the middle size. His com-
plexion was very fair. His eyes were of a dark blue
color, and small, but sprightly. He had a squint
with one of them.* His features were in general
good and regular. His countenance was manly, and
his voice exceeding strong, yet both were softened
with an uncommon degree of sweetness. He was always very clean and neat, and often said pleasantly,
" that a Minister of the Gospel ought to be without
spot." His deportment was decent and easy, without
the least stiffness or formality : and his engaging polite manner made his company universally agreeable.
In his youth he was very slender, and moved his body
with great agility to action, suitable to his discourse ;

but

* Occasioned either by the ignorance, or the carelessness of
the nurse who attended him in the measles, when he was
about four years old,

but about the fortieth year of his age, he began to grow corpulent ; which however was folely the effect of his difeafe, being always, even to a proverb, remarkable for his moderation both in eating and drinking. Several prints have been done of him, which exhibit a very bad likenefs. The beft refemblance of him in his younger years, before he became corpulent, is that mezzotinto fcraping which reprefents him at full length, with one hand on his breaft, and holding a fmall Bible in the other ; but the late paintings, the one by Mr. Hone, and the other by Mr. Ruffell, as they are the beft pictures that ever were done of him, are certainly the jufteft likeneffes of his perfon. An elegant copper-plate of the firft, by Mr. Picot, is given with this account of his life ; and a very fine mezzotinto fcraping of the laft is juft publifhed, done by Mr. Watfon. Mr. Ruffell's painting, from which the fcraping is taken, was the laft picture which Mr. WHITEFIELD fat for, and was drawn only two years before he died. Both the copper plate and the fcraping will no doubt be very acceptable to Mr. WHITEFIELD's friends, as the one will be an ornament to the clofet, and the other to the parlor.

In reviewing the life of this extraordinary man, the following particulars appear very remarkable.

FIRST, we are ftruck with his unwearied diligence in the offices of religion, and his confcientious improvement of every portion of his time. Early in the morning he rofe to his Mafter's work, and all the day long was employed in a continual fucceffion of different duties. Take a view of his public conduct ; here he is engaged either in preaching the gofpel, in vifiting and giving counfel to the afflicted, in inftructing the ignorant, or in celebrating the praifes of GOD. Obferve his behavior in private company : there

T 2

there you hear him introducing, upon all occasions, and among all sorts of people, discourse that tended to edification. And if you follow him to his retirements, you see him writing devout meditations upon the occurrences of the day, or letters to his Christian acquaintance, full of piety and zeal. What a gloomy idea must a stranger to vital piety entertain of a life spent in this manner? He will think it must have been not only joyless and disgusting, but intolerably burthensome. Far otherwise did it appear in the experience of this servant of CHRIST. He felt the greatest enjoyment when engaged in a constant round of social and religious duties. In these whole weeks passed away like one day. And when he was visited with any distress or affliction, preaching, as he tells us himself, was his catholicon, and prayer his antidote against every trial. The pleasure of a man of business in successfully pushing his trade, or of a philosopher when pursuing his favorite studies, may give us some faint conception of the joys which he felt: yet so ardent were his desires after the heavenly happiness, that he often longed to finish his work, and to go home to his SAVIOR.*

AGAIN, we are justly surprized at his frequent and fervent preaching under all the disadvantages of a sickly constitution, and the many fits of illness with which he was suddenly seized. It must indeed be confessed, that change of air, frequent travelling on horseback, and the many voyages he made, might contribute

---

* " Blessed be GOD, the prospect of death is pleasant to my soul. I would not live here always. I want to be gone.

" Sometimes it arises from a fear of falling. Sometimes from a prospect of future labours and sufferings. But these are times when my soul hath such foretastes of GOD, that I long more eargerly to be with Him; and the prospect of the happiness which the spirits of just men made perfect now enjoy, often carries me, as it were, into another world."

contribute to the prefervation of his health and vigor:
but when we confider what exertion of voice was
neceffary to reach his large congregations; that he
preached generally twice or thrice every day, and
often four times on the Lord's day; but above all,
what wafte of ftrength and fpirits every fermon muft
have coft him, through the earneftnefs of his delivery;
it is truly aftonifhing how his conftitution could hold
out fo long.*

But there is another circumftance not lefs remarkable than either of the former, which is, the
uncommon defire that all forts of people expreffed to
attend his preaching; and that not upon the firft or
fecond vifit only, but at every fucceeding opportunity.
Wherever he went, prodigious numbers flocked to
hear him. His congregations often confifted of four
or five thoufand: in populous places they fwelled to
ten, fometimes fourteen; and upon fome occafions the
concourfe was fo great, that they have been computed
to be from twenty to thirty thoufand.

It is wonderful to think how he commanded the
attention of fuch multitudes; with what compofure
they liftened, when he began to fpeak; how they
hung upon his lips, and were often diffolved in tears;
and this was the cafe with perfons of the moft hardy
and rugged, as well as thofe of fofter tempers.

His eloquence was indeed very great, and of the
trueft and nobleft kind. He was utterly devoid of all
appearance of affectation. He feemed to be quite
unconfcious of the talents he poffeffed. The importance of his fubject, and the regard due to his hearers,
engroffed all his concern. He fpake like one who
did not feek their applaufe, but was concerned for
their beft interefts, and who, from a principle of unfeigned love, earneftly endeavored to lead them in
the right way. And the effect in fome meafure corresponded

* "I preach till I fweat through and through."

responded to the design. They did not amuse themselves with commending his discourses ; but being moved and persuaded by what he said, entered into his views, felt his passions, and were willing, for that time at least, to comply with all his requests. This was especially remarkable at his charity-sermons,* when the most worldly-minded were made to part with their money in so generous a manner, that when they returned to their former temper, they were ready to think that it had been conjured from them by some inexplicable charm. The charm, however, was nothing else than the power of his irresistible eloquence, in which respect it is not easy to say, whether he was ever excelled either in ancient or modern times.

He had a strong and musical voice, and a wonderful command of it. His pronunciation was not only proper, but manly and graceful. Nor was he ever at a loss for the most natural and strong expressions. Yet these in him were but lower qualities. The grand sources of his eloquence were an exceeding lively imagination, which made people think they saw what he described ; an action still more lively if possible, by which, while every accent of his voice spoke to the ear, every feature of his face, every motion of his hands, and gesture spoke to the eye ; so that the most dissipated and thoughtless found their attention involuntarily fixed, and the dullest and most ignorant could not but understand. He had likewise a certain elevation of mind, which raised him equally above praise and censure, and added great authority to whatever he said.† But what was perhaps the most important

portant

---

* Which he preached for a great many others, besides his own orphans in Georgia. See his Life.

† " The Lord only knows how he will be pleased to dispose of me ; great afflictions I am sure of having ; and a sudden

portant of all, he had a heart deeply exercifed in all the focial, as well as the pious and religious affections, and was at the fame time moft remarkably communicative, by which means he was peculiarly fitted to awaken like feelings in others, and to fympathize with every one that had them.

This laft, fome have thought was the diftinguifhing part of his character. It was certainly, however, an eminent part of it. In his Journals and Letters, an impartial reader will find inftances thereof almoft in every page : fuch as, lively gratitude to God in the firft place, and to all whom God had ufed as inftruments of good to him : fincere love in dealing fo plainly with his correfpondents about the intereft of their fouls : frequent and particular interceffion for his friends, his enemies and all mankind : great delight in the fociety of Chriftian acquaintance ; many very forrowful partings and joyful meetings with his friends : tender-heartednefs to the afflicted : the pleafure in procuring and adminiftering feafonable fupply to the indigent: and condefcenfion to people of the loweft rank, to inftruct and converfe with them for their good, in as kind and fociable manner, as if he had been their brother or intimate friend. Thefe are manifeft proofs that he had a heart eafily fufceptible of every humane, tender, and compaffionate feeling. And this was certainly a great mean of enabling him fo ftrongly to affect the hearts of others.

Had his natural talents for oratory been employed in fecular affairs, and been fomewhat more improved by the refinements of art, and the embellifhments of erudition, it is poffible they would foon have advanced him to diftinguifhed wealth and renown. But

his

fudden death, bleffed be God, will not be terrible. I know that my Redeemer liveth. I every day long to fee Him, that I may be free from the remainder of fin, and enjoy him, without interruption, for ever.

his fole ambition was to ferve a crucified Savior, in the miniftry of the golpel. And being early convinced of the great hurt that has been done to Chriftianity, by a bigoted fpirit, he infifted not upon the peculiar* tenets of a party. but upon the univerfally interefting doctrines of Holy Scripture, concerning the ruin of mankind by fin, and their recovery by Divine Grace ; doctrines, the truth of which, he himfelf had deeply felt.   To make men fenfible of the mifery of their alienation from God ; and of the neceffity of juftifica-tion by faith in the Lord Jesus Christ, of regenera-tion by the Holy Spirit, and of a life of devotednefs to God, was the principal aim of all his difcourfes. " The only Methodifm, I defire to know, (fays he,)† is a holy method of dying to ourfelves, and of living to God." By this defcription. he was far from intend-ing to confine true religion to the exercifes of devo-tion.   By " living to God" he meant a conftant en-deavour after conformity to the Divine Will in all things.   For, fays he in another§ place, " It is a great miftake to fuppofe religion confifts only in faying our prayers.   Every Chriftian lies under a neceffity to have fome particular calling whereby he may be a ufeful member of the fociety to which he belongs.   A man is no further holy than he is relatively holy : and he only will adorn the Gofpel of our Lord Jesus Christ in all things, who is careful to perform all the civil offices of life, with a fingle eye to God's glory, and from a principle of lively faith in Jesus

Christ

---

* " I love all that love our Lord Jesus Christ."
" Oh how do I long to fee bigotry and party-zeal taken away, and all the Lord's fervants more knit together."
" I wifh all names among the Saints of God, were fwal-lowed up in that one of Chriftian."

† Preface to the Journals, in the edition of 1736.

§ Journals, May, 1739.

CHRIST our Savior. This is the morality which we preach." He used also to give this definition of true religion, " that it is a universal morality founded upon the love of GOD, and faith in the LORD JESUS CHRIST." Licentiousness and luxury, and all sorts of time wasting and dissipating amusements, how fashionable so ever, he constantly inveighed against. These were the topics on which he employed his eloquence.

BUT not to dwell any longer on his accomplishments as an orator, and the excellent purposes to which, through the grace of GOD, he devoted them ; one thing remains to be mentioned, of an infinitely higher order than any human powers whatever : and that is, the power of GOD, which so remarkably accompanied the labors of his servant, and without which both scripture and experience teach us, that all external means, however excellent, are ineffectual and vain.   It is here Mr. WHITEFIELD is most to be envied, were it lawful to envy any man.   When we consider the multitudes that were not only awakened, but brought under lasting religious impressions by his ministry; and the multitudes that were wrought upon in the same manner by the ministry of others, excited by his * example, both in Great Britain and America, we are naturally led into the same sentiments with Mr. Wesley in his funeral sermon, " What an honor hath it pleased GOD to put upon his faithful servant ! Have we read or heard of any person since the Apostles, who testified the gospel of the grace of GOD, through so widely extended a space, through so large a part of the habitable world ? Have we read or heard of any person, who called so many thousands, so many myriads of sinners to repentance.   Above all, have we read or heard of any who has been a blessed instrument in his hand of bringing so many sinners from darkness to light, and from the power of Satan to God ?"   ·THIS

* See Hist. Coll. of the Succefs of the Gospel, Vol. II.

THIS excellent character joined to talents fo extraordinary, and to labors, which GOD was pleafed to blefs with almoft unequalled fuccefs, was fhaded with fome infirmities.   And what elfe could be expected in the prefent condition of humanity? Thefe have been fufficiently laid open in the preceding Narrative of his Life.   And it ought to be obferved, that as there was fomething very amiable in the franknefs and unreferv- ednefs which prevented his concealing them ; fo thro' his openefs to conviction, his teachablenefs,† and his readinefs to confefs and correct his miftakes, they be- came ftill fewer and fmaller, decreafed continually as he advanced in knowledge and experience.

IT would be unjuft to his memory not to take no- tice

---

† " May GOD reward you for watching over my foul.   It is difficult, I believe, to go through the fiery trial of popu- larity and applaufe, untainted."

" When I am unwilling to be told of my faults, correfpond with me no more.   If I know any thing of my heart, I love thofe moft who are moft faithful to me in this refpect.   Hence- forward, dear Sir, I befeech you by the mercies of GOD in CHRIST JESUS, fpare me not."

" We muft be helps to each other on this fide eternity.— Nothing gives me more comfort, next to the affurance of the eternal continuance of GOD's love, than the pleafing reflection of having fo many Chriftian friends to watch with my foul. I wifh they would finite me friendly, and reprove me oftener than they do."

" I rejoice that you begin to know yourfelf.   If poffible, Satan will make us think more highly of ourfelves than we ought to think.   I can tell this by fatal experience.   It is not fudden flafhes of joy, but having the humility of CHRIST JE- SUS, that muft denominate us Chriftians.   If we hate reproof, we are fo far from being true followers of the LAMB of GOD, that in the opinion of the wifeft of men, we are brutifh."

" O my dear brother, ftill continue faithful to my foul ; do not hate me in your heart ; in any wife reprove me.

" You need make no apology for your plain dealing.   I love thofe beft who deal moft fincerely with me.   Whatever errors I have been, or fhall be guilty of, in my miniftry, I hope the LORD will fhew me, and give me grace to amend."

tice upon this occasion of that uniformity of sentiment which runs through all his sermons and writings, after he was thoroughly enlightened in the truth. Indeed, when he first set out in the ministry, his youth and inexperience led him into many expressions which were contrary to sound doctrine, and which made many of the sermons he first printed, justly exceptionable; but reading, experience, and a deeper knowledge of his own heart, convinced him of his errors, and upon all occasions he avowed his belief of the thirty-nine Articles of the Church of England, and the Standards of the Church of Scotland, as expresly founded on the word of GOD. He loved his friend, but he would not part with a grain of sacred truth for the brother of his heart. Thus we see him constrained to write and print against the Arminian tenets of Mr. John Wesley, whom he loved in the bowels of CHRIST JESUS. And it appears from several other tracts in the 4th Vol. of his Works, that he neglected no opportunity of stepping forth as a bold champion, in defence of that faith which was once delivered to the saints.

EXTRACTS

U

EXTRACTS

FROM

Some of the FUNERAL SERMONS *which were Preached on the Occasion of his* DEATH.

MANY Sermons were preached upon occasion of his death, both in America and England. From these, though they contain nothing materially different from the above accounts, yet the reader will probably not be displeased to see the following extracts ; as they not only set the character of Mr. WHITEFIELD, in a variety of lights, but are so many testimonies to it, by witnesses of undoubted credit, in different parts of the world.

THE first was preached by Mr. Parsons, the very day on which he died,* from Phil. i. 21. " To me to live

---

* Early next morning, Mr. Sherburn of Portsmouth, sent Squire Clarkson and Dr. Haven with a message to Mr. Parsons, desiring Mr. WHITEFIELD's remains might be buried in his own new tomb, at his own expence : and in the evening several gentlemen from Boston came to Mr. Parsons, desiring the body might be carried there. But as Mr. WHITEFIELD had repeatedly desired he might be buried before Mr. Parsons' pulpit, if he died at Newbury-Port, Mr. Parsons thought himself obliged to deny both of these requests. The following account of his interment, is subjoined to this sermon, viz. " October 2, 1770. At one o'clock all the bells in town were tolled for half an hour, and all the vessels in the harbor gave their proper signals of mourning. At two the bells tolled a
　　　　　　　　　　　　　　　　　　　　　　　second

live is Chrift, and to die is gain." And this is the character he gives of his departed friend.

"CHRIST became a principle of fpiritual life in his foul, while he was an Under-graduate at the Univerfity in Oxford. Before his conveﬁon he was a Pharifee of the Pharifees, as ftrict as ever Paul was, before GOD met him on his way to Damafcus, according to his own declaration in his laft fermon, which I heard him preach at Exeter, vefterday. He was, by means of reading, a very fearching, puritanical writer, convinced of the rottennefs of all the duties he had done, and the danger of a felf-righteous foundation of hope. When he heard CHRIST fpeak to him in the Gofpel, he cried, "LORD, what wilt thou have me to do?' And it feems as if, at that time, it had been made known to him that he was a chofen veffel, to bear the name of JESUS CHRIST through the Britiﬁ Nation and her Colonies: to ftand before Kings and Nobles, and all forts of people, to preach CHRIST and him crucified. From that time.

second time. At three the bells called to attend the funeral. The Rev. Dr. Samuel Haven of Portfmouth, the Rev. Meffieurs Daniel Rogers, of Exeter, Jedidiah Jewet, and James Chandler, of Rowley, Mofes Parfons, of Newbury, and Edward Bafs, of Newbury Port, were pall-bearers. The proceffion was from the Rev. Mr. Parfons', of Newbury-Port, where Mr. WHITEFIELD died. Mr. Parfons and his family, together with many other refpectable perfons, followed the corpfe in mourning. The proceffion was only one mile, and then the corpfe was carried into the Prefbyterian church, and placed on the bier in the broad-alley; when the Rev. Mr. Rogers made a very fuitable prayer in the prefence of about fix thoufand perfons, within the walls of the church, while many thoufands were on the outfide, not being able to find admittance. Then, the third hymn of the fecond book of Dr. Watts' Spiritual Songs was fung by the congregation. After this, the corpfe was put into a new tomb, before Mr. Parfons' pulpit, which the gentlemen of the congregation had prepared for that purpofe; and before it was fealed, the Rev. Mr. Jewet gave a fuitable exhortation, &c." In

time the dawns of falvation had living power in his
heart, and he had an ardent defire to furnifh himfelf
for the Gofpel miniftry. To this end, befides the
ufual ftudies at the College, he gave himfelf to reading the holy Scriptures, to meditation and prayer;
and

In Reverendum Virum

GEORGIUM WHITEFIELD,

Laboribus facris olim abundantem; nunc vero, ut bene fpe-
ratur, cœleftem et immortalem vitam cum CHRISTO
agentem,

EPITAPHIUM.

(Auctore THOMA GIBBONS, S. T. P.)

Electum et divinum vas, WHITEFIELD, fuifti-
    Ingenio pollens, divitiifque facris:
IUs opibus populo longe lateque tributis,
    Tandem perfrueris lætitia fuperum
Inque hanc intrafti, Domino plaudente miniftrum,
    Expertum in multis, affiduumque bonum:
Ecce mei portus, et clara palatia cœli
    Deliciis plenis omnia aperta tibi.
Dum matutinam Stellam, quam dulce rubentem!
    Vivificos rorefque offa fepulta manent.

ENGLISHED THUS:

A veffel chofen and divine, replete
With Nature's gifts, and Grace's richer ftores,
Thou WHITEFIELD waft: thefe thro' the world difpens'd,
In long laborious travels, thou at length
Haft reach'd the realms of reft, to which thy LORD
Has welcom'd thee with his immenfe applaufe.
All hail, my fervant, in thy various trufts
Found vigilant and faithful: See the ports,
See the eternal kingdoms of the fkies,
With all their boundlefs glory, boundlefs joy,
Open'd for thy reception and thy blifs.
Mean-time, the body in its peaceful cell
Repofing from its toils, awaits the Star,
Whofe living luftres lead that promis'd morn,
Whofe vivifying dews thy moulder'd corfe
Shall vifit, and immortal life infpire.

and particularly, he read Mr. Henry's Annotations on the Bible, upon his knees before GOD.

" SINCE my first acquaintance with him, which is about thirty years ago, I have highly esteemed him, as an excellent Christian, and an eminent Minister of the Gospel. An heart so bent for CHRIST, with such a sprightly, active genius, could not admit of his stated, fixed residence, in one place, as the pastor of a particular congregation ; and therefore, he chose to itinerate from place to place, and from one country to another ; which indeed was much better suited to his talents, than a fixed abode would have been. I often considered him as an angel flying through the midst of heaven, with the everlasting Gospel, to preach unto them that dwell on the earth ; for he preached the uncorrupted word of GOD, and gave solemn warnings against all corruptions of the Gospel of CHRIST.*   When he came the first time to Bolton, the venerable Dr. Coleman, (with whom I had a small acquaintance) condescended to write to me, ' That the wonderful man was come, and they had had a week of Sabbaths ; that his zeal for CHRIST was extraordinary ; and yet he recommended himself to his many thousand hearers, by his engagedness for holiness and souls.' I soon had opportunity to observe that wherever he flew, like a flame of fire, his ministry gave a general alarm to all sorts of people, though before, they had, for a long time, been amazingly sunk down into dead formality. It
was

* This may be a proper place to mention what the compiler is just now informed of. The late Dr. Grosvenor, who was reputed one of the most eminent divines of his time, upon hearing Mr. WHITEFIELD preach at Charles-square, Hoxton, about the year 1741, expressed himself in these very strong terms, in the presence of a very respectable gentleman now living, " That if the Apostle Paul had preached to this auditory, he would have preached in the same manner."

was then a time in New-England, that real Christians generally had slackened their zeal for CHRIST, and fallen into a remiss and careless frame of spirit ; and hypocritical professors were sunk into a deep sleep of carnal security.   Ministers, and their congregations, seemed to be at ease.   But his preaching appeared to be from the heart, though too many who spake the same things, preached as if it were indifferent, whether they were received or rejected.   We were convinced that he believed the message he brought us, to be of the last importance.   Nevertheless, as soon as there was time for reflection, the enemies of CHRIST began to cavil and hold up some of his sallies, as if they were unpardonable faults.   By such means he met with a storm as tempestuous as the troubled sea, that casts up mire and dirt.   Some of every station were too fond of their old way of formality, to part with it, for such a despised cause as living religion.   But the Spirit of CHRIST set home the message of the LORD upon the consciences of some, and shook them off their false hopes : but many began to find fault, and some to write against his evangelizing through the country, while others threatened firebrands, arrows, and death.   Yet GOD gave room for his intense zeal to operate, and fit objects appeared, wherever he went, to engage him in preaching CHRIST, and him crucified.

In his repeated visits to America, when his services had almost exhausted his animal spirits, and his friends were ready to cry, Spare thyself, his hope of serving CHRIST, and winning souls to him, animated and engaged him to run almost any risque. Neither did he ever cross the Atlantic, on an itinerating ministry, without visiting his numerous brethren here, to see how religion prospered amongst them : and we know that his labors have been unwearied among us, and to the applause of all his hearers ;

and,

THE REV. GEORGE WHITEFIELD. 223

and, through the infinite mercy of God, his labors have fometimes been crowned with great fuccefs, in the converfion of finners, and the edification of faints. And though he often returned from the pulpit very feeble, after public preaching, yet his engaging fweetnefs of converfation, changed the fufpicions of many, into paffionate love and friendfhip.

"In many things his example is worthy of imitation ; and, if in any thing he exceeded or came fhort, his integrity, zeal for God, and love to Christ and his Gofpel, rendered him, in extenfive ufefulnefs, more than equal to any of his brethren. In preaching here, and through moft parts of America, he has been in labors more abundant, approving himfelf a minifter of God, in much patience, in afflictions, in watchings, in faftings ; by purenefs, by the Holy Ghost, by love unfeigned ; as forrowful, yet always rejoicing; as having nothing, yet poffeffing all things. And God, that comforteth thofe that are caft down, has often comforted us by his coming : and not by his coming only, but by the confolation wherewith he was comforted in us, fo that we could rejoice the more.

"His popularity exceeded all that I ever knew ; and, though the afthma was fometimes an obftruction to him, his delivery and entertaining method was fo inviting to the laft, that it would command the attention of the vaft multitudes of his hearers. An apprehenfion of his concern to ferve the Lord Jesus Christ, and to do good to the fouls of men, drew many thoufands after him, who never embraced the doctrines he taught. He had fomething fo peculiar in his manner, expreffive of fincerity in all he delivered, that it conftrained the moft abandoned to think, he believed what he faid was not only true, but of the laft importance to fouls ; and by adapted texts adduced, and inftances of the grace of God, related

                                        agreeable

agreeable thereto, he often surprized his most judicious hearers.

"His labors extended not only to New England, and many other Colonies in British America, but were eminent and more abundant in Great Britain. Many thousands at his Chapel and Tabernacle in London, and in other places, were witnesses that he faithfully endeavored to restore the interesting doctrines of the Reformation, and the purity of the Church to its primitive glory. Some among the learned, some of the mighty and noble have been called, by his ministry, to testify for the Gospel of the grace of God. The force of his reasonings against corrupt principles, and the easy method he had in exposing the danger of them, have astonished the most that heard him, in all places where he preached. How did he lament and withstand the modern, unscriptural notions of religion and salvation, that were palmed upon the churches of every denomination! The affecting change from primitive purity to fatal heresy, together with the sad effects of it in mere formality and open wickedness, would often make him cry, as the Prophet did in another case, ' How is the gold become dim, and the most fine gold changed! How hath the LORD covered the daughter of Zion with a cloud in his anger, and cast down from heaven to earth the beauty of Israel.'

"It is no wonder that this Man of God should meet with enemies, and with great opposition to his ministry; for hell trembled before him. It is no more than may be always expected of the devil, that he should stir up his servants, to load the most eminent ministers of CHRIST with calumny, and most impudent lies; and represent them as the filth, and offscouring of all things. All this may be, and often has been done, under a pretence of great concern for the honor of CHRIST, and the preservation of Gospel-order.

order. When Satan's kingdom totters and begins to fall, he can find men enough to cry, The Church is in danger! and that, he knows, is sufficient with many, to hide his cloven foot, and make him appear as an angel of light.

"THROUGH a variety of such labors and trials, our worthy friend, and extensively useful servant of CHRIST, Mr. WHITEFIELD, passed, both in England and America: but the LORD was his Sun, to guide and animate him, and his shield to defend and help him unto the end: neither did he count his own life dear, so that he might finish his course with joy, and the ministry that he had received of the LORD JESUS, to testify the Gospel of the grace of GOD. The last sermon that he preached, though under the disadvantage of a stage in the open air, was delivered with such clearness, pathos, and eloquence, as to please and surprise the surrounding thousands. And as he had been confirmed by the grace of GOD, many years before, and had been waiting and hoping for his last change, he then declared, that he hoped it was the last time he should ever preach. Doubtless, he then had such clear views of the blessedness of open vision, and the complete fruition of GOD in CHRIST, that he felt the pleasures of heaven in his raptured soul, which made his countenance shine like the unclouded sun."

THE next sermon was preached by Dr. Pemberton of* Boston, October, 11, 1770, upon 1. Pet. i. 4.

"To

* The following lines are a part of a poem on Mr. WHITEFIELD, which is published along with this sermon, written by a Negro servant-girl of seventeen years of age ; and who has been but nine years from Africa, belonging to Mr. J. Wheatley of Boston.

"He pray'd that grace in every heart might dwell ;
He long'd to see America excel ;

He

" To an inheritance—reserved in heaven for you."
In which he says :

" I am not fond of funeral panegyrics. But
where persons have been distinguishingly honored by
heaven, and employed to do uncommon service for
God's church upon earth, it would be criminal ingrat-
itude to suffer them to drop into the dust without the
most respectful notice. ' The memory of the just is
blessed !' Posterity will view Mr. WHITEFIELD, in
many respects, as one of the most extraordinary characters of the present age. His zealous, incessant, and
successful labors, in Europe and America, are without
a parallel.

" DEVOTED early to GOD, he took orders as soon
as the constitution of the established Church in England

He charg'd its youth to let the grace divine
Arise, and in their future actions shine.
He offer'd that he did himself receive,
A greater gift not GOD himself can give. .
He urg'd the need of Him to every one ;
It was no less than GOD's co-equal Son.
Take Him, ye wretched, for your only good ;
Take Him, ye starving souls, to be your food.
Ye thirsty, come to this life-giving stream ;
Ye preachers, take Him for your joyful theme,
Take Him, my dear Americans, he said,
Be your complaints in his kind bosom laid.
Take him, ye Africans ; he longs for you :
Impartial Savior is his title due.
If you will choose to walk in grace's road,
You shall be Sons, and Kings, and Priests, to GOD.
Great Countess ! we Americans revere
Thy name, and thus condole thy grief sincere.
New-England, sure doth feel ; the Orphan's smart
Reveals the true sensations of his heart.
His lonely Tabernacle sees no more
A WHITEFIELD landing on the British shore.
Then let us view him in yon azure skies,
Let every mind with this lov'd object rise.
Thou tomb, shall safe retain thy sacred trust,
Till life divine re-animates his dust."

gland allowed. His firſt appearance in the work of the miniſtry was attended with ſurprizing ſuccefs. The largeſt churches in London were not able to contain the numbers that perpetually flocked to hear his awakening difcourfes. The crowds daily increaſed. He was ſoon forced into the fields, followed by multitudes, who hung with ſilent attention upon his lips, and with avidity received the word of life. The SPIRIT of GOD, in uncommon meafure, defcended upon the hearers. The ſecure were awakened to a ſalutary fear of divine wrath ; and inquiring minds were directed to JESUS, the only Savior of a revolted world. The vicious were viſibly reclaimed, and thofe who had hitherto reſted in a form of godlinefs, were made acquainted with the power of a divine life. The people of GOD were refreſhed with the confola‑tion of the bleſſed SPIRIT, and rejoiced to fee their exalted Maſter, going on from conquering to conquer ; and ſinners of all orders and characters, bowing to the ſceptre of a crucified SAVIOR.

His zeal could not be confined within the Britiſh iſlands. His ardent defire for the welfare of immortal ſouls, conveyed him to the diſtant ſhores of America. We beheld a new ſtar arife in the hemifphere of thefe weſtern churches ; and its ſalutary influences were diffufed through a great part of the Britiſh ſettlements in thefe remote regions. We heard with pleaſure, from a divine of the Epifcopal communion, thofe great doctrines of the Gofpel, which our venerable anceſtors brought with them from their native country. With a ſoul elevated, above a fond attachment to forms and ceremonies, he inculcated that pure and unadulterated religion, for the prefervation of which our fathers baniſhed themfelves into an uncultivated defert. In his repeated progreſſes through the Colonies, he was favored with the ſame ſuccefs which attended him on the other ſide of the Atlantic.

He

He preached from day to day in thronged affemblies; yet his hearers never difcovered the leaft wearinefs, but always followed him with increafing ardor.— When in the pulpit, every eye was fixed upon his expreffive countenance ; every ear was charmed with his melodious voice, all forts of perfons were captivated with the propriety and beauty of his addrefs.

BUT it is not the fine fpeaker, the accomplifhed orator, that we are to celebrate from the facred defk ; thefe engaging qualities, if not fanctified by divine grace, and confecrated to the fervice of heaven, are as the founding brafs, and the tinkling cymbal. When mifimproved, inftead of conveying happinefs to mankind, they render us more illuftrioufly miferable.

"The gifts of nature, the acquifitions of art, which adorned the character of Mr. WHITEFIELD, were devoted to the honor of GOD, and the enlargement of the Kingdom of our divine REDEEMER.— While he preached the Gofpel, the HOLY GHOST was fent down to apply it to the confciences of the hearers ; the eyes of the blind were opened, to behold the glories of the compaffionate SAVIOR ; the ears of the deaf were unftopped to attend to the invitations of incarnate love ; the dead were animated with a divine principle of life ; many in all parts of the land, were turned from darknefs to light, and from the power of Satan unto GOD. Thefe doctrines which we had been inftructed in from our infancy by our faithful paftors, feemed to acquire new force, and were attended with uncommon fuccefs when delivered by him. His difcourfes were not trifling fpeculations, but contained the moft interefting truths ; they were not an empty play of wit, but folemn addreffes to the hearts of men.

"To convince finners that they were by nature children of wrath ; by practice, tranfgreffors of the divine law ; and in confequence of this, expofed to
the

the vengeance of offended heaven ; to difplay the tranfcendent excellency of a SAVIOR, and perfuade awakened minds to confide in his merits and righteoufnefs, as the only hope of a guilty world ; to imprefs upon the profeffors of the Gofpel the neceffity, not only of an outward reformation, but an internal change, by the powerful influences of the SPIRIT ; to lead the faithful to a zealous practice of the various duties of the Chriftian life, that they may evidence the fincerity of their faith, and adorn the doctrine of GOD their SAVIOR ; thefe were the reigning fubjects of his pulpit-difcourfes.

" IF finners were converted ; if faints were built up in faith, holinefs, and comfort, he attained his utmoft aim.

HE was no contracted bigot, but embraced Chriftians of every denomination in the arms of his charity, and acknowledged them to be children of the fame Father, fervants of the fame Mafter, heirs of the fame undefiled inheritance.

" THAT I am not complimenting the dead, but fpeaking the words of truth and fobernefs, I am perfuaded I have many witneffes in this affembly.

" HE was always received by multitudes with pleafure, when he favored thefe parts with his labors ; but he never had a more obliging reception than in his laft vifit. Men of the firft diftinction in the Province, not only attended his miniftry, but gave him the higheft marks of their refpect. With what faithfulnefs did he declare unto as the whole counfel of GOD ? With what folemnity did he reprove us for our increafing degeneracy ? With what zeal did he exhort us, to remember from whence we were fallen, and repent and do our firft works, left GOD fhould come and remove our candleftick out of its place ?

" ANIMATED

W

"ANIMATED with a God-like defign of promoting the temporal and fpiritual happinefs of mankind, after the example of his Divine Mafter, he went about doing good. In this he perfevered with unremitting ardor and affiduity till death removed him to that reft which remains for the people of GOD. Perhaps no man, fince the apoftolic age, preached oftener or with greater fuccefs*.

" If we view his private character, he will appear in a moft amiable point of light. The polite gentleman ; the faithful friend ; the engaging companion ; above all, the fincere Chriftian, were vifible in the whole of his deportment.

" WITH

* As a fpecimen of his indefatigable labours in the work of the miniftry, I have fet down an account of the Sermons he preached after his arrival at Newport, Rhode-Ifland, to the time of his death. He failed from New-York, Tuefday, July 31, P. M. arrived at Newport, Friday Auguft 3, A. M. and preached

Auguft, 4. At Newport
       5. Newport
       6. Newport
       7. Newport
       8. Newport
       9. Providence
      10. Providence
      11. Providence
      12. Providence
      13. Attleborough
      14. Wrentham
      15. Bofton
      16. Bofton
      17. Bofton
      18. Bofton
      19. Malden
      20. Bofton
      21. Bofton
      22. Bofton
      23. Bofton

Auguft 24. At Bofton
       25. Bofton
       26. Medford
       27. Charleftown
       28. Cambridge
       29. Bofton
       30. Bofton
       31. Roxbury-Plain
Septm. 1. Milton
       2. Roxbury
       3. Bofton
       5. Salem
       6. Marblehead
       7. Salem
       8. Cape-Ann
       9. Ipfwich
      10. Newburyport
      11. Newburyport
      12. Rowley
      13. Rowley.

" From

" WITH large opportunities of accumulating wealth, he never difcovered the leaft tincture of avarice. What he received from the kindnefs of his friends, he generoufly employed in offices of piety and charity. His benevolent mind was perpetually forming plans of extenfive ufefulnefs.—The Orphan-houfe, which many years ago he erected in Georgia, and the College he was founding in that Province at the time of his death, will be lafting monuments of his care, that religion and learning might be propagated to future generations.

" I HAVE not, my brethren, drawn an imaginary portrait, but defcribed a character exhibited in real life. I have not mentioned his natural abilities, which were vaftly above the common ftandard.—I confider him principally in the light of a Chriftian, and a minifter of JESUS CHRIST, in which he fhone with a fuperior luftre, as a ftar of the firft magnitude.

" AFTER all I am not reprefenting a perfect man ; there are fpots in the moft fhining characters upon earth. But this may be faid of Mr. WHITEFIELD with juftice, that after the moft public appearances for above thirty years, and the moft critical
cal

" From the thirteenth of September to the feventeenth, he was detained from public fervice by a fevere indifpofition. When recovered he preached

Septm. 17. At Bofton	*Septm.* 19 At Bofton
18. Bofton	20. Newton.

" The twenty-firft of September he departed from Bofton upon a tour to the eaftward, pretty much indifpofed. But on the twenty-third he preached

Septm. 23. At Portfmouth, New-Hampfhire	*Septm.* 26. At Kittery
24. Portfmouth	27. Old-York
25. Portfmouth	28. Portfmouth
	29. Exeter.

cal examination of his conduct, no other blemish could be fixed upon him, than what arose from the common frailties of human nature, and the peculiar circumstances which attended his first entrance into public life.

" The imprudencies of unexperienced youth, he frequently acknowledged from the pulpit with a frankness which will for ever do honor to his memory. He took care to prevent any bad consequences that might flow from his unguarded censures in the early part of his ministry. The longer he lived, the more he evidently increased in purity of doctrine, in humility, meekness, prudence, patience, and the other amiable virtues of the Christian life."

Another Funeral Sermon on Mr. Whitefield was preached by Mr. Ellington, at Savannah in Georgia, November 11, 1770, upon Heb. xi. 26. " Esteeming the reproach of Christ greater riches than the treasures of Egypt: for he had respect unto the recompence of the reward." In which are the following passages.*

" The receiving the melancholy news of the much lamented death of a particular friend to this Province, a person who was once minister of this Church, is the reason of this discourse ; and my choice of this subject before us is to pay my grateful respect to the memory of this well known, able minister of the New Testament, and faithful-servant of the most high God, the Rev. George Whitefield; whose life was justly esteemed, and whose death will be greatly regretted, by the sincerely religious part of

* " Savannah-church was decently hung with mourning, by the legislative body of the Province."

The same public marks of regard were shewn at one of the churches in Philadelphia, of which Mr. Sproutt is pastor, which, by desire of the session and committee, was put into mourning Also, at their desire and expence, the bells of Christ Church, in that city, were rung muffled.

of mankind of all denominations, as long as there is one remaining on earth, who knew him, to recollect the fervor of spirit, and holy zeal with which he spake, when preaching the everlasting Gospel ; and every other part of his difinterefted conduct, confiftent with the minifterial character in life and converfation.   Mr. WHITEFIELD's Works praife him loud enough ; I am not able to fay any thing that can add greater luftre to them.   May every one that minifters in holy things, and all who partake of their miniftrations, have equal right to the characteriftic in the text as he had.

" IT is the ruling opinion of many, that the offence of the crofs is long fince ceafed, and that whatever evil treatment fome of the fingular turn may meet with, it is only the fruit of their own doings, and the reward of their own work. whereby they raife the refentment of mankind againft them for uncharitable flander, and fpiritual abufe.   But whoever knoweth any thing of the Gofpel, and hath experienced it to be the power of GOD unto falvation, knoweth this is the language of perfons who are unacquainted with the depravity of their nature, and through the degeneracy of their hearts, are unwilling to be difturbed ; therefore are faying to the Minifters of CHRIST, ' Prophecy unto us fmooth things.'   But the Minifters of the Gofpel are to be fons of thunder, and fo to utter their voice, and conduct their lives, as to prove the nature of their work.

" OUR dear and reverend friend was highly honored for many years in being an happy inftrument to do this fuccefsfully.   With what a holy zeal he proceeded, long before he was publicly ordained to the facred office, has been long attefted ; and no perfon has been able to contradict the teftimony. No fooner did he appear in the work of the fanctu-

ary

ary, but he foon convinced his numerous auditories, that his ALMIGHTY LORD who had given him the commiffion, had by his grace wrought him for the felf-fame thing; and through the HOLY SPIRIT, attending his endeavors made him a workman that needed not to be afhamed. One would think his great fuccefs in his public labors, the frequent opportunities he embraced of doing good, by the relief of people in diftrefling circumftances, every occafion he took to ufe his influence for the good of mankind, and the whole of his behavior through a life of fifty-fix years, being (fo far as the frailty of our prefent ftate will admit) unblameable and unreproveable, fhould have exempted him from contempt and reproach. But, quite the contrary, there was fo near a refemblance with his bleffed Mafter, that obliged him to bear his reproach. He has fuffered with him on earth, and he is now glorified with him in heaven. He has labored abundantly, and he has been as liberally reproached and maligned from every quarter. Clergy and laity have whet their tongues like a fword againft him, and bent their bows to fhoot their arrows; but the LORD, amongft all, has known and approved his righteous fervant. Though it is well known he has had opportunity long fince to enjoy epifcopal emolument, yet, in his opinion (and it will be found he judged like a wife man in the end) finners, through his inftrumentality, being turned unto the LORD, and becoming his joy, and crown of rejoicing, in the day of our LORD JESUS, was efteemed a greater honor than any this world could afford him. His longing defire for the falvation of immortal fouls, would not admit of his being confined within the diftrict of any walls; though it muft be acknowledged he never thought of commencing field preacher, till his invidious enemies refufed him church-pulpits, with indignation of fpirit unbecoming

the

the loweſt and vulgar claſs of mankind, much leſs
men profeſſing themſelves preachers of godlineſs.—
Though he has, throughout the whole courſe of his
miniſtry, given ſufficient proof of his inviolable attachment to our happy eſtabliſhment, he was deſirous
to countenance the image of Chriſt, wherever he ſaw
it, well knowing, that political inſtitutions in any
nation whatever, ſhould not deſtroy the bleſſed union,
or prevent the communion which ought to ſubſiſt
throughout the Holy Catholic Church, between real
and ſincere Chriſtians of all denominations. Some
people may retain ſuch a veneration for apoſtolic
phraſes as to ſuppoſe they ought not to be applied to
other perſons; ſorry am I to obſerve, that few de-
ſerve the application. But of Mr. WHITEFIELD we
may ſay with the ſtricteſt truth, in journeyings often,
in perils of robbers, in perils of his own countrymen,
in perils in the city, in perils in the wildneſs, in
perils in the ſea, in perils among falſe brethren, in
wearineſs and painfulneſs, he hath approved himſelf
a miniſter of GOD. All who knew and were acquainted with him, ſoon diſcovered in him every
mark of good ſenſe and good manners; his company
and converſation was ſo enlivening and entertaining,
and at the ſame time ſo inſtructive and edifying, that
no perſon with the leaſt degree of common ſenſe,
could behave improperly in his preſence. In him
met (which do not often meet in one perſon) the finiſhed and compleat gentleman, and the real and true
Chriſtian. Why then did he take pleaſure in reproaches and ſubmit to the taunts and inſults both of
the vulgar and politer part of mankind? He had
reſpect to the recompence of reward. Though the
believer's work will never entitle him to a reward
of debt, yet the reward of grace will always excite
a holy deſire to render ſomething unto the LORD:
What wouldſt thou have me do? is the inceſſant en-

quiry

quiry of that foul, who by the merits of the REDEEM-
ER's death, and the virtue of his precious blood, is
redeemed from fin, and made a partaker of the inheritance incorruptible, undefiled, and that fadeth not
away. Faith operates by good works: and let all
the men of the world fay to the contrary, or put ever
fo bafe a conftruction upon our doctrine, it will evidence itfelf by thefe good fruits. It was from thefe
principles that Mr. WHITEFIELD acted, and they
were productive of the defired effects; not only in
alms-giving, this was but a fmall matter, when compared with the happier and more important attempt
which he made for the good of mankind, at the ha-
zard of his life, and the expence of an unblemifhed
character. How he has preached with fhowers of
ftones, and many other inftruments of malice and re-
venge about his ears, many of his furviving friends
can witnefs; but having the falvation of finners at
heart, and a great defire to refcue them from the
power of eternal death; he refolved to fpend and be
fpent for the fervice of precious and immortal fouls;
and fpared no pains, and refufed no labor, fo that he
might but adminifter to their real and eternal good:
And glory be to our good GOD, he hath perfevered
and endured to the end of his life, having refpect
unto the recompence of reward. Surely nothing
elfe could fupport him under fuch a weight of care,
and enable him amidft it all, for fo many years, to
bear it with fo much cheerfulnefs. The worthy inhabitants of this Province do not want my attefation,
either to the lofs the Province has fuftained, or to the
defire he has had for its profperity. His indefatigable endeavors to promote it, and the many fervent
prayers he has night and day offered for it, fpeak
loud enough. Happy omens we would hope in favor
of it, both as to its temporal increafe, and fpiritual
profperity. May GOD raife up fome ufeful men to

fupply

supply his place, and carry on unto perfection what he hath so disinterestedly begun, that the institution he hath founded in this Province, may be of public utility to the latest posterity ! As to his death, little more can be said of it, than has been communicated to the public already. He died like a hero in the field of battle ; he has been fighting the battles of the LORD of Hosts upwards of thirty years, against the world, sin, and Satan ; and he hath been a conqueror, he hath fought succesfully ; many, very many converted sinners are the trophies of his victory : but now his warfare is accomplished, the Captain of his salvation hath granted him a discharge, he is entered' into his everlasting rest, and is reaping the benefits of a life sincerely dedicated to the service of the once crucified, but now exalted JESUS. He preached the day before his decease : though his death was sudden, he was not surprized ; the morning of his departure, not many hours before his spirit took its flight to the regions of blifs, he prayed to the GOD of his salvation, and committed his departing soul into his hands, as his faithful CREATOR, and all merciful REDEEM.R.—Soon after he said, ' I am near my end ;' then fell asleep ; he fainted, and died ! not one sigh, or groan ; the LORD heard his prayer, and granted him his request, and gave him an easy dismission out of time into eternity : sudden death was his desire, and sudden death was to him sudden glory. He has fought the good fight ; few, if any, since the Apostles, have been more extensively useful, or labored more abundantly. Thousands, I believe I may with propriety say, in England, Scotland, and America, have great reason to bless GOD for his ministrations ; for he hath travelled far and wide, proclaiming the glad tidings of salvation, through faith in a crucified SAVIOR. Adorable EMMANUEL, make thou up the lofs of him to thy Church and people!

Let

Let a double portion of thy Spirit be poured out upon the remaining Ministers! Let that holy fire which burnt so bright in thy departed servant, warm each of their hearts! And, O thou LORD of the harvest, send forth more such true and faithful laborers into thy harvest!"

A NUMBER of Funeral Sermons were preached for him in England as well as in America. In one by Mr. D. Edwards, November 11, 1770, upon Heb. xi. 4. "By it he being dead, yet speaketh," we have the following character of Mr. WHITEFIELD.

"1. THE ardent love he bore to the LORD JESUS CHRIST was remarkable. This divine principle constrained him to an unwearied application to the service of the Gospel, and transported him, at times, in the eyes of some, beyond the bounds of sober reason. He was content to be a fool for CHRIST's sake; to be despised, so CHRIST might be honored; to be nothing, that JESUS might be all in all. He had such a sense of the incomparable excellence of the person of CHRIST, of his adorable condescension in taking our nature upon him, and enduring the curses of the holy law; his complete suitableness and sufficiency; as the wisdom, righteousness, sanctification and redemption of his people, that he could never say enough of him. He was so convinced of the happy tendency and efficacy of this principle in his own mind, that he made use of it, and proposed it to others, in the room of a thousand arguments, whenever he would inculcate the most unreserved obedience to the whole will of GOD, or stir up believers to a holy diligence in adorning the doctrine of GOD our SAVIOR in all things; inspired by this principle, nothing frightened or flattered him from his duty.

"2. ANOTHER pleasing ingredient in his character, and a sure evidence of the former, was love to the souls of mankind. He rejoiced in their prosperity

rity as one that had found great spoil ; and with St. Paul was willing to spend and be spent in promoting their happiness. He loved all who loved JESUS CHRIST in sincerity, however they might differ in some circumstantials. He embraced all opportunities to expose the malignant leaven of a party, and to remove prejudices and misapprehensions which good people too often entertain of one-another, when under the influence of a sectarian humor.

" 3. HIS attachment to the great doctrines of the Gospel was inflexible ; having known their worth, and experienced their power in his own heart, he plainly saw, that though they were unacceptable to the carnal heart, yet they bore the plain impress of the infinite wisdom of GOD. Those important truths, which tend to humble the sinner, to exalt CHRIST, and promote holiness in heart and life, were his darling subjects. He did not disguise Gospel truths by some artful sweetening, to render them more palatable to men of corrupt minds : he studied to preach the word in its purity, plainness, and simplicity. The warmth of his zeal disgusted many who make a mighty outcry about candor and charity, and are willing to extend it to every sentiment, except the truths in which the Apostles gloried. It was his love to the truths of GOD, and the souls of men, that led him to expose those who plead for the rectitude and excellency of human nature ; deny the proper Godhead of JESUS CHRIST, justification by faith in his righteousness imputed, or the New-Birth, and the absolute necessity of the operations of the HOLY GHOST. Faith and holiness were ever united together in his system, in opposition to those who pretend to faith without obedience to the law of GOD as the rule of life. He knew errors in the great truths of the Gospel are not indifferent, but dreadful and fatal ; he knew it was not candor and charity to say that errors in judg-

ment

ment are not hurtful, but the greatest unmercifulness and cruelty; therefore he often reproved such sharply.

ALTHOUGH he was so tenacious of the foundation-truths of the Gospel, yet none more candid in things that are not essential; herein he was full of gentleness and forbearance. In things indifferent he became all things to all men.*

" 4. To the foregoing particulars in Mr. WHITE-FIELD's character, I may add his zeal. His Christian zeal was like the light of the sun, which did warm, shine, and cherish, but knew not to destroy; full of generous philanthropy and benevolence, his zeal made him exceeding earnest and importunate in his addresses to saints and sinners. His zeal returned blessings for curses, and prayers for ill treatment : it kindled in him a becoming indignation against the errors, follies, and sins of the times ; it led him to weep bitterly over those who would not be persuaded to fly from the wrath to come : it made him bold and intrepid in the cause of GOD, and kept him from that flatness and deadness which is too visible in some good ministers. In these things he was an example to ministers of every denomination : and, if the limits of my discourse would admit, I could mention many things, as to his great charity to the poor, his humility, &c."

On Sunday, November 18, 1770, a Sermon was preached on his death at the Chapel in Tottenham-Court-Road, and at the Tabernacle near Moor fields, by the Rev. Mr. John Wesley.† The text was Numb. xxiii.

* As to the difference between essentials and non essentials in religion, Mr. Edwards refers to the Rev. Mr. Newton's " Review of Ecclesiastical History, so far as it concerns the progress, declensions, and revivals of Evangelical Doctrine and Practice."

† LONDON CHRONICLE, November 19, 1770. " Yesterday the Rev. Mr. Wesley preached a Funeral Sermon on Mr. WHITE-

xxiii. 10. "Let me die the death of the righteous, and let my laft end be like his." And in the fermon, after giving fome particulars of his life and death, Mr. Wefley fays,

" 1. We are next to take fome view of his charac-ter. A little fketch of this was foon after his death, publifhed in the Bofton Gazette ; an extract of which is fubjoined : " Little can be faid of him, but what every friend to vital Chriftianity, who has fat under his miniftry, will atteft. In his public labors he has for many years aftonifhed the world with his elo-quence and devotion. With what divine pathos did he perfuade the impenitent finner to embrace the practice of piety and virtue : filled with the SPIRIT of grace, he fpoke from the heart, and with a fervency of zeal, perhaps unequalled, fince the days of the apoftles, adorned the truths he delivered with the moft graceful charms of rhetoric and oratory. From the pulpit he was unrivalled in the command of an ever crowded auditory. Nor was he lefs agreeable and inftructive in his private converfation ; happy in a remarkable eafe of addrefs, willing to communicate, ftudious to edify : may the rifing generation catch a fpark of that flame which fhone with fuch diftin-guifhed luftre in the fpirit and practice of this faithful fervant of the moft high GOD.'

" 2. A MORE particular and equally juft character of him, has appeared in one of the Englifh papers.* It might not be difagreeable to you, to add the fub-ftance of this likewife : ' The character of this truly pious

WHITEFIELD's death, in the morning at the Chapel; and in the afternoon at the Tabernacle : the infide of each place was lined with black cloth, and an efcutcheon hung on the pulpits. The multitudes that went with a defign to hear the Sermon exceed all belief. The Chapel and Tabernacle were both filled as foon as they were opened."

* LONDON CHRONICLE, November 8, 1770.

X

pious perfon, muft be deeply impreffed on the heart
of every friend to vital religion. In fpite of a tender
and delicate conftitution, he continued to the laft day
of his life, preaching with a frequency and fervor
that feemed to exceed the natural ftrength of the
moft robuft. Being called to the exercife of his
function at an age, when moft young men are only
beginning to qualify themfelves for it, he had not
time to make a very confiderable progrefs in the
learned languages : but this defect was amply fup-
plied by a lively and fertile genius, by fervent zeal,
and by a forcible and moft perfuafive delivery. And
though in the pulpit he often found it needful, by
the terrors of the Lord, to perfuade men, he had
nothing gloomy in his nature, being fingularly chear--
ful, as well as charitable and tender-hearted. He
was as ready to relieve the bodily as the fpiritual
neceffities of thofe who applied to him. It ought
alfo to be obferved, that he conftantly enforced upon
his audience every moral duty, particularly induftry
in their feveral callings, and obedience to their fupe-
riors. He endeavored by the moft extraordinary
efforts of preaching in different places, and even in
the open fields, to roufe the lower clafs of people,
from the laft degree of inattention and ignorance, to
a fenfe of religion. For this, and his other labors,
the name of George Whitefield will long be
remembered with efteem and veneration.'

"3. That both thefe accounts are juft and impartial, will readily be allowed ; that is, as far as
they go : but they go little farther than the outfides
of his character : they fhew you the preacher, but
not the man, the Chriftian, the faint of God. May
I be permitted to add a little on this head, from a
perfonal knowledge of near forty years ? Indeed, I
am thoroughly fenfible how difficult it is to fpeak on
fo delicate a fubject ; what prudence is required to
avoid

avoid both extremes, to fay neither too little, nor too much? Nay, I know it is impoſſible to fpeak at all, to fay either leſs or more, without incurring from fome the former, from others the latter cenſure. Some will ſeriouſly think that too little is ſaid; and others, that it is too much: but without attending to this, I will ſpeak juſt what I know, before him to whom we are all to give an account.

"4. MENTION has already been made of his unparalleled zeal, his indefatigable activity, his tender heartedneſs to the afflicted, and charitableneſs toward the poor. But ſhould we not likewiſe mention his deep gratitude to all whom GOD had uſed as inſtruments of good to him? Of whom he did not ceaſe to ſpeak in the moſt reſpectful manner, even to his dying day. Should we not mention that he had an heart ſuſceptible of the moſt generous and the moſt tender friendſhip? I have frequently thought, that this, of all others, was the diſtinguiſhing part of his character. How few have we known of ſo kind a temper, of ſuch large and flowing affections. Was it not principally by this, that the hearts of others were ſo ſtrangely drawn and knit to him? Can any thing but love beget love? This ſhone in his very countenance, and continually breathed in all his words, whether in public or private. Was it not this, which, quick and penetrating as lightning, flew from heart to heart? Which gave that life to his ſermons, his converſations, his letters? Ye are witneſſes.

"5. BUT away with the vile miſconſtruction of men of corrupt minds, who know of no love, but what is earthly and ſenſual. Be it remembered, at the ſame time, that he was endued with the moſt nice and unblemiſhed modeſty. His office called him to converſe very frequently and largely with women as well as men, and thoſe of every age and condition.

But

But his whole behavior toward them, was a practical comment, on that advice of St. Paul to Timothy, ' Intreat the elder women as mothers, the younger as sisters, with all purity.'

" 6. MEAN-TIME, how suitable to the friendliness of his spirit, was the frankness and openness of his conversation ? Although it was as far removed from rudeness on the one hand, as from guile and disguise on the other. Was not this frankness at once a fruit and a proof of his courage and intrepidity ? Armed with these, he feared not the faces of men ; but used great plainness of speech, to persons of every rank and condition, high and low, rich and poor ; endeavoring only by manifestation of the truth, to commend himself to every man's conscience in the sight of GOD.

" 7. NEITHER was he afraid of labor or pain, any more than of what man could do unto him, being equally

'Patient in bearing ill and doing well.'

And this appeared, in the steadiness wherewith he pursued whatever he undertook, for his Master's sake : witness one instance for all, the Orphan-house in Georgia, which he began and perfected, in spite of all discouragements. Indeed, in whatever concerned himself, he was pliant and flexible : in this case he was easy to be intreated, easy to be either convinced or persuaded ; but he was immoveable in the things of GOD, or wherever his conscience was concerned. None could persuade any more than affright him to vary in the least point from that integrity, which was inseparable from his whole character, and regulated all his words and actions. Herein he did

' Stand as an iron pillar strong,
And stedfast as a wall of brass.'

" 8. IF it be enquired, What was the foundation of this integrity, or of his sincerity, courage, patience,

and

and every other valuable and amiable quality ? it is
eafy to give the anfwer. It was not the excellence
of his natural temper ; not the ftrength of his under-
ftanding : it was not the force of education : no, nor
the advice of his friends. It was no other than faith
in a bleeding LORD ; faith of the operation of GOD.
It was a lively hope of an inheritance incorruptible,
undefiled, and that fadeth not away. It was the
love of GOD, fhed abroad in his heart by the HOLY
GHOST, which was given unto him, filling his foul
with tender, difinterefted love to every child of man.
From this fource arofe that torrent of eloquence
which frequently bore down all before it. From this,
that aftonifhing force of perfuafion, which the moft
hardened finners could not refift. This it was, which
often made his head as waters, and his eyes a foun-
tain of tears. This it was which enabled him to
pour out his foul in prayer, in a manner peculiar to
himfelf, with fuch fulnefs and eafe united together,
with fuch ftrength and variety both of fentiment
and expreffion.

"9. I MAY clofe this head with obferving, what
an honor it pleafed GOD to put upon his faithful fervant, by allowing him to declare his everlafting Gofpel, in fo many various countries, to fuch numbers of
people, and with fo great an effect, on fo many of
their precious fouls ! Have we read or heard of any
perfon fince the Apoftles, &c." (See the conclufion
of this paragraph in page 215, immediately before
the quotations from Funeral Sermons.)

* ON the fame day (November 18, 1770) the
Rev. Mr. Venn preached at the Countefs of Huntingdon's

* AN HYMN.

Servant of GOD, well done !
  Thy glorious warfare's paft :
The battle's fought, the race is won,
And thou art crown'd at laft ;

X 2

don's Chapel at Bath, on Ifaiah viii. 18. "Behold I,
and the children whom the LORD hath given me, are
for figns and for wonders in Ifrael ; from the LORD
of Hofts, which dwelleth in Mount Zion." And of
Mr. WHITEFIELD he fays : "Though the children
of CHRIST are all for figns and for wonders in Ifrael,
yet do they differ as one ftar differs from another ftar
in glory. Talents, grace, and zeal, eminently digni-
fy fome, and draw the eyes of men upon them. In
the foremoft of this rank, doubtlefs, is the Rev. Mr.
WHITEFIELD to be placed ; for his doctrine was the
doctrine

Of all thy heart's defire
  Triumphantly poffeft ;
Lodg'd by the minifterial quire
  In thy REDEEMER's breaft.

II

In condefcending love
  Thy ceafelefs prayer he heard,
And bade thee fuddenly remove
  To thy compleat reward :
Ready to bring the peace,
  Thy beauteous feet were fhod,
When mercy fign'd thy foul's releafe,
  And caught thee up to GOD.

III.

With faints enthron'd on high
  Thou doft thy LORD proclaim,
And ftill to GOD falvation cry,
  Salvation to the LAMB !
O happy, happy foul,
  In extafies of praife,
Long as eternal ages roll,
  Thou feeft thy SAVIOR's face.

IV.

Redeem'd from earth and pain,
  Ah ! when fhall we afcend,
And all in JESUS' prefence reign
  With our tranflated friend !
Come, LORD, and quickly come !
  And when in Thee compleat,
Receive thy longing fervants home,
  To triumph at thy feet !

doctrine of the Reformers, of the Apostles, and of
Christ : it was the doctrine of free grace, of God's
everlasting love. Through Jesus he preached the
forgiveness of sins, and perseverance in holy living, through his faithfulness and power engaged to
his people. And the doctrine which he preached,
he eminently adorned by his zeal, and by his works.
For if the greatness, extent, success, and disinterested-
ness of a man's labor can give him distinction amongst
the children of Christ, we are warranted to affirm,
that scarce any one of his ministers, since the Apostles'
days, has exceeded ; scarce any one has equalled Mr.
Whitefield.

"What a sign and wonder was this man of God
in the greatness of his labors ! One cannot but stand
amazed, that his mortal frame could, for the space of
near thirty years, without interruption, sustain the
weight of them. For what is so trying to the human
frame, in youth especially, as long-continued, frequent and violent straining of the lungs ? Who, that
knows their structure, would think it possible, that
a person, little above the age of manhood, should
speak in the compass of a single week (and that for
years) in general, forty hours, and in very many
weeks, sixty, and that to thousands ; and after this
labor, instead of taking any rest, should be offering
up prayers, intercessions, with hymns and spiritual
songs, as his manner was in every house to which he
was invited. The history of the Church of Christ af-
fords but very few instances of men thus incessantly
employing their whole strength, and as it were, every
breath they drew, in the business of their sacred function. And the truth is, that in point of labor, this
extraordinary servant of God did as much in a few
weeks, as most of those who exert themselves, are
able to do in the space of a year. Thus laboring
not by fits and starts, but with constancy and perseverance,

verance, and ardor unabated, his mortal frame, about
nine years since, began to sink under the weight of
so much work. If, with the length and frequency of
Mr. WHITEFIELD's preaching, we consider the in-
tenseness of voice and spirit with which he spoke, the
greatness of his labors will appear perfectly astonish-
ing : he knew not how to speak with less zeal, in his
whole manner, than became the subjects of his discourse. The total ruin of the human race by the fall ;
the complete recovery of believers in CHRIST, his
dying love, and the unsearchable riches of his grace,
to be known experimentally in this life, though fully
to be displayed in the next; and the infatuation of
sinners, led captive by their lusts down to the cham-
bers of death : these grand truths, of more weight
than words can paint, fired his whole soul ; they
transported him as much as earthly spirits are transported into vehemence, when they contend person-
ally for their own property ; he cried out therefore,
as his dear LORD was wont to do, with a voice audible
to an amazing distance : hence, in a thousand instances, where the cause of GOD more coolly pleaded,
would have been neglected. he gained it a hearing,
and carried the day : for the unusual earnestness of
the speaker roused the most stupid and lethargic : it
compelled them to feel ; the matter must be moment-
ous indeed, which the speaker was urging as a man
would plead for his own life. Early and often his
body suffered for this very violent exertion of his
strength : early and often his inside has bled a considerable quantity, and cried out, spare thyself: but,
prodigal of life, in the best of causes, he would give
himself no rest : expecting very soon to finish his
course, and infinitely desirous to save the souls condemned to die ; he perished. Though this may be
blamed as an excess it was an excess far above the
reach of a selfish mind, or an ordinary faith.

" EQUAL

"EQUAL to the greatnefs and intenfenefs of his labors, was their extent. The abilities and grace of moft teachers, have full employ in a fmall diftrict, nor have common men talents for more. But when GOD lights up in the breaft, an apoftolic zeal for his own glory, an apoftolic love for the fouls of men, it feems reafonable to conclude, fuch an inftrument is defigned for the moft extenfive ufefulnefs.

"ACCORDINGLY the compafs of Mr. WHITE- FIELD's labors, exceeds any thing that others can pretend to. Not only in the fouth, the weft, and north of England, did he lift up his voice, faying, 'Repent, for the Kingdom of Heaven is come:' but in Wales, in Scotland, in Ireland, and America, from Georgia to Bofton, vaft multitudes in each country were witneffes of his zeal for the falvation of fouls.

"AND to crown all, he was abundantly fuccefsful in his vaft labors, and difinterefted too. The feals of his miniftry, from firft to laft, I am perfuaded, are more than would be credited, could the number be' fixed. This is certain, his amazing popularity was only from his ufefulnefs: for he no fooner opened his mouth as a preacher, than GOD commanded an extraordinary bleffing upon his word. The people were fo deeply impreffed with the fenfe of divine things from what he delivered, that, to his own great furprize, they followed him from church to church, until the largeft churches in London could no longer contain a fourth part of the crowds, which preffed to hear the word of GOD from his lips.

"SHOULD any one fay, few in comparifon, be- fides low, ignorant, common people, were his fol- lowers; I would anfwer, the fouls of the poor and ignorant, are to the full as precious as thofe of the rich and learned: and the mob have fhown the jufteft difcernment, and have received the truth; whilft men of wealth, and learning, and education, have tram-

pled

pled it under their feet. Witnefs the chief Scribes and Pharifees who rejected both the Baptist and the Savior, when the common people justified GOD, and gave them both the honor of being fent from him. Indeed in every age, we fee the Scripture fulfilled, ‘ Not many rich, not many mighty, not many wife men after the flefh are called ; but GOD hath chosen the poor, rich in faith, and heirs of the Kingdom.'

“ HOWEVER, when the fiercenefs of prejudice was worn off, numbers, who at first defpifed him, taught to do fo by grofs flanders, were happy under his ministry. And this honor was put upon him even to the laft He had a much larger audience ftatedly to hear him, than any man in the whole kingdom, perhaps in all Chriftendom.

“ AND that this vaft multitude of people were gathered, juft as the primitive churches of CHRIST, by the truth they heard, and the fpiritual benefit they received under his word, is evident beyond a reafonable doubt. For if you trace his progrefs through the various cities and countries where he preached the Gofpel, you will find, as the cafe was with St. Paul, fo it was with this fervant of CHRIST. Many were turned by him from darknefs to light, from the power of Satan to GOD, receiving remiffion of their fins and an inheritance among thofe that are fanctified, through faith in CHRIST. Enquire of the effects of his labors, from the only proper judges, thofe who live in the religious world, and they will aver, that many within their own knowledge, fmall as that circle muft be, confefs they owe their own felves to this faithful witnefs for his LORD. Add to this, that the letters he received of grateful acknowledgment from perfons of all ages and conditions in life, for the fpiritual bleffings he had conveyed to them, would fill whole volumes. Nay, it is a well known fact, that the converfion of men's fouls

has

has been the fruit of a single sermon from his lips ; so eminently was he made of GOD, a fisher of men. But he was not more succefsful than he was difinterefted in his labors ; for though a vaft multitude, (which muft ever be the cafe with thofe whom GOD is pleafed remarkably to own) followed him, he had ftill no ambition to ftand as the head of a party. His great object was to exalt CHRIST crucified ; and when his hearers were brought to the knowledge of falvation, his point was gained and his foul was fatisfied.— Hence neither in his fermons, nor more private exhortations, did he caft difparaging reflections upon other preachers of CHRIST. No bafe fuggeftion dropt from his mouth. as if to differ from him muft be owing to blindnefs in the judgment, or coldnefs of the heart for the interefts of holinefs. Truly cordial and catholic in his love for all who appeared to love the LORD JESUS in fincerity, he never defired to fee his congregation increafed by thofe who had evangelical paftors of their own. Further, in proof of his difintereftednefs, confider what he gained by his labors. The fcourge of the tongue was let loofe upon him, and his name was loaded with the foulest calumnies ; he was often in tumults, and more than once in danger of his life, by the rage of the people ; he wore himfelf away in the fervice of fouls ; and when he died, he died quite exhaufted by much fpeaking ; but in his death. he received an immediate anfwer to his own prayer, " That if it were confiftent with the Divine Will, he might finifh that day, his Mafter's work.'

" FOR fuch a life, and fuch a death, (though in tears under our great lofs) we muft yet thank GOD. And though we are allowed to forrow, becaufe we fhall never fee or hear him again, we muft rejoice that millions have heard him fo long, fo often, and to fuch good effect ; that out of this mafs of people,

multitudes

multitudes are gone before him, we doubt not, to hail his entrance into the world of glory·; and that in every period of life, from childhood to hoary age, many of his children in the LORD are still to follow; all to be his crown of rejoicing : the only effectual, everlasting confutation of his adverfaries; that he ran not in vain, nor labored in vain.''

THERE were many other fermons preached on occasion of Mr. WHITEFIELD's death; in which the defcriptions of his character are the fame in fubftance with thofe already given.*

To

* Such as, by the Rev. Meff. Whitaker and Smith of Charlefton; Sprout of Philadelphia; Langford, Elliott, W. M. and probably others, which have not come to the Compiler's knowledge.

The Rev. Mr. De Courcy, alfo wrote fome Elegiac lines, among which are the following :

Soon as the SPIRIT's unction from above,
Throughout his foul diffus'd the SAVIOR's love,
A fire enkindled in his eager breaft,
With pity burn'd to finners loft—
Straight like a trumpet, he his voice did raife,
The wonders of redeeming love to praife;
Of health regardlefs, all things did forego,
That finners JESUS' boundlefs grace may know;
Where-e'er he preach'd, attentive crowds were feen,
Aftonifh'd at his youth and zealous mien :
Let Kennington, Blackheath, Moorfields declare,
How oft the gofpel-trumpet founded there.
Nor could his zeal the vaft Atlantic bound—
Throughout the weftern world he CHRIST difplays,
And joyful news to Georgia's coaft conveys.
There Orphans yet unborn, fhall weeping tell
How mourn'd, the founder of Bethefda fell—
The love of JESUS was his darling theme;
And heaven he felt in that dear precious name :
Hence when his heart with facred ardor glow'd,
His tongue in prompteft elocution flow'd.
With what compaffion, energy, and fire,
Would he the guilty heart for CHRIST require !

Oft

To be the subject of so many funeral sermons, both at home and abroad, is something singular; though quite suitable to his extraordinary manner of life. But it was still more singular, to have a sermon preached upon his personal and ministerial character, in his own life-time, and when he was but

twenty-

Oft whilst his Master's glorious grace he show'd,
An arrow dip'd in JESUS' precious blood,
Th' aspiring sinner in the dust brought low,
And forc'd him at the bleeding cross to bow—
Whene'er he meant the power of sin to kill,
And carnal hearts with purest love to fill,
Transgressors he to Calvary's summit led,
Where JESUS, spotless victim, bowed his head.
But, as a glass, the sinners guilt to show,
The Law he brought with all its curse and woe;
The conscience wounded with this flaming sword,
While Sinai seem'd to thunder in his word.
But—whilst each terror of the LORD, and threat,
With zeal and faithfulness he did repeat,
He all dissolv'd in sorrow would appear,
While plenteous flow'd the sympathetic tear;
Like JESUS, who o'er bloody Salem mourn'd,
While wrath divine against it vengeful burn'd—
In prayer, with a peculiar gift endow'd,
Reverent before the throne of grace he bow'd;
In tears, like Jacob, with the Angel strove,
Prevail'd, like Israel, with the GOD of Love.—
For all he pray'd—and all in love receiv'd,
With heart capacious, who in CHRIST believ'd.
    In him there dwelt a spirit generous, bold,
Unaw'd by threatenings, unallur'd by gold.
Preferments, honors, ease, he deem'd but loss,
Vile and contemptible for JESUS' Cross.
Inur'd to scandal, injuries, and pain,
To him to live was CHRIST ; to die was gain."

IN a note upon the last paragraph, the author says, "Whoever is acquainted with Mr. WHITEFIELD's life, well knows that I have not exaggerated matters. For in a visit to Ireland, he was solicited by the Primate of that kingdom, to

accept

twenty fix years of age. This fermon was preached
by the Rev. Mr Jofiah Smith, of Charlefton, South-
Carolina, and was publifhed at Bofton, with a recommendatory preface, by the Rev. Dr. Colman and Mr.
Cooper, in the year 1740. Of this it is worth while
to make a fhort extract,* after all that has been faid;
that by comparing it with the funeral fermons, the
reader may fee how confiftent and uniform Mr.
WHITEFIELD's conduct was, from that early period
of his miniftry, till his death.

AFTER fpeaking of his doctrine concerning Original Sin—Juftification by faith alone—Regeneration
—The inward feelings of the Spirit—Mr. Smith
adds, " As to the manner of his preaching—With
what a flow of words did he fpeak to us, upon the
great concern of our fouls ! in what a flaming light
did he fet out eternity before us ! How earneftly did
he prefs CHRIST upon us ! How clofe, ftrong and
pungent were his applications to the confcience ;
mingling light and heat ; pointing the arrows of the
ALMIGHTY at the hearts of finners, while he poured
in the balm on the wounds of the contrite ! How
bold and courageous did he look ? He was no flat-
terer. He taught the way of GOD in truth, and
regarded not the perfons of men. The politeft and
moft modifh of our vices, he ftruck at, the moft
fafhionable entertainments ; regardlefs of every one's
prefence, but His in whofe name he fpake.

                                          " As

accept of fome confiderable church-preferment ; but declined
the offer, becaufe he looked upon himfelf as called to an itinerant life ; and what makes this circumftance the more remarkable, is, that Mr. WHITEFIELD, at that time, had no
profpect whatever, as to temporals."

SEE alfo, a Paftoral on Mr. WHITEFIELD, faid to be written
by the Hon. and Rev. Mr. Shirley ; an Elegy, containing a
fhort Hiftory of his Life, by the Rev. Mr. Knight of Halifax;
and another Elegy, and a Monody, by anonymous authors.

* A large Extract both of the Preface and Sermon, is to be
found in Prince's Chriftian Hiftory, No. XCIX.

" As to his perfonal character, while he preaches up faith alone in our juftification before God, he is careful to maintain good works. Thefe things the grace of God teaches us. And how much of this doctrine has he tranfcribed into his life ! How rich has he been in all good works ! What an eminent pattern of piety towards God ! How holy and un-blameable in all converfation and godlinefs ! How feafonable, how much to the ufe of edifying all his difcourfes ! How naturally does he turn them to religion ? How much is he given to devotion himfelf, and how does he labor to excite it in others !

" He affects no party in religion, nor fets himfelf at the head of any. He is not bigoted to the leffer rites and forms of religion. while zealous enough in all its effentials. He profeffes love to good men of every denomination. His heart feems fet upon doing good. He goes about his great Mafter's work with diligence and application, and with fuch chearfulnefs as would make one in love with a life of religion. He is proof againft reproach and invective. When he is reviled, he revileth not again ; but prays hear-tily for all his enemies.

' He renders to all their due. While zealous for the things of God, is a friend to Cæfar. And for charity, as it confifts in compaffion and acts of beneficence, we have few men like minded. Had he been under any criminal influence of a mercenary temper ; had he collected monies for himfelf in his journies, under the pretext of doing it for the poor, as was flanderoufly reported, he had certainly a fair opportunity to enrich himfelf. But we have feen ; and plain fact cannot be denied : that he cafts all into the treafury, and ferves the tables of the poor with it. Strolling, and vagabond orphans, without father, and without mother, without purfe, and without friend, he feeks out, picks up, and adopts into his

family.

family. He is now building accommodations, and laying the beft foundation for their fupport and maintenance." Thus far Mr. J. Smith, who had the pleafure of feeing this character of his friend verified in the whole of his future life ; and who, in his Funeral Sermon upon him at Charlefton, October 28, 1770, has this remarkable expreffion, concerning a vifit he made to Mr. WHITEFIELD at his Orphanhoufe : " It was a fcene that made me think I was in heaven."

By a paper, written with Mr. WHITEFIELD's own hand, of the contents of his imperfect manuscript, frequently quoted in the above account of his life, it appears that if he had lived to finifh it, the conclufion would have been, " Reflections upon the whole, containing arguments to prove the divinity of the work ; and anfwers to objections againft Field-preaching—Lay preaching—Irregularities—and the blemifhes that have attended it."

As he did not live to execute this defign, the Reader is referred to what has been publifhed upon the fubject, by the Rev. Meffieurs Jonathan Edwards, Hobby, Shurtliff, &c. The Rev. Mr. Newton preached a fermon at Olney, November 11, 1770, on John v. 35. " He was a burning and a fhining light."— In which he fpeaks of Mr. WHITEFIELD ; an extract of which follows : " Some minifters are burning and fhining lights in a peculiar and eminent degree. Such a one, I doubt not, was the fervant of GOD whofe death we now lament. I have had fome opportunities of looking over the Hiftory of the Church in paft ages, and I am not backward to fay, that I have not read or heard of any perfon, fince the Apoftles' days, of whom it may more emphatically be faid, ' He was a burning and a fhining light," than the late Mr. WHITEFIELD, whether we confider the warmth of his zeal, the greatnefs of his minifterial

talents,

talents, or the extenfive ufefulnefs with which the LORD honored him.   I do not mean to praife the man, but the LORD, who furnifhed him, and made him what he was.   He was raifed up to fhine in a dark place.   The ftate of religion, when he firft appeared in public, was very low in our eftablifhed church.   I fpeak the truth, though to fome it may be an offenfive truth.   The doctrines of Grace, were feldom heard from the pulpit, and the life and power of godlinefs were little known.   Many of the moft fpiritual among the Diffenters, were mourning under the fenfe of a great fpreading declenfion on their fide : what a change has taken place throughout the land, within a little more than thirty years, that is, fince the time when the firft fet of defpifed minifters came from Oxford ; and how much of this change has been owing to GOD's blefling on Mr. WHITE-FIELD's labors, is well known to many who have lived tl·ugh this period ; and can hardly be denied by thofe who are leaft willing to allow it.   Firft, He was a burning light.   He had an ardent zeal for GOD, an enflamed defire for the falvation of finners. So that no labors could weary him, no difficulties or oppofition difcourage him, hardly any limits could confine him ; not content with the bounds of a county, or a kingdom, this meffenger of good tidings preached the everlafting Gofpel in almoft every confiderable place in England, Scotland and Ireland, and throughout the Britifh empire in America, which is an extent of more than a thoufand miles.   Moft of thefe places he vifited again and again ; nor did he confine his attention to places of note, but in the former part of his miniftry, was ready to preach to few, as well as to many, wherever a door was opened ; though in the latter part of his life, his frequent illnefs, and the neceffity of his more immediate charge, confined him more at home.   In fome of his moft

early

early excursions, the good Providence of GoD led him here, and many, I truft, were made willing to rejoice in his light, and have reafon to blefs GoD, that ever they faw and heard him. Secondly, He was a fhining light : his zeal was not like wild-fire, but directed by found principles, and a found judgment. In this part of his character, I would obferve, 1ft. Though he was very young, when he came out, the LORD foon gave him a very clear view of the Gofpel. In the fermons he publifhed foon after his firft appearance, there is the fame evangelical ftrain obfervable, as in thofe which he preached in his advanced years. Time and obfervation, what he felt, and what he faw, enlarged his experience, and gave his preaching an increafing ripenefs and favor, as he grew older in the work ; but from firft to laft he preached the fame Gofpel, and was determined to know nothing but JESUS CHRIST, and him crucified. 2dly, His fteadinefs and perfeverance in the truth was the more remarkable, confidering the difficulties and fnares he was fometimes befet with. But the LORD kept him fteady, fo that neither the example, nor friendfhip, nor importunity of thofe he dearly loved, were capable of moving him.

3dly. THE LORD gave him a manner of preaching, which was peculiarly his own. He copied from none, and I never met any one who could imitate him with fuccefs. They who attempted, generally made themfelves difagreeable. His familiar addrefs, the power of his action, his marvellous talent in fixing the attention even of the moft carelefs, I need not defcribe to thofe who have heard him, and to thofe who have not, the attempt would be vain. Other minifters could, perhaps, preach the gofpel as clearly, and in general fay the fame things, but, I believe, no man living could fay them in his way. Here I always
thought

thought him unequalled, and I hardly expect to fee
his equal while I live.

" 4th. But that which finished his character as a
shining light, and is now his crown of rejoicing,
was the fingular fuccefs which the Lord was pleafed
to give him in winning fouls ; what numbers entered
the kingdom of glory before him, and what numbers
are now lamenting his lofs, who were awakened by
his miniftry ? It feemed as if he never preached in
vain. Perhaps there is hardly a place, in all the extenfive compafs of his labors, where fome may not be
found who thankfully acknowledge him as their fpiritual father. Nor was he an awakening preacher
only, wherever he came; if he preached but a fingle
difcourfe, he ufually brought a feafon of refrefhment
and revival with him. to thofe who had already received the truth. Great as his immediate and perfonal ufefulnefs was, his occafional ufefulnefs (if I may
fo call it) was perhaps much greater. Many have
caufe to be thankful for him, who never faw or heard
him. I have already obferved, that there was fomething peculiar in his manner of preaching, in which
no perfon of found judgment would venture to imitate him. But notwithftanding this, he was in other
refpects, a fignal and happy pattern and model for
preachers. He introduced a way of clofe and lively
application to the confcience, for which I believe
many of the moft admired and eminent preachers
now living, will not be afhamed, or unwilling to
acknowledge themfelves his debtors."

There was alfo a Sermon preached on the occafion by the Rev. Mr. Samuel Brewer, of Stepney,
London, which his modefty would not permit him to
print. And many others of the minifters, both of the
Church, and among the Diffenters in England, in
their Sermons and Prayers upon the news of Mr.

Whitefield's

WHITEFIELD's death, bewailed the lofs of fo great a man, and fo faithful and fuccefsful a fervant of CHRIST.*

ON the 6th of February, 1771, the executors having received the probate of Mr. WHITEFIELD's Will, Mr. Keen, who was perfectly acquainted with every particular of his temporal affairs, immediately publifhed it, with the following preamble :

AS we make no doubt the numerous friends of the late Rev. Mr. GEORGE WHITEFIELD will be glad of an opportunity of feeing a genuine copy of his laft Will and Teftament : his Executors have favored us with a copy of the fame, tranfmitted to them from the Orphan-houfe in Georgia, and which they have proved in the Prerogative Court of Canterbury. And as it was Mr. WHITEFIELD's conftant declaration he never meant to raife either a purfe or a party, it is to be remarked, that almoft the whole money he died poffeffed of, came to him within two or three years of his death in the following manner, viz. Mrs. Thomfon, of Tower-Hill, bequeathed him 500l. By the death of his Wife, including a Bond of 300l. he got 700l. Mr. Whitmore bequeathed him 100l. and Mr. Winder 100l. and it is highly probable, that had he lived to reach Georgia from his late northern tour, he would have much leffened the above fums, by difpofing of them in the fame noble and difinterefted manner that all the public or private fums he has been entrufted with, have been.

' GEORGIA.

* Among thefe were the Rev. Mr. Romaine, Mr. Madan, Dr. Gibbons, and Dr. Trotter.

' GEORGIA.

'By his Excellency *James Wright*, Efq Captain-
'General, Governor and Commander in Chief of
' his Majefty's faid Province of GEORGIA, Chancel-
' lor and Vice-Admiral of the fame.

To all to whom thefe prefents fhall come greeting:
Know ye, that Thomas Moodie, who hath certified
the annexed copy from the original, in the Secretary's Office, is Deputy-Secretary of the faid Province,
and therefore all due faith and credit is and ought to
be, had and given to fuch his certificate.

In teftimony whereof, I have hereunto fet my
hand, and caufed the Great Seal of this his Majefty's
faid Province to be put and affixed, dated at Savannah the tenth day of December, in the year of our
LORD 1770, and in the eleventh year of the reign
of his Majefty King George the Third.
            By his Excellency's command,
                            J. WRIGHT.
                THO. MOODIE, D. Secretary.'

"In the name of the FATHER, SON and HOLY
GHOST, three Perfons, but one GOD ; I GEORGE
WHITEFIELD, Clerk, at prefent refiding at the Orphan
houfe Academy, in the Province of Georgia, in North-
America, being through infinite mercy in more than
ordinary bodily health, and a perfect, found and compofed mind, knowing the certainty of death, and yet
the uncertainty of the time, I fhall be called by it to
my long wifhed-for home, do make this my laft Will
and Teftament, in manner and form following, viz.
Imprimis, In fure and certain hope of a refurrec-
tion to eternal life, through our LORD JESUS CHRIST,
I commit my body to the duft, to be buried in the
                                                    moft

moſt plain and decent manner ; and knowing in whom
I have believed, and being perſuaded that he will
keep that which I have committed unto him, in the
fulleſt aſſurance of faith I commend my ſoul into the
hands of the ever-loving, altogether lovely, never-
failing JESUS, on whoſe complete and everlaſting
righteouſneſs I entirely depend, for the juſtification of
my perſon and acceptance of my poor, worthleſs,
though, I truſt ſincere performances, at that day
when he ſhall come in the glory of his FATHER, his
own glory and the glory of his holy Angels, to judge
both the quick and dead.   In reſpect to my outward American concerns, which I have engaged in
ſimply and ſolely for his great Name's ſake, I leave
that building commonly called the Orphan-houſe, at
Betheſda, in the Province of Georgia, together with
all the other buildings lately erected thereon, and
likewiſe all other buildings, lands, negroes, books,
furniture, and every other thing whatſoever which I
now ſtand poſſeſſed of in the Province of Georgia
aforeſaid, to that elect Lady, that mother in Iſrael,
that mirror of true and undefiled religion, the Right
Honorable SELINA, Counteſs Dowager of Huntingdon ; deſiring, that as ſoon as may be, after my deceaſe, the plan of the intended Orphan houſe, Betheſ-
da-College, may be proſecuted, or, if not practicable,
or eligible, to purſue the preſent plan of the Orphan-
houſe Academy, on its old foundation and uſual channel ; but if her Ladyſhip ſhould be called to enter into
her glorious reſt before my deceaſe, I bequeath all
the buildings, lands, negroes, and every thing before-
mentioned, which I now ſtand poſſeſſed of, in the Province of Georgia, aforeſaid, to my dear firſt fellow-
traveller and faithful, invariable friend, the Honorable JAMES HABERSHAM, Eſq. Preſident of his Majeſty's Honorable Council : and ſhould he ſurvive her
Ladyſhip, I earneſtly recommend him as the moſt
                                                 proper

proper person to succed her Ladyship, or to act for her during her Ladyship's life time, in the affairs of the Orphan house Academy. With regard to my outward affairs in England; whereas there is a building commonly called the Tabernacle, set apart many years ago for Divine Worship, I give and bequeath the said Tabernacle, with the adjacent house in which I usually reside, when in London, with the stable and coach-house in the yard adjoining, together with all books, furniture, and every thing else whatsoever, that shall be found in the house and premises aforesaid : and also the building commonly called Tottenham Court Chapel, together with all the other buildings, houses, stable, coach house, and every thing else whatsoever which I stand possessed of in that part of the town, to my worthy, trusty, tried friends Daniel West, Esq. in Church-street, Spitalfields, and Mr. Robert Keen, Woolen-Draper, in the Minories, or the longer survivor of the two. As to the monies, which a kind Providence, especially of late, in a most unexpected way, and unthought of means, have vouchsafed to entrust me with; I give and bequeath the sum of one hundred pounds sterling to the Right Honorable Countess Dowager of Huntingdon aforesaid, humbly beseeching her Ladyship's acceptance of so small a mite, as a pepper-corn of acknowledgment for the undeserved, unsought-for honor her Ladyship conferred upon me, in appointing me, less than the least of all, to be one of her Ladyship's Domestic Chaplains. Item, I give and bequeath to my dearly beloved friend, the Honorable James Habersham aforesaid, my late Wife's gold watch, and ten pounds for mourning ; to my dear old friend, Gabriel Harris, Esq. of the city of Gloucester, who received and boarded me in his house, when I was helpless and destitute, above thirty-five years ago, I give and bequeath the sum of fifty pounds ; to my humble,

faithful

faithful fervant and friend, Mr. Ambrofe Wright, if
in my fervice and employ, either in England or America, or elfewhere, at the time of my deceafe, I give
and bequeath the fum of five hundred pounds ; to my
brother, Mr. Richard Whitefield, I give and bequeath
the fum of fifty pounds ; to my brother, Mr. Thomas
Whitefield, I give and bequeath the fum of fifty
pounds, to be given him at the difcretion of Mr. Robert Keen ; to my brother-in-law, Mr. James Smith,
Hofier, in the city of Briftol, I give and bequeath the
fum of fifty pounds, and thirty pounds alfo for family
mourning ; to my niece, Mrs. Frances Hartford, of
Bath, I give and bequeath the fum of fifty pounds,
and twenty pounds for family mourning ; to Mr. J.
Crane, now a faithful fteward at the Orphan-houfe
Academy, I give and bequeath the fum of forty pounds;
to Mr. Benjamin Stirk, as an acknowledgment of his
paft fervices at Bethefda, I give and bequeath the
fum of ten pounds for mourning ; to Peter Edwards,
now at the Orphan-houfe Academy, I give and bequeath the fum of fifty pounds ; to William Trigg,
at the fame place, I give and bequeath the fum of
fifty pounds ; both the fums aforefaid to be laid out,
or laid up for them, at the difcretion of Mr. Ambrofe
Wright : to Mr. Thomas Adams, of Rodborough,
in Gloucefterfhire, my only furviving firft fellow-laborer, and beloved much in the LORD, I give and bequeath the fum of fifty pounds ; to the Rev. Mr.
Howel Davis, of Pembrokefhire, in South Wales, that
good foldier of JESUS CHRIST ; to Mr. Torial Jofs,
Mr. Cornelius Winter, and all my other dearly beloved prefent ftated affiftant-preachers at Tabernacle
and Tottenham-Court Chapel, I give and bequeath
ten pounds each for mourning : to the three brothers
of Mr Ambrofe Wright, and the wife of his brother
Mr. Robert Wright, now faithfully and fkilfully laboring and ferving at the Orphan-houfe Academy, I

give

give and bequeath the fum of ten pounds each for mourning; to Mr. Richard Smith, now a diligent attendant on me, I give and bequeath the fum of fifty pounds, and all my wearing apparel which I fhall have with me in my journey through America, or on my voyage to England, if it fhould pleafe an all-wife God to fhorten my days in either of thofe fituations. Finally, I give and bequeath the fum of one hundred pounds, to be diftributed at the difcretion of my executors, herein after mentioned, for mourning among my old London fervants, the poor widows at Tottenham Court Chapel, and the Tabernacle poor, efpecially my old trufty, difinterefted friend and fervant, Mrs. Elizabeth Wood. All the other refidue, if there be any refidue, of monies, goods, and chattels, or whatever profits may arife from the fale of my books, or any manufcripts that I may leave behind, I give and bequeath to the Right Honourable the Countefs Dowager of Huntingdon, or, in cafe of her Ladyfhip's being deceafed at the time of my departure, to the Honorable James Haberfham, Efq. before mentioned, after my funeral expences and juft debts are difcharged, towards paying off my arrears that may be due on the account of the Orphan-houfe Academy, or for annual prizes, as a reward for the beft three orations that fhall be made in Englifh on the fubjects mentioned in a paper annexed to this my Will. And I do hereby appoint the Honourable James Haberfham, Efq. aforefaid, to be my executor, in refpect to my affairs in the Province of Georgia, and my trufty, tried, dearly beloved friends, Charles Hardy, Efq. Daniel Weft, Efq. and Mr. Robert Keen, to be executors of this my laft Will and Teftament, in refpect of my affairs in England, begging each to accept of a mourning ring. To all my other Chriftian benefactors, and more intimate acquaintance, I leave my moft hearty thanks and bleffing, af-

Z   furing

suring them that I am more and more convinced of the undoubted reality, and infinite importance of the grand gospel-truths which I have from time to time delivered; and am so far from repenting my delivering them in an itinerant way, that had I strength equal to my inclination, I would preach them from pole to pole, not only because I have found them to be the power of GOD to the salvation of my own soul, but because I am as much assured that the Great Head of the Church hath called me by his word, providence and SPIRIT, to act in this way, as that the sun shines at noon-day. As for my enemies, and misjudging, mistaken friends, I most freely and heartily forgive them, and can only add, that the last tremendous day will soon discover what I have been, what I am, and what I shall be, when time itself shall be no more; and therefore, from my inmost soul, I close all, by crying, Come, LORD JESUS, come quickly; even so, LORD JESUS, Amen and Amen.

GEORGE WHITEFIELD.

" This was written with the Testator's own hand, and at his desire, and in his presence, sealed, signed, and delivered, at the Orphan house Academy, in the Province of Georgia, before these witnesses, *Anno Domini*, March the twenty second, one thousand; seven hundred and seventy.
Signed,   ROBERT BOLTON.
                 THOMAS DIXON.
                 CORNELIUS WINTER.

" N. B. I also leave a mourning ring to my honored and dear friends and disinterested fellow-labourers, the Rev. Messrs. John and Charles Wesley, in token of my indissoluble union with them, in heart and Christian affection, notwithstanding our difference in judgment about some particular points of doctrine.—

Grace

Grace be with all them, of whatever denomination, that love our LORD JESUS, our common LORD, in sincerity."

Georgia, Secretary's Office.

" A true copy, taken from the original in this office, examined and certified : and I do further certify that the same was duly proved; and the Honourable James Habersham, Esq. one of the executors therein named, was duly qualified as executor before his Excellency James Wright, Esq. Governor and Ordinary of the said Province, this 10th day of December 1770.

THO. MOODIE, D. Sec."

Concerning the manner in which Mr. WHITEFIELD's Tabernacle and Chapel are at present supplied, the compiler has received the following information :

HAVING by his Will left both of his places of worship, his houses, library, and all things appertaining thereto, to two of his executors in survivorship, they have been enabled; through the abundant goodness of GOD, to carry on the work in the same manner as in Mr. WHITEFIELD's life-time, without the least diminution either of the largeness of the congregations, or the visible power of GOD attending the ministry there. And as neither of them are ministers, but engaged in extensive business, it appears the more wonderful, and shews the work to be begun and carried on by the power of GOD alone; and it is their earnest prayer and study, that it may be transmitted down, and faithful ministers and upright persons raised to carry it on when their heads are laid in the dust. Two of his fellow-labourers were taken off by death, whilst he was last abroad, viz. the Rev. Mr. Howel Davies, a clergyman, and Mr. Thomas Adams, a layman ; and a little before, Mr. Middleton, all tried and faithful ministers : but

the

the LORD hath wonderfully raised up others in their stead. The present ministers are chiefly these, the Rev. Mr. Kinsman of Plymouth, the Rev. Mr. Edwards of Leeds, the Rev. Mr. Knight of Halifax, and the Rev. Mr. Ashburner, of Pool in Dorsetshire : these visit London once, and if wrote for, twice a year. The constant ones upon the spot are, Mr. Jols and Mr. Brooksbanks. The Rev. Mr. De Courcy, and the Rev. Mr. Piercy, and other Clergymen, have often assisted. Besides these, the proprietors have been favoured with the occasional labours of Mr. Rowland Hill, and Mr. Heath of Plymouth : also of many worthy Clergymen and dissenting ministers from the country, who esteemed it their privilege to preach to very large, serious, and attentive congregations, whose hearts have been filled with thankfulness, and at the same time engaged in prayer for every such minister ; and an unusual blessing has commonly attended both sowers and reapers ; and it is the earnest desire of the proprietors that the pleasure of the LORD may thus prosper in their hands. They propose, thro' the blessing of GOD, to let the pulpits be open to every disinterested minister who may occasionally come to town, of good moral character, sound in the faith, of moderate Calvinistical Principles, without distinction of parties or denominations, whose talents are suitable to preach with life and power to large congregations. And hope for the concurrence of all well-wishers to the prosperity of Zion.

END OF THE MEMOIRS.

AN

E N Q U I R Y

INTO.

The first and chief Reason, why the generality of
Christians fall so far short of the holiness and
devotion of Christianity.

(Extracted from Mr. WHITEFIELD's Tracts.)

SINCE Christian devotion is nothing less than a life wholly
devoted unto GOD, and persons who are free from the
necessities of labour and employments, are to consider themselves as devoted to GOD in a higher degree ; it may now reasonably be enquired, how it comes to pass, that the lives
even of the moral and better sort of people, are in general
so directly contrary to the principles of Christianity? I answer, because the generality of those who call themselves
Christians, are destitute of a true living faith in JESUS CHRIST;
for want of which, they never effectually intended to please
GOD in all the actions of life, as the happiest and best thing in
the world.

To be partaker of such a faith, is every-where represent-
ed in scripture, as a fundamental and necessary part of true
piety. For without a living faith in the righteousness of JESUS
CHRIST, our persons cannot be justified, and consequently
none of our performances acceptable in the sight of GOD. It
is this faith that enables us to overcome the world, and to
devote ourselves without reserve to promote the glory of Him,
who has loved and given himself for us. And therefore it is
purely for want of such a faith, that you see such a mixture
of sin and folly even in the lives of the better sort of people :
It is for want of this faith, that you see Clergymen given to
pride, and covetousness, and worldly enjoyments : It is for
want of such a faith, that you see Women, who profess devotion, yet living in all the folly and vanity of dress, wasting
their time in idleness and pleasures, and in all such instances
of state and equipage as their estate will reach. Let but a
Woman feel her heart full of this faith, and she will no more
desire to shine at balls and assemblies, or to make a figure a-
mong those that are most finely dressed, than she will desire
to dance upon a rope to please spectators: For she will then

Z 2 know,

know, that the one is as far from the true nature, wifdom, and excellency of the Chriftian fpirit, as is the other.

Let a Clergyman be but thus pious, and he will converfe as if he had been brought up by an Apoftle; he will no more think and talk of noble preferment, than of noble eating, or a glorious chariot. He will no more complain of the frowns of the world, or a fmall cure, or the want of a patron, than he will complain of the want of a laced coat, or of a running horfe. Let him but have fuch a faith in love for GOD, as will conftrain him to make it his bufinefs to ftudy to pleafe GOD in all his actions, as the happieft and beft thing in the world, and then he will know, that there is nothing noble in a Clergyman, but burning zeal for the falvation of fouls; nor any thing poor in his profeffion but idlenefs and a worldly fpirit.

Further, let a Tradefman but have fuch a faith, and it will make him a faint in his fhop; his every-day bufinefs will be a courfe of wife and reafonable actions, made holy to GOD, by flowing from faith, proceeding from love, and by being done in obedience to his will and pleafure. He will therefore not chiefly confider, what arts, or methods, or application will fooneft make him greater and richer than his brethren, that he may remove from a fhop, to a life of ftate and pleafure; but he will chiefly confider, what arts, what methods, and what application can make worldly bufinefs moft conducive to GOD's glory, and his neighbour's good; and confequently make a life of trade, to be a life of holinefs, devotion, and undiffembled piety.

It was this faith that made the primitive Chriftians fuch eminent inftances of religion; and that made the goodly fellowfhip of the faints in all ages, and all the glorious army of confeffors and martyrs. And if we will ftop and afk ourfelves, why we are not as pious as the primitive Chriftians, and faints of old were? our own hearts muft tell us, that it is becaufe we never yet perhaps earneftly fought after, and confequently were never really made partakers of, that precious faith, whereby they were conftrained to intend to pleafe GOD in all their actions, as the beft and happieft thing in the world.

Here then let us judge ourfelves fincerely; let us not vainly content ourfelves with the common diforders of our lives, the vanity of our expences, the folly of our diverfions, the pride of our habits, the idlenefs of our lives, and the wafting of our time; fancying that thefe are only fuch imperfections as we neceffarily fall into, through the unavoidable weaknefs and frailty of our nature; but let us be affured, that thefe
habitual

habitual diforders of our common life, are fo many demonftrable proofs, that we never yet truly accepted of the LORD
JESUS and his righteoufnefs by a living faith, and never really.
intended, as a proof and evidence of fuch a faith, to pleafe
GOD in all the actions of our life, as the beft thing in the
world.

Though this be a matter we can eafily pafs over at prefent,
whilft the health of our bodies, the paffions of our minds, the
noife, and hurry, and pleafures, and bufinefs of the world,
lead us on with "eyes that fee not, and ears that hear not:"
yet at death, it will fet itfelf before us in a dreadful magnitude; it will haunt us like a difmal ghoft, and our confciences
will never let us take our eyes from it, unlefs they are feared
as with a red hot iron, and GOD fhall have given us over to a
reprobate mind.

PENITENS was a bufy notable tradefman, and very profper-
ous in his dealings; but died in the thirty-fifth year of his
age.

A little before his death, when the doctors had given him
over, fome of his neighbours came one evening to fee him;
at which time he fpake thus to them.

"I fee (fays he) my friends, the tender concern you have
for me, by the grief that appears in your countenances, and
I know the thoughts that you now have of me. You think
how melancholy a cafe it is, to fee fo young a man, and in
fuch flourifhing bufinefs, delivered up to death. And perhaps,
had I vifited any of you in my condition, I fhould have had
the fame thoughts of you. But now, my friends, my thoughts
are no more like your thoughts, than my condition is like
yours. It is no trouble to me now to think that I am to die
young, or before I have raifed an eftate. Thefe things are
funk into fuch mere nothings, that I have no name little
enough to call them by. For if in a few days, or hours, I am
to leave this carcafe to be buried in the earth, and to find myfelf either for ever happy in the favour of GOD, or eternally
feparated from all light and peace; can any words fufficiently exprefs the littlenefs of every thing elfe?

Is there any dream, like the dream of life, which amufes us
with the neglect and difregard of thefe things? Is there any
folly like the folly of our manly ftate, which is too wife and
bufy to be at leifure for thefe reflections?

When we confider death as a mifery, we generally think of
it as a miferable feparation from the enjoyments of this life.
We feldom mourn over an old man that dies rich, but we lament the young, that are taken away in the progrefs of their
fortunes.

fortunes. You yourselves look upon me with pity, not that you think I am going unprepared to meet the Judge of quick and dead, but that I am to leave a prosperous trade in the flower of my life.

This is the wisdom of our manly thoughts. And yet what folly of the silliest children, is so great as this? For what is there miserable or dreadful in death, but the consequences of it? When a man is dead, what does any thing signify to him, but the state he is then in?.

Our poor friend Lepidus, you know died as he was dressing himself for a feast;—do you think it is now part of his trouble, that he did not live till that entertainment was over? Feasts, and business, and pleasures, and enjoyments, seem great things to us, whilst we think of nothing else; but as soon as we add death to them, they all sink into littleness not to be expressed; and the soul that is separated from the body, no more laments the loss of business, than the losing of a feast.

If I am now going to the joys of God, could there be any reason to grieve, that this happened to me before I was forty years of age. Can it be a sad thing to go to heaven, before I have made a few more bargains, or stood a little longer behind a counter: :

And if I am to go amongst lost spirits, could there be any reason to be content, that this did not happen to me till I was old and full of riches.

If good angels were ready to receive my soul, could it be any grief to me that I was dying on a poor bed in a garret ?.

And if God has delivered me up to evil spirits, to be dragged by them to places of torment, could it be any comfort to me, that they found me upon a bed of state? When you are as near death as I am, you will know, that all the different states of life, whether of youth or age, riches or poverty, greatness or meanness, signify no more to you, than whether you die in a poor or stately apartment.

The greatness of the things which follow death, makes all that goes before it sink into nothing.

Now, that judgment is the next thing which I look for, and everlasting happiness or misery is come so near to me, all the enjoyments and prosperities of life seem as vain and insignificant, and to have no more to do with my happiness, than the clothes that I wore when I was a little child.

What a strange thing! that a little health, or the poor business of a shop, should keep us so senseless of these great things that are coming so fast upon us !

Just

Just as you came into my chamber, I was thinking with myself, what numbers of souls there are in the world, in my condition at this very time, surprized with a summous to the other world, some taken from their shops and farms, others from their sports and pleasures; these at suits at law, those at gaming-tables; some on the road, others at their own firesides; and all seized at an hour when they thought nothing of it; frighted at the approach of death; confounded at the vanity of all their labours, designs and projects; astonished at the folly of their past lives, and not knowing which way to turn their thoughts, to find any comfort. Their consciences flying in their faces, bringing all their sins to remembrance, tormenting them with the deepest convictions of their own folly, presenting them with the sight of the angry Judge, and the worm that never dies, the fire that is never quenched, the gates of hell, the powers of darkness, and the bitter pains of eternal death.

O my friends! bless God that you are not of this number; and take this along with you, that there is nothing but a real faith in the LORD JESUS, and a life of true piety, or a death of great stupidity, that can keep off these apprehensions.

Had I now a thousand worlds, I would give them all for one moment's scriptural assurance that I had really received the LORD JESUS by a living faith into my heart, and for one more year's continuance in life, that I might evidence the sincerity of that faith, by presenting unto God, one year of such devotion and good works, as I am persuaded I have hitherto never done.

Perhaps, when you consider that I have lived free from scandal and debauchery, and in the communion of the church, you wonder to see me so full of remorse and self-condemnation at the approach of death.

But alas! what a poor thing is it, to have lived only free from murder, theft and adultery, which is all that I can say of myself. Was not the slothful servant, that is condemned in the gospel, thus negatively good? And did not the SAVIOUR of mankind tell the young man, who led a more blameless and moral life than I have done, that yet one thing he lacked.

But the thing that now surprizes me above all wonders, is this, that till of late I never was convinced of that reigning, soul-destroying sin of unbelief; and that I was out of a state of salvation, notwithstanding my negative goodness, my seemingly strict morality, and attendance on public worship and the holy sacrament. It never entered into my head or heart,

that

that the righteoufnefs of Jesus Christ alone, could recommend me to the favour of a fin-avenging God, and that I muft
be born again of God, and have Christ formed in my heart,
before I could have any well guarded affurance that I was a
Chriftian indeed, or have any folid foundation whereon I
might build the fuperftructure of a truly holy and pious life.

Alas! I thought I had faith in Christ, becaufe I was born
in a Chriftian country, and faid in my creed, that " I believed on Jesus Christ his only Son our Lord." I thought I
was certainly regenerate and born again, and was a real
Chriftian, becaufe I was baptized when I was young, and received the holy facrament in my adult age. But alas! little
did I confider that faith is fomething more than the world generally thinks of; a work of the heart, and not merely of the
head, and that I muft know and feel that there is no other name
given under heaven whereby I can be faved, but that of Jesus
Christ.

It is true indeed, you have frequently feen me at church
and the facrament; but alas! you little think what remorfe
of confcience I now feel for fo frequently faying, " the remembrance of our fins is grievous unto us, and the burden
of them is intolerable," when I never experienced the meaning of them in all my life. You have alfo feen me join with
the minifter when he faid, " we do not approach thy table
trufting on our own righteoufnefs; but all this while I was
utterly ignorant of God's righteoufnefs, which is by faith in
Christ Jesus, and was going about to eftablifh a righteoufnefs
of my own. It is true indeed, I have kept the fafts, and
feafts of the church, and have called Christ, Lord, Lord;
but little did I think, that no one could call Christ truly
Lord, but by the Holy Ghost. I have attended upon ordi-
nations, and heard the Bifhop afk the candidates, " whether
they were called by the Holy Ghost; I have ferioufly attended to the minifter, when he exhorted us to pray for true
repentance and God's Holy Spirit; but alas, I never enquired whether I myfelf had received the Holy Ghost, to
fanctify and purify my heart, and work a true evangelical repentance on my foul. I have prayed in the litany that I might
bring forth fruits of the Spirit, but alas, my whole life has
been nothing but a dead life, a round of duties, and model of
performances, without any living faith for their foundation.
I have profeffed myfelf a member of the church of England;
I have cried out, " The temple of the Lord, the temple of
the Lord," and in my zeal have exclaimed againft Diffenters; but little did I think, that I was ignorant all this while
of

of most of her essential articles, and that my practice, as well as the want of a real experience of a work of regeneration and true conversion, when I was using her offices, and reading her homilies, gave my conscience the lie.

O my friends! a form of Godliness without the power, and dead morality not founded on a living faith in the LORD JESUS CHRIST, is such a dreadful delusion, so contrary to the lively oracles of GOD, that did not I know (though alas, how late!) that the righteousness of JESUS CHRIST was revealed in them, and that there was mercy to be found with GOD, if we venture by a real faith on that righteousness, though at the eleventh hour, I must now sink into total despair.

Penitens was here going on, but had his mouth stopped by a convulsion, which never suffered him to speak any more. He lay convulsed about twelve hours, and then gave up the ghost.

Now if every reader would imagine this *Penitens* to have been some particular acquaintance or relation of his, and fancy that he saw and heard all which is here described; that he stood by his bed-side when his poor friend lay in such distress and agony, lamenting the want of a living faith in JESUS CHRIST, as the cause of a dead, lifeless, indevout life: besides this, he should consider, how often he himself might have been surprized in the same formal dead state, and made an example to the rest of the world; this double reflection, both upon the distress of his friend, and the goodness of that GOD, which ought to have led him to repentance, would in all likelihood set him upon seeking and earnestly praying for such a faith, of which *Penitens* felt himself void, and constrain him to let the LORD have no rest, till he should be pleased to apply the righteousness of his dear SON to his sin-sick soul, and enable him henceforward to study, out of love, to glorify him in all the actions of his future life, as the best and happiest thing in the world.

THIS therefore being so useful a meditation, I shall here leave the reader, I hope seriously engaged in it.

FINIS.